PENGUIN (Ⓟ) CLASSICS

THE LEAVENWORTH CASE

ANNA KATHARINE GREEN (1846–1935), often referred to as "The Mother of the Detective Novel," was born on November 11, 1846, to Katherine Ann Whitney Green and James Wilson Green. Her mother died while Green was still young, and her father moved the family from Brooklyn to Connecticut, Albany, and finally Buffalo. At her stepmother's urging, Green attended Ripley Female College in Vermont, where she met Ralph Waldo Emerson, with whom she later corresponded. On November 25, 1884, Green married Charles Rohlfs, an actor seven years her junior, though Green's father forced him to give up acting before the wedding. With him she designed award-winning furniture. Her first novel, *The Leavenworth Case*, was published in 1878, nine years before the debut of Sherlock Holmes, and became the standard by which new detective stories were measured. She went on to publish thirty-six novels, several more of them starring Ebenezer Gryce of *The Leavenworth Case*, before she died in Buffalo at eighty-eight years old. She was also the creator of Amelia Butterworth, the intrepid spinster who helped inspire Agatha Christie's Miss Marple.

MICHAEL SIMS is the author of several nonfiction books, including *Apollo's Fire*, which National Public Radio chose as one of the best science books of the year; *Adam's Navel*, which was a *New York Times* Notable Book and a *Library Journal* Best Science Book; and most recently *In the Womb: Animals*, a companion book to a National Geographic Channel TV series. For Penguin Classics he has edited *The Annotated Archy and Mehitabel*; *Arsène Lupin, Gentleman-Thief*; and *The Penguin Book of Gaslight Crime*. His work has appeared in the *Washington Post*, *Orion*, *New Statesman*, *Chronicle of Higher Education*, and many other periodicals, as well as on radio. Learn more at www.michaelsimsbooks.com.

ANNA KATHARINE GREEN

The Leavenworth Case

Introduction by
MICHAEL SIMS

PENGUIN BOOKS

PENGUIN BOOKS

Published by the Penguin Group

Penguin Group (USA) Inc., 375 Hudson Street,
New York, New York 10014, U.S.A.
Penguin Group (Canada), 90 Eglinton Avenue East, Suite 700, Toronto,
Ontario, Canada M4P 2Y3 (a division of Pearson Penguin Canada Inc.)
Penguin Books Ltd, 80 Strand, London WC2R 0RL, England
Penguin Ireland, 25 St Stephen's Green, Dublin 2, Ireland
(a division of Penguin Books Ltd)
Penguin Group (Australia), 250 Camberwell Road,
Camberwell, Victoria 3124, Australia
(a division of Pearson Australia Group Pty Ltd)
Penguin Books India Pvt Ltd, 11 Community Centre,
Panchsheel Park, New Delhi - 110 017, India
Penguin Group (NZ), 67 Apollo Drive, Rosedale, North Shore 0632,
New Zealand (a division of Pearson New Zealand Ltd)
Penguin Books (South Africa) (Pty) Ltd, 24 Sturdee Avenue,
Rosebank, Johannesburg 2196, South Africa

Penguin Books Ltd, Registered Offices:
80 Strand, London WC2R 0RL, England

First published in the United States of America by G. P. Putnam's Sons 1878
This edition with an introduction by Michael Sims published in Penguin Books 2010

5   7   9   10   8   6   ●

Introduction copyright © Michael Sims, 2010
All rights reserved

LIBRARY OF CONGRESS CATALOGING IN PUBLICATION DATA
Green, Anna Katherine, 1846–1935.
The Leavenworth case / Anna Katherine Green : introduction by Michael Sims.
p.   cm.—(Penguin classics)
ISBN 978-0-14-310612-8
1. Sisters—Fiction.   2. Merchants—Crimes against—Fiction.
3. Inheritance and succession—Fiction.   4. Police—New York (State)—New York—Fiction.
5. Murder—Investigation—Fiction.   I. Title.
PS2732.L4 2010
813'.4—dc22   2009052296

Printed in the United States of America
Set in Sabon

Contents

THE LEAVENWORTH CASE

BOOK I
THE PROBLEM

BOOK II
HENRY CLAVERING

BOOK III
HANNAH

BOOK IV
THE PROBLEM SOLVED

Introduction

The first time I opened *The Leavenworth Case*, I couldn't put it down. I had found a century-old edition in green buckram with crossed red keys embossed on the cover—nothing valuable, just a reading copy whose cloth and paper gave antique pleasure, but still not a volume I ought to hold in one hand while scrambling eggs with the other. Yet I couldn't stop reading. I took the book with me to a doctor's office and even read a page or two at traffic lights. I had enjoyed her later stories about the young socialite detective Violet Strange, but this was my introduction to Anna Katharine Green's entertaining skills as a novelist. And this nineteenth-century bestseller was her first novel.

From the opening page, the story gallops off like a runaway hansom cab. Soon readers find themselves caught up in a trial scene worthy of *Perry Mason* or *Law & Order*—a coroner's inquest held, as was customary in the late nineteenth century, at the scene of the crime. After this surprising episode, the story grows ever trickier, with revelations and cliff-hangers galore. Green keeps the dialogue lively and mostly convincing, especially for its era. Some critics disparage her characters' occasional florid speeches, but if outbreaks of Victorian emotion were fatal, all of Dickens's characters would have expired long ago. Aside from her modern sense of pacing, Green draws us back to her books for all the virtues that we think of as Victorian, those that keep us returning to, say, Wilkie Collins: atmosphere, plot, color, and sheer narrative energy. Now and then her storytelling is as leisurely as you would expect from a nineteenth-century novel, but mostly the story dashes at a pace that dazzled her contemporaries. She zips through many scenes like an indie film director. Watch this cinematic jump cut:

> The answer came in the shape of an envelope thrust under the door. Raising it, I found it to be a note. It was from Mr. Gryce, and ran thus:
> "Come at once; Hannah Chester is found."
>
> "Hannah found?"
> "So we have reason to think."
> "When? Where? by Whom?"
> "Sit down, and I will tell you."
> Drawing up a chair in a flurry of hope and fear, I sat down by Mr. Gryce's side.
> "She is not in the cupboard," that personage exclaimed, observing without doubt how my eyes went traveling about the room in my anxiety and impatience.

The Leavenworth Case was published in 1878, nine years before the debut of a cocky English private detective named Sherlock Holmes. Anna Katharine Green was unquestionably a pioneer, but even she was not the first woman to write a detective novel. Apparently that honor goes to American dime novelist Metta Victoria Fuller Victor, who published *The Dead Letter* in 1867 under the pseudonym Seeley Regester. And Regester's novel was preceded by a story published in January 1866 in the *Australian Journal*—"The Dead Witness," which appeared under the pseudonym "W. W.," which hid the identity and gender of a young Irish-born writer named Mary Fortune.

But Green was much the better writer of the three. Her plotting was outrageously sneaky, and her characterizations quick and often witty. *The Leavenworth Case* became one of the best-selling novels of the nineteenth century, launching not only the first major detective novelist—her career would span forty-five years—but also the first series of such novels about an ongoing character. Green became so well known that, during his tour of America in the 1890s, Arthur Conan Doyle sought a meeting with her.

When Green wrote her sophisticated and confident first

book, the genre was still young. Most critics cite Edgar Allan Poe's 1841 "Murders in the Rue Morgue" as the genesis of detective fiction. Of course, practically every story since Cain and Abel has included crime; and rudimentary detection shows up in, for example, Voltaire's novel *Zadig* and E. T. A. Hoffmann's story "Mademoiselle de Scuderi." But Poe brought them all together. His influences included the felony-ridden stories of French novelist Honoré de Balzac, who drew some of his own inspiration from the hawkeyed trackers in James Fenimore Cooper's tales of American Indians. It was Poe who introduced the first private consulting detective, C. Auguste Dupin, as well as other trappings that Conan Doyle would later purloin to furnish his Sherlock Holmes adventures—an egotistical amateur, an admiring narrator, inept official police, and an outré murder. The genre reached adolescence in the detective novels that Balzac's countryman Émile Gaboriau began publishing in 1866, several of them starring Monsieur Lecoq, based upon a real-life criminal-turned-policeman named Eugène François Vidocq. Soon after her debut, Anna Katharine Green was called the American Gaboriau.

Ahead of the pack as usual, it was also Poe who established the now standard last scene in detective stories, a retrospective explanation by the detective that casts the story's events in a new light. This innovation launched one of the great aesthetic pleasures of the genre: the last-minute reconfiguring of events into a second story underlying the one that you thought you were reading. From this first novel, Anna Katharine Green proved a master at such conjuring.

In 1846, after living in Manhattan and moving to Indiana and back, a restless attorney named James Wilson Green and his pregnant wife, Katherine Ann Whitney Green, settled their three children in Brooklyn Heights, on the bluff across the East River from Manhattan. In their house opposite the Plymouth Church, Anna Catherine Green was born on November 11. Not until the age of thirty-two, when she published her first book, would she change the spelling of her middle name to more closely resemble her mother's first name.

Brooklyn Heights was bustling. Walt Whitman lived there

and edited the *Brooklyn Eagle*. A decade before, the census had reported sixty-four lawyers working in Brooklyn, but James Green practiced in Manhattan near the U.S. courthouse. The Plymouth Church was the pulpit of the famous Presbyterian orator Henry Ward Beecher. Three years after arriving and immediately joining the church, the Greens would name their fifth child after Beecher—just before his church burned down. That same tragic summer, leaving three older children, a three-year-old Anna, and a newborn, Katherine Green died in a cholera epidemic. The baby lived only two more weeks, and Anna became the charge of her sixteen-year-old sister. James Green gathered his children around him and became ever more the guardian patriarch.

He also continued his peripatetic lifestyle, taking the family to Connecticut and Albany before settling in Buffalo in 1857. Financial troubles were haunting the New York City area; thanks largely to the Erie Canal, however, Buffalo was a bustling iron-and-steel town that was trying to outgrow its frontier roughness. Green prospered. While tightly controlling his children's lives, he gave them material comforts and education. In time he married a woman who encouraged her bright stepdaughter to write down her rhymes and narratives. It was in this cold industrial town that young Anna began her habit of walking alone, reciting to herself the poems she wrote. Her older brother had a toy printing press and played publisher to her author.

Unlike most fathers of his era, James Green sent his daughters to college, although only a few specialized universities even accepted female students at the time. In 1863, after graduating from public high school in Buffalo, Anna Green left for Poultney, Vermont, where she attended Ripley Female College, which is now Green Mountain College. At Ripley she met Ralph Waldo Emerson. She was drawn toward writing poetry, and her professors encouraged her. She became president of the Washington Irving Association, and like Irving she would set most of her writing in New York or at least in the northeastern United States. Employment was not an option for a middle-class young woman, so after graduation Green returned home—although home kept moving, to various places around New York and finally back to Brooklyn Heights. Five years after

graduating, Green sent several poems to Emerson, who replied
with only modest encouragement:

> [T]hey clearly indicate a good degree attained in power of ex-
> pression. . . . I think one is to be congratulated on every degree of
> success of this kind. . . . But it is quite another question whether
> it is to be made a profession,—whether one may dare leave all
> other things behind, & write. . . .

Discouraged, Green looked to other avenues of expression.
Her stepmother again encouraged her to write fiction. Throughout her young life, she had observed her father's career—his
remarks about courts and attorneys, his interactions with colleagues and police. Later she remembered riding in the back-
seat of a carriage and listening to her father chatting in the front
with the police chief as their horse clopped along the streets.
Gradually she began to wonder if she might write a novel along
the lines of Wilkie Collins—a suspenseful tale about crime and
lawyers and detectives. She began to draw upon her knowledge
of her father's profession and the wealthier people whose lives
she had glimpsed, making notes toward characters and scenes,
thinking about the legalities of wills and marriages. The daughter of a strong-willed father, she worked female dependence
and inheritance laws into the story.

For six long years, afraid that she would be unable to complete
a novel, Anna Green worked in secret, filling school notebooks
as she evolved the story that would become *The Leavenworth
Case.* Writing with various inks and on various colored papers,
working at the mountains and seashore, in Brooklyn, even on
trains, she accumulated a 150,000-word manuscript that she
later described as "like Joseph's coat of many colors." She waited
until it was two-thirds complete before showing it to her father
and the rest of the family. He liked it and encouraged her but also
immediately assumed the role of editor, advising a number of
deletions and additions. "I felt grateful to my father for his kindness in helping me," she recalled later, "but I must confess that
the way he tore some of my most cherished construction all to
pieces was almost disheartening. However, I reconstructed and
pieced together the parts which he had condemned, and set about

completing my work." He insisted that before going to a publisher, she surrender the manuscript to the critical legal eye of a judge he knew; but when the judge completed his reading, he had a single minor critique—that the author had used the word *equity* in a colloquial rather than a precise legal sense. She changed her wording.

Through a contact of her father's, the manuscript was submitted to New York publisher George Putnam, who insisted that Green cut sixty thousand words. Frustrated but eager to please, she did so, and Putnam published the book in 1878. It quickly became astonishingly popular. Later Wilkie Collins himself exclaimed over its virtues:

> Her powers of invention are so remarkable—she has so much imagination and so much belief (a most important qualification for our art) in what she says. . . . Dozens of times reading the story I have stopped to admire the fertility of invention, the delicate treatment of incident—and the fine perception of event on the personages of the story.

Soon Yale assigned Green's first novel to its law students, as a demonstration of the risks of circumstantial evidence. The book was so well known six years later, when Green married a young aspiring actor named Charles Rohlfs—who later became an acclaimed furniture designer—that Rohlfs said he felt as if he had married *The Leavenworth Case*. She was thirty-seven, he twenty-eight. She came from an old New England family and had become famous and wealthy; his parents were German immigrants, and he was just starting out. But in real life as in fiction, Anna Katharine Green seldom followed expectations.

Wherever you turn in the history of detective stories, Green's influence shows up. In Agatha Christie's 1963 novel *The Clocks*, for example, Hercule Poirot holds forth about various early crime stories. He applauds *The Mystery of the Yellow Room*, the 1907 impossible-crime novel by Gaston Leroux of *Phantom of the Opera* fame, and of course lauds the Sherlock Holmes stories. Then he says of *The Leavenworth Case*, "One savours its period atmosphere, its studied and deliberate melodrama." Christie herself had savored the novel since the age of eight, when her sister Madge read it to her. When she published her own first novel in 1920, *The Mysterious Affair at Styles*, she too created an elderly male detective, the vainglorious Poirot. Considering Christie's fondness for Green's writing, surely she read the later Ebenezer Gryce novels—including *That Affair Next Door* and other cases that Gryce shared with the first meddlesome spinster sleuth in detective fiction, Amelia Butterworth, a worthy ancestor of Miss Jane Marple (in fact, a more rounded, amusing, and believable character).

Christie adopted Green's habit of telling a story mostly in dialogue and even her gimmick of having characters misconstrue what they overhear. Christie, Conan Doyle, and others also followed Green's example in employing what would later be called a multimedia text. In *Leavenworth,* Green includes two scene diagrams and two samples of handwriting, one of which is reversed because it appears scratched on a windowpane.

The atmosphere and melodrama that Christie admired owe something to the so-called sensation novels—books such as Wilkie Collins's *The Woman in White*, Ellen Wood's *East Lynne*, and Mary Elizabeth Braddon's *Lady Audley's Secret*, all of which appeared between 1859 and 1862. Green chose not to follow directly in their path, but she learned from them. Such books tore away the comforting notion that scandal and melodrama belonged only to Gothic settings; sensation writers brought violent events and family secrets out of haunted castles and into drawing rooms. They were so popular that W. S. Gilbert parodied them in his 1871 comic opera *A Sensation Novel.*

Green's first and longest-running series detective, Ebenezer Gryce, advances beyond two particular ancestors. In 1852 Charles Dickens created Inspector Bucket, a secondary character in *Bleak House* but the first important fictional detective. He investigates the mysterious past of Lady Dedlock. Middle-aged, sharp-eyed Bucket seems to materialize in a room like a phantom, so quiet is his approach; and he looks at one character, as Dickens remarks with his usual offhand genius for simile, "as if he were going to take his portrait." Bucket's intense gaze belies his lethargic pose. Then in 1868 came Sergeant Cuff in *The Moonstone*, by Dickens's friend Wilkie Collins, the king of sensation writers. Cuff is "a grizzled, elderly man, so miserably lean that he looked as if he had not got an ounce of flesh on his bones in any part of him," and his eyes, "of a steely light gray, had a very disconcerting trick, when they encountered your eyes, of looking as if they expected something more from you than you were aware of yourself."

By the time Green started writing, readers were already assuming that a detective character's raison d'être in a novel was his literal and symbolic penetrating gaze. When she created Ebenezer Gryce a decade after *The Moonstone*, Green amusingly rejected this idea in the very first chapter:

> Mr. Gryce, the detective, was not the thin, wiry individual with a shrewd eye that seems to plunge into the core of your being and pounce at once upon its hidden secret that you are doubtless expecting to see. Mr. Gryce was a portly, comfortable personage with an eye that never pounced, that did not even rest—on you. If it rested anywhere, it was always on some insignificant object in your vicinity, some vase, inkstand, book or button. These things he would seem to take into his confidence, make the repositories of his conclusions, but you—you might as well be the steeple on Trinity Church, for all the connection you ever appeared to have with him or his thoughts.

Tireless, rheumatic, and sardonic, Gryce is a wonderful character who stands comfortably beside other great eccentrics in the field. "Oh, beautiful!" he exclaims when pieces of evidence fit together. The narrator asks him, "Whom do you suspect?" and Gryce replies with the kind of oracular ambiguity later immortalized by Sherlock Holmes, "Everyone and nobody." This remark sounds like a cliché because it has since become one; but readers heard it here first. Green's detective even propounds a manifesto that would be strikingly reminiscent of Holmes had not Gryce said it a decade before the debut of the sage of Baker Street: "Now it is a principle which every detective recognizes the truth of, that if of a hundred leading circumstances connected with a crime, ninety-nine of these are acts pointing to the suspected party with unerring certainty but the hundredth equally important act one which that person could not

have performed, the whole fabric of suspicion is destroyed."
And Gryce distinguishes between inquisition and investigation
with a single remark: "It is not enough to look for evidence
where you expect to find it."

Unlike Bucket and Cuff, Gryce has something of a Watson to
tell his story in *The Leavenworth Case*, although he appears only
in this one novel: our narrator, Everett Raymond. But the story's
camera-eye doesn't follow Gryce all the time, because Raymond
is no passive admirer dogging his master's footsteps. He has an
agenda of his own. He is an intelligent, passionate, and impul-
sive lawyer who hounds across the countryside sniffing for clues
because, as you will soon discover, he falls for one of Leavenworth's beautiful nieces. Raymond is an excellent point-of-view
character. Driven by emotion but determined to employ his professional brain in the cause of justice, he pays close attention,
thinks aloud, and inaugurates what will become a detective story
tradition: he regularly summarizes the clues glimpsed so far.

These were not the only genre conventions that Green established; she also provides the aforementioned diagrams of crime
scenes and wraps up the story with a trap-laden assembly of
suspects. Throughout *The Leavenworth Case*, while her characters are caught up in the tempest, the author calmly presents
the crime as a puzzle to be worked out. Book I is called "The
Problem" and Book IV "The Problem Solved." Green liked the
mathematical-sounding word *problem*, and she would use it
again elsewhere, including in the title of a 1915 story collection
about a female detective, *The Golden Slipper, and Other Prob-
lems for Violet Strange*. In this case the problem is a SHOCK-
ING MURDER, as one headline shouts before adding in a stage
whisper, "Mr. Leavenworth, the Well-Known Millionaire,
Found Dead in His Room." This kind of lighthearted, escapist
detective story is more fun when the victim is wealthy. Riches
increase the motivation and also furnish an exotic setting—"the
glow of satin, glitter of bronze, and glimmer of marble," as Everett Raymond remarks. The author turns Horatio Leavenworth's Gilded Age palace into the New York City version of an
English country house, replete with butler, maids, cook, amanuensis, and, of course, the eccentric and reclusive millionaire and
his beautiful orphaned nieces. Throughout her career, she would

often build a story around a single family or a single setting. In this characteristic too, Agatha Christie would follow her model, gradually expanding it to include brilliant variations such as *Murder on the Orient Express*.

I find it interesting that Green is no less preoccupied with class structure than her later colleagues across the Atlantic. During the 1870s, as Green was writing *The Leavenworth Case*, the notorious Mrs. Astor was directing the selection of four hundred old-family New Yorkers who would become the new American aristocracy and be permitted to enter the sacred precincts of her Fifth Avenue ballroom. The servants in the Leavenworth household reflect the influx of Irish immigrants in the decades following the potato famine; by 1890, there would be more Irish in New York than in Dublin. Leavenworth's glum secretary, in contrast, is distinctly middle class, precisely attuned to the distinctions between himself and the rest of the staff.

When Ebenezer Gryce wants to persuade the narrator to spy for him—that is, to watch for evidence behind the scenes—he explains first that there is one disguise that he himself cannot execute convincingly: "I have never by any possibility of means succeeded with one class of persons at all. I cannot pass myself off for a gentleman. Tailors and barbers are no good; I am always found out." Everett Raymond is a gentleman who became an attorney, and the policeman cannot possibly join him in this exclusive club. Gryce says to him, "Now you, I dare say, have no trouble———was born one, perhaps. Can even ask a lady to dance without blushing, eh?" When Raymond later complains that there was simply no way to stop a woman from mailing a certain epistle, Gryce mutters, "That is because you are a gentleman." Raymond doesn't deny his elevated position; he happily observes the world from the height of privilege. When a humble laborer professes himself dazzled by a lady's beauty, Raymond thinks, "I could but wonder over a loveliness capable of swaying the low as well as the high."

Sometimes, like Jane Austen, Anna Katharine Green describes characters more in terms of the overall implications of their social status than with actual physical description. Consider the young man "whose sleek appearance, intelligent eye, and general air of trustworthiness, seemed to proclaim him to be, what in fact he was, the confidential clerk of a responsible mercantile house." Arthur Conan Doyle, and therefore Sherlock Holmes, interpreted the world via more specific details of status—a racing form protruding from a goose-monger's pocket, the double line on a typist's plush sleeve.

In her social-criticism mode, while confidently employing a male narrator, Green has fun with stereotypes about her own gender. "Women," mutters one of Gryce's assistants, "are a mystery." Raymond himself advises a client, "Of old, the modes of getting a wife were the same as those of acquiring any other species of property, and they are not materially changed at the present time." The dependent legal status of women plays an important role in the story. Yet Green opposed the women's suffrage movement. Throughout her life she remained socially conservative, fond of old-fashioned clothes and furnishings, and sympathetic to women's issues but resistant to what she saw as radical or unseemly behavior. In 1917, at the height of World War I—when she was in her seventies and famous and rich—Green wrote a public letter to the *New York Times* urging men to vote against granting women the right to vote, because it would confuse government, encourage immodesty, provoke marital discord, and unnecessarily add to the traditional burdens of women.

Although Raymond is the narrator and Gryce the official detective, another character grows ever more important as the story progresses—"the horrible, blood-curdling *it*," as Raymond exclaims, "that yesterday was a living, breathing man." Although Horatio Leavenworth is dead before the story opens, "Death by murder is in a way not an end but a beginning," as Ruth Rendell observes in one of her Inspector Wexford novels. "The lives of the naturally dead may be buried with them," says Rendell, but murder victims' lives are exposed, one piece at a time, until they take on "the character of a celebrity's biography." In fiction as in reality, old sins cast long shadows. "One must go farther back than this murder," muses Raymond about the death of Horatio Leavenworth, "to find the root of a mistrust so great. . . ."

After *The Leavenworth Case*, Anna Katharine Green's fame grew through more than three dozen books in the mystery field, from *A Strange Disappearance* in 1880 to *The Step on the Stair* in 1923. She quickly developed a work schedule, beginning to write around 9:00 a.m. and working into the afternoon, only to often return again after dinner, when she would read her day's work aloud for her husband and children and governess to critique. She was her own most severe critic, of course, and often paused in reading to jot marginal notes on the pages. Ebenezer Gryce returned in several novels and some stories, and three times he was joined by the quick-witted spinster, Amelia Butterworth. After her first couple of novels, Green published a volume of twenty-six early poems, *The Defence of the Bride*. "Vigorous productions," *Harper's* magazine called the poems, and the reviewer added the highest compliment he could imagine, proclaiming this young woman's poetry to be absolutely masculine in its power and concision. Later Green also published a drama, *Risifi's Daughter*.

Green's seemingly risky choice of husband proved as wise as her determination to pursue a career instead of sitting quietly in the parlor and chatting about fashion. Besides acting now and then—in Shakespeare and Molière and a stage version of *The Leavenworth Case*—Charles Rohlfs became an acclaimed industrial designer and furniture designer. In a recent article, art historian Joseph Cunningham called Rohlfs "one of the most enigmatic and celebrated American designers of the early twentieth century," and went on to examine the ways that his wife collaborated with him on much of his best-known work. A desk chair they designed together is in the Metropolitan Museum of Art in New York. Together, Green and Rohlfs raised three children; two sons embraced the new century to the point of becoming pilots.

Green didn't publish any more books after 1923, but even this date was in the modern era that critics often call the Golden Age of detective fiction. Agatha Christie had published her first Poirot novel three years earlier and was moving toward becoming the Anna Katharine Green of the twentieth century. Before the end of the decade, such influential forces as Raymond Chandler and Ellery Queen would appear. Upon Green's death on

April 11, 1935, at the age of eighty-eight, *Publishers Weekly* reported that her first book had sold more than a million copies.

Her grave, in Forest Lawn Cemetery in Buffalo, bears her name incised next to others on a single large family stone labeled ROHLFS. There is no mention of her fame. But literary characters, unlike their creators, live beyond the grave. The mortal remains of Anna Katharine Green rest underground, but Amelia Butterworth and Ebenezer Gryce and Violet Strange are still cavorting in the minds of readers. A century and a third after their first appearance, the characters in *The Leavenworth Case* stand poised to reenact the drama. Turning the first page, you will open the door at the firm of Veeley, Carr & Raymond and find ambitious young Everett Raymond seated behind a desk. Someone is coming in to announce the shocking murder of Mr. Leavenworth.

MICHAEL SIMS

Suggestions for Further Reading

"Anna Katharine Green Tells How She Manufactures Her Plots." *Literary Digest* 58 (July 1918): 48.

Bargainnier, Earl F., ed. 10 *Women of Mystery*. Bowling Green, OH: Bowling Green State University Popular Press, 1981.

Christie, Agatha. *Agatha Christie: An Autobiography*. New York: Dodd, Mead, 1977. Christie describes her early fondness for Green's books.

Cunningham, Joseph. "Anna Katharine Green and Charles Rohlfs: Artistic Collaborators." *Antiques*, December 2008.

Green, Anna Katharine. "Why Human Beings Are Interested in Crime." *American Magazine* 87, no. 2 (February 1919): 38–39, 82–86.

———. "Women Must Wait." *New York Times*, October 30, 1917, 14.

Hatch, Mary R. P. "An American Gaboriau." *The Daily Inter Ocean* 18, no. 119 (July 21, 1889): 21.

Haycraft, Howard. *Murder for Pleasure: The Life and Times of the Detective Story*. 1941, revised 1951. Reprint, New York: Carroll & Graf, 1984.

Maida, Patricia D. *Mother of Detective Fiction: The Life and Works of Anna Katharine Green*. Bowling Green, OH: Bowling Green State University Popular Press, 1989. Maida's book provided much of the personal information about Green that appears in the introduction to the present volume.

Murch, Alma E. *The Development of the Detective Novel*. Westport, CT: Greenwood, 1981.

Nickerson, Catherine Ross. *The Web of Iniquity: Early Detective Fiction by American Women*. Chapel Hill: Duke University Press, 1998.

Snyder, Ruth. "Life's Facts as Startling as Fiction, Says Writer, 76." *The Indianapolis Sunday Star*, May 13, 1928, 16.

Steinbrunner, Chris, and Otto Penzler. *Encyclopedia of Mystery and Detection*. New York: McGraw-Hill, 1976. This essential volume provides a great deal of background on early detective fiction.

WEB SITES

http://www.ladybluestocking.com/index.htm. This site features facsimile dust jackets for vintage books, including many of Green's.

http://motherofmystery.com/articles/plots. This excellent site provides access to online versions of numerous articles by and about Anna Katharine Green, including most of those cited above.

http://tarlton.law.utexas.edu/lpop/green.html. This site, hosted by the Tarlton Law Library's Law in Popular Culture Collection, at the University of Texas at Austin, features a Green chronology and bibliography.

The Leavenworth Case

BOOK I

THE PROBLEM

CHAPTER I

"A Great Case"

A deed of dreadful note.
—MACBETH.

I had been a junior partner in the firm of Veeley, Carr & Raymond, attorneys and counselors at law, for about a year, when one morning, in the temporary absence of both Mr. Veeley and Mr. Carr, there came into our office a young man whose whole appearance was so indicative of haste and agitation that I involuntarily rose as he approached, and advanced to meet him.

"What is the matter, sir?" I inquired. "You have no bad news to tell me, I hope?"

"I have come to see Mr. Veeley; is he in?"

"No," I replied; "he was unexpectedly called away this morning to Washington; he cannot be home before tomorrow, but if you will make your business known to me——"

"To you, sir?" interrupted he, turning a very cold, but steady eye on mine; then seeming to be satisfied with his scrutiny, continued: "There is no reason why I shouldn't; my business is no secret. I came to inform him that Mr. Leavenworth is dead."

"Mr. Leavenworth!" I exclaimed, falling back a step. Mr. Leavenworth was an old client of our firm, to say nothing of his being the particular friend of Mr. Veeley.

"Yes, murdered; shot through the head by some unknown person while sitting at his library table."

"Shot! Murdered!" I could scarcely believe my ears. What! The genial, whole-souled old gentleman, who but a week before had stood in that very spot, twitting me with my bachelorhood and asking me in the same breath to come to his house and see what he had there to show me! I stared at the man beside me, half incredulously.

"How? When?" I gasped.

"Last night. At least so we suppose. He was not found till

this morning. I am Mr. Leavenworth's private secretary," he explained, "and live in the family. It was a dreadful shock," he went on, "especially to the ladies."

"Dreadful!" I repeated. "Mr. Veeley will be overwhelmed by it."

"They are all alone," continued he in a low business-like way I afterward found to be inseparable from the man; "the Misses Leavenworth I mean—Mr. Leavenworth's nieces; and as an inquest is to be held there today, it is deemed proper they should have someone present capable of advising them. As Mr. Veeley was their uncle's best friend, they naturally sent me for him, but he being absent, I don't know what to do or where to go."

"Well," replied I, "I am a stranger to the ladies, but if I can be of any assistance to them, my respect for their uncle is such——"

The expression of the secretary's eye stopped me. Without seeming to wander from my face, its pupil had suddenly dilated till it appeared to embrace my whole person within its scope.

"I don't know," remarked he finally, a slight frown testifying to the fact that he was not altogether pleased with the turn affairs were taking. "Perhaps it would be best. The ladies must not be left alone——"

"Say no more," interrupted I; "I will go." And sitting down I dispatched a hurried message to Mr. Veeley, after which, and the few other preparations necessary, I accompanied the secretary to the street.

"Now," said I, "tell me all you know of this frightful affair."

"All I know? A few words will do that. I left him last night sitting as usual at his library table, and found him this morning, seated in the same place, almost in the same position, but with a bullet hole in his head as large as the end of my little finger."

"Dead?"

"Stone dead."

"Horrible!" I exclaimed. Then, after a moment: "Could it have been a suicide?"

"No. The pistol with which the deed was committed is not to be found."

"But if it was a murder, there must have been some motive. Mr. Leavenworth was too benevolent a man to have enemies, and if robbery was intended——"

"There was no robbery. There is nothing missing," he again interrupted. "The whole affair is a mystery."

"A mystery?"

"An utter mystery."

Turning, I looked at my informant curiously. The inmate of a house in which a mysterious murder had occurred was rather an interesting object. But the good-featured and yet totally unimpressive countenance of the man beside me offered but little basis for even the wildest imagination to work upon, and glancing almost immediately away I asked:

"Are the ladies very much overcome?"

He took at least a half-dozen steps before replying.

"It would be unnatural if they were not," he said at last; and whether it was the expression of his face at the time or the nature of the reply itself, I felt that in speaking of these ladies to this uninteresting, self-possessed secretary of the late Mr. Leavenworth, I was somehow treading upon dangerous ground. As I had heard they were very accomplished women, I was not altogether pleased at this discovery. It was, therefore, with a certain consciousness of relief that I saw a Fifth Avenue stage approach.

"We will defer our conversation," said I. "Here's the stage."

But once seated within it, we soon discovered that all intercourse upon such a subject was impossible. Employing the time, therefore, in running over in my mind what I knew of Mr. Leavenworth, I found that my knowledge was limited to the bare fact of his being a retired merchant of great wealth and fine social position, who in default of possessing children of his own, had taken into his home two nieces, one of whom had already been declared his heiress. To be sure I had heard Mr. Veeley speak of his eccentricities, giving as an instance this very fact of his making a will in favor of one niece to the utter exclusion of the other, but of his habits of life and connection with the world at large, I knew little or nothing.

There was a great crowd in front of the house when we arrived there, and I had barely time to observe that it was a corner dwelling of unusual depth as well as width, when I was seized by the throng and carried quite to the foot of the broad stone steps. Extricating myself, though with some difficulty, owing to the importunities of a boot-black and butcher boy, who seemed to think that by clinging to my arms they might be able to smuggle themselves into the very scene of the tragedy, I mounted the steps, and finding the secretary by some unaccountable good fortune close to my side, hurriedly rang the bell. Immediately the door opened, and a face I recognized as that of one of our city detectives appeared in the gap.

"Mr. Gryce!" I exclaimed.

"The same," replied he. "Come in, Mr. Raymond." And drawing us quietly into the house, he shut the door with a grim smile on the disappointed crowd without. "I trust you are not surprised to see me here," said he, holding out his hand, with a side-glance at my companion.

"No," returned I. Then with a vague idea that I ought to introduce the young man at my side, continued, "This is Mr. ——, Mr. ——, —excuse me, but I do not know your name," I said, turning with a glance of inquiry to my companion. "The private secretary of the late Mr. Leavenworth," I hastened to add.

"Oh," returned he, "the secretary! The coroner has been asking for you, sir."

"The coroner is here, then?" said I.

"Yes, the jury have just gone upstairs to view the body; would you like to follow them?"

"No," said I. "It is not necessary. I have merely come in the hope of being of some assistance to the young ladies. Mr. Veeley is away."

"And you thought the opportunity too good to be lost," he went on; "just so. Still, now that you are here and as the case promises to be a marked one, I should think that, as a rising young lawyer, you would wish to make yourself acquainted with it in all its details. But follow your own judgment."

I made an effort and overcame my repugnance. "I will go," said I.

"Very well, then," he replied, "follow me."

But just as I set foot on the stairs I heard the jury descending, so drawing back with Mr. Gryce into the recess between the reception room and parlor, I had time to remark:

"The young man says that it could not have been the work of a burglar."

"Indeed!" fixing his eye on a door-knob near by.

"That nothing has been found missing——"

"And that the fastenings to the house were all found secure this morning; just so."

"He did not tell me that. In that case"—and I shuddered—"the murderer must have been in the house all night."

Mr. Gryce smiled darkly at the door-knob.

"It has a dreadful look!" exclaimed I.

Mr. Gryce immediately frowned at the door-knob.

And here let me say that Mr. Gryce, the detective, was not the thin, wiry individual with a shrewd eye that seems to plunge into the core of your being and pounce at once upon its hidden secret that you are doubtless expecting to see. Mr. Gryce was a portly, comfortable personage with an eye that never pounced, that did not even rest—on you. If it rested anywhere, it was always on some insignificant object in your vicinity, some vase, inkstand, book or button. These things he would seem to take into his confidence, make the repositories of his conclusions, but you—you might as well be the steeple on Trinity Church, for all the connection you ever appeared to have with him or his thoughts. At present, then, Mr. Gryce was, as I have already suggested, on intimate terms with the door-knob.

"A dreadful look," I repeated.

His eye shifted to the button on my sleeve.

"Come," he said, "the coast is clear at last."

Leading the way, he mounted the stairs, but stopped on the upper landing. "Mr. Raymond," said he, "I am not in the habit of talking much about the secrets of my profession, but in this case everything depends upon getting the right clue at the start. We have no common villainy to deal with here; genius has been at work. Now sometimes an absolutely uninitiated mind will intuitively catch at something which the most highly trained intellect will miss. If such a thing should occur, remember that

I am your man. Don't go round talking, but come to me. For this is going to be a great case, mind you, a great case. Now come on."

"But the ladies?"

"They are in the rooms above; in grief, of course, but tolerably composed, for all I hear." And advancing to a door, he pushed it open and beckoned me in.

All was dark for a moment but presently, my eyes becoming accustomed to the place, I saw that we were in the library.

"It was here that he was found," said he; "in this room and upon this very spot." And advancing he laid his hand on the end of a large, baize-covered table that, together with its attendant chairs, occupied the center of the room. "You see for yourself that it is directly opposite this door," and, crossing the floor, he paused in front of the threshold of a narrow passage-way, opening into a room beyond.* "As the murdered man was discovered sitting in this chair, and consequently with his back toward the passage-way, the assassin must have advanced through the doorway to deliver his shot, pausing let us say about here." And Mr. Gryce planted his feet firmly upon a certain spot in the carpet, about a foot from the threshold before mentioned.

"But——" I hastened to interpose.

1. *Library Table.*   2. *Chair.*   3. *Passage-way.*
4. *Bed.*   5. *Shaving Stand.*

This diagram is for those who are interested in the details of this affair.

"There is no room for but," he cried. "We have studied the situation." And without deigning to dilate upon the subject, he turned immediately about and stepping swiftly before me led the way into the passage named. "Wine closet, clothes closet, washing apparatus, towel-rack," explained he, waving his hand from side to side as we hurried through, finishing with "Mr. Leavenworth's private apartment," as that room in all its elegance opened upon us.

Mr. Leavenworth's private apartment! It was here then that *it* ought to be, the horrible blood-curdling *it* that yesterday was a living, breathing man. Advancing to the bed that was hung with heavy curtains, I raised my hand to put them back when Mr. Gryce, drawing them from my clasp, disclosed lying upon the pillow a cold, a calm face looking so natural I involuntarily started.

"His death was too sudden to distort the features," said he, turning the head to one side in a way to make visible a ghastly wound in the back of the cranium. "Such a hole as that sends a man out of the world without much notice. The surgeon will convince you it could never have been inflicted by himself. It is a case of deliberate murder."

Horrified, I drew hastily back, when my glance fell upon a door situated directly opposite me in the side of the wall toward the hall. It appeared to be the only outlet from the room with the exception of the passage through which we had entered, and I could not help wondering if it was through there the assassin had come on his roundabout course to the library. But Mr. Gryce, seemingly observant of my glance, though his own was fixed upon the chandelier, made haste to remark, as if in reply to the inquiry in my face:

"Found locked on the inside; may have come that way and may not: we don't pretend to say."

Observing now that the bed was undisturbed in its arrangement, I remarked: "He had not retired then?"

"No; the tragedy must be ten hours old. Time for the murderer to have studied the situation and provided for all contingencies."

"The murderer? Whom do you suspect?" I whispered.

He looked impassively at the ring on my finger.

"Everyone and nobody. It is not for me to suspect but to detect." And dropping the curtain into its former position he led me from the room.

The coroner's inquest being now in session, I felt a strong desire to be present, so requesting Mr. Gryce to inform the ladies that, Mr. Veeley being absent from town, I had come as one of his partners to render them any assistance they might require on so melancholy an occasion, I proceeded to the large parlor below and took my seat among the various perons there assembled.

CHAPTER 2

The Coroner's Inquest

The baby figure of the giant mass
Of things to come.
    —TROILUS AND CRESSIDA.

For a few minutes I sat dazed by the sudden flood of light that greeted me from the many open windows, then as the strongly contrasting features of the scene before me began to impress themselves upon my consciousness, I found myself experiencing something of the same sensation of double personality, which years before had followed an enforced use of ether. As at that time it appeared to me that I was living two lives at once, in two distinct places, with two separate sets of incidents going on, so now did I seem to be divided between two irreconcilable trains of thought; the gorgeous house, its elaborate furnishing, the little glimpses of yesterday's life as seen in the open piano with its sheet of music held in place by a lady's dainty fan, occupying my attention fully as much as the aspect of the throng of incongruous and impatient people huddled about me.

Perhaps one reason of this lay in the extraordinary splendor of the room I was in; the glow of satin, glitter of bronze and glimmer of marble meeting the eye at every turn. But I am rather inclined to think that it was mainly due to the force and eloquence of a certain picture that confronted me from the opposite wall. A sweet picture—sweet enough and poetic enough to have been conceived by the most idealistic of artists: simple too—vision of a young, golden-haired, blue-eyed coquette, dressed in the costume of the First Empire, standing in a woodpath looking back over her shoulder as at someone following—yet with such a dash of something not altogether saint-like in the corners of her meek eyes and baby-like lips, that it impressed me with the individuality of life. Had it not been for the open dress with its waist almost beneath the armpits, the hair cut short on the forehead and the perfection of the neck and shoulders, I should have taken it for a literal portrait of one of the ladies of the house. As it was, I could not rid myself of the idea that one, if not both, of Mr. Leavenworth's nieces looked down upon me from the eyes of this entrancing blonde with the beckoning glance and forbidding hand. So vividly did this fancy impress me, that I half shuddered as I looked, wondering if this sweet creature did not know what had occurred in this house since the happy yesterday, that she should stand there smiling so invitingly—when suddenly I became aware that I had been watching the little crowd of men about me with as complete an attention as if there were nothing else in the room but themselves. That the face of the coroner, sternly intelligent and attentive, was as distinctly imprinted upon my mind as that of this lovely picture, or the clearer-cut and more noble features of the sculptured Psyche, shining in mellow beauty from the crimson-hung window at his right. Yes, even that the various countenances of the jurymen clustered before me, commonplace and insignificant as most of them were, the trembling forms of the excited servants crowded into a far corner, and the still more disagreeable aspect of the pale-faced seedy reporter, seated at a small table and writing with a ghoul-like avidity that made my flesh creep, were each and all as fixed an element in the remarkable scene before me as the splendor of the surroundings which made their presence such a nightmare of discord and unreality.

I have spoken of the coroner. As fortune would have it he

was no stranger to me. I had not only seen him before, but had had frequent conversation with him, in fact knew him. His name was Hammond, and he was universally regarded as a man of more than ordinary acuteness, fully capable of conducting an important examination with the necessary skill and address. Interested as I was, or rather was likely to be in this particular inquiry, I could not but congratulate myself upon our good fortune in having so intelligent a coroner.

As for his jurymen, they were, as I have intimated, very much like all other bodies of a similar character. Picked up at random from the streets, but from such streets as Fifth and Sixth Avenues, they presented much the same appearance of average intelligence and refinement as might be seen in the chance occupants of one of our city stages rolling down Broadway, with its quota of business men. Indeed, I marked but one amongst them all who seemed to take any interest in the inquiry, as an inquiry; all the rest appearing to be actuated in the fulfillment of their duty by the commoner instincts of pity and indignation.

Dr. Maynard, the well-known surgeon of Thirty-sixth Street, was the first witness called. His testimony was mainly concerning the nature of the wound found in the murdered man's head. As some of the facts presented by him are likely to prove of importance to us in our narrative, I will proceed to give a synopsis of what he said.

Prefacing his remarks with some account of himself, and the manner in which he had been summoned to the house by one of the servants, he went on to state that upon his arrival he found the deceased lying on a bed in the second-story front room, with the blood clotted about a pistol wound in the back of the head; having evidently been carried there from the adjoining apartment some hours after death. It was the only wound discovered on the body, and having probed it, he had found and extracted the bullet which he now handed to the jury. It was lying in the brain, having entered the base of the skull, passed obliquely upward, and at once struck the *medulla oblongata*, causing instant death. The fact of the ball having entered the brain in this peculiar manner, he deemed worthy of note, since it would produce not only instantaneous death but an utterly

motionless one. Further, from the position of the bullet hole
and the direction taken by the bullet, it was manifestly impossible that the shot should have been fired by the man himself, even if the condition of the hair about the wound did not
completely demonstrate the fact that the shot was fired from a
point some three feet or four feet distant. Still further, considering the angle at which the bullet had entered the skull, it was
evident that the deceased must not only have been seated at the
time, a fact about which there could be no dispute, but he must
also have been engaged in some occupation which drew his
head forward. For, in order that the ball should enter the head
of a man sitting erect at the angle seen here, at 45°, it would be
necessary not only for the pistol to be held very low down, but
in a peculiar position; while if the head had been bent forward
as in the act of writing, a man holding a pistol naturally, with
the elbow bent, might very easily fire a ball into the brain at
the angle observed.

Upon being questioned in regard to the bodily health of Mr.
Leavenworth, he replied that the deceased appeared to have
been in good condition at the time of his death, but that not
being his attendant physician, he could not speak conclusively
upon the subject without further examination; and to the remark of a juryman observed that he had not seen pistol or
weapon lying upon the floor, or indeed anywhere else in either
of the above-mentioned rooms.

I might as well add here what he afterward stated, that from
the position of the table, the chair and the door behind it, the
murderer, in order to satisfy all the conditions imposed by the
situation, must have stood upon or just within the threshold of
the passage-way leading into the room beyond. Also, that as
the ball was small and from a rifled barrel, and thus especially
liable to deflections while passing through bones and integu-
ments, it seemed to him evident that the victim had made no
effort to raise or turn his head when advanced upon by his destroyer; the fearful conclusion being that the footstep was an
accustomed one, and the presence of its possessor in the room
either known or expected.

The physician's testimony being ended, the coroner picked
up the bullet which had been laid on the table before him, and

for a moment rolled it contemplatively between his fingers,
then drawing a pencil from his pocket, hastily scrawled a line
or two on a piece of paper and calling an officer to his side,
delivered some command in a low tone. The officer taking up
the slip, looked at it for an instant knowingly, then catching up
his hat left the room. Another moment, and the front door
closed on him, and a wild halloo from the crowd of urchins
without told of his appearance in the street. Sitting where I
did, I had a full view from the window of the corner. Looking
out, I saw the officer stop there, hail a cab, hastily enter it, and
disappear in the direction of Broadway.

CHAPTER 3

Facts and Deductions

> Confusion now hath made his master-piece;
> Most sacrilegious murder hath broke ope
> The Lord's anointed temple and stolen thence
> The life of the building.
>
> —Macbeth.

Turning my attention back into the room where I was, I found
the coroner consulting a memorandum through a very impres-
sive pair of gold eye-glasses.

"Is the butler here?" he asked.

Immediately there was a stir among the group of servants in
the corner, and an intelligent-looking though somewhat pompous Irishman stepped out from their midst and confronted the
jury. "Ah," thought I to myself as my glance encountered his
precise whiskers, steady eye and respectfully attentive though
by no means humble expression, "here is a model servant who
is likely to prove a model witness." And I was not mistaken.
Thomas, the butler, was in all respects one in a thousand—and
he knew it.

The coroner, upon whom, as upon all others in the room, he seemed to have made the like favorable impression, proceeded without hesitation to interrogate him.

"Your name, I am told, is Thomas Dougheity?"

"Yes, sir."

"Well, Thomas, how long have you been employed in your present situation?"

"It must be a matter of two years now, sir."

"You are the person who first discovered the body of Mr. Leavenworth?'"

"Yes, sir; I and Mr. Harwell."

"And who is Mr. Harwell?"

"Mr. Harwell is Mr. Leavenworth's private secretary, sir; the one who did his writing."

"Very good. Now at what time of the day or night was it that you made this discovery?"

"It was early, sir; early this morning, about eight."

"And where?"

"In the library, sir, off Mr. Leavenworth's bedroom. We had forced our way in, feeling anxious about his not coming to breakfast."

"You forced your way in; the door then was locked?"

"Yes, sir."

"On the inside?"

"That I cannot tell; there was no key in the door."

"Where was Mr. Leavenworth lying when you first found him?"

"He was not lying, sir. He was seated at the large table in the center of the room, his back to the bedroom door; leaning forward, his head on his hands."

"How was he dressed?"

"In his dinner suit, sir, just as he came from the table last night."

"Were there any evidences in the room that a struggle had taken place?"

"No, sir."

"Any pistol on the floor or table?"

"No, sir."

"Any reason to suppose that robbery had been attempted?"

"No, sir. Mr. Leavenworth's watch and purse were both in his pockets."

Being asked to mention who was in the house at the time of the discovery, he replied: "The young ladies, Miss Mary Leavenworth and Miss Eleanore, Mr. Harwell, Kate the cook, Molly the upstairs girl, and myself."

"The usual members of the household?"

"Yes, sir."

"Now tell me whose duty it is to close up the house at night."

"Mine, sir."

"Did you secure it as usual, last night?"

"I did, sir."

"Who unfastened it this morning?"

"I, sir."

"How did you find it?"

"Just as I left it."

"What, not a window open nor a door unlocked?"

"No, sir."

By this time you could have heard a pin drop. The certainty that the murderer, whoever he was, had not left the house, at least till after it was opened in the morning, seemed to weigh upon all minds. Forewarned as I had been of the fact, I could not but feel a certain degree of emotion at having it thus brought before me; and moving so as to bring the butler's face within view, searched it for some secret token that he had spoken thus emphatically in order to cover up his own dereliction of duty. But it was unmoved in its candor, and sustained the concentrated gaze of all in the room like a rock.

Being now asked when he had last seen Mr. Leavenworth alive, he replied. "At dinner last night."

"He was, however, seen later by some of you?"

"Yes, sir; Mr. Harwell says he saw him as late as half-past ten in the evening."

"What room do you occupy in this house?"

"A little one on the basement floor."

"And where do the other members of the household sleep?"

"Mostly on the third floor, sir; the ladies in the large back rooms, and Mr. Harwell in the little one in front. The girls sleep above."

"There was then no one on the same floor with Mr. Leaven-worth?"

"No, sir."

"At what hour did you go to bed?"

"Well, I should say about eleven."

"Did you hear any noise in the house either before or after that time, that you remember?"

"No, sir."

"So that the discovery you made this morning was a surprise to you?"

"Yes, sir."

Requested now to give a more detailed account of that discovery, he went on to say that it was not till Mr. Leavenworth failed to come to his breakfast at the call of the bell, that any suspicion arose in the house that all was not right. Even then they waited some time before doing anything, but as minute after minute went by and he did not come, Miss Eleanore grew very anxious, and finally left the room saying she would go to see what was the matter, but soon returned looking very much frightened, saying she had knocked at her uncle's door, and had even called to him, but could get no answer. At which he and Mr. Harwell had gone up and together tried both doors, and finding them locked, burst open that of the library, when they saw Mr. Leavenworth as he had already said, sitting at the table, dead.

"And the ladies?"

"Oh, they followed us up and came into the room and Miss Eleanore fainted away."

"And the other one, Miss Mary I believe they call her?"

"I don't remember anything about her. I was so busy fetching water for Miss Eleanore, I didn't notice."

"Well, how long was it before Mr. Leavenworth was carried into the next room?"

"Almost immediate, as soon as Miss Eleanore recovered and that was as soon as ever the water touched her lips."

"Who proposed that the body should be carried from the spot?"

"She, sir. As soon as ever she stood up she went over to it and looked at it and shuddered, and then calling Mr. Harwell and me, bade us carry him in and lay him on the bed and go for the doctor, which we did."

"Wait a moment; did she go with you when you went into the other room?"

"No, sir."

"What did she do?"

"She stayed by the library table."

"What doing?"

"I couldn't see; her back was to me."

"How long did she stay there?"

"She was gone when we came back."

"Gone from the table?"

"Gone from the room."

"Humph! When did you see her again?"

"In a minute. She came in at the library door as we went out."

"Anything in her hand?"

"Not as I see."

"Did you miss anything from the table?"

"I never thought to look, sir. The table was nothing to me. I was only thinking of going for the doctor, though I knew it was of no use."

"Whom did you leave in the room when you went out?"

"The cook, sir, and Molly, sir, and Miss Eleanore."

"Not Miss Mary?"

"No, sir."

"Very well. Have the jury any questions to put to this man?"

A movement at once took place in that profound body.

"I would like to ask a few," exclaimed a weazened-faced, excitable little man whom I had before noticed shifting in his seat in a restless manner, strongly suggestive of an intense but hitherto repressed desire to interrupt the proceedings.

"Very well, sir," returned Thomas.

But the juryman stopping to draw a deep breath, a large and decidedly pompous man who sat at his right hand seized the opportunity to inquire in a round listen-to-me sort of voice:

"You say you have been in the family for two years. Was it what you might call a united family?"

"United?"

"Affectionate, you know—on good terms with each other." And the juryman lifted a very long and heavy watch chain that hung across his vest as if that as well as himself had a right to a suitable and well-considered reply.

The butler, impressed perhaps by his manner, glanced uneasily around. "Yes, sir, as far as I know."

"The young ladies were attached to their uncle?"

"Oh, yes, sir."

"And to each other?"

"Well, yes, I suppose so; it's not for me to say."

"You suppose so. Have you any reason to think otherwise?" And he doubled the watch chain about his fingers as if he would double its attention as well as his own.

Thomas hesitated a moment. But just as his interlocutor was about to repeat his question, he drew himself up into a rather stiff and formal attitude and replied:

"Well, sir, no."

The juryman, for all his self-assertion, seemed to respect the reticence of a servant who declined to give his opinion in regard to such a matter, and drawing complacently back, signified with a wave of his hand that he had no more to say.

Immediately the excitable little man, before mentioned, slipped forward to the edge of his chair and asked this time without hesitation: "At what time did you unfasten the house this morning?"

"About six, sir."

"Now could anyone leave the house after that time without your knowledge?"

Thomas glanced a trifle uneasily at his fellow-servants, but answered up promptly and as if without reserve.

"I don't think it would be possible for anybody to leave this house after six in the morning without either myself or the cook's knowing of it. Folks don't jump from second-story windows in broad daylight, and as to leaving by the doors, the front door closes with such a slam all the house can hear it from top to bottom, and as for the back door, no one that goes out of that can get clear of the yard without going by the kitchen window, and no one can go by that kitchen window without the cook's a-seeing of them, that I can just swear to." And he cast a half quizzing, half malicious look at the round, red-faced individual in question, strongly suggestive of late and unforgotten bickerings over the kitchen coffee-urn and castor.

This reply, which was of a nature calculated to deepen the forebodings which had already settled upon the minds of those present, produced a visible effect. The house found locked and no one seen to leave it! Evidently, then, we had not far to look for the assassin.

Shifting on his chair with increased fervor, if I may so speak, the juryman glanced sharply around. But perceiving the renewed interest on the faces about him, he declined to weaken the effect of the last admission by any further questions. Settling, therefore, comfortably back, he left the field open for any other juror who might choose to press the inquiry. But no one seeming to be ready to do this, Thomas in his turn evinced impatience, and at last looking respectfully around inquired:

"Would any other gentleman like to ask me anything?" No one replying, he threw a hurried glance of relief toward the servants at his side, then while each one marveled at the sudden change that had taken place in his countenance, withdrew with an eager alacrity and evident satisfaction for which I could not at the moment account.

But the next witness proving to be none other than my acquaintance of the morning, Mr. Harwell, I soon forgot both Thomas and the doubts his last movement had awakened in the interest which the examination of so important a person as the secretary and right-hand man of Mr. Leavenworth was likely to create.

Advancing with the calm and determined air of one who realized that life and death itself might hang upon the words he would be called upon to utter, Mr. Harwell took his stand before the jury with a degree of dignity that was not only highly prepossessing in itself, but to me who had not been over and above pleased with him in our first interview, admirable and surprising. Lacking, as I have said, any distinctive quality of face or form agreeable or otherwise—being what you might call in appearance a negative sort of person, his pale regular features, dark well-smoothed hair and simple whiskers all belonging to a recognized type and very commonplace—there was still visible on this occasion at least a certain self-possession in his carriage which went far toward making up for the want of impressiveness in his countenance and expression. Not that even this was in any way remarkable. Indeed there was nothing remarkable about the man, any more than there is about a thousand others you meet every day on Broadway, unless you except the look of concentration and solemnity which pervaded his whole person; a solemnity which at this time would not have been noticeable, perhaps, if it had not appeared to be the habitual expression of one who in his short life had seen more of sorrow than joy, less of pleasure than care and anxiety.

The coroner, to whom his appearance one way or the other seemed to be a matter of no moment, addressed him immediately and without reserve.

"Your name?"

"James Trueman Harwell."

"Your business?"

"I have occupied the position of private secretary and amanuensis to Mr. Leavenworth for the past eight months."

"You are the person who last saw Mr. Leavenworth alive, are you not?"

The young man raised his head with a haughty gesture that well-nigh transfigured it.

"Certainly not; as I am not the man who killed him."

This answer, which seemed to introduce something akin to levity or badinage into an examination the seriousness of which we were all beginning to realize, produced an immediate revulsion of feeling toward the man who, in face of facts revealed and to be revealed, could so lightly make use of it. A hum of disapproval swept through the room, and in that one remark, James Harwell lost all that he had previously won by the self-possession of his bearing and the unflinching regard of his eye. He seemed himself to realize this, for he lifted his head still higher, though his general aspect remained unchanged.

"I mean," the coroner exclaimed, evidently nettled that the

young man had been able to draw such a conclusion from his words, "that you were the last one to see him previous to his assassination by some unknown individual?"

The secretary folded his arms, whether to hide a certain tremble that had seized him or by that simple action to gain time for a moment's further thought, I could not then determine. "Sir," he replied at length, "I cannot answer yes or no to that question. In all probability I was the last so to see him, but in a house as large as this I cannot be sure of even so simple a fact as that." Then observing the unsatisfied look on the faces around, added slowly: "It is my business to see him late."

"Your business? Oh, as his secretary, I suppose?"

He gravely nodded.

"Mr. Harwell," the coroner went on, "the office of private secretary in this country is not a common one. Will you explain to us what your duties were in that capacity; in short, what use Mr. Leavenworth had for such an assistant and how he employed you?"

"Certainly. Mr. Leavenworth was, as you perhaps know, a man of great wealth. Connected with various societies, clubs, institutions, etc., besides being known far and near as a giving man, he was accustomed every day of his life to receive numerous letters, begging and otherwise, which it was my business to open and answer; his private correspondence always bearing a mark upon it which distinguished it from the rest. But this was not all I was expected to do. Having in his early life been engaged in the tea-trade, he had made more than one voyage to China, and was consequently much interested in the question of international communication between that country and our own. Thinking that in his various visits there he had learned much which if known to the American people would conduce to our better understanding of the nation, its peculiarities and the best manner of dealing with it, he has been engaged for some time in writing a book on the subject, which same it has been my business for the last eight months to assist him in preparing, by writing at his dictation, three hours out of the twenty-four, the last hour being commonly taken from the evening, say from half-past nine to half-past ten; Mr. Leavenworth being a very methodical man and accustomed to regulate his own life and that of those about him with almost mathematical precision."

"You say that you were accustomed to write at his dictation evenings. Did you do this as usual last evening?"

"I did, sir."

"What can you tell us of his manner and appearance at the time? Were they in any way unusual?"

A frown crossed the secretary's brow.

"As he probably had no premonition of his doom, how should there have been any change in his manner?"

This giving the coroner an opportunity to revenge himself for his discomfiture of a moment before, he said somewhat severely:

"It is the business of a witness to answer questions, not to put them."

The secretary flushed and the account stood even.

"Very well then, sir; if Mr. Leavenworth felt any forebodings of his end, he did not reveal them to me. On the contrary, he seemed to be more absorbed in his work than usual. One of the last words he said to me was: 'In a month we will have this book in press, eh, Trueman?' I remember this particularly, as he was filling his wineglass at the time. He always drank one glass of wine before retiring, it being my duty to bring the decanter of sherry from the closet the last thing before leaving him. I was standing with my hand on the knob of the hall door, but advanced as he said this and replied, 'I hope so indeed, Mr. Leavenworth.' 'Then join me in drinking a glass of sherry,' he said, motioning me to procure another glass from the closet. I did so, and he poured me out the wine with his own hand. I am not especially fond of sherry, but the occasion was a pleasant one and I drained my glass. I remember being slightly ashamed of doing so, for Mr. Leavenworth set his down half full. It was half full when we found him this morning."

Do what he would (and being a reserved man, he appeared anxious to control his emotion), the horror of his first shock seemed to overwhelm him here. Pulling his handkerchief from his pocket he wiped his forehead. "Gentlemen, that is the last action of Mr. Leavenworth I ever saw. As he set the glass down on the table, I said good night to him and left the room."

The coroner, with a characteristic imperviousness to all expressions of emotion, leaned back and surveyed the young man with a scrutinizing glance. "And where did you go then?" he asked.

"To my own room."

"Did you meet anybody on the way?"

"No, sir."

"Hear anything or see anything unusual?"

The secretary's voice fell a trifle. "No, sir."

"Mr. Harwell, think again. Are you ready to swear that you neither met anybody, heard anybody nor saw anything which lingers yet in your memory as unusual?"

His face grew quite distressed. Twice he opened his lips to speak and as often closed them without doing so. At last with an effort he replied:

"I saw one thing, a little thing, too slight to mention, but it was unusual, and I could not help thinking of it when you spoke."

"What was it?"

"Only a door half open."

"Whose door?"

"Miss Eleanore Leavenworth's." His voice was almost a whisper now.

"Where were you when you observed this fact?"

"I cannot say exactly. Probably at my own door, as I did not stop on the way. If this frightful occurrence had not taken place I should never have thought of it again."

"When you went into your room did you close your door?"

"I did, sir."

"How soon did you retire?"

"Immediately."

"Did you hear nothing before you fell asleep?"

Again that indefinable hesitation.

"Barely nothing."

"Not a footstep in the hall?"

"I might have heard a footstep."

"Did you?"

"I cannot swear I did."

"Do you think you did?"

"Yes, I think I did. To tell the whole, I remember hearing, just as I was falling into a doze, a rustle and a footstep in the hall, but it made no impression upon me and I dropped asleep."

"Well?"

"Some time later I woke, woke suddenly, as if something had startled me, but what, a noise or move, I cannot say. I remember rising up in my bed and looking around, but hearing nothing further soon yielded to the drowsiness which possessed me and fell into a deep sleep. I did not awaken again till morning."

Here requested to relate how and when he became acquainted with the fact of the murder, he substantiated, in all particulars, the account of the murder already given by the butler; which subject being exhausted, the coroner went on to ask if he had noted the condition of the library table after the body had been removed.

"Somewhat, yes, sir."

"What was on it?"

"The usual properties, sir; books, paper, a pen with the ink dried on it, besides the decanter and the wineglass from which he drank the night before."

"Nothing more?"

"I remember nothing more."

"In regard to that decanter and glass," broke in the juryman of the watch and chain, "did you not say that the latter was found in the same condition in which it was at the time you left Mr. Leavenworth sitting in his library?"

"Yes, sir, very much."

"Yet he was in the habit of drinking a full glass?"

"Yes, sir."

"An interruption must, then, have ensued very close upon your departure, Mr. Harwell."

A cold bluish pallor suddenly broke out upon the young man's face. He started and for a moment looked as if struck by some horrible thought. "That does not follow, sir," he articulated with some difficulty. "Mr. Leavenworth might"—but suddenly stopped as if too much distressed to proceed.

"Go on, Mr. Harwell, let us hear what you have to say."

"There is nothing," he returned faintly as if battling with some strong emotion.

As he had not been answering a question, only volunteering an explanation, the coroner let it pass, but I saw more than one pair of eyes roll suspiciously from side to side as if many there felt they had at last found some sort of a clue in this man's emotion. The coroner, ignoring in his easy way both the emotion and the universal excitement it had produced, now proceeded to ask—"Do you know whether the key to the library was in its place or not when you left the room last night?"

"No, sir; I did not notice."

"The presumption is, it was?"

"I suppose so."

"At all events the door was locked in the morning, and the key gone?"

"Yes, sir."

"Then whoever committed this murder locked the door on passing out and took away the key?"

"It would seem so."

The coroner turning, faced the jury with an earnest look. "Gentlemen," said he, "there seems to be a mystery in regard to this key which must be looked into."

Immediately a universal murmur swept through the room testifying to the acquiescence of all present. The little jury-man rising hastily proposed that an instant search should be made for it, but the coroner, turning upon him with what I should denominate as a quelling look, decided that the inquest should proceed in the usual manner, till the verbal testimony was all in.

"Then allow me to ask a question," said the irrepressible. "Mr. Harwell, we are told that upon the breaking in of the library door this morning, Mr. Leavenworth's two nieces followed you into the room."

"One of them, sir, Miss Eleanore."

"Is Miss Eleanore the one who is said to be Mr. Leavenworth's sole heiress?" the coroner here interposed.

"No, sir, that is Miss Mary."

"That she gave orders," pursued the juryman, "for the removal of the body into the farther room?"

"Yes, sir."

"And that you obeyed her by helping to carry it in?"

"Yes, sir."

"Now in thus passing through the rooms did you observe anything to lead you to form a suspicion of the murderer?"

The secretary shook his head. "I have no suspicion," he said emphatically.

Somehow I did not believe him. Whether it was the tone of his voice, the clutch of his hand on his sleeve—and the hand will often reveal more than the countenance—I felt that this man was not to be relied upon in making this assertion.

"I would like to ask Mr. Harwell a question," said a juryman who had not yet spoken. "We have had a detailed account of what looks like the discovery of a murdered man. Now, murder is never committed without some motive. Does the secretary know whether Mr. Leavenworth had any secret enemy?"

"I do not."

"Everyone in the house seemed to be on good terms with him?"

"Yes, sir," with a little quaver of dissent in the assertion however.

"Not a shadow lay between him and any other member of his household, as far as you know?"

"I am not ready to say that," he returned, quite distressed. "A shadow is a very slight thing. There might have been a shadow——"

"Between him and whom?"

A long hesitation. "One of his nieces, sir."

"Which one?"

Again that defiant lift of the head. "Miss Eleanore."

"How long has this shadow been observable?"

"I cannot say."

"You do not know the cause?"

"I do not."

"Nor the extent of the feeling?"

"No, sir."

"You open Mr. Leavenworth's letters?"

"I do."

"Has there been anything in those lately received by him

that, recurring to your memory now, might seem to throw any light upon this deed?"

It actually seemed as if he never would answer. Was he simply pondering over his reply or was the man turned to stone?

"Mr. Harwell, did you hear the juryman?" inquired the coroner.

"Yes, sir; I was thinking."

"Very well; now answer."

"Sir," he replied, turning and looking the juryman full in the face and in that way revealing his unguarded left hand to my gaze, "I have opened Mr. Leavenworth's letters as usual for the last two weeks, and I can think of nothing in them bearing in the least upon this tragedy."

The man lied; I knew it instantly. The clenched hand pausing irresolute, then making up its mind to go through with the lie firmly, was enough for me.

"Mr. Harwell, this is undoubtedly true according to your judgment," said the coroner; "but Mr. Leavenworth's correspondence will have to be searched for all that."

"Of course," he replied carelessly, "that is only right."

This remark ended Mr. Harwell's examination for the time. As he sat down I made note of four things.

That Mr. Harwell himself, for some reason not given, was conscious of a suspicion which he was anxious to suppress even from his own mind.

That a woman was in some way connected with it, a rustle as well as a footstep having been heard by him on the stairs.

That a letter had arrived at that house and not long since which if found would be likely to throw some light upon this subject.

That Eleanore Leavenworth's name came with difficulty from his lips; this evidently unimpressible man manifesting more or less emotion whenever he was called upon to utter it.

CHAPTER 4

A Clue

Something is rotten in the State of Denmark.

—HAMLET.

The cook of the establishment being now called, that portly, ruddy-faced individual stepped forward with alacrity, displaying upon her good-humored countenance such an expression of mingled eagerness and anxiety that more than one person present found it difficult to restrain a smile at her appearance. Observing this and taking it as a compliment, being a woman as well as a cook, she immediately dropped a curtsy, and opening her lips was about to speak when the coroner, rising impatiently in his seat, took the word from her mouth by saying sternly:

"Your name?"

"Katherine Malone, sir."

"Well, Katherine, how long have you been in Mr. Leavenworth's service?"

"Shure, it is a good twelvemonth now, sir, since I came, on Mrs. Wilson's ricommindation, to that very front door, and——"

"Never mind the front door, but tell us why you left this Mrs. Wilson?"

"Shure, and it was she as left me, being as she went sailing to the ould country the same day when on her ricommindation I came to this very front door——"

"Well, well! no matter about that. You have been in Mr. Leavenworth's family a year?"

"Yes, sir."

"And liked it? Found him a good master?"

"Och, sir, niver have I found a better, worse luck to the villain as killed him. He was that free and ginerous, sir, that many's the time I have said to Hannah——" She stopped with a sudden comical gasp of terror, looking at her fellow-servants like one who had incautiously made a slip. The coroner, observing this, inquired hastily:

"Hannah? Who is Hannah?"

The cook, drawing her roly-poly figure up into some sort of shape in her efforts to appear unconcerned, exclaimed boldly: "She? Oh, only the ladies' maid, sir."

"But I don't see anyone here answering to that description. You didn't speak of anyone by the name of Hannah, as belonging to the house," said he, turning to Thomas.

"No, sir," the latter replied with a bow and a sidelong look at the red-cheeked girl by his side. "You asked me who were in the house at the time the murder was discovered, and I told you."

"Oh," cried the coroner satirically, "used to police courts, I see." Then turning back to the cook, who had all this while been rolling her eyes in a vague fright about the room, inquired: "And where is this Hannah?"

"Shure, sir, she's gone."

"How long since?"

The cook caught her breath hysterically. "Since last night."

"What time last night?"

"Troth, sir, and I don't know. I don't know anything about it."

"Was she dismissed?"

"Not as I know on; her clothes is here."

"Oh, her clothes are here. At what hour did you miss her?"

"I didn't miss her. She was here last night, and she isn't here this morning, and so I says she's gone."

"Humph!" cried the coroner, casting a slow glance down the room, while everyone looked about him as if he had suddenly stumbled upon a door in a closed wall.

"Where did this girl sleep?"

The cook, who had been fumbling uneasily with her apron, looked up.

"Shure, we all sleeps at the top of the house, sir."

"In one room?"

Slowly: "Yes, sir."

"Did she come up to the room last night?"

"Yes, sir."

"At what hour?"

"Shure it was ten when we all came up. I heard the clock a-striking."

"Did you observe anything unusual in her appearance?"

"She had a toothache, sir."

"Oh, a toothache; what then? Tell me all she did."

But at this the cook broke into tears and wails.

"Shure, she didn't do nothing, sir. It wasn't her, sir, as did anything, don't you believe it. Hannah is a good girl, and honest, sir, as ever you see. I am ready to swear on the Book that she never put her hand to the lock of his door. What should she for? She only went down to Miss Eleanore for some toothache drops, her face was paining her that awful; and oh, sir——"

"There, there," interrupted the coroner, "I am not accusing Hannah of anything. I only asked you what she did after you reached your room. She went downstairs, you say. How long after you went up?'"

"Troth, sir, I couldn't tell; but Molly says——"

"Never mind what Molly says. *You* didn't see her go down?"

"No, sir."

"Nor see her come back?"

"No, sir."

"Nor see her this morning?"

"No, sir; how could I when she's gone?"

"But you did see last night that she seemed to be suffering with toothache?"

"Yes, sir."

"Very well; now tell me how and when you first became acquainted with the fact of Mr. Leavenworth's death."

But her replies to this question, while over-garrulous, contained but little information, and seeing this, the coroner was on the point of dismissing her, when the little juror, remembering an admission she had made of having seen Miss Eleanore Leavenworth coming out of the library door a few minutes after Mr. Leavenworth's body had been carried into the next room, asked if her mistress had anything in her hand at the time.

"I don't know, sir. Faith!" she suddenly exclaimed. "I believe she did have a piece of paper. I recollect, now, seeing her put it in her pocket."

The next witness was Molly, the upstairs girl.

Molly O'Flanagan, as she called herself, was a rosy-cheeked, black-haired, pert girl of about eighteen, who under ordinary circumstances would have found herself able to answer, with a due degree of smartness, any question which might have been addressed to her. But fright will sometimes cower the stoutest heart, and Molly, standing before the coroner at this juncture, presented anything but a reckless appearance, her naturally rosy cheeks blanching at the first word addressed to her, and her head falling forward on her breast in a confusion too genuine to be dissembled, and too transparent to be misunderstood.

As her testimony related mostly to Hannah, and what she knew of her and her remarkable disappearance, I shall confine myself to a mere synopsis of it.

As far as she, Molly, knew, Hannah was what she had given herself out to be, an uneducated girl of Irish extraction, who had come from the country to act as lady's maid and seamstress to the two Misses Leavenworth. She had been in the family for some time, before Molly herself in fact; and though by nature remarkably reticent, refusing to tell anything about herself or her past life, she had managed to become a great favorite with all in the house. But she was of a melancholy nature and fond of brooding, often getting up at night to sit and think in the dark; "as though she was a lady!" exclaimed Molly.

This habit being a singular one for a girl in her station, an attempt was made to win from the witness further particulars in regard to it. But Molly, with a toss of her head, confined herself to the one statement. She used to get up at night and sit in the window, and that was all she knew about it.

Drawn away from this topic, during the consideration of which a little of the sharpness of Molly's disposition had asserted itself, she went on to state in connection with the events of the past night that Hannah had been ill for two days or more with a swelled face; that last night it had given her so much trouble she got out of bed, and dressing herself—Molly was closely questioned here, but insisted upon the fact that Hannah had fully dressed herself, even to arranging her collar and ribbon—lighted a candle, and made known her intention of going down to Miss Eleanore for aid.

"Why Miss Eleanore?" a juryman here asked.

"Oh, she was the one who always gave out medicines and such-like to the servants."

Urged to proceed, she went on to state that that was all she knew about it. Hannah did not come back, nor was she to be found in the house at breakfast time.

"You say she took a candle with her," said the coroner. "Was it in a candlestick?"

"No, sir; loose like."

"Why did she take a candle? Does not Mr. Leavenworth burn gas in his halls?"

"Yes, sir; but we put the gas out as we came up, and Hannah is afraid of the dark."

"If she took a candle it must be lying somewhere about the house. Now has anybody seen a stray candle?"

"Not as I knows on, sir."

"*Is this it?*" exclaimed a voice over my shoulder.

It was Mr. Gryce, and he was holding up into view a half-burned paraffin candle.

"Yes, sir; lor,' where did you find it?"

"In the grass of the carriage yard, half-way from the kitchen door to the street," he returned quietly.

Sensation. A clue, then, at last. Something had been found which seemed to connect this mysterious murder with the outside world. Instantly the back door assumed the chief position of interest. The candle found lying in the yard seemed to prove not only that Hannah had left the house shortly after descending from her room, but had left it by the back door, which we now remembered was only a few steps from the iron gate opening into the side street. But Thomas, being recalled, repeated his assertion that not only the back door, but all the lower windows of the house, had been found by him securely locked and bolted at six o'clock that morning. Inevitable conclusion—someone had locked and bolted them after the girl. Who? Alas! that had now become the very serious and momentous question.

CHAPTER 5

Expert Testimony

> And often-times, to win us to our harm,
> The instruments of darkness tell us truths;
> Win us with honest trifles, to betray us
> In deepest consequence.
>
> —MACBETH.

In the midst of the universal gloom that had now fallen upon all present, there came a sharp ring at the bell. Instantly all eyes turned toward the parlor door, when it slowly opened, and the officer who had been sent off so mysteriously by the coroner an hour before entered with a young man at his side, whose sleek appearance, intelligent eye and general air of trustworthiness seemed to proclaim him to be, what in fact he was, the confidential clerk of a responsible mercantile house.

Advancing without apparent embarrassment, though each and every eye in the room was fixed upon him with lively curiosity, he made a slight bow to the coroner.

"You have sent for a man from Bohn & Co.," he said. Strong and immediate excitement. Bohn & Co. was the well-known pistol and ammunition store of Broadway.

"Yes, sir," returned the coroner. "We have here a bullet, which we would be glad to have you examine. You are fully acquainted with all matters connected with your business?"

The young man merely elevating an expressive eyebrow took the bullet carelessly in his hand.

"Can you tell us from what make of pistol that was delivered?"

The young man rolled it slowly round between his thumb and forefinger, and then laid it down. "It is a No. 32 ball, usually sold with the small pistol made by Smith & Wesson."

"A small pistol!" exclaimed the butler, jumping up from his

seat. "Master used to keep a little pistol in his stand drawer. I have often seen it. We all knew about it."

Great and irrepressible excitement, especially among the servants. "That's so," I heard a heavy voice exclaim, "I saw it once myself—master was cleaning it." It was the cook who spoke.

"In his stand drawer?" the coroner inquired.

"Yes, sir; at the head of his bed."

An officer was sent to examine the stand drawer. In a few moments he returned, bringing a small pistol which he laid down on the coroner's table, saying: "Here it is."

Immediately everyone sprang to his feet, but the coroner, handing it over to the clerk from Bohn's, inquired if that was of the make before mentioned. Without hesitation he replied: "Yes, Smith & Wesson, you can see for yourself," and he proceeded to examine it.

"Where did you find this pistol?" asked the coroner of the officer.

"In the top drawer of a shaving table that stands at the head of Mr. Leavenworth's bed. It was lying in a velvet case together with a box of cartridges, one of which I bring as a sample," and he laid it down beside the bullet.

"Was the drawer locked?"

"Yes, sir; but the key was not taken out."

Interest had now reached its climax. A universal cry swept through the room, "Is it loaded?"

The coroner frowning on the assembly, with a look of great dignity, remarked:

"I was about to ask that question myself, but first I must request order." An immediate calm followed. Everyone was too much interested to interpose any obstacle in the way of gratifying his curiosity.

"Now, sir!" exclaimed the coroner.

The clerk from Bohn's, taking out the cylinder, held it up. "There are seven chambers here, and they are all loaded."

A murmur of disappointment followed this assertion.

"But," he quietly said after a momentary examination of the face of the cylinder, "they have not all been loaded long. A bullet has been recently shot from one of these chambers."

"How do you know?" cried one of the jury.

"How do I know, sir?" said he, turning to the coroner. "Will you be kind enough to examine the condition of this pistol?" And he handed it over to that gentleman. "Look first at the barrel; it is clean and bright, you will say, and shows no evidence of a bullet having passed out of it very lately; that is because it has been cleaned. But now observe the face of the cylinder: what do you see there?"

"I see a faint line of smut near one of the chambers."

"Just so; show it to the gentlemen."

It was immediately handed down.

"That faint line of smut on the edge of one of the chambers is the telltale, sirs. A bullet passing out always leaves smut behind. The man who fired this, remembering the fact, cleaned the barrel, but forgot the cylinder." And stepping aside he folded his arms.

"Jerusalem!" spoke out a rough, hearty voice, "isn't that wonderful!" It was a countryman who had stepped in from the street, and now stood all agape in the doorway.

It was a rough but not altogether unwelcome interruption. A smile passed round the room, and each man seemed to breathe easier. Order being at last restored, the officer was requested to describe the position of the stand, and its distance from the library table.

"The library table is in one room and the stand in another. To reach the former from the latter, one would be obliged to cross Mr. Leavenworth's bedroom in a diagonal direction, pass through the passage-way separating that one apartment from the other, and——"

"Wait a moment; how does this table stand in regard to the door which leads from the bedroom into the hall?"

"One might enter that door, pass directly round the foot of the bed to the stand, procure the pistol, and cross half-way over to the passage-way, without being seen by anyone sitting or standing in the library beyond."

"Holy Virgin!" exclaimed the horrified cook, throwing her apron over her head as if to shut out some dreadful vision. "Hannah niver would have the pluck for that, niver, niver!"

But Mr. Gryce, laying a heavy hand on the woman, forced her back into her seat, reproving and calming her at the same time with a dexterity that was marvelous to behold. "I beg your pardons," she cried deprecatingly to those around, "but it niver was Hannah, niver."

The clerk from Bohn's here being dismissed, those assembled took the opportunity of making some change in their position, after which the name of Mr. Harwell was again called. That person rose with manifest reluctance. Evidently the preceding testimony had either upset some theory of his, or indubitably strengthened some unwelcome suspicion.

"Mr. Harwell," the coroner began, "we are told of the existence of a pistol belonging to Mr. Leavenworth, and upon searching, we discover it in his room. Did you know of his possessing such an instrument?"

"I did."

"Was it a fact generally known in the house?"

"So it would seem."

"How was that? Was he in the habit of leaving it around where anyone could see it?"

"I cannot say, I can only acquaint you with the manner in which I myself became cognizant of its existence."

"Very well, do so."

"We were once talking about firearms. I have some taste that way, and have always been anxious to possess a pocket pistol. Saying something of the kind to him one day, he rose from his seat and bringing this from its place in his stand drawer, showed it to me."

"How long ago was this?"

"Some few months since."

"He has owned this pistol, then, for some time?"

"Yes, sir."

"Is that the only occasion upon which you have ever seen it?"

"No, sir"—the secretary blushed—"I have seen it once since."

"When?"

"About three weeks ago."

"Under what circumstances?"

The secretary drooped his head, a certain drawn look making itself suddenly visible on his countenance. He even unfolded his arms and pressed his hands together, looking all the while into the coroner's face, from under his half-closed lids, with an expression that was almost like an appeal.

"Gentlemen," he asked after a moment's hesitation, "will you not excuse me?"

"It is impossible," returned the coroner.

His face grew even more pallid and deprecatory. "I am obliged to introduce the name of a lady," said he hesitatingly.

"We are very sorry," remarked the coroner.

The young man turned fiercely upon him, and I could not help wondering that I had ever thought him commonplace. "Of Miss Eleanore Leavenworth," he exclaimed.

At that name, so uttered, everyone started but Mr. Gryce; he was engaged in holding a close and confidential confab with his finger-tips, and did not appear to notice.

"Surely it is contrary to the rules of decorum and the respect we all feel for the lady herself, to introduce her name into this discussion," Mr. Harwell went on hurriedly. But the coroner still insisting upon an answer, he refolded his arms, a movement indicative of resolution with him, and began in a low forced tone to say:

"It is only this, gentlemen. One afternoon about three weeks since, I had occasion to go to the library at an unusual hour. Crossing over to the mantelpiece for the purpose of procuring a penknife which I had carelessly left there in the morning, I heard a noise in the adjoining room. Knowing that Mr. Leavenworth was out and supposing that the ladies had gone with him, I took the liberty of looking to see who was there; when what was my astonishment to behold Miss Eleanore Leavenworth standing at the side of her uncle's bed, with this pistol in her hand. Confused at my indiscretion, I attempted to escape without being observed, but in vain, for just as I set foot on the threshold of the door, she turned around and, detecting me, called me by name, and upon my advancing, asked me if I would not explain the pistol to her. Gentlemen, in order to do so, I was obliged to take it in my hand; and that, sirs, is the only other occasion upon which I ever saw or handled the pistol of Mr. Leavenworth."

Drooping his head he waited in indescribable agitation for the next question.

"She asked you to explain the pistol to her; what do you mean by that?"

"I mean," continued he faintly, catching his breath in a vain effort to appear calm, "how to load, aim and fire it."

A flash, like the glare of sudden lightning, shot across the faces of all present. Even the coroner showed sudden signs of emotion, and sat staring at the bowed form and pale countenance of the man before him with a peculiar look of surprised compassion, that could not fail of producing its effect, not only upon the young man himself, but upon all who saw him.

"Mr. Harwell," he inquired at length, "have you anything to add to the statement you have just made?"

The secretary sadly shook his head.

"Mr. Gryce," I here whispered, clutching that person by the arm and dragging him down to my side; "assure me, I entreat you——" but he would not let me finish.

"The coroner is about to ask for the young ladies," he quickly interposed. "If you desire to fulfill your duty toward them, be ready, that's all."

Fulfill my duty! The simple words recalled me to myself. What had I been thinking of? Was I mad? Instantly the present with its doubt and horror rolled away from me like a scroll, leaving only a tender picture of the lovely cousins bowed in anguish over the remains of one who had been dear as a father to them. As the vision deepened and impressed itself upon me, I slowly rose, and upon demand being made for Miss Mary and Miss Eleanore Leavenworth, advanced and said that, as a friend of the family—a pretty lie, which I hope will not be laid up against me—I begged the privilege of going for the ladies and escorting them down.

Instantly a dozen eyes flashed upon me, and I experienced the embarrassment of one who, by some unexpected word or action, has drawn upon himself the concentrated attention of a whole room.

But, the permission sought being almost immediately accorded, I was speedily enabled to withdraw from my rather trying position, finding myself almost before I knew it in the hall; my face aflame, my heart beating with excitement and these words of Mr. Gryce's ringing in my ears: "Third floor, rear room, first door at the head of the stairs. You will find the young ladies expecting you."

CHAPTER 6

Side-Lights

Oh! she has beauty might ensnare
A conqueror's soul, and make him leave his crown
At random, to be scuffled for by slaves.

—OTWAY.

Third floor, rear room, first door at the head of the stairs! What was I about to see there!

Mounting the lower flight and shuddering by the library wall, that to my troubled fancy seemed written all over with horrible suggestions, I took my way slowly upstairs, revolving in my mind many things, among which an admonition uttered long ago by my mother occupied a prominent place:

"My son, remember that a woman with a secret may be a fascinating study, but she can never be a safe or even a satisfactory companion."

A sentence wise, no doubt, but wholly uncalled for under the circumstances; for certainly I had no intention of especially interesting myself in these women. Yet notwithstanding all my efforts to elude it, it continued to haunt me, till the sight of the door to which I had been directed put every other thought to flight save this, that I was about to meet the stricken nieces of a brutally murdered man.

Pausing only long enough on the threshold to compose myself for the interview, I lifted my hand to knock, when a rich clear voice rose from within, and I heard distinctly uttered these ominous words: "I do not accuse your hand, though I know of none other which would or could have done this; but your heart, your head, your will, those I do and must accuse in my secret mind at least, and it is well that you should know it."

Struck as if by a blow, I staggered back. Good God! what depths of horror and depravity were about to open before me! Shuddering and sick, I cowered there, my hands over my ears, when suddenly I felt a touch on my arm, and turning saw Mr. Gryce standing close beside me with his finger on his lip, and the last flickering shadow of a flying emotion fading from his steady, almost compassionate countenance.

"Come, come," whispered he; "I see you don't begin to know what kind of a world you have got into. Rouse yourself; remember they are waiting down below."

"But who is it? Who was it that spoke?"

"That we shall soon see," exclaimed he shortly. And without waiting to meet, much less answer my appealing look, he struck his hand against the door, and flung it wide open.

Instantly a flush of loveliest color burst upon us. Blue curtains, blue carpets, blue walls. It was like a glimpse of azure heaven let unexpectedly into the depths of a gloomy prison. Fascinated by the splendor before me, and drawn almost from myself by the suddenness of the vision, I stepped impetuously forward, but instantly paused again, overcome and impressed by the exquisite picture which opened before me.

Seated in an easy chair of embroidered satin, but rousing from her half-recumbent position, like one who was in the act of launching a powerful invective, I beheld a glorious woman. Fair, pale, proud, delicate; looking like a lily in the thick creamy-tinted wrapper that alternately clung to and swayed from her richly-molded figure; with her Grecian front, crowned with the palest of pale tresses, lifted and flashing with power; one quivering hand clasping the arm of her chair, the other outstretched and pointing toward some distant object in the room—her whole appearance was so splendid, so startling, so extraordinary, that I held my breath in surprise, actually for the moment doubting if it were a living woman I beheld, or some famous pythoness conjured up from ancient story, to express in one tremendous gesture the supreme indignation of outraged womanhood.

"Miss Mary Leavenworth," whispered that ever-present voice over my shoulder.

Ah! Mary Leavenworth—and I felt a sudden thrill of relief! This beautiful creature, then, was not the Eleanore who could load, aim, and fire a pistol. Turning my head, I followed the guiding of that uplifted hand, now frozen into its place by a new emotion, the emotion of being interrupted in the midst of direful and pregnant revelation, and saw—but no, here description fails me; Eleanore Leavenworth must be painted by other hands than mine. I could sit half the day and dilate upon the subtle grace, the pale magnificence, the perfection of form and feature which make Mary Leavenworth the wonder of all who behold her, but Eleanore—I could as soon paint the beatings of my own heart. Beguiling, terrible, grand, pathetic, that face of faces flashed upon my gaze, and instantly the moonlight loveliness of her cousin faded from my memory, and I saw only Eleanore—only Eleanore from that moment on forever.

When my glance first fell upon her, she was standing by the side of a small table with her face turned toward her cousin, and her two hands resting, the one upon her breast, the other on the table, in an attitude of antagonism. But before the sudden pang which shot through me at the sight of her beauty had subsided, her head had turned, her gaze had encountered mine; all the horror of the situation had burst upon her, and instead of a haughty woman drawn up to receive and trample upon the insinuation of another, I beheld, alas! a trembling, panting human creature, conscious that a sword hung above her head, and without a word to say why it should not fall and slay her.

It was a pitiable change; a heart-rending revelation. I turned from it as from a confession. But just then, her cousin, who had apparently regained her self-possession at the first betrayal of emotion on the part of the other, stepped forward, and holding out her hand, inquired:

"Is not this Mr. Raymond? How kind of you, sir. And you?"

turning to Mr. Gryce; "you have come to tell us we are wanted below, is it not so?"

It was the voice I had heard through the door, but modulated to a sweet, winning, almost caressing tone.

Glancing hastily at Mr. Gryce, I looked to see how he was affected by it. Evidently much, for the bow with which he greeted her words was lower than ordinary, and the smile with which he met her earnest look, both deprecatory and reassuring. He did not look toward her cousin, though her deathly conscious eyes were fixed upon his face with an inquiry in their depths more agonizing than the utterance of any cry would have been. Knowing Mr. Gryce as I did, I felt that nothing could promise worse or be more significant, than this same transparent disregard of one who seemed to fill the room with her terror. And struck with pity, I forgot that Mary Leavenworth had spoken, forgot her very presence in fact, and turning hastily away, took one step toward her cousin, when Mr. Gryce's hand falling on my arm stopped me.

"Miss Leavenworth speaks," said he.

Recalled to myself, I turned my back upon what had so interested me even while it repelled, and forcing myself to make some sort of reply to the fair creature before me, offered my arm and led her toward the door.

Immediately the pale, proud countenance of Mary Leavenworth softened almost to the point of smiling: and here let me say, there never was a woman who could smile and not smile like Mary Leavenworth. Looking in my face with a frank and sweet appeal in her eyes, she murmured:

"You are very good. I do feel the need of support, the occasion is so horrible, and my cousin there"—here a little gleam of alarm flickered into her eyes—"is so very strange today."

"Humph!" thought I to myself, "where is the grand indignant pythoness with the unspeakable wrath and menace in her countenance, whom I saw when I first entered the room?" Could it be that she was trying to beguile us from our conjectures, by making light of her former expressions! Or was it possible that she had deceived herself so far as to believe us unimpressed by the weighty accusation overheard by us at a moment so critical?

But Eleanore Leavenworth, leaning on the arm of the detective, soon absorbed all my attention. She had regained in a manner also, by this time, her self-possession, but not so entirely as her cousin. Her step faltered as she endeavored to walk, and the hand which rested on his arm trembled like a leaf. "Would to God I had never entered this house!" said I to myself. And yet, before the exclamation was half uttered, I became conscious of a secret rebellion against the thought, an emotion, shall I say, of thankfulness, that I, and not another, was the one to break in upon their privacy, overhear that significant remark, and—shall I acknowledge it?—follow Mr. Gryce and the trembling, swaying figure of Eleanore Leavenworth downstairs. Not that I felt the least relenting in my soul toward guilt. Crime had never looked so black; revenge, selfishness, hatred, cupidity, never seemed more loathsome, and yet—but why enter into the consideration of my feelings at that time? They cannot be of interest; besides, who can fathom the depths of his own soul, or untangle for others the secret cords of repulsion and attraction which are, and ever have been, a mystery and wonder to himself. Enough that, supporting upon my arm the clinging, half-fainting form of one woman, but with my attention and interest with another, I descended the stairs of the Leavenworth mansion, and entered again the dreaded presence of those inquisitors of the law, who had been so impatiently awaiting us.

As I once more crossed that threshold, and faced the eager countenances of those I had left so short a time before, I felt as if ages had elapsed in the interval, so much can a human soul experience in the short space of a few over-weighted moments.

CHAPTER 7

Mary Leavenworth

For this relief much thanks.
—HAMLET.

Have you ever observed the effect of the sunlight bursting suddenly upon the earth from behind a mass of heavily surcharged clouds? If so, you can have some idea of the sensation produced in that room, by the entrance of these two beautiful ladies. Possessed of a loveliness that would have been conspicuous in all places and under all circumstances, Mary at least, if not her less striking, though by no means less interesting cousin, could never have entered any assemblage without drawing to herself the wondering attention of all present. But heralded as here by the most fearful of tragedies, what could you expect from a collection of men such as I have already described, but overmastering wonder and incredulous admiration? Nothing, perhaps, and yet at the first murmuring sound of amazement and satisfaction, I felt my soul recoil in disgust.

Making haste to seat my now trembling companion in the most retired spot I could find, I looked around for her cousin.

But Eleanore Leavenworth, weak as she had appeared in the interview above, showed at this moment neither hesitation nor embarrassment. Advancing upon the arm of the detective, whose suddenly assumed air of persuasion in the presence of the jury was anything but reassuring, she stood for an instant gazing calmly upon the scene before her. Then bowing to the coroner with a grace and condescension that seemed at once to place him on the footing of a politely endured intruder in this home of elegance, she took the seat which her own servants hastened to procure for her with an ease and dignity that rather recalled the triumphs of the drawing room than the self-consciousness of a scene such as that in which we were. Palpable acting though this was, it was not without its effect.

Instantly the murmurs ceased, the obtrusive glances fell, and something like a forced respect made itself visible upon the countenances of all present. Even I, impressed as I had been by her very different demeanor in the room above, experienced a sensation of relief; and was more than startled when upon turning to the lady at my side, I beheld her eyes riveted upon her cousin with an inquiry in their depths that was anything but encouraging. Fearful of the effect this look might have upon those about us, I hastily seized her hand, which, clenched and unconscious, hung over the edge of her chair, and was about to beseech her to have care, when her name, called in a slow impassive way by the coroner, roused her from her abstraction. Hurriedly withdrawing her gaze from her cousin, she lifted her face to the jury and I saw a gleam pass over it that brought back my early fancy of the pythoness. But it passed, and it was with an expression of great modesty that she settled herself to respond to the demand of the coroner, and answer the first few opening inquiries.

But what can express the anxiety of the moment to me? Gentle as she now appeared, she was capable of great wrath, as I knew. Was she going to reiterate her suspicions here? Did she hate as well as mistrust her cousin? Would she dare assert in this presence and before the world, what she found it so easy to utter in the privacy of her own room and the hearing of the one person concerned? Did she wish to? Her own countenance gave me no clue to her intentions, and in my anxiety I turned once more to look at Eleanore. But she, in a dread and apprehension I could easily understand, had recoiled at the first intimation that her cousin was to speak; and now sat with her face covered from sight, by hands that were blanched to an almost deathly whiteness.

The testimony of Mary Leavenworth was short. After some few questions mostly referring to her position in the house and her connection with its deceased master, she was asked to relate what she knew of the murder itself, and of its discovery by her cousin and the servants.

Lifting up a brow that seemed never to have known till now the shadow of care or trouble, and a voice that whilst low and womanly, rang like a bell through the room, she replied:

"You ask me, gentlemen, a question which I cannot answer of my own personal knowledge. I know nothing of this murder or of its discovery, save what has come to me through the lips of others."

My heart gave a bound of relief and I saw Eleanore Leavenworth's hand drop from her brow like stone, while a flickering gleam as of hope fled over her face and then died away like sunlight leaving marble.

"For strange as it may seem to you," Mary earnestly continued, the shadow of a past horror revisiting her countenance, "I did not enter the room where my uncle lay. I did not even think of doing so; my only impulse was to fly from what was so horrible and heart-rending. But Eleanore went in and she can tell you———"

"We will question Miss Eleanore Leavenworth later," interrupted the coroner, but very gently for him. Evidently the grace and elegance of this sweet woman were making their impression. "What we want to know is what *you* saw. You say, then, that you cannot tell us of anything that passed in the room at the time of the discovery?"

"No, sir."

"Only what occurred in the hall?"

"Nothing occurred in the hall," she remarked innocently.

"Did not the servants pass in from the hall, and your cousin come out there, after her revival from the fainting fit that overcame her at the first sight of her uncle?"

Mary Leavenworth's violet eyes opened wonderingly.

"Yes, sir; but that was nothing."

"You remember, however, that she did come out into the hall?"

"Yes, sir."

"With a paper in her hand?"

"Paper?" and she wheeled suddenly and looked at her cousin. "Did you have a paper, Eleanore?"

The moment was intense. Eleanore Leavenworth, who at the first mention of the word paper had started perceptibly, rose to her feet at this naïve appeal, and opening her lips seemed about to speak, when the coroner, with a strict sense of what was regular, lifted his hand with decision and said:

"You need not ask your cousin, miss; but let us hear what you have to say yourself."

Immediately Eleanore Leavenworth sank back, a pink spot breaking out on either cheek; while a slight murmur testified to the disappointment of those in the room who were more anxious to have their curiosity gratified, than the forms of law adhered to.

Satisfied with having done his duty, and disposed to be easy with so charming a witness, the coroner repeated his question. "Tell us, if you please, if you saw any such thing in her hand?"

"I? Oh, no, no; I saw nothing."

Being now questioned in relation to the events of the previous night, she had no new light to throw upon the subject. She acknowledged that her uncle was perhaps a little reserved at dinner, but no more so than anyone might be, who was not perfectly well, or who had any ordinary care or anxiety upon his mind.

Asked if she had seen her uncle again that evening, she said no, that she had been detained in her room. That the sight of him sitting in his seat at the head of the table was the very last remembrance she had of him.

There was something so touching, so forlorn, and yet so unobtrusive in this simple recollection of hers, that a look of sympathy passed slowly round the room. I even detected Mr. Gryce softening toward the inkstand. But Eleanore Leavenworth sat unmoved.

"Was your uncle on ill terms with anyone?" was now asked. "Had he valuable papers or secret sums of money in his possession?"

To all these inquiries she returned an equal negative.

"Has your uncle met any stranger lately, or received any important letter during the last few weeks, that might seem in any way to throw light upon this mystery?"

There was the slightest perceptible hesitation in her voice as she replied: "No, not to my knowledge; I don't know of any such." But here stealing a side-glance at Eleanore, she evidently saw something that reassured her, for she hastened to add:

"I believe I may go further than that, and say positively no.

My uncle was in the habit of confiding in me, and I should have known if anything of importance to him had occurred."

Questioned in regard to Hannah, she gave that person the best of characters, knew of nothing which could have led either to her strange disappearance, or to her connection with crime. Could not say whether she kept any company or had any visitors, only knew that no one with any such pretensions came to the house. Finally, when asked when she had last seen the pistol which Mr. Leavenworth always kept in his stand drawer, she returned, not since the day he bought it, Eleanore, and not herself, having the charge of her uncle's apartments.

It was the only thing she had said which, even to a mind freighted like mine, would seem to point to any private doubt or secret suspicion, and this, uttered in the careless manner in which it was, would have passed without comment, if Eleanore herself had not directed at that moment a very much aroused and inquiring look upon the speaker.

But it was time for the inquisitive juror to make himself heard again. Edging to the brink of his chair, he drew in his breath with a vague awe of Mary's beauty almost ludicrous to see, and asked if she had properly considered what she had just said.

"I hope, sir, I consider all that I say at such a time as this," was her earnest reply.

The little juror drew back, and I looked to see her examination terminate, when suddenly his ponderous colleague of the watch chain, catching the young lady's eye, inquired:

"Miss Leavenworth, did your uncle ever make a Will?"

Instantly every man in the room was in arms, and even she could not prevent the slow blush of injured pride from springing to her cheek. But her answer was given firmly and without any show of resentment.

"Yes, sir," she returned simply.

"More than one?"

"I never heard of but one."

"Are you acquainted with the contents of that Will?"

"I am. He made no secret of his intentions to anyone."

The juryman lifted his eye-glass and looked at her. Her grace was little to him, her beauty or her elegance. "Perhaps then, you can tell me who is the one most likely to be benefited by his death?"

The brutality of this question was too marked to pass unchallenged. Not a man in that room, myself included, but frowned with sudden disapprobation. But Mary Leavenworth, drawing herself up, looked her interlocutor calmly in the face, and restrained herself to say:

"I know who would be the greatest losers by it. The children he took to his bosom in their helplessness and sorrow; the young girls he enshrined with the halo of his love and protection, when love and protection were what their immaturity most demanded; the women who looked to him for guidance when childhood and youth were past—these, sir, these are the ones to whom his death is a loss, in comparison to which all other losses which may come to them must ever seem trivial and unimportant."

It was a noble reply to the basest of insinuations, and the juryman drew back rebuked; but here another of them, one who had not spoken before, but whose appearance was not only superior to the rest, but also almost imposing in its gravity, leaned from his seat and in a solemn voice said:

"Miss Leavenworth, the human mind cannot help forming impressions. Now have you, with or without reason, felt at any time a suspicion as to who the murderer of your uncle might be?"

It was a frightful moment. To me and to one other, I am sure it was not only frightful but agonizing. Would her courage fail? Would her determination to shield her cousin remain firm in the face of duty and at the call of probity? I dared not hope it.

But Mary Leavenworth, rising to her feet, looked judge and jury calmly in the face, and, without raising her voice, giving it an indescribably clear and sharp intonation, replied:

"No; I have neither suspicion nor reason for any. The assassin of my uncle is not only entirely unknown to, but completely unsuspected by me."

It was like the removal of a stifling pressure. Amid a universal outgoing of the breath, Mary Leavenworth stood aside and Eleanore was called in her place.

CHAPTER 8

Circumstantial Evidence

"O dark, dark, dark!"

And now that the interest was at its height; that the veil which shrouded this horrible tragedy seemed about to be lifted, if not entirely withdrawn, I felt a desire to fly the scene, to leave the spot, to know no more. Not that I was conscious of any particular fear that this woman was going to betray herself. The cold steadiness of her now fixed and impassive countenance was sufficient warranty in itself against the possibility of any such catastrophe. But if indeed the suspicions of her cousin were the offspring; not only of hatred, but of knowledge; if that face of beauty was in truth only a mask, and Eleanore Leavenworth was what the words of her cousin, and her own after behavior would seem to imply, how could I bear to sit there and see the frightful serpent of deceit and sin evolve itself from the bosom of this white rose! And yet, such is the fascination of uncertainty, that although I saw something of my own feelings reflected in the countenances of many about me, not a man in all that assemblage showed any disposition to depart, I least of all.

The coroner, upon whom the blonde loveliness of Mary had impressed itself to Eleanore's apparent detriment, was the only one in the room who showed himself unaffected at this moment. Turning toward the witness with a look which, while respectful, had a touch of austerity in it, he began:

"You have been an inmate of Mr. Leavenworth's family from childhood, they tell me, Miss Leavenworth?"

"From my tenth year," returned she.

It was the first time I had heard her voice, and it surprised me, it was so like, and yet so unlike that of her cousin. Similar in tone, it lacked its expressiveness, if I may so speak, sounding without vibration on the ear and ceasing without an echo.

"Since that time you have been treated like a daughter, they tell me?"

"Yes, sir, like a daughter indeed; he was more than a father to both of us."

"You and Miss Mary Leavenworth are cousins, I believe. When did she enter the family?"

"At the same time that I did. Our respective parents were victims of the same disaster. If it had not been for our uncle, we should have been thrown, children as we were, upon the world. But he"—here she paused, her firm lips breaking into a half-tremble—"but he in the goodness of his heart adopted us into his family, and gave us what we had both lost, a father and a home."

"You say that he was a father to you as well as to your cousin—that he adopted you. Do you mean by that, that he not only surrounded you with present luxury, but gave you to understand that the same should be secured to you after his death; in short, that he intended to leave any portion of his property to you?"

"No, sir; I was given to understand, from the first, that his property would be bequeathed by will to my cousin."

"Your cousin was no more nearly related to him than yourself, Miss Leavenworth; did he never give you any reason for this evident partiality?"

"None but his pleasure, sir."

Her answers up to this point had been so straightforward and satisfactory that a gradual confidence seemed to be taking the place of the rather uneasy doubts which had from the first circled about this woman's name and person. But at this admission, uttered as it was in a calm unimpassioned voice, not only the jury, but myself, who had so much truer reason for mistrusting her, felt that actual suspicion in her case must be very much shaken before the utter lack of motive which this reply so clearly betokened.

Meanwhile the coroner continued: "If your uncle did for you all that you say, you must have become very much attached to him?"

"Yes, sir," her mouth taking a sudden determined curve.

"His death, then, must have been a great shock to you?"

"Very, very great."

"Enough of itself to make you faint away, as they tell me you did, at the first glimpse you had of his body?"

"Enough, quite."

"And yet you seemed to be prepared for it?"

"Prepared?"

"The servants say you were much agitated at finding your uncle did not make his appearance at the breakfast table."

"The servants!" Her tongue seemed to cleave to the roof of her mouth; she could hardly speak.

"That when you returned from his room you were very pale."

Was she beginning to realize that there was some doubt, if not actual suspicion, in the mind of the man who could assail her with questions like these? I had not seen her so agitated since that one memorable instant up in her room. But her mistrust, if she felt any, did not long betray itself. Calming herself by a great effort, she replied with a quiet gesture:

"That is not so strange. My uncle was a very methodical man; the least change in his habits would be likely to awaken our apprehensions."

"You were alarmed, then?"

"To a certain extent I was."

"Miss Leavenworth, who is in the habit of overseeing the regulation of your uncle's private apartments?"

"I am, sir."

"You are doubtless, then, acquainted with a certain stand in his room containing a drawer?"

"Yes, sir."

"How long is it since you had occasion to go to this drawer?"

"Yesterday," visibly trembling at the admission.

"At what time?"

"Near noon, I should judge."

"Was the pistol he was accustomed to keep there in its place at that time?"

"I presume so; I did not observe."

"Did you turn the key upon closing the drawer?"

"I did."

"Take it out?"

"No, sir."

"Miss Leavenworth, that pistol, as you have perhaps observed, lies on the table before you. Will you look at it?" And lifting it up into view, he held it toward her.

If he had meant to startle her by the sudden action, he amply succeeded. At the first sight of the murderous weapon she shrank back, and a horrified, but quickly suppressed shriek burst from her lips. "Oh, no, no!" she moaned, flinging out her hands before her.

"I must insist upon your looking at it, Miss Leavenworth," pursued the coroner. "When it was found just now, all the chambers were loaded."

Instantly the agonized look left her countenance. "Oh, then——" She did not finish, but put out her hand for the weapon.

But the coroner, looking at her steadily, continued: "It has been lately fired off for all that. The hand that cleaned the barrel forgot the cartridge-chamber, Miss Leavenworth."

She did not shriek again, but a hopeless, helpless look slowly settled over her face, and she seemed about to sink, but like a flash the reaction came, and lifting her head with a steady, grand action I have never seen equalled, she exclaimed: "Very well, what then?" The coroner laid the pistol down; men and women glanced at each other, everyone seemed to hesitate to proceed. I heard a tremulous sigh at my side, and turning, beheld Mary Leavenworth staring at her cousin with a startled flush on her cheek, as if she began to recognize the fact that others beside herself felt that there was something unexplained about this woman. At last the coroner summoned up courage to continue.

"You ask me, Miss Leavenworth, upon the evidence given, what then? Your question obliges me to say that no burglar, no hired assassin, would have used this pistol for a murderous purpose, and then taken the pains not only to clean it, but to reload it, and lock it up again in the drawer from which he had taken it."

She did not reply to this, but I saw Mr. Gryce make a note of it with that peculiar emphatic nod of his.

"Nor," he went on even more gravely, "would it be possible for anyone who was not accustomed to pass in and out of Mr. Leavenworth's room, at all hours, to enter his door so late at night, procure this pistol from its place of concealment, traverse his apartment, and advance so closely upon him as the facts show to have been necessary—without causing him at least to turn his head to one side, which, in consideration of the doctor's testimony, we cannot believe he did."

It was a frightful suggestion, and we looked to see Eleanore Leavenworth recoil. But that expression of outraged feeling was left for her cousin to exhibit. Starting indignantly from her seat, Mary cast one hurried glance around her, and opened her lips to speak, but Eleanore, slightly turning, motioned her to have patience, and replied in a cold and calculating voice: "You are not sure, sir, that this *was* done. If my uncle, for some purpose of his own, had fired the pistol off yesterday, let us say—which is surely possible if not probable—the like results would be observed, and the same conclusions drawn."

"Miss Leavenworth," the coroner went on, "the ball has been extracted from your uncle's head."

"Ah!"

"It corresponds with those in the cartridges found in his stand-drawer, and is of the number used with this pistol."

Her head fell forward on her hands, her eyes sought the floor, her whole attitude expressed disheartenment. Seeing it, the coroner grew still more grave.

"Miss Leavenworth," said he, "I have now some questions to put you concerning last night. Where did you spend the evening?"

"Alone in my own room."

"You, however, saw your uncle or your cousin during the course of it?"

"No, sir; I saw no one after leaving the dinner table—except Thomas," she added after a moment's pause.

"And how came you to see him?"

"He came to bring me the card of a gentlemen who called."

"May I ask the name of the gentleman?"

"The name on the card was Mr. Le Roy Robbins."

The matter seemed trivial, but the sudden start given by the lady at my side made me remember it.

"Miss Leavenworth, when seated in your room are you in the habit of leaving your door open?"

A startled look at this, quickly suppressed. "Not in the habit, no, sir."

"Why did you leave it open last night?"

"I was feeling warm."

"No other reason?"

"I can give no other."

"When did you close it?"

"Upon retiring."

"Was that before or after the servants went up?"

"After."

"Did you hear Mr. Harwell when he left the library and ascended to his room?"

"I did, sir."

"How much longer did you leave your door open after that?"

"I—I—a few minutes a—I cannot say," she added hurriedly.

"Cannot say? Why, do you forget?"

"I forget just how long after Mr. Harwell came up, I closed it."

"Was it more than ten minutes?"

"Yes."

"More than twenty?"

"Perhaps." How pale her face was, and how she trembled!

"Miss Leavenworth, according to evidence, your uncle came to his death not very long after Mr. Harwell left him. If your door was open, you ought to have heard if anyone went to his room or any pistol shot was fired. Now did you hear anything?"

"I heard no confusion, no, sir."

"Did you hear anything?"

"Not any pistol shot."

"Miss Leavenworth, excuse my persistence, but did you hear anything?"

"I heard a door close."

"What door?"

"The library door."

"When?"

"I do not know." She clasped her hands hysterically; "I cannot say. Why do you ask me so many questions?"

I leaped to my feet; she was swaying, almost fainting. But before I could reach her, she had drawn herself up again and resumed her former demeanor. "Excuse me," said she, "I am not myself this morning. I beg your pardon," and she turned steadily to the coroner. "What was it you asked?"

"I asked," and his voice grew thin and high—evidently her manner was beginning to tell against her—"when it was you heard the library door shut?"

"I cannot fix the precise time, but it was after Mr. Harwell came up and before I closed my own."

"And you heard no pistol shot?"

"No, sir."

The coroner cast a quick look at the jury, who almost to a man dropped their eyes as he did so.

"Miss Leavenworth, we are told that Hannah, one of the servants, started for your room late last night after some medicine. Did she come there?"

"No, sir."

"When did you first learn of her remarkable disappearance from this house during the night?"

"This morning before breakfast. Molly met me in the hall, and asked how Hannah was. I thought the inquiry a strange one, and so questioned her. A moment's talk made the conclusion plain that the girl was gone."

"What did you think when you became assured of this fact?"

"I did not know what to think."

"No suspicion of foul play crossed your mind?"

"No, sir."

"You did not connect the fact with that of your uncle's murder?"

"I did not know of this murder then."

"And afterward?"

"Oh, some thought of the possibility of her knowing something about it may have crossed my mind. I cannot say."

"Can you tell us anything of this girl's past history?"

"I can tell you no more in regard to it than my cousin has done."

"Do you not know what made her so sad at night?"

Her cheek flushed angrily; was it at his tone or at the question itself? "No, sir; she never confided her secrets to my keeping."

"Then you cannot tell us where she would be likely to go upon leaving this house?"

"Certainly not."

"Miss Leavenworth, we are obliged to put another question to you. We are told that you were the one who ordered your uncle's body to be removed from where it was found, into the next room."

She bowed her head.

"Didn't you know that it is not proper to disturb the body of a person found dead, except in the presence and under the authority of the proper officer?"

"I did not consult my knowledge, sir, in regard to the subject, only my feelings."

"Then I suppose it was your feelings that prompted you to remain standing by the table at which he was murdered instead of following the body in and seeing it properly deposited? Or perhaps," he went on with relentless sarcasm, "you were too much interested just then in the piece of paper you took away, to think much of the proprieties of the occasion?"

"Paper?" lifting her head with determination. "Who says that I took a piece of paper from the table? I am sure I have not."

"One witness has sworn that he saw you bending over the table upon which there were lying several papers, another, that when she met you a few minutes later in the hall, you were in the act of putting a piece of paper in your pocket. The inference follows, Miss Leavenworth."

This was a home thrust and we looked to see some show of agitation, but her haughty lip never quivered.

"You have drawn the inference, and you must prove the fact."

The answer was stateliness itself, and we were not surprised to see the coroner look a trifle baffled; but recovering himself, he said:

"Miss Leavenworth, I must ask you again, whether you did or did not take anything from that table?"

She folded her arms; "I decline answering the question," she said quietly.

"Pardon me," he rejoined, "it is necessary that you should."

Her lip took a still more determined curve. "When any suspicious paper is found in my possession, it will be time enough then for me to explain how I came by it."

This defiance seemed to quite stagger the coroner. "Do you realize to what this refusal is liable to subject you?"

She drooped her head. "I am afraid that I do; yes, sir."

Mr. Gryce lifted his hand and softly twirled the tassel of the window-curtain.

"And you still persist?"

She absolutely disdained to reply.

The coroner did not press it further.

It had now become evident to all, that Eleanore Leavenworth not only stood upon her defense, but was perfectly aware of her position and prepared to maintain it. Even her cousin, who until now had preserved some sort of composure, began to show signs of strong and uncontrollable agitation, as if she found it one thing to utter an accusation herself, and quite another to see it working its way to light in the countenances of the men about her.

"Miss Leavenworth," the coroner continued, changing the line of attack, "you have always had free access to your uncle's apartments, have you not?"

"Yes, sir."

"Might even have entered his room late at night, crossed it and stood at his side, without disturbing him sufficiently to cause him to turn his head?"

"Yes"; her hands pressing themselves painfully together.

"Miss Leavenworth, the key to the library door is missing."

She made no answer.

"It has been testified to, that previous to the actual discovery of the murder, you visited the door of the library alone. Will you tell us if the key was then in the lock?"

"It was not."

"Are you certain?"

"I am."

"Now, was there anything peculiar about this key, either in size or shape?"

She strove to repress the sudden terror which this question produced, glanced carelessly around at the group of servants stationed at her back and trembled. "It was a little different from the others," she murmured at last.

"In what respect?"

"The handle was broken."

"Ah, gentlemen, the handle was broken," the coroner observed, looking toward the jury.

Mr. Gryce seemed to take the information to himself, for he gave another of his quick nods.

"You would, then, recognize this key, Miss Leavenworth, if you should see it?"

She cast a startled look at him, as if she expected to behold it in his hand, but seeming to gather courage at not finding it produced, replied quite easily:

"I think I should, sir."

"Very well then," said he, waving his hand in dismissal. "That is all, gentlemen," continued he, looking at the jurymen, "you have heard the testimony of the members of the household, and——" But here Mr. Gryce, quietly advancing, touched him on the arm. "One moment," said he, and stooping, he whispered a few words in the coroner's ear, then recovering himself, stood with his right hand in his breast pocket and his eye upon the chandelier.

I scarcely dared to breathe. Had he repeated to the coroner the words he had inadvertently overheard in the hall above? But a glance at the latter's face satisfied me that nothing so important as that had transpired. He looked not only tired but a trifle annoyed.

"Miss Leavenworth," said he, turning again in her direction, "you have declared that you were not with your uncle last evening, did not visit his room. Do you repeat the assertion?"

"I do."

He glanced at Mr. Gryce, who immediately drew from his breast a handkerchief curiously soiled. "It is strange, then," remarked he, "that this handkerchief of yours, in the hands of the officer, should have been found this morning in that room."

The girl uttered a cry; then while Mary's face hardened into a sort of strong despair Eleanore tightened her lip and coldly replied: "I do not see that it is so very strange. I was in that room early this morning."

"And you dropped it then?"

A distressed blush crossed her face; she did not reply.

"Soiled in this way?" he went on.

"I know nothing about the soil. What is it? Let me see."

"In a moment; what we now wish, is to know how it came to be in your uncle's apartment."

"There are many ways. I might have left it there, days ago. I have told you that I was in the habit of visiting his room. But first, let me see if it is my handkerchief." And she held out her hand.

"I presume so, as I am told it has your initials embroidered in the corner," he returned, as Mr. Gryce passed it to her.

But she with horrified voice interrupted him. "These dirty spots—what are they? They look like——"

"Like what they are," said the coroner. "If you have ever cleaned a pistol you must know what they are, Miss Leavenworth."

She let the handkerchief fall convulsively from her hand, and stood staring at it, lying before her on the floor. "I know nothing about it, gentlemen," she said. "It is my handkerchief, but——" For some cause she did not finish her sentence, but again repeated: "Indeed, gentlemen, I know nothing about it." This closed her testimony.

Kate, the cook, was now recalled, and asked to tell when she last washed the handkerchief.

"This, sir; this handkerchief? Oh, some time this week, sir," throwing a deprecatory glance at her mistress.

"What day?"

"Well, I wish I could forget, Miss Eleanore, but I can't. It is the only one like it in the house. I washed it day before yesterday."

"When did you iron it?"

"Yesterday morning," half-choking over the words.

"And when did you take it to her room?"

The cook threw her apron over her head. "Yesterday afternoon with the rest of the clothes, just before dinner. Indade, I could not help it, Miss Eleanore," whispered she; "it was the truth."

Eleanore Leavenworth frowned. That somewhat contradictory evidence had very sensibly affected her; and when a moment later, the coroner, having dismissed the witness, turned toward her, and inquired if she had anything further to say in regard to this matter, in the way of explanation or otherwise, she threw her hands up almost spasmodically, slowly shook her head, and without word or warning fainted quietly away in her chair.

A commotion, of course, followed, during which I noticed that Mary did not hasten to her cousin, but left it for Molly and Kate to do what they could toward her resuscitation. In a few moments this was in so far accomplished, that they were enabled to lead her from the room. As they did so, I observed a tall man rise and follow her out.

A momentary silence ensued, soon broken, however, by an impatient stir as our little juryman rose and proposed that the jury should now adjourn for the day. This seeming to fall in with the coroner's views, he announced that the inquest would stand adjourned till three o'clock the next day, when he trusted all the jurors would be present.

A general rush followed, that in a few minutes emptied the room of all but Miss Leavenworth, Mr. Gryce and myself.

CHAPTER 9

A Discovery

His rolling Eies did never rest in place,
But walkte each where for feare of hid mischance,
Holding a lattis still before his Face,
Through which he still did peep as forward he did pace.
—FAERIE QUEENE.

Miss Leavenworth, who appeared to have lingered from a vague terror of everything and everybody in the house not under her immediate observation, shrank from my side the moment she found we were left comparatively alone, and retiring to a distant corner, gave herself up to grief. Turning my attention, therefore, in the direction of Mr. Gryce, I found that person busily engaged in counting his own fingers with a troubled expression upon his countenance, which may or may not have been the result of that arduous employment.

But at my approach, satisfied perhaps that he possessed no more than the requisite number, he dropped his hands and greeted me with a faint smile that was, considering all things, too suggestive to be pleasant.

"Well," said I, taking my stand before him, "I cannot blame you. You had a right to do as you thought best, but how had you the heart? Was she not sufficiently compromised without your bringing out that wretched handkerchief, which may or may not have dropped in that room, but whose presence there, soiled though it was with pistol grease, is certainly no proof that she herself was connected with this murder?"

"Mr. Raymond," returned he, "I have been detailed as police officer and detective to look after this case, and I propose to do it."

"Of course," I hastened to reply, "I am the last man to wish you to shirk your duty; but you cannot have the temerity to declare, that this young and tender creature can by any possibility be considered as at all likely to be implicated in a crime so monstrous and unnatural. The mere assertion of another woman's suspicions on the subject ought not——"

But here Mr. Gryce interrupted me. "You talk when your attention should be directed to more important matters. That other woman, as you are pleased to designate the fairest ornament of New York society, sits over there in tears; go and comfort her."

Looking at him in amazement, I hesitated to comply, but seeing he was in earnest, crossed to Mary Leavenworth and sat down by her side. She was weeping, but in a slow unconscious way, as if grief had been mastered by fear. The fear was too undisguised and the grief too natural for me to doubt the genuineness of either.

"Miss Leavenworth," said I, "any attempt at consolation on the part of a stranger must seem at a time like this the most bitter of mockeries, but do try and consider that circumstantial evidence is not always absolute proof."

Starting like one caught back from the verge of a precipice, just as destruction seemed inevitable, she turned her eyes upon me with a slow comprehensive gaze wonderful to see in orbs so tender and womanly.

"No," murmured she, "circumstantial evidence is not absolute proof, but Eleanore does not know this. She is so intense; she cannot see but one thing at a time. She has been running her head into a noose and oh——" Pausing she clutched my arm with a passionate grasp. "Do you think there is any danger? Will they——" She could not go on.

"Miss Leavenworth," whispered I with a warning look toward the detective, "what do you mean?"

Like a flash her glance followed mine, an instant change taking place in her bearing.

"Your cousin may be intense," I went on as if nothing had occurred, "but I do not know to what you refer, when you say that she has been running her head into a noose."

"I mean this," returned she firmly; "that wittingly or unwittingly, she has so parried and met the questions which have been put to her in this room, that anyone listening to her would give her the credit of knowing more than she ought to of this horrible affair. She acts"—Mary whispered, but not so low but that every word could be distinctly heard in all quarters of the room—"as if she were anxious to conceal something. But she is not, I am sure she is not. Eleanore and I are not good friends, but all the world could never make me believe that she has any more knowledge of this murder than I have. Won't somebody tell her, then—won't you—that her manner is a mistake, that it is calculated to arouse suspicion, that it has already done so? And, oh, tell her from me——" she went on, her voice sinking to a low whisper now—"what you have just said, that circumstantial evidence is not always absolute proof."

I surveyed her with great astonishment. What an actress this woman was!

"You request me to tell her this," said I: "wouldn't it be better for you to speak to her yourself?"

"Eleanore and I hold little or no confidential communication," replied she.

I could easily believe that, and yet I was puzzled. Indeed, there was something incomprehensible in her whole manner. Not knowing what else to say, I remarked: "That is unfortunate. She ought to be told that the straightforward course is the best by all means."

Mary Leavenworth only wept. "Oh, why has this awful trouble come to me who have always been so happy before!"

"Perhaps for the very reason that you have always been so happy."

"It was not enough that dear uncle should die in this horrible manner; but she, my own cousin, had to——"

I touched her arm, and the action seemed to recall her to herself. Stopping short she bit her lip.

"Miss Leavenworth," I whispered, "you should hope for the best. Besides, I honestly believe that you are disturbing yourself unnecessarily. If nothing fresh transpires, a mere prevarication or so of your cousin's will not suffice to injure her."

I said this to see if she had any reason to doubt the future. I was amply rewarded.

"Anything fresh? How could there be anything fresh, when she is perfectly innocent?"

Suddenly a thought seemed to strike her.

"Mr. Raymond," said she, wheeling round in her seat till her lovely, perfumed wrapper brushed my knee, "why didn't they ask me more questions? I could have told them Eleanore never left her room last night."

"You could?" What was I to think of this woman?

"Yes; my room is nearer the head of the stairs than hers; to have gone down, she would have been obliged to pass my door. I should have heard her, don't you see?"

Ah, was that all?

"That does not follow," I answered sadly. "Can you give no other reason?"

"I would say whatever was necessary," she whispered.

I started back. Yes, this woman would lie now to save her cousin, had lied during the inquest, but then I felt grateful, and now I was simply horrified.

"Miss Leavenworth," said I, "nothing can justify one in violating the dictates of his own conscience, not even the safety of one we do not altogether love."

"No!" returned she; and her lip took a tremulous curve; the lovely bosom heaved and she softly looked away.

If Eleanore's beauty had made one jot less of an impression on my fancy, or her frightful situation awakened one iota less of anxiety in my breast, I should have been a lost man from that moment.

"I did not mean to do anything very wrong," murmured she; "do not think too badly of me."

"No, no," said I; and there is not a man living who would not have said the same in my place.

What more might have passed between us on this subject I cannot say, for just then the door opened and a man entered whom I recognized as the one who had followed Eleanore Leavenworth out a short time before.

"Mr. Gryce," said he, pausing just inside the door, "a word if you please."

The detective nodded, but did not hasten toward him; instead of that, walked deliberately away to the other end of the room, where he lifted the lid of an inkstand he saw there, muttered some unintelligible words into it, and speedily shut it again.

Immediately the uncanny fancy seized me, that if I should leap to that inkstand, open it and peer in, I should surprise and capture a bit of confidence he had entrusted to it. But I restrained my foolish impulse, and contented myself with noting the subdued look of respect with which the gaunt subordinate watched the approach of his superior.

"Well?" inquired the latter as he reached him, "what now?"

The man shrugged his shoulders and drew his principal through the open door. Once in the hall their voices sank to a whisper, and as their backs only were visible, I turned to look at my companion. She was pale but composed.

"Has he come from Eleanore?"

"I do not know; I fear so. Miss Leavenworth," said I, "can it be possible that your cousin has anything in her possession that she desires to conceal?"

"Then you think she is trying to conceal something?"

"I do not say so. But there was considerable talk about a paper——"

"They will never find any paper or anything else suspicious in Eleanore's possession," interrupted she. "In the first place, there was no paper of importance enough"—I saw Mr. Gryce's form suddenly stiffen—"for anyone to think of concealment. Don't I know? Was I not my uncle's confidante?"

"I do not suppose there was," suggested I, "as far as your knowledge goes. But could she not have been acquainted with something——"

She drew back coldly. "There was nothing to be acquainted with, Mr. Raymond. We lived the most methodical and domestic of lives. I cannot understand for my part why so much should be made out of this. My uncle undoubtedly came to his death by the hand of some intended burglar. That nothing was stolen from the house, is no proof that a burglar never entered it. As for the doors and windows being locked, will you take the word of an Irish servant as infallible upon such a point as that? I cannot. I believe the assassin to be one of a gang who make their living by breaking into houses, and if you cannot honestly agree with me, do try and consider such an explanation as possible if not for the sake of the family credit, why, then"—and she turned her face with all its fair beauty upon mine, eyes, cheeks, mouth all so exquisite and winsome—"why, then, for mine."

Instantly Mr. Gryce turned toward us. "Mr. Raymond, will you be kind enough to step this way?"

Glad to escape from my present position, I hastily obeyed.

"What has happened?" I inquired.

"We propose to take you into our confidence," murmured Mr. Gryce easily. "Excuse me, Mr. Raymond, Mr. Fobbs."

I bowed to the man I saw before me, and stood uneasily waiting. Anxious as I was to know what we really had to fear, I still intuitively shrank from any communication with one whom I looked upon as a spy.

"A matter of some importance," continued Mr. Gryce. "It is not necessary for me to remind you that it is in confidence, is it?"

"No."

"I thought not. Mr. Fobbs, you may proceed."

Instantly the whole appearance of the man Fobbs changed. Assuming an expression of lofty importance, he laid his large hand outspread upon his heart and commenced.

"Detailed by Mr. Gryce to watch the movements of Miss Eleanore Leavenworth, I left this room upon her departure from it, and followed her and the two servants who conducted her upstairs to her own apartment. Once there——"

Mr. Gryce interrupted him. "Once there? Where?"

"Her own room, sir."

"Where situated?"

"At the head of the stairs."

"That is not her room. Go on."

"Not her room? Then it *was* the fire she was after," cried he, clapping himself on the knee.

"The fire?"

"Excuse me, I am ahead of my story. She did not appear to notice me much, though I was right behind her. It was not until she had reached the door of this room—which was not her room," he interpolated dramatically—"and turned to dismiss her servants, that she seemed conscious that she was followed. Looking at me then with an air of great dignity, quickly eclipsed, however, by an expression of patient endurance, she walked in, leaving the door open behind her in a courteous way that I cannot sufficiently commend."

I could not help frowning. Honest as the man appeared, this was evidently anything but a sore subject with him. Observing me frown, he softened his manner.

"Not seeing any other way of keeping her under my eye, and thus performing my duty creditably, except by entering the room, I followed her in and took a seat in a remote corner. She flashed one look at me as I did so, and commenced pacing the room in a restless kind of way I'm not altogether unused to. At last she stopped abruptly, right in the middle of the room. 'Get me a glass of water,' she gasped; 'I'm faint again— quick! the stand in the corner.' Now in order to get that glass of water it was necessary for me to pass behind a dressing-mirror that reached almost to the ceiling and I naturally hesitated. But she turned and looked at me, and—well, gentlemen, I think either of you would have hastened to do what she asked; or at least"—with a doubtful look at Mr. Gryce—"have given your two ears for the privilege, even if you didn't succumb to the temptation."

"Well, well!" exclaimed Mr. Gryce impatiently.

"I am going on," said he. "I stepped out of sight, then, for a moment, but it seemed long enough for her purpose, for when I emerged, glass in hand, she was kneeling at the grate full five feet from the spot where she had been standing, and was fumbling with the waist of her dress in a way that convinced me she had something concealed there which she was anxious to dispose of. I eyed her pretty closely as I handed her the glass of water, but she was gazing into the grate with a look on her face such as I don't remember ever seeing before, and didn't appear to notice. Drinking barely a drop, she gave it back, and in another moment was holding out her hands over the fire. 'Oh, I am so cold,' murmured she, 'so cold.' And I verily believe she was. At any rate she shivered most naturally. But there were a few dying embers in the grate, and when I saw her thrust her hand again into the folds of her dress, I became distrustful of her intentions, and drawing a step nearer, looked over her shoulder, when I distinctly saw her drop something into the grate that clinked as it fell. Suspecting what it was, I was about to interfere, when she sprang to her feet, seized the scuttle of coal that was upon the hearth, and with one move emptied the whole upon the dying embers. 'I want a fire,' she cried, 'a fire.' 'That is hardly the way to make one,' I returned, carefully taking the coal out with my hands, piece by piece, and putting it back into the scuttle, till——"

"Till what?" I asked, seeing him and Mr. Gryce exchange a hurried look.

"Till I found this," opening his large hand and showing me *a broken-handled key.*

CHAPTER 10

Mr. Gryce Receives New Impetus

There's nothing ill
Can dwell in such a temple.
—TEMPEST.

This astounding discovery, thus made, was dreadful to me. It was true then. Eleanore, the beautiful, the lovesome, was—I did not, could not finish the sentence, even in the silence of my own mind.

"You look surprised," said Mr. Gryce, glancing curiously toward the key. "Now I ain't. A woman does not thrill and blush and equivocate and faint for nothing; especially such a woman as Miss Leavenworth."

"A woman who could do such a deed would be the last to thrill, equivocate, and faint," retorted I. "Give me the key; let me see it."

He complacently put it in my hand. "It is the one we want," said he. "No getting out of that."

I returned it. "If she declares she is innocent, I will believe her."

He stared with great amazement. "You have strong faith in the women," laughed he. "I hope you will live to find them worthy of it."

I had no reply for this, and a short silence ensued, first broken by Mr. Gryce. "There is but one thing left to do," said he. "Fobbs, you will have to request Miss Leavenworth to come down. Do not alarm her, only see that she comes. To the reception-room," added he as the man drew off.

No sooner were we left alone than I made a move to return to Mary, but he stopped me.

"Come and see it out," whispered he. "She will be down in a moment; see it out, you had best."

Glancing back, I hesitated; but the prospect of beholding Eleanore again drew me in spite of myself. Telling him to wait, I returned to Mary's side to make my excuses.

"What is the matter—what has occurred?" said she breathlessly.

"Nothing as yet to disturb you much. Do not be alarmed." But my face betrayed me.

"There is something," said she.

"Your cousin is coming down."

"Down here?" and she shrank visibly.

"No, to the reception-room."

"I do not understand. It is all dreadful, and no one tells me anything."

"Miss Leavenworth," I essayed, "I pray God there may be nothing to tell. Judging from your present faith in your cousin, there will not be. Take comfort, then, and believe that I will inform you if anything occurs which you ought to know."

Giving her a look of reassurance, I left her crushed against the crimson pillows of the sofa on which she sat, and rejoined Mr. Gryce. We had scarcely entered the reception-room when Eleanore Leavenworth came in.

More languid than she was an hour before, but haughty still, she slowly advanced, and meeting my eyes, gently bent her head.

"I have been summoned here," said she, directing herself exclusively to Mr. Gryce, "by an individual whom I take to be in

your employ. If so, may I request that you will make your
wishes known at once, as I am quite exhausted and am in great
need of rest."

"Miss Leavenworth," returned Mr. Gryce, rubbing his
hands together and staring in quite a fatherly manner at the
door-knob, "I am very sorry to trouble you, but the fact is I
wish to ask you——"

But here she stopped him. "Anything in regard to the key
which that man has doubtless told you he saw me drop into
the ashes?"

"Yes, miss."

"Then I must refuse to answer any questions concerning it. I
have nothing to say on the subject, unless it is this"—giving
him a look full of suffering, but full of a certain sort of courage
too—"that he was right if he told you I had the key in hiding
about my person, and that I attempted to conceal it in the ashes
of the grate."

"Still, miss——"

But she had already withdrawn to the door. "I pray you
to excuse me," said she. "No argument you could advance
would make any difference in my determination, therefore it
would be but a waste of energy on your part to attempt any."
And with a flitting glance in my direction, that was not without its appeal, she quietly left the room. For a moment Mr.
Gryce stood gazing after her with a look of great interest, then
bowing almost to the ground in his homage, he hastily followed
her out.

I had scarcely recovered from the surprise occasioned by this
unexpected movement, when a quick step was heard in the
hall, and Mary, flushed and anxious, appeared at my side.

"What is it?" said she. "What has Eleanore been saying?"

"Alas!" I answered, "she has not said anything. That is the
trouble, Miss Leavenworth. Your cousin preserves a reticence
upon certain points that is very painful to witness. She ought
to understand that if she persists in doing this, that——"

"That what?" There was no mistaking the fearful anxiety
that prompted this question.

"That she cannot avoid the trouble that will ensue."

For a moment she stood gazing at me with great horror-stricken incredulous eyes; then sinking back into a chair, flung her hands over her face with the cry:

"Oh, why were we ever born! Why were we allowed to live! Why did we not perish with those who gave us birth!"

In the face of anguish like this, I could not keep still.

"Dear Miss Leavenworth," I essayed, "there is no cause for such despair as this. The future looks dark, but not impenetrable. Your cousin will listen to reason, and in explaining——"

But she, deaf to my words, had again risen to her feet and stood before me in an attitude almost appalling.

"Some women in my position would go mad!" she whispered, "mad, mad!"

I looked at her with growing wonder. I thought I knew what she meant. She conceived that she had given us the clue, which had led to this suspicion of her cousin, and that in this way the trouble which hung over their heads was of her own making. I endeavored to soothe her, but my efforts were all unavailing. Absorbed in her own anguish, she paid but little attention to me. Satisfied at last that I could do nothing more for her, I turned to go; the movement seemed to arouse her.

"I am sorry to leave," said I, "without having afforded you any comfort. Believe me that I am very anxious to assist you. Is there no one I can send to your side; no woman friend or relative? It is sad to leave you alone in this house at such a time."

"And do you suppose," said she, "that I intend remaining here? Why, I should die. Here tonight?" and the long shudders shook her very frame.

"It is not at all necessary," broke in a bland voice over our shoulders, "that you should do so, Miss Leavenworth."

I turned with a start. Mr. Gryce was not only at our back, but had evidently been there for some moments. Seated in an easy chair near the door, one hand in his pocket, the other caressing the arm of his chair, he met our gaze with a side-long smile that seemed at once to beg pardon for the intrusion, and to assure us that it was made with no unworthy motive. "Everything will be properly looked after, miss; you can leave with perfect safety."

I expected to see her resent this interference, but instead of that she manifested a certain satisfaction in beholding him there.

Drawing me to one side she whispered: "You think this Mr. Gryce very clever, do you not?"

"Well," replied I cautiously, "he ought to be to hold the position he does. The authorities evidently repose great confidence in him."

Stepping from my side as suddenly as she had approached it, she crossed the room and stood before Mr. Gryce.

"Sir," said she, gazing at him with a glance of entreaty, "I hear that you have great talents; that you can ferret out the real criminal from a score of doubtful characters, and that nothing can escape the penetration of your eye. If this is so, have pity on two orphan girls suddenly bereft of their guardian and protector, and use your acknowledged skill in finding out who has committed this crime. It would be folly in me to endeavor to hide from you that my cousin in her testimony has given cause for suspicion; but I here declare that I believe her to be as innocent of wrong as I am myself, and I am only endeavoring to turn the eye of justice from the guiltless to the guilty when I entreat you to look elsewhere for the culprit who committed this deed." Pausing, she held her two hands out before him. "It must have been some common burglar or desperado; can you not bring him, then, to justice?"

Her attitude was so touching, her whole appearance so earnest and appealing, that I saw Mr. Gryce's countenance brim with suppressed emotion, though his eye never left the coffee-urn upon which it had fixed itself at her first approach.

"You must find out—you can," she went on. "Hannah, the girl who is gone, must know all about it. Search for her, then, ransack the world, do anything; my property is at your disposal. I will offer a large reward for the detection of the burglar who did this deed."

Mr. Gryce slowly rose. "Miss Leavenworth," said he, and then stopped; the man was actually agitated. "Miss Leavenworth, I did not need your very touching appeal to incite me to my utmost duty in this case. Personal and professional pride were in themselves sufficient. But since you have honored me with this expression of your wishes, I will not conceal from you that I shall feel a certain increased interest in the affair from this hour. What mortal man can, I will do, and if in one month from this day I do not come to you for my reward, Ebenezer Gryce is not the individual I have always taken him to be."

"And Eleanore?"

"We will mention no names," said he, gently waving his hand to and fro.

A few minutes later I left the house with Miss Leavenworth, she having testified her wish that I would accompany her to the home of her friend Mrs. Gilbert, with whom she had decided to take refuge. As we rolled away in the carriage Mr. Gryce had been kind enough to provide for us, I noticed my companion cast a look of regret behind her, as if she could not help feeling some compunction at this desertion of her cousin. But this expression was soon changed for the alert look of one who dreads to see a certain face start up from some unknown quarter. Glancing up and down the street, peering furtively into doorways as we passed, starting and trembling if a sudden figure appeared on the curbstone, she did not seem to breathe with perfect ease till we had left the Avenue behind us and entered upon Thirty-seventh Street. Then all at once her natural color returned and, leaning gently toward me, she asked if I had a pencil and piece of paper I could give her. I fortunately possessed both. Handing them to her, I watched her with some little curiosity, while she wrote two or three lines, wondering she should choose such a time and place for the purpose.

"A little note I wish to send," she remarked, glancing at the almost illegible scrawl with an expression of doubt. "Couldn't you stop the carriage a moment while I direct it?"

I did so, and in another instant the leaf which I had torn from my note-book was folded, directed, and sealed with a stamp which she had taken from her own pocket-book.

"That is a crazy-looking epistle," she murmured, as she laid it, direction downwards, in her lap.

"Why not wait, then," I suggested, "till you arrive at your destination, where you can seal it properly, and direct it at your leisure?"

"Because I am in haste. I wish to mail it now. Look, there is a box on the corner; please ask the driver to stop once more."

"Shall I not post it for you?" I asked, holding out my hand.

But she shook her head, and without waiting for my assistance, opened the door on her own side of the carriage and leaped to the ground. Even then she paused to glance up and down the street, before venturing to drop it into the box. But when it was done she looked brighter and more hopeful than I had yet seen her. And when a few moments later she turned to bid me good-bye in front of her friend's house, it was with almost a cheerful air she put out her hand and entreated me to call on her the next day and inform her how the inquest progressed.

I shall not attempt to disguise from you the fact that I spent all that long evening in going over the testimony given at the inquest, endeavoring to reconcile what I had heard with any other theory than that of Eleanore's guilt. Taking a piece of paper, I jotted down the leading causes of suspicion as follows:

1. Her late disagreement with her uncle, and evident estrangement from him, as testified to by Mr. Harwell.

2. The mysterious disappearance of one of the servants of the house.

3. The forcible accusation of her cousin—overheard, however, only by Mr. Gryce and myself.

4. Her equivocation in regard to that handkerchief of hers, found stained with pistol smut on the scene of the tragedy.

5. Her refusal to speak in regard to the paper which she was supposed to have taken from Mr. Leavenworth's table immediately upon the removal of the body.

6. The finding of the library key in her possession.

"A dark record," I involuntarily cried as I looked it over, but even in doing so began jotting down on the other side of the sheet the following explanatory notes:

1. Disagreements and even estrangements between relatives are common. Cases where such disagreements and estrangements have led to crime, rare.

2. The disappearance of Hannah pointed no more in one direction than in another.

3. If Mary's private accusation of her cousin was forcible and convincing, her public declaration that she neither knew nor suspected who might be the author of this crime was equally so. To be sure the former possessed the advantage of being uttered spontaneously, but it was likewise true that it was spoken under momentary excitement, without foresight of the consequences, and possibly without due consideration of the facts.

4, 5. An innocent man or woman, under the influence of terror, will often equivocate in regard to matters that seem to incriminate them.

But the key! What could I say to that? Nothing. With that key in her possession and unexplained, Eleanore Leavenworth stood in an attitude of suspicion, which even I, who was so averse to believing her guilty, was forced to recognize. Brought to this point, I thrust the paper into my pocket and took up the evening *Express*. Instantly my eye fell upon these words:

SHOCKING MURDER.

MR. LEAVENWORTH, THE WELL-KNOWN MILLIONAIRE, FOUND DEAD IN HIS ROOM.

NO CLUE TO THE PERTPETRATOR OF THE DEED.

THE AWFUL CRIME COMMITTED WITH A PISTOL— EXTRAORDINARY FEATURES OF THE AFFAIR.

Ah! here at least was one comfort; her name was not yet mentioned as that of a suspected party. But what might not the morrow bring? I thought of Mr. Gryce's expressive look as he handed me that key, and shuddered.

"She must be innocent; she cannot be otherwise," I reiterated to myself, and then pausing, asked what warranty I had of this. Only her beautiful face; only, only her beautiful face. Abashed, I dropped the newspaper, and went downstairs with the wild idea, I believe, of encountering on the step the telegraph boy, whom I expected every moment with a message from Mr. Veeley. By some great good fortune I did, and taking the telegram from his hand, I opened it on the doorstep. It was from the proprietor of the hotel at which Mr. Veeley was then stopping and ran thus:

Washington, D.C.

MR. EVERETT RAYMOND,

Mr. Veeley is lying at my house ill. Have not shown him telegram, fearing results. Will do so as soon as advisable.

THOMAS LOWORTHY.

I went in musing. Why this sudden sensation of relief on my part? Could it be that I had unconsciously been guilty of cherishing a latent dread of my senior's return? Why, who else could know so well the secret springs which governed this family? Who else could so effectively put me upon the right track? Was it possible that I, Everett Raymond, hesitated to know the truth in any case? No, that should never be said; and, sitting down again, I drew out the memoranda I had made, and looking them carefully over, wrote against No. 6 the word "Suspicious" in good round characters. There! No one could say after that I was a man to be blinded by a bewitching face, from seeing what, in one with no claims to comeliness, would be considered at once an almost indubitable evidence of guilt.

And yet after it was all done, I found myself repeating aloud as I gazed at it: "If she declares that she is innocent, I will believe her." So completely are we the creatures of our own predilections.

CHAPTER II

The Summons

The pink of courtesy.
—ROMEO AND JULIET.

The morning papers contained a more detailed account of the murder than those of the evening before. Reading over the evidence given at the inquest with almost feverish haste, I sought for the one thing I most dreaded to see; but it was not there. Hannah, the seamstress and lady's maid, whose remarkable disappearance was as yet unaccounted for, was mentioned as the possible accomplice of the murderer, if not the virtual assassin; but Eleanore's name was not so much as hinted at in this connection.

The final paragraph in the *Times* ran thus:

"The detectives are upon the track of the missing girl."

And in the *Herald* I read the following notice:

"*A Liberal Reward* will be given by the relatives of Horatio Leavenworth, Esq., deceased, for any news of the whereabouts of one Hannah Chester, disappeared from the house —— Fifth Avenue since the evening of March 4. Said girl was of Irish extraction; in age about twenty-five, and may be known by the following characteristics: Form tall and slender; hair dark brown with a tinge of red; complexion fresh; features delicate and well made; hands small but with the fingers much pricked by the use of the needle; feet large and of a coarser type than the hands. She had on when last seen a checked gingham dress, brown and white, and was supposed to have wrapped herself in a red-and-green blanket shawl, very old. Beside the above distinctive marks, she had upon her right-hand wrist the scar of a large burn; also a pit or two of smallpox upon the left temple."

This paragraph turned my thoughts in a new direction. Oddly enough I had expended very little thought upon this girl, and yet how apparent it was that she was the one upon whose testimony, if given, the whole case in reality hinged. I could not agree with those who considered her as personally implicated in the murder. An accomplice, conscious of what was before her, would have stopped to put what money she had into her pocket before engaging in such an enterprise, and this the inspection of her trunk had proved her not to have done. But if, on the contrary, she had unexpectedly come upon the assassin at his work, how could she have been hustled from the house without creating a disturbance loud enough to have been heard by the ladies, one of whom had her door open? An innocent girl's first impulse upon such an occasion would have been to scream, and yet no scream was heard; she simply disappeared. What were we to think, then? That the person seen by her was one both known and trusted? I would not consider that possibility, so laying down the paper, I endeavored to put away all further consideration of the affair till I had acquired more facts upon which to base a theory. But who can control his thoughts when over-excited upon any one theme? All the morning I found myself turning the case over in my mind, arriving ever at one of two conclusions. Hannah Chester must be found, or Eleanore Leavenworth must explain when and by what means the key of the library door came into her possession.

At two o'clock I started from my office to attend the inquest, but being delayed on the way, missed arriving at the house until after the delivery of the verdict. This was a disappointment to me, especially as I thus lost the opportunity of seeing Eleanore Leavenworth, she having retired to her room immediately upon the dismissal of the jury. But Mr. Harwell was visible, and from him I heard what the verdict had been.

"Death by means of a pistol-shot from the hand of some person unknown."

This result of the inquest was a great relief to me. I had feared worse. Nor could I help seeing that for all his studied self-command, the pale-faced secretary shared in my satisfaction.

What was less of a relief to me was the fact, soon communicated, that Mr. Gryce and his subordinates had left the premises immediately upon the delivery of the verdict. Mr. Gryce was not the man to forsake an affair like this while anything of importance connected with it remained unexplained. Could it be he meditated any decisive action? Somewhat alarmed, I was about to hurry from the house for the purpose of learning what his intentions were, when a sudden movement in the front lower window of the house on the opposite side of the way arrested my attention, and looking closer I detected the face of Mr. Fobbs peering out from behind the curtain. The sight assured me I was not wrong in my estimate of Mr. Gryce; and struck with pity for the desolate girl left to meet the exigencies of a fate, to which this watch upon her movements was but the evident precursor, I stepped back and sent her a note in which, as Mr. Veeley's representative, I proffered my services in case of any sudden emergency, saying I was always to be found in my rooms between the hours of six and eight. This done, I proceeded to the house in Thirty-seventh Street, where I had left Miss Mary Leavenworth the day before.

Ushered into the long and narrow drawing room which of late years has been so fashionable in our up-town houses, I found myself almost immediately in the presence of Miss Leavenworth. "Oh," said she with an eloquent cry of welcome, "I had begun to think I was forsaken." And advancing impulsively, she held out her hand. "What is the news from home?"

"A verdict of murder, Miss Leavenworth."

Her eyes did not lose their question.

"Perpetrated by party or parties unknown."

A look of relief broke softly across her features.

"And they are all gone?" exclaimed she in a bright, keen way, that showed me how animated she must have been in former days.

"I found no one in the house that did not belong there," I returned.

"Oh, then we need have no more trouble, need we?"

I glanced hastily up and down the room.

"There is no one here," she cried.

And still I hesitated. At length in an awkward way enough, I turned toward her and said:

"I do not wish either to offend or to alarm you, but I must

say that I think it is your duty to return to your own home tonight."

"Why?" she stammered. "Is there any particular reason for my doing so? Do you not know that I cannot be in the same house with Eleanore?"

"I do not know that, nor can I stop to consider the question. She is your cousin, has been brought up to regard you as a sister; it is not worthy of you to desert her in the time of her necessity. You will see it as I do, if you will allow yourself a moment's dispassionate thought."

"Dispassionate thought is hardly possible under the circumstances," returned she with a smile of bitter irony.

But before I could reply to this, she softened and asked if I was very anxious she should return, and when I replied: "More so than I could say," trembled and looked for a moment as if she were half-inclined to yield, but suddenly broke into tears, crying it was impossible, and that I was cruel to ask it.

I drew back baffled and sore. "Pardon me," said I, "I have indeed transgressed the bounds allotted to me. I will not do so again; you have doubtless many friends, let some of them advise you."

She turned upon me, all fire. "The friends you speak of would cringe and bow and urge me to do as I please. You alone have the courage to command me to do what is right."

"Excuse me," said I. "I do not command; I only entreat."

She made no reply, but began pacing the room, her eyes fixed, her hands working convulsively. "You little know what you ask," said she. "I feel as though the very atmosphere of that house would destroy me, but—— Why cannot Eleanore come here?" she suddenly inquired. "I know Mrs. Gilbert will be quite willing, and I could keep my room, and we need not meet."

"You forget there is another call at home besides the one I have already mentioned. Tomorrow afternoon your uncle is to be buried."

"Oh, yes; poor, poor uncle!"

"You are the head of the household," I now ventured, "and the proper one to attend to the final offices toward one who has done so much for you."

There was something strange in the look which she gave me. "It is true," she murmured. Then with a grand turn of her body and a quick air of determination, "I am desirous of being worthy of your good opinion; I will go back to my cousin, Mr. Raymond."

I felt my spirits rise a little; I took her by the hand. "May that cousin have no need of the comfort which I am now sure you will not shrink from giving her if necessity calls."

Her hand dropped from mine. "I mean to do my duty," she responded.

As I descended the stoop, I met a certain thin and fashionably-dressed young man, who gave me a very sharp look as he passed. As he wore his clothes a little too conspicuously for the perfect gentleman, and as I had some remembrance of having seen him at the inquest, I set him down for a man in Mr. Gryce's employ, and hastened on toward the Avenue when what was my surprise to find on the corner another person who, while pretending to be on the look-out for a car, cast upon me, as I approached, a furtive glance of intense inquiry. As this latter was undoubtedly a gentleman, I felt some annoyance, and walking quietly up to him, asked if he found my countenance familiar that he scrutinized it so closely.

"I find it a very agreeable one," he returned, and bowing with a Chesterfieldian grace, walked from me down the Avenue.

Irritated and a trifle ashamed, I stood for a moment watching him, trying to determine who and what he might be. For he was not only a gentleman, but a marked one; possessing features of extraordinary beauty as well as a form of great elegance. Not so very young, having seen, as I should judge, full forty years of mingled pleasure and disappointment, he still bore the impress of youth's strongest emotions, not a curve of his chin nor a glance of his eye betraying in any way the slightest leaning toward ennui, though face and figure were of that type which seems most to invite and cherish it.

"He can have no connection with the police force," thought I; "nor is it by any means certain that he knows me, or is interested in my affairs, but I shall not soon forget him for all that."

The summons from Eleanore Leavenworth came about eight

o'clock in the evening. It was brought by Thomas, and read as follows:

"Come, oh, come; I——" there breaking off in a tremble, as if the pen had fallen from a nerveless hand.

It did not take me long to find my way to her home.

CHAPTER 12

Eleanore

Constant you are—
. . . And for secrecy
No lady closer.
—HENRY IV.

No, 'tis slander,
Whose edge is sharper than the sword whose tongue
Outvenoms all the worms of Nile.
—CYMBELINE.

The door was opened by Molly. "You will find Miss Eleanore in the drawing room, sir," she said, ushering me in.

Fearing I knew not what, I hurried to the room thus indicated, feeling as never before the sumptuousness of the magnificent hall with its antique flooring, carved woods and bronze ornamentations—the mockery of *things* for the first time forcing itself upon me. Laying my hand on the drawing room door, I listened. All was silent.

Slowly pulling it open I lifted the heavy satin curtains hanging before me to the floor, and looked within. What a picture met my eyes!

Sitting in the light of a solitary gas-jet, whose faint glimmering just served to make visible the glancing satin and stainless marble of the gorgeous apartment, I beheld Eleanore Leavenworth.

Pale as the sculptured image of the Psyche that towered above her from the mellow dusk of the bow-window near which she sat, beautiful as it, and almost as immobile, she crouched with rigid hands frozen in forgotten entreaty before her, apparently insensible to sound, movement or touch; a silent figure of despair in presence of an implacable Fate.

Impressed by the scene, I stood with my hand upon the curtain, hesitating if to advance or retreat, when suddenly a sharp tremble shook her impassive frame, the rigid hands unlocked, the stony eyes softened, and springing to her feet she uttered a cry of satisfaction, and advanced toward me.

"Miss Leavenworth!" exclaimed I, starting at the sound of my own voice.

She paused and pressed her hands to her face, as if the world and all that she had forgotten had rushed back upon her at this simple utterance of her name.

"What is it?" asked I.

Her hands fell heavily. "Do you not know?" she cried. "They—they are beginning to say that I——" She paused and clutched her throat. "Read," she murmured, pointing to a newspaper lying on the floor at her feet.

I stooped and lifted what showed itself at first glance to be the *Evening Telegram*. It needed but a single look to inform me to what she referred. There, in startling characters, I beheld:

THE LEAVENWORTH MURDER.

LATEST DEVELOPMENTS IN THE MYSTERIOUS CASE.

A MEMBER OF THE MURDERED MAN'S OWN FAMILY STRONGLY SUSPECTED OF THE CRIME.

THE MOST BEAUTIFUL WOMAN IN NEW YORK UNDER A CLOUD.

PAST HISTORY OF MISS ELEANORE LEAVENWORTH.

I was prepared for it; had schooled myself for this very thing, you might say; and yet I could not help recoiling. Dropping the

paper from my hand, I stood before her, longing and yet dread-
ing to look into her face.

"What does it mean?" she gasped. "What, what does it
mean? Is the world mad?" And her eyes, fixed and glassy,
stared into mine as if she found it impossible to grasp the sense
of this outrage.

I shook my head, I could not reply.

"To accuse me," she murmured. "Me—me," striking her
breast with her clenched hand; "who loved the very ground he
trod upon, who would have cast my own body between him
and the deadly bullet if I had only known his danger. Oh,"
cried she, "it is not a slander they utter, but a dagger which
they thrust into my heart."

Overcome by this, but determined not to show my compassion until more thoroughly convinced of her complete innocence, I replied, after a pause:

"This seems to strike you with great surprise, Miss Leavenworth; were you not, then, able to foresee what must follow
your determined reticence upon certain points? Did you know
so little of human nature as to imagine that, situated as you
are, you could keep silence in regard to any matter connected
with this crime without arousing the antagonism of the crowd,
to say nothing of the suspicions of the police?"

"But—but——"

I hurriedly waved my hand. "When you defied the coroner
to find any suspicious paper in your possession; when"—I
forced myself to speak—"you refused to tell Mr. Gryce how
you came in possession of the key——"

She drew hastily back, a heavy pall seeming to fall over her
with my words.

"Don't," she whispered, looking agonizedly about her. "Don't!
Sometimes I think the walls have ears, the very shadows seem to
listen."

"Ah," returned I, "do you, then, hope to keep from the world
what is known to the detectives?"

She did not answer.

"Miss Leavenworth," I went on, "I am afraid that you do not
comprehend your position. Try to look at the case for a mo-

ment in the light of an unprejudiced person; try to see for yourself the necessity of explaining——"

"But I cannot explain," she murmured huskily.

"Cannot!"

I do not know whether it was the tone of my voice or the
word itself, but that simple expression seemed to affect her like
a blow upon the face.

"Oh!" she cried, shrinking back, "you do not, cannot doubt
me, too? I thought that you——" and stopped. "I did not
dream that I——" and stopped again. Suddenly her whole form
quivered. "Oh, I see," she murmured, "you have mistrusted me
from the first; the appearances against me have been too
strong;" and she sank inert, lost in the depths of her shame and
humiliation. "Ah, but now I am forsaken!" she murmured.

The appeal went to my heart. Starting forward, I exclaimed,
"Miss Leavenworth, I am but a man; I cannot see you so distressed. Say that you are innocent, and I will believe you, without regard to appearances."

Springing erect, she towered upon me. "Can anyone look in
my face and accuse me of guilt?" Then as I sadly shook my
head, she hurriedly gasped: "You want further proof!" and quivering like a suddenly-awakened deer, she sprang to the door.

"Come, then," she cried, "come!" her eyes flashing full of
resolve upon me.

Aroused, appalled, moved in spite of myself, I crossed the
room to where she stood, but she was already in the hall. Hastening after her, filled with a fear I dared not express, I stood at
the foot of the stairs; she was half-way to the top. Following
her into the hall above, I saw her form standing erect and noble
at the door of her uncle's bedroom.

"Come!" she again cried, but this time in a calm and reveren-
tial tone; and flinging the door open before her she passed in.

Subduing the wonder which I felt, I slowly followed her.
There was no light in the room of death, but the flame of the
gas-burner at the far end of the hall shone weirdly in, and by
its glimmering I beheld her kneeling at the shrouded bed, her
head bowed above that of the murdered man, her hand upon
his breast.

"You have said that if I declared my innocence you would believe me," exclaimed she, lifting her head as I entered. "See here," and laying her cheek against the pallid brow of her dead benefactor, she kissed the clay-cold lips softly, wildly, agonizedly, then leaping to her feet, cried in a subdued but thrilling tone:"Could I do that if I were guilty? Would not the breath freeze on my lips, the blood congeal in my veins, the life faint away at my heart? Son of a father loved and reverenced, can you believe me to be a woman stained with crime when I can do this?" And kneeling again she cast her arms over and about that inanimate form, looking in my face at the same time with an expression no mortal touch could paint, nor tongue describe.

"In olden times," she went on, "they used to say that a dead body would bleed if its murderer came in contact with it. What, then, would happen here if I, his daughter, his cherished child, loaded with benefits, enriched with his jewels, warm with his kisses, should be the thing they accuse me of? Would not the body of the outraged dead burst its very shroud and repel me?"

I could not answer; in the presence of some scenes, the tongue forgets its functions.

"Oh!" she went on, "if there is a God in Heaven who loves justice and hates a crime, let Him hear me now. If I, by thought or action, with or without intention, have been the means of bringing this dear head to this pass; if so much as the shadow of guilt, let alone the substance, lies upon my heart and across these feeble woman's hands, may His wrath speak in righteous retribution to the world, and here upon the breast of the dead let this guilty forehead fall, never to rise again!"

An awed silence followed this invocation. It seemed to me as if the world stood still to listen; then a long, long sigh of utter relief rose tremulously from my breast, and all the feelings hitherto suppressed in my heart, the exceeding great awe, the boundless interest, the unspeakable compassion, hope, longing tenderness, that had against my better judgment, reason, and prejudice, made their way into my heart, burst their bonds, and leaning toward her I took her hand in mine.

"You do not, cannot, believe me tainted by crime now?" she

whispered, the smile which does not stir the lips, but rather emanates from the countenance like the flowering of an inner peace, breaking softly out on cheek and brow.

"Crime!" the word broke uncontrollably from my lips; "crime!"

"No," she said calmly, "the man does not live who could accuse me of aught, *here.*"

For reply I took her hand which lay in mine, and placed it on the breast of the dead.

Softly, slowly, gratefully, she bowed her head.

"Now let the struggle come," she whispered. "There is one who will believe in me, however dark appearances may be."

CHAPTER 13
The Problem

But who would force the soul, tilts with a straw
Against a champion cased in adamant.
—WORDSWORTH.

When we re-entered the parlor below, the first sight that met our eyes was Mary, standing wrapped in her long cloak in the center of the room. She had arrived during our absence, and now awaited us with lifted head and countenance fixed in its proudest expression. Looking in her face, I realized what the embarrassments of this meeting must be to these women, and would have retreated, but something in the attitude of Mary Leavenworth seemed to forbid my doing so. At the same time determined that the opportunity should not pass without some sort of reconcilement between them, I stepped forward, and bowing to Mary, said:

"Your cousin has just succeeded in doing what you have expressed yourself so desirous of accomplishing, Miss Leavenworth; convinced me of her entire innocence in regard to this whole matter. I am now ready to join Mr. Gryce, heart and soul, in finding out the true culprit."

"I should have thought that it would have been sufficient for anyone to have looked Eleanore Leavenworth in the face, to know her guiltless of crime." And lifting her head with a proud gesture, she fixed her eyes steadfastly on mine.

I felt the blood flash to my brow, but before I could speak, her voice rose again still more coldly than before.

"It is hard for a delicate girl, reared in the lap of love and luxury, unused to aught but adulation and sincerest expressions of regard, to be obliged to assure the world of her innocence in respect to the committal of a great crime. Eleanore has my sympathy." And sweeping her cloak from her shoulders with a quick gesture, she turned her gaze for the first time upon her cousin.

Instantly Eleanore advanced as if to meet it, and I could not but feel that for some reason this moment possessed an importance for them, which I was scarcely competent to measure. But if I found myself unable to realize its significance, I at least responded to its intensity. And indeed it was an occasion to remember. To have beheld two such women, either of whom must have been considered the model of her time, face to face and drawn up in evident antagonism, would have been a sight to move the dullest sensibilities. But there was something more in it than that. It was the shock of all the most passionate emotions of the human soul; the meeting of waters of whose depth and force I could only guess by the effect. Eleanore was the first to recover. Drawing back with the cold haughtiness which, alas, I had almost forgotten in the display of later and softer emotions, she exclaimed:

"There is something better than sympathy, and that is justice," and turned as if to go. "I will confer with you in the reception-room, Mr. Raymond."

But Mary, springing forward, caught her back with one powerful hand. "No," she cried, "you shall confer with *me*. I have something to say to you, Eleanore Leavenworth." And taking her stand in the center of the room she waited.

I glanced at Eleanore, saw this was no place for me, and hastily withdrew. For ten long minutes I paced the floor of the reception-room, a prey to a thousand doubts and conjectures. What was the secret of this home? What had given rise to the deadly mistrust continually manifested between these cousins fitted by Nature for the completest companionship and the most cordial friendship? It was not a thing of today or yesterday. No sudden flame could awake such concentrated heat of emotion as that of which I had just been the unwilling witness. One must go further back than this murder to find the root of a mistrust so great, that the struggle it caused made itself felt even where I stood, though nothing but the faintest murmur came to my ears through the closed doors.

Presently the drawing room curtain was raised, and Mary's voice was heard in distinct articulation.

"The same roof can never shelter us both after this. Tomorrow, you or I find another home." And blushing and panting, she stepped into the hall and advanced to where I stood. But at the first sight of my face, a change came over her; all her pride seemed to dissolve, and flinging out her hands as if to forbid me to look, she fled from my side, and rushed weeping upstairs.

I was yet laboring under the oppression caused by this painful termination of the strange scene, when the parlor curtain was again lifted, and Eleanore entered the room where I was. Pale but calm, showing no evidences of the struggle she had just been through, unless it was a little extra weariness about the eyes, she sat down by my side, presenting such a contrasted picture to herself as seen by me upon my first entrance, that I could only look and marvel. Whether it was that with the consciousness one soul thoroughly believed in her she had received a fresh influx of strength, or whether it was that in her interview with the dead she had found a new endurance and patience, I cannot say; I only know that a new creature confronted me now, a resigned, earnest and forbearing woman, who might be called upon to endure ignominy, but who felt, and was determined that others should feel, it was an ignominy brought about by circumstances; a concomitant of her fate, and not a thing that tainted her spirit or touched her soul—as a great queen, overcome by the force of a brutish conquerer, might submit her arms to the chains without feeling herself less a queen and great, because the iron of a base victor ground itself into her flesh.

Meeting my gaze with one unfathomable in its courage, she said after a pause: "Tell me where I stand; let me know the worst at once; I fear that I have not indeed comprehended my own position."

Rejoiced to hear her say this, I hastened to comply. I began by placing before her the whole case as it appeared to an unprejudiced person; enlarged upon the causes of suspicion, and pointed out in what regard some things looked dark against her, which perhaps to her own mind were easily explainable and of small account; tried to make her see the importance of her decision and finally wound up with an appeal. Would she not confide in me?

"But I thought you were satisfied?" she inquired, trembling.

"And so I am; but I am but one, and I want the whole world to view you as I do."

"I fear that can never be," she said sadly. "The finger of suspicion never forgets the way it has once pointed. My name is tainted forever."

"And you will submit to this when a word——"

"I am thinking that any word of mine now would make very little difference," she murmured.

I looked away, the vision of Mr. Fobbs in hiding behind the curtains of the opposite house recurring painfully to my mind.

"If the affair looks as bad as you intimate," pursued she, "it is scarcely probable that Mr. Gryce will care much for any interpretation of mine in regard to the matter."

"Mr. Gryce would be glad to know where you procured that key, if only to assist him in turning his inquiries in the right direction."

She did not reply, and a weight settled again upon my heart.

"It is worth your while to satisfy him," I pursued, "and though it may compromise someone you desire to shield——"

She rose, a light flaming suddenly across her face. "I shall never divulge to anyone how I came in possession of that key." And sitting again, she locked her hands in fixed resolve before her.

I rose in my turn and paced the floor, the fang of a deadly serpent striking deep down into my heart.

"Mr. Raymond, if the worst should come, and all who love me should plead on bended knees for me to tell, I should never do it."

"Then," said I, determined not to disclose my secret thought, but equally resolved to find out if possible her motive for this silence, "you desire to defeat the cause of justice."

She neither spoke nor moved.

"Miss Leavenworth," I now said, "this determined shielding of another at the expense of your own good name is no doubt generous of you, but your friends and the lovers of truth and justice cannot accept such a sacrifice."

She started haughtily. "Sir!" she said.

"If you will not assist us," I went on calmly, determinedly, "we must do without your aid. That you were the adopted child of Mr. Veeley's friend, would have been sufficient to have nerved me to exert myself to the utmost to clear your name from the shadows enveloping it; but after the scene I have just witnessed above; after the triumphant assurance which you have forced upon me not only of your innocence, but your horror of the crime and its consequences, I should feel myself less than a man if I did not sacrifice even your own good opinion in urging your cause and clearing your character from this foul aspersion."

Again that heavy silence.

"What do you propose to do?" she asked at last.

Crossing the room, I stood before her. "I propose," said I, "to relieve you utterly and forever from suspicion, by finding out and revealing to the world the true culprit."

I expected to see her recoil, so positive had I become by this time as to whom that culprit was. But instead of that, she merely folded her hands still more tightly and exclaimed:

"I doubt if you will be able to do that, Mr. Raymond."

"Doubt if I will be able to put my finger upon the guilty man, or doubt if I will be able to bring him to justice?"

"I doubt," she said with strong effort, "if anyone ever knows who is the guilty person in this case."

"There is one who knows," I said with a desire to test her.

"One?"

"The girl Hannah is acquainted with the mystery of that night's evil doings, Miss Leavenworth. Find Hannah, and we find one who can point out to us the assassin of your uncle."

"That is mere supposition," she said, but I saw the blow had told.

"Your cousin has offered a large reward for the girl, and the whole country is on the look out. Within a week we shall see her in our midst."

A change took place in her expression and bearing.

"The girl cannot help me," she said.

Baffled by her manner, I drew back. "Is there anything or anybody that can?"

She slowly looked away.

"Miss Leavenworth," I continued with renewed earnestness, "you have no brother to plead with you, you have no mother to guide you, let me then entreat in default of nearer and dearer friends, that you will rely sufficiently upon me to tell me one thing."

"What is it?" she asked.

"Whether you took the paper imputed to you from the library table."

She did not instantly respond, but sat looking earnestly before her with an intentness which seemed to argue that she was weighing the question as well as her reply. Finally, turning toward me, she said:

"In answering you, I speak in confidence. Mr. Raymond, I did."

Crushing back the sigh of despair that arose to my lips, I went on.

"I will not inquire what the paper was"—she waved her hand deprecatingly—"but this much more you will tell me. Is that paper still in existence?"

She looked me steadily in the face.

"It is not."

I could with difficulty forbear showing my disappointment. "Miss Leavenworth," I now said, "it may seem cruel for me to press you at this time; nothing less than my strong realization of the peril in which you stand would induce me to run the risk of incurring your displeasure, by asking what under other circumstances would seem puerile and insulting questions. You have told me one thing which I strongly desired to know; will you also inform me what it was you heard that night while sitting in your room, between the time of Mr. Harwell's going upstairs and the closing of the library door of which you made mention at the inquest?"

I had pushed my inquiries too far, and I saw it immediately.

"Mr. Raymond," she returned, "influenced by my desire not to appear utterly ungrateful to you, I have been led to reply in confidence to one of your urgent appeals, but I can go no further. Do not ask me, then."

Stricken to the heart by her look of reproach, I answered with some sadness that her wishes should be respected. "Not but what I intend to make every effort in my power to discover the true author of this crime," said I, "that is a sacred duty which I feel myself called upon to perform; but I will ask you no more questions nor urge any further appeal upon you. What is done shall be accomplished without your assistance, and if I succeed in what I here undertake, I will ask for no further reward than this; that you will then acknowledge what you must now believe, my motives to have been pure and my action disinterested."

"I am ready to acknowledge that today," she began, but paused, and looked with almost agonized entreaty in my face. "Mr. Raymond, cannot you leave things as they are? Won't you? I don't ask for assistance, nor do I want it; I would rather——"

But I would not listen. "Guilt has no right to profit by the generosity of the guiltless. The hand that struck this blow shall not be accountable for the loss of a noble woman's honor and happiness as well. I shall do what I can, Miss Leavenworth."

As I walked down the Avenue that night, feeling like an adventurous traveler that in a moment of desperation has set his foot upon a plank stretching in narrow perspective over a chasm of immeasurable depth, this problem evolved itself from the shadows before me.

How, with no other clue than the persuasion that Eleanor Leavenworth was engaged in shielding another at the expense of her own good name, was I to combat the prejudices of Mr. Gryce, find out the real assassin of Mr. Leavenworth, and free an innocent woman from the suspicion that had, not without some show of reason, fallen upon her?

BOOK II

HENRY CLAVERING

CHAPTER 1

Mr. Gryce at Home

Nay, but hear me.
—MEASURE FOR MEASURE.

That the guilty person for whom Eleanore Leavenworth stood ready to sacrifice herself was one for whom she had formerly cherished affection, I could no longer doubt, nothing less than love or the strong sense of duty growing out of that passion, whether living or dead, seeming to offer incentive enough for her action. Obnoxious as it was to all my prejudices, one name alone, that of the commonplace secretary with his sudden heats and changeful manners, his odd ways and studied self-possession, would recur to my mind whenever I asked myself who this person could be.

Not that without some such light as had fallen upon the affair through Eleanore's own behavior, I should have selected this man as one in any way open to suspicion; the peculiarity of his manner at the inquest not being marked enough to counteract the improbability of one in his relations to the deceased finding sufficient motive for a crime so manifestly without favorable results to himself. But if love had entered as a factor into the affair, what might not be expected? James Harwell, simple amanuensis to a retired tea-merchant, was one man; James Harwell, swayed by a passion for a woman beautiful as Eleanore Leavenworth, was another; and in placing him upon the list of those parties open to suspicion, I felt that I was only doing what was warranted by a proper consideration of probabilities.

But between casual suspicion and actual proof, what a gulf! To believe James Harwell capable of guilt, and to find evidence enough to accuse him of it, were two very different things. I felt myself instinctively shrink from the task before I had fully made up my mind to attempt it, some relenting thought of his unhappy position, if innocent, forcing itself upon me, and making my very distrust of him seem personally ungenerous, if not absolutely unjust. If I had liked the man better, I should not have been so ready to look upon him with doubt.

But Eleanore must be saved at all hazards. Once delivered up to the blight of suspicion, who could tell what the results might be; the arrest of her person, perhaps, a thing which, once accomplished, would cast a shadow over her young life that it would take more than time to utterly dispel. The accusation of an impecunious secretary would be less horrible than this. I determined to make an early call upon Mr. Gryce.

Meanwhile, the contrasted pictures of Eleanore standing with her hand upon the breast of the dead, her face upraised and reflecting the glory of the heaven she invoked, and Mary fleeing a short half-hour later indignantly from her presence, haunted me and kept me awake long after midnight. It was like a double vision of light and darkness that, while contrasting, neither assimilated nor harmonized. I could not flee from it. Do what I would, the two pictures followed me, filling my soul with alternate hope and distrust, till I knew not whether to place my hand with Eleanore on the breast of the dead and swear implicit faith in her truth and purity, or to turn my face like Mary, and fly from what I could neither comprehend nor reconcile.

Expectant of difficulty I started next morning upon my search for Mr. Gryce, with strong determination not to allow myself to become flurried by disappointment or discouraged by premature failure. My business was to save Eleanore Leavenworth, and to do that, it was necessary for me to preserve not only my equanimity but my self-possession. The worst fear I anticipated was that matters should reach a crisis before I could acquire the right, or obtain the opportunity, to interfere. However, the fact of Mr. Leavenworth's funeral being announced for that day, gave me some comfort in that direction; my knowledge of Mr. Gryce being sufficient, as I thought, to warrant me in believing that he would wait till after that ceremony before proceeding to extreme measures.

I do not know that I had any very definite ideas of what a detective's home should be, but when I stood before the neat three-story brick house to which I had been directed, I could not but acknowledge there was something in the aspect of its half-open shutters over closely-drawn curtains of spotless purity, highly suggestive of the character of its inmate.

A pale-looking youth with vivid locks of red hair hanging straight down over either ear, answered my rather nervous ring. To my inquiry as to whether Mr. Gryce was in, he gave a kind of snort, which might have meant no, but which I took to mean yes.

"My name is Raymond, and I wish to see him."

He gave me one glance that took in every detail of my person and apparel, and pointed to a door at the head of the stairs. Not waiting for further directions, I hastened up, knocked at the door he had designated, and went in. The broad back of Mr. Gryce stooping above a desk that might have come over in the *Mayflower,* it was so old-fashioned, confronted me.

"Well!" he exclaimed, "this is an honor," and rising he opened with a squeak and shut with a bang the door of an enormous stove that occupied the center of the room. "Rather chilly day, eh?"

"Yes," I returned, eyeing him closely to see if he was in a communicative mood. "But I have had but little time to consider the state of the weather. My anxiety in regard to this murder——"

"To be sure," he interrupted, fixing his eyes upon the poker, though not with any hostile intention, I am sure. "A puzzling piece of business enough. But perhaps it is otherwise to you. I see you have something to communicate."

"Yes," said I, "I have, though I doubt if it is of the nature you expect. Mr. Gryce," pursued I, drawing up a little closer to his side, "since I saw you last my convictions upon a certain point have been strengthened into an absolute belief. The subject of your suspicions is an innocent woman."

If I had expected him to betray any surprise at this, I was destined to be disappointed. "That is a very pleasing belief," he murmured. "I honor you for entertaining it, Mr. Raymond."

I suppressed a movement of anger. "So thoroughly is it mine," said I, determined to arouse him in some way, "that I have come here today to ask you in the name of justice and of common humanity to suspend action in that direction till we can look around and see if there is not a truer scent to go upon."

But there was no more show of curiosity than before. "Indeed!" exclaimed he, "that is a singular request to come from a man like you."

I was not to be discomposed. "Mr. Gryce," I went on, "a woman's name once tarnished remains so forever. Eleanore Leavenworth is of too noble a make to be thoughtlessly dealt with in a crisis so momentous as this. If you will give me your attention, I promise you shall not regret it."

He smiled and allowed his eyes to roam from the poker to the arm of my chair. "Very well," remarked he, "I hear you, say on."

I drew my notes from my pocket-book and laid them on the table.

"What, memoranda!" he exclaimed. "Unsafe, very; never put your plans on paper."

Taking no heed of the interruption, I went on.

"Mr. Gryce, I have had opportunities which you have lacked for studying this woman. I have seen her in a position which no guilty person could occupy, and I am assured, beyond all doubt, that not only her hands, but her heart, is pure from this crime. She may have some knowledge of its secrets; that I do not presume to deny. The key seen in her possession would refute me if I did. But what if she has? You can never desire to see so lovely a being brought to shame for withholding information which she evidently considers it her duty to keep back, when by a little patient finesse we may succeed in our purposes without it."

"But," interposed the detective, "say this is so, how are we to arrive at the knowledge we want, without following out the only clue which has yet been given us?"

"You will never reach it by following out any clue given you by Eleanore Leavenworth."

His eyebrows lifted expressively, but he said nothing.

"Miss Eleanore Leavenworth has been used by someone acquainted with her firmness, generosity, and perhaps love. Let us discover who possesses sufficient power over her to control her to this extent, and we find the man we seek."

"Humph!" came from Mr. Gryce's compressed lips, and no more.

Determined that he should speak, I waited.

"You have, then, someone in your mind," remarked he at last almost flippantly.

"I mention no names," I returned. "All I want is further time."

"You are, then, intending to make a personal business of this matter?"

"I am."

He gave a long, low whistle. "May I ask," he inquired at length, "whether you expect to work entirely upon your own hook, or whether if a suitable coadjutor were provided, you would disdain his assistance and slight his advice."

"I desire nothing more than to have you for my colleague."

The smile upon his face deepened ironically. "You must feel very sure of yourself," said he.

"I am very sure of Miss Leavenworth," I retorted.

The reply seemed to please him. "Let us hear what you propose doing."

I did not immediately answer. The truth was I had formed no plans.

"It seems to me," he continued, "that you have undertaken a rather difficult task for an amateur. Better leave it to me, Mr. Raymond, better leave it to me."

"I am sure," I returned, "that nothing would please me better——"

"Not," he interrupted, "but that a word from you now and then would be welcome. I am not an egotist. I am open to suggestions, as for instance now, if you could conveniently inform me of all you have yourself seen and heard in regard to this matter, I should be most happy to listen."

Relieved to find him so amenable, I asked myself what I really had to tell; not much that he would consider vital. However, it would not do to hesitate now.

"Mr. Gryce," said I, "I have but few facts to give beyond those already known to you. Indeed, it is not so much facts I possess as convictions. That Eleanore Leavenworth not only never committed this crime, but was in utter ignorance of it until its completion, I am assured. That the real perpetrator is likewise known to her, I am equally certain, and that for some reason she considers it a sacred duty to shield the assassin even at the risk of her own safety, follows as a matter of course from the facts. Now with such data, it cannot be a very difficult task for you or me to work out satisfactorily to our own minds, at least, who this person can be. A little more knowledge of the family——"

"You know nothing of its secret history then?"

"Nothing."

"Do not even know whether those girls are engaged to be married, or possess lovers?"

"I do not," returned I, rather wincing at this direct putting into words of my own inner thought.

He remained a moment silent. "Mr. Raymond," cried he at last, "have you any idea of the disadvantages under which a detective labors? For instance now, you imagine that I can insinuate myself into all sorts of society perhaps, but you are mistaken. Strange as it may appear, I have never by any possibility of means succeeded with one class of persons at all. I cannot pass myself off for a gentleman. Tailors and barbers are no good; I am always found out."

He looked so dejected that I could scarcely forbear smiling, notwithstanding my secret care and anxiety.

"I have even employed a French valet, who understood dancing and whiskers, but it was all of no avail. The first gentleman I approached stared at me, real gentleman I mean, none of your American dandies, and I had no stare to return; I had forgotten that emergency in my confabs with Pierre Camille Marie Make-face."

Amused, but a little discomposed by this sudden turn in the conversation, I looked at Mr. Gryce inquiringly.

"Now you, I dare say, have no trouble——" he exclaimed, "was born one, perhaps. Can even ask a lady to dance without blushing, eh?"

"Well," I commenced——

"Just so," he replied, "now I can't. I can enter a house, bow to the mistress of it, let her be as elegant as she will, so long as I have a writ of arrest in my hand or some such professional matter

upon my mind, but when it comes to visiting in kid gloves, raising a glass of champagne in response to a toast—and such-like, I
am absolutely good for nothing." And he plunged his two hands
into his hair, and looked dolefully at the head of the cane I carried in my hand. "But it is much the same with the whole of us.
When we are in want of a gentleman to work for us, we have to
go outside of our profession."

I thought I began to see what he was driving at, but held my
peace, vaguely conscious that I was likely to prove a necessity
to him after all.

"Mr. Raymond," he now said almost abruptly, "do you
know a gentleman by the name of Clavering, at present resid-
ing at the Hoffman House?"

"Not that I am aware of."

"He is very polished in his manners; would you mind making his acquaintance?"

I followed Mr. Gryce's example and stared at the chimney-
piece. "I cannot answer till I understand matters a little better,"
I returned at length.

"There is not much to understand," he replied. "Mr. Henry
Clavering, a gentleman and a man of the world, resides at the
Hoffman House. He is a stranger in town, without being strange,
drives, walks, smokes, but never visits, looks at the ladies but
was never seen to bow to one. In short, a person whom it is
desirable to know, but whom, being a proud man with something of the old-world prejudice against Yankee freedom and
forwardness, I could no more get near to than I could the Em-
peror of Austria."

"And you wish——"

"He would make a very agreeable companion for a rising
young lawyer of good family and undoubted respectability. I
have no doubt that if you yourself undertook to cultivate him,
you would find him well worth the trouble."

"But——"

"Might even desire to take him into familiar relations—by
degrees you know—confide in him, and——"

"Mr. Gryce," I interrupted hastily, "I can never consent to
plot for any man's friendship for the sake of betraying him to
the police."

"It is essential to your plans to make the acquaintance of Mr. Clavering," he replied dryly.

"Oh," I returned, a light breaking in upon me, "he has some connection with this case, then?"

Mr. Gryce smoothed his coat-sleeve thoughtfully. "I don't know that it will be necessary for you to betray him. You wouldn't object to being introduced to him?"

"No."

"Nor if you found him pleasant, to converse with him?"

"No."

"Not even if in the course of conversation you should come across something that might serve as a clue in your efforts to save Eleanore Leavenworth?"

The no I uttered this time was less assured; the part of a spy was the very last one I desired to play in the coming drama.

"Well, then," he went on, ignoring the doubtful tone in which my assent had been given, "I advise you to immediately take up your quarters at the Hoffman House."

"I doubt if that would do," I said. "If I am not mistaken, I have already seen this gentleman and spoken to him."

"Where?"

"Describe him first."

"Well, he is tall, finely formed, of very upright carriage, with a handsome dark face, brown hair streaked with gray, a piercing eye and a smooth address. A very imposing personage, I assure you."

"I have reason to think I have seen him," I returned, and in a few words told him when and where.

"Humph!" said he at the conclusion, "he is evidently as much interested in you as we in him. How's that? I think I see," he cried again after a moment's thought. "Pity you spoke to him; it may have created an unfavorable impression, and everything depends upon your meeting without any distrust."

He rose and paced the floor.

"Well, we must work slow, that is all. Give him a chance to see you in other and better lights. Drop into the Hoffman House reading-room. Talk with the best men you meet while there, but not too much or too indiscriminately. Mr. Clavering is fastidious, and will not feel honored by the attentions of one who is hail-fellow-well-met with everybody. Show yourself for what you are, and leave all advances to him; he'll make them."

"Supposing we are under a mistake, and the man I met on the corner of Thirty-seventh Street was not Mr. Clavering?"

"I should be greatly surprised, that's all."

Not knowing what further objection to make, I remained silent.

"And this head of mine would have to put on its thinking-cap," he pursued jovially.

"Mr. Gryce," said I, anxious to show that all this talk about an unknown party had not served to put my own plans from my mind, "there is one person of whom we have not spoken."

"No?" he exclaimed softly, wheeling around until his broad back confronted me. "And who may that be?"

"Why, who but Mr.——." I could get no further. What right had I to mention any man's name in this connection, unless I possessed sufficient evidence against him to make such mention justifiable? "I beg your pardon," said I, "but I think I will hold to my first impulse and speak no names."

"Harwell?" he ejaculated easily.

The quick blush rising to my face, involuntarily assented.

"I see no reason why we shouldn't speak of him," he went on, "that is, if there is anything to be gained by it."

"His testimony at the inquest was honest, you think?"

"It has not been disproved."

"He is a peculiar man."

"And so am I," the detective returned.

I felt myself slightly nonplussed, and, conscious of appearing at a disadvantage, lifted my hat from the table and prepared to take my leave, but suddenly thinking of Hannah, turned and asked if there was any news of her.

He seemed to debate with himself, hesitating so long that I began to doubt if this man intended to confide in me after all, when suddenly he brought his two hands down before him and exclaimed vehemently:

"The evil one himself is in this business. If the earth had opened and swallowed up this girl, she couldn't have more effectually disappeared."

I experienced a sinking of the heart. Eleanore had said,

"Hannah can do nothing for me." Could it be that the girl was indeed gone, and forever?

"I have innumerable agents at work, to say nothing of the general public, and yet not so much as a whisper has come to me in regard to her whereabouts or situation. I am only afraid we shall find her floating in the river some fine morning, without a confession in her pocket."

"Everything hangs upon that girl's testimony," I remarked.

He gave a short grunt. "What does Miss Leavenworth say about it?"

"That the girl cannot help her."

I thought he looked a trifle surprised at this, but he covered it with a nod and an exclamation. "She must be found for all that," said he, "and shall, if I have to send out Q."

"Q?"

"An agent of mine who is a living interrogation point; so we called him Q, which is short for query." Then as I turned again to go: "When the contents of the will are made known, come to me."

The will! I had forgotten the will.

CHAPTER 2

Ways Opening

It is not and it cannot come to good.
—HAMLET.

I attended the funeral of Mr. Leavenworth, but did not see the ladies either before or after the ceremony. I had, however, a few moments' conversation with Mr. Harwell, which, without eliciting anything new, provided me with food for abundant conjecture. For he had asked, almost at first greeting, if I had seen the telegram of the night before, and when I responded in the affirmative, turned such a look of mingled distress and appeal upon me, that I was tempted to ask how such a fright-ful insinuation against a young lady of reputation and breed-ing could ever have got into the papers. It was his reply that struck me.

"That the guilty party might be driven by remorse to own himself the true culprit, I suppose."

A curious remark to come from a person who had no knowl-edge or suspicion of the criminal and his character; and I would have pushed the conversation further, but the secretary, who was a man of few words, drew off at this, and could be induced to say no more. Evidently it was my business to culti-vate Mr. Clavering, or anyone else who could throw any light upon the secret history of these girls.

That evening I received notice that Mr. Veeley had arrived home but was in no condition to consult with me upon so painful a subject as the murder of Mr. Leavenworth. Also a line from Eleanore giving me her address but requesting me at the same time not to call unless I had something of impor-tance to communicate, as she was too ill to receive visitors. The little note affected me. Ill, alone, and in a strange home—it was pitiful!

The next day, pursuant to the wishes of Mr. Gryce, I stepped into the Hoffman House and took a seat in the reading-room. I had been there but a few moments when a gentleman entered whom I immediately recognized as the same I had spoken to on the corner of Thirty-seventh Street and Sixth Avenue. He must have remembered me also, for he seemed to be slightly embar-rassed at seeing me, but recovering himself took up a paper and soon became to all appearance lost in its contents, though I could feel his handsome black eye upon me studying my fea-tures, figure, apparel and movements with a degree of interest that astonished as much as it disconcerted me. I felt that it would be injudicious on my part to return his scrutiny, anxious as I was to meet his eye and learn what emotion had so fired his curiosity in regard to a perfect stranger; so I rose and, cross-ing to an old friend of mine who sat at a table opposite, com-menced a desultory conversation, in the course of which I took occasion to ask if he knew who the handsome stranger was. Dick Furbish was a society man and knew everybody.

"His name is Clavering, and he comes from London. I don't know anything more about him, though he is everywhere you go, if you except private houses. He has not been received into society yet, waiting for letters of introduction perhaps."

"A gentleman?"

"Undoubtedly."

"One you speak to?"

"Oh, yes, I talk to him, but it's little he says to me." I could not help smiling at the grimace with which Dick accompanied this remark. "Which same goes to prove," he went on, "that he is the real thing."

Laughing this time outright, I left him, and in a few minutes sauntered from the room.

As I mingled again with the crowd on Broadway, I found myself wondering immensely over this slight experience. That this unknown gentleman from London, who went everywhere except into private houses, could be in any way connected with the affair I had so at heart, seemed not only improbable but absurd, and for the first time I felt tempted to doubt the sagacity of Mr. Gryce in recommending him to my attention.

The next day I repeated the experiment, but with no greater success than before. Mr. Clavering came into the room, but seeing me, did not remain. I began to realize it was no easy matter to make his acquaintance. To atone for my disappointment I called on Mary Leavenworth in the evening. She received me with almost a sister-like familiarity.

"Ah," cried she, after introducing me to an elderly lady at her side—some connection of the family, I believe, who had come to remain with her for a while—"you are here to tell me Hannah is found, is it not so?"

I shook my head, sorry to disappoint her. "No," said I, "not yet."

"But Mr. Gryce was here today, and he told me that he hoped she would be heard from within twenty-four hours."

"Mr. Gryce here?"

"Yes, he came to report to me how matters were progressing— not that they seemed to have advanced very far," she continued mournfully.

"You could hardly have expected that yet," returned I. "You must not be so easily discouraged."

"But I cannot help it; every day, every hour that passes in this uncertainty is like a mountain weight here," and she laid one trembling hand upon her bosom. "I would have the whole world at work if it were possible. I would leave no stone un-turned, I——"

"What would you do?" I murmured.

"Oh, I don't know," cried she, her whole manner suddenly changing, "nothing perhaps." Then before I could reply to this—"Have you seen Eleanore today?"

I answered in the negative.

She did not seem satisfied, but waited till her friend left the room before saying more, then with an earnest look inquired if I knew whether Eleanore was well.

"I fear she is not," I returned.

"It is a great trial to me," she murmured, "Eleanore being away. Not," resumed she, noting, perhaps, my incredulous look, "that I would have you think I wish to disclaim my share in bringing about the present unhappy state of things. I am willing to acknowledge that I was the first to propose a separa-tion. But it is none the easier to bear on that account."

"It is not as hard for you as for her," said I.

"Not as hard? Why? Because she is left comparatively poor while I am rich—is that what you would say? Ah," she went on without waiting for my answer, "would that I could per-suade Eleanore to share my riches with me. Willingly would I bestow upon her the half I have received, but I fear she could never be induced to accept it."

"Under the circumstances it would be wiser that she should not."

"Just what I thought," Mary returned, "yet it would ease me of a great weight if she would. This fortune, suddenly thrown into my lap, sits like an incubus upon me, Mr. Raymond. When the will was read today which makes me the possessor of so much wealth, I could not but feel that a heavy, binding pall had settled upon me, spotted with blood and woven of horrors. Ah, how different from the feelings with which I have been accustomed to anticipate this day. For, Mr. Raymond," she went on with a hurried gasp, "dreadful as it seems now, I have been reared to look forward to this hour with pride, if not with actual longing. Money has been made so much of in my small world. Not that I wish in this evil time of retribution to lay blame upon anyone, least of all upon my uncle, but from the day twelve years ago when for the first time he took us in his arms, and looking down upon our childish faces, exclaimed: 'The light-haired one pleases me best, she shall be my heiress'—I have been petted, cajoled and spoiled, called little princess, and uncle's darling, till it is only strange that I retain in this prejudiced breast any of the impulses of generous womanhood; yes, though I was aware from the first that whim alone had raised this distinction between myself and cousin, a distinction which superior beauty, worth or accomplishments could never have drawn, Eleanore being more than my equal in all these things." Pausing, she choked back the sudden sob that rose in her throat, with an effort at self-control that was at once touching and admirable. Then while her eyes stole to my face, she murmured in a low appealing voice—"If I have faults, you see there is some slight excuse for them, arrogance, vanity and selfishness being considered in the gay young heiress as no more than so many assertions of a laudable dignity. Ah, ah," she exclaimed bitterly. "Money alone has been the ruin of us all!" Then with a falling of her voice—"And now it has come to me with its heritage of evil, and I—I would give it all for—but this is weakness. I have no right to afflict you with my griefs. Pray forget all I have said, Mr. Raymond, or regard my complaints as the utterances of an unhappy girl loaded down with sorrows and oppressed by the weight of many perplexities and terrors."

"But I do not wish to forget," replied I. "You have spoken some good words, manifested much noble emotion. Your possessions cannot but prove a blessing to you if you enter upon them with such feelings as these."

But with a quick gesture, she replied: "Impossible! they cannot prove a blessing." Then, as if startled at her own words, bit her lip and hastily added—"Very great wealth is never a blessing.

"And now," said she with a total change of manner, "I wish

to address you on a subject which may strike you as ill-timed, but which, nevertheless, it is essential for me to mention, if the purpose I have at heart is ever to be accomplished. My uncle, as you know, was engaged at the time of his death in writing a book on Chinese customs and prejudices. It was a work he was anxious to see published, and naturally I desire to carry out his wishes; but in order to do so, I find it necessary not only to interest myself in the matter now—Mr. Harwell's services being required and it being my wish to dismiss that gentleman as soon as possible—but to find someone competent to supervise its completion. Now I have heard—I have been told that you were the one of all others to do this, and though it is difficult if not improper for me to ask so great a favor of one who but a week ago was a perfect stranger to me, it would afford me the keenest pleasure if you would consent to look over this manu-script and tell me what is necessary to be done."

The timidity with which these words were uttered proved her to be in earnest, and I could not but wonder at the strange coincidence of this request with my secret wishes, it having been a question with me for sometime how I was to gain free access to this house without in any way compromising either its inmates or myself. I did not know then what I afterward learned, that Mr. Gryce had been the one to recommend me to her favor in this respect. But whatever satisfaction I may have experienced, I felt myself in duty bound to plead my incompe-tence for a task so entirely out of the line of my profession, and to suggest the employment of someone better acquainted with such matters than myself. But she would not listen to me.

"Mr. Harwell has notes and memoranda in plenty," she ex-claimed, "and can give you all the information necessary. You will have no difficulty, indeed you will not."

"But cannot Mr. Harwell himself do all that is requisite? He seems to be a clever and diligent young man."

But she shook her head. "He thinks he can," she murmured, "but I know uncle never trusted him with the composition of so much as a single sentence, and I wish to do just as he would have done in this case."

"But perhaps he will not be pleased—Mr. Harwell, I mean—with the intrusion of a stranger into his work."

She opened her eyes with astonishment. "That makes no difference," she said. "Mr. Harwell is in my pay and has nothing to say about it. But he will not object. I have already consulted him and he expresses himself as satisfied with the arrangement."

"Very well," said I, "then I will promise to consider the subject. I can at any rate look over the manuscript and give you my opinion in regard to its condition."

"Oh, thank you," said she, with the prettiest gesture of satisfaction. "How kind you are, and what can I ever do to repay you? But would you like to see Mr. Harwell himself?" and she moved toward the door, but suddenly paused, whispering, with a short shudder of remembrance. "He is in the library, do you mind?"

Crushing down the sick qualm that arose at the mention of that spot, I replied in the negative.

"The papers are all there, and he can work better in his old place, he says, than anywhere else, but if you wish, I can call him down."

But I would not listen to it, and myself led the way to the foot of the stairs.

"I have sometimes thought I would lock up that room," she went on hurriedly, "but something restrains me. I can no more do so than I can leave this house; a power beyond myself forces me to confront all its horrors. And yet," she went on, "I suffer continually from terror. Sometimes in the darkness of the night—— But," she suddenly cried, "I will not distress you. I have already said too much; come," and with a sudden lift of the head she mounted the stairs.

Mr. Harwell was seated, when we entered that fatal room, in the one chair of all others that I expected to see unoccupied, and as I beheld his meager figure bending where such a little while before his eyes had encountered the outstretched form of his murdered employer, I could not but marvel over the unimaginativeness of the man, who, in the face of such memories, could not only appropriate that very spot for his own use, but pursue his avocations there with so much calmness and evident precision. But in another moment I discovered that the disposition of the light in the room made that one seat the only desirable one for his purpose, and instantly my wonder changed to admiration at this quiet surrender of personal feeling to the requirements of necessity.

He looked up mechanically as we came in, but did not rise, his countenance wearing the absorbed expression which bespeaks the preoccupied mind.

"He is utterly oblivious," Mary whispered; "that is a way of his. I doubt if he knows who or what it is that has disturbed him." And advancing into the room, she passed across his line of vision as if to call attention to herself, and said, "I have brought Mr. Raymond upstairs to see you, Mr. Harwell. He has been so kind as to accede to my wishes in regard to the completion of the manuscript now before you."

Slowly Mr. Harwell rose, wiped his pen and put it away, manifesting, however, a reluctance in doing so, that proved this interference to be in reality anything but agreeable to him. Observing this, I did not wait for him to speak, but took up the pile of manuscript which I saw arranged in one mass on the table, saying:

"This seems to be very clearly written. If you will excuse me, I will glance over it and see something of its general character."

He bowed, uttered a word or so of acquiescence, then, as Mary left the room, awkwardly reseated himself and took up his pen.

Instantly the manuscript and all connected with it vanished from my thoughts, and Eleanore, her situation and the mystery surrounding this family, returned upon me with renewed force. Looking the secretary steadily in the face, I remarked:

"I am very glad of this opportunity of seeing you a moment alone, Mr. Harwell, if only for the purpose of saying——"

"Anything in regard to the murder?"

"Yes——" I began.

"Then," replied he respectfully but firmly, "you must pardon me. It is a disagreeable subject which I cannot bear to think of, much less discuss."

Disconcerted and, what was more, convinced of the impossibility of obtaining any information from this man, I abandoned the attempt, and taking up the manuscript once more, endeavored to master in some small degree the nature of its contents.

Succeeding beyond my hopes, I opened a short conversation with him in regard to it, and finally, coming to the conclusion I could accomplish what Miss Leavenworth desired, left him and descended again to the reception-room.

When, an hour or so later, I withdrew from the house, it was with the feeling that one obstacle had been removed from my path at all events. If I failed, it would not be from lack of opportunity of studying the inmates of this dwelling.

CHAPTER 3

The Will of a Millionaire

Our remedies oft in ourselves do lie,
Which we ascribe to Heaven.
—ALL's WELL THAT ENDS WELL.

The next morning's *Tribune* contained a synopsis of Mr. Leavenworth's will. Its provisions were a surprise to me, for while the bulk of his immense estate was, according to the general understanding, given to his niece Mary, it appeared by a codicil attached to his will some five years before that Eleanore was not entirely forgotten, a handsome bequest, though not a large one, having been left her. After listening to the various comments of my associates on the subject, I proceeded to the house of Mr. Gryce in obedience to his request to call upon him as soon as possible after the publication of the will.

"Good morning," he remarked as I entered, but whether addressing me or the frowning top of the desk before which he was sitting it would be difficult to say. "Won't you sit?" nodding with a curious back movement of his head toward a chair in his rear.

I drew up the chair to his side. "I am curious to know," I remarked, "what you have to say about this will and its probable effect upon the matters we have in hand."

"What is your own idea in regard to it?"

"Well, I think upon the whole it will make but little difference in public opinion. Those who thought Eleanore guilty before will feel that they possess now greater cause than ever to doubt her innocence; while those who have hitherto hesitated to suspect her will not consider that the comparatively small amount bequeathed her would constitute an adequate motive for so great a crime."

"You have heard men talk; what seems to be the general opinion among those you converse with?"

"That the motive of the tragedy will be found in the partiality shown in so singular a will, though how, they do not profess to know."

Mr. Gryce suddenly became interested in one of the small drawers before him.

"And all this has not set you thinking?" said he.

"Thinking?" returned I. "I don't know what you mean. I am sure I have done nothing but think for the last three days. I——"

"Of course—of course," cried he. "I didn't mean to say anything disagreeable. And so you have seen Mr. Clavering?"

"Just seen him, no more."

"And are you going to assist Mr. Harwell in finishing Mr. Leavenworth's book?"

"How did you learn that?"

He only smiled.

"Yes," said I; "Miss Leavenworth has requested me to do her that little favor."

"She is a queenly creature!" exclaimed he in a burst of enthusiasm. Then with an instant return to his business-like tone—"You are going to have opportunities, Mr. Raymond. Now, there are two things I want you to find out; first, what is the connection between these ladies and Mr. Clavering——"

"There is a connection, then?"

"Undoubtedly. And, secondly, what is the cause of the unfriendly feeling which evidently exists between the cousins."

I drew back and pondered the position offered me. A spy in a fair woman's house! How could I reconcile it with my natural instincts as a gentleman?

"Cannot you find someone more suitable to learn these secrets for you!" I asked at length. "The part of a spy is anything
but agreeable to my feelings, I assure you."

Mr. Gryce's brows fell.

"I will assist Mr. Harwell in his efforts to arrange Mr. Leavenworth's manuscript for the press," I said, "I will give Mr.
Clavering an opportunity to form my acquaintance, and I will
listen if Miss Leavenworth chooses to make me her confidant
in any way. But any hearkening at doors, surprises, unworthy
feints or ungentlemanly subterfuges I herewith disclaim as outside of my province; my task being to find out what I can in an
open way, and yours to search into the nooks and corners of
this most wretched business."

"In other words, you are to play the hound and I the mole;
just so, I know what belongs to a gentleman."

"And now," said I, "what news of Hannah."

He shook both hands high in the air. "None," cried he.

I cannot say I was greatly surprised that evening when, upon
descending from an hour's labor with Mr. Harwell, I encountered Miss Leavenworth standing at the foot of the stairs. There
had been something in her bearing the night before which prepared me for another interview this evening, though her manner of commencing it was a surprise. "Mr. Raymond," said
she, looking down with an appearance of embarrassment, "I
want to ask you a question. I believe that you are a good man
and will answer it conscientiously—as a brother would," she
murmured, lifting her eyes for a moment to my face. "I know it
will sound strange, but remember that I have no adviser but
you, and I must ask someone. Mr. Raymond, do you think a
person could do something that was very wrong and yet grow
to be thoroughly good afterward?"

"Certainly," I replied, "if he were truly sorry for his fault."

"But say it was more than a fault, say it was an actual harm;
would not the memory of that one evil hour cast a shadow
over the life which the soul could never escape from?"

"That depends," said I, "upon the nature of the harm and its
effect upon others. If one had irreparably injured a fellow-being
it would be hard, I should think, to live a happy life afterward,

though the fact of not living a happy life ought to be no reason why one should not live a good one."

"But to live a good life would it be necessary to reveal the evil you had done? Cannot one go on and do right without confessing to the world that he had once committed a great wrong?"

"Yes, unless by its confession he can in some way make reparation."

My answer seemed to trouble her. Drawing back, she stood for one moment in a thoughtful attitude before me, her beauty shining with almost a statuesque splendor in the glow of the porcelain-shaded lamp at her side. Nor, though she presently roused herself, leading the way into the drawing room with a gesture that was allurement itself, did she recur to this topic again, but rather seemed to strive in the conversation that followed to make me forget what had already passed between us. That she did not succeed, was owing to my intense and unfailing interest in her cousin.

As I descended the stoop I saw Thomas, the butler, leaning over the area gate. Immediately I was seized with an impulse to interrogate him in regard to a matter which had more or less interested me ever since the inquest, and that was, who was the Mr. Robbins who had called upon Eleanore the night of the murder? But Thomas was decidedly uncommunicative. He remembered such a person called, but could not describe his looks any further than to say that he was not a small man.

I did not press the matter.

CHAPTER 4

The Beginning of Great Surprises

*Vous regardez une étoile pour deux motifs, parce qu'elle
est lumineuse et parce qu'elle est impénétrable. Vous
avez auprès de vous un plus doux rayonnement et un
plus grand mystère, la femme.*

—LES MISÉRABLES.

And now followed days in which I seemed to make little or no
progress. Mr. Clavering, disturbed perhaps by my presence,
forsook his usual haunts, thus depriving me of all opportunity
of making his acquaintance in any natural manner, while the
evenings spent at Miss Leavenworth's were productive of little
else than constant suspense and uneasiness.

The manuscript required less revision than I supposed, Mr.
Leavenworth being one of the men who believe in finishing as
you go, but in the course of making such few changes as were
necessary I had ample opportunity of studying the character of
Mr. Harwell. I found him to be neither more nor less than an
excellent amanuensis. Stiff, unbending and somber, but true to
his duty and reliable in its performance, I learned to respect
him, and even to like him, and this, too, though I saw the lik-
ing was not reciprocated, whatever the respect may have been.
He never spoke of Eleanore Leavenworth or, indeed, mentioned
the family or its trouble in any way, till I began to feel that all
this reticence had a cause deeper than the nature of the man,
and that if he did speak, it would be to some purpose. This
suspicion, of course, kept me restlessly eager in his presence. I
could not forbear giving him sly glances now and then, to see
how he acted when he believed himself unobserved, but he was
ever the same, a passive, diligent, unexcitable worker.

This continual beating against a stone wall, for thus I felt
it to be, became at last almost unendurable. Clavering shy, and
the secretary unapproachable—how was I to gain anything?
The short interviews I had with Mary did not help matters.

Haughty, constrained, feverish, pettish, grateful, appealing, everything at once and never twice the same, I learned to dread, even while I coveted an interview. She appeared to be passing through some crisis which occasioned her the keenest suffering. I have seen her when she thought herself alone throw up her hands with the gesture which we use to ward off a coming evil, or shut out some hideous vision. I have likewise beheld her standing with her proud head abased, her nervous hands drooping, her whole form sinking and inert, as if the pressure of a weight she could neither upbear nor cast aside had robbed her even of the show of resistance. But that was only once. Ordinarily she was at least stately in her trouble. Even when the softest appeal came into her eyes, she stood erect, and retained her expression of conscious power. Even, the night she met me in the hall with feverish cheeks, and lips trembling with eagerness, only to turn and fly again without giving utterance to what she had to say, she comported herself with a fiery dignity that was well-nigh imposing.

That all this meant something I was sure, and so I kept my patience alive with the hope that some day she would make a revelation. Those quivering lips would not always remain closed, the secret involving Eleanore's honor and happiness would be divulged by this restless being, if by no one else. Nor was the memory of that extraordinary, if not cruel, accusation I had heard her make enough to destroy this hope—for hope it had grown to be—so that I found myself insensibly shortening my time with Mr. Harwell in the library, and extending my *tête-à-tête* visits with Mary in the reception-room, till the imperturbable secretary was forced to complain that he was often left for hours without work.

But as I say, days passed and a second Monday evening came round without seeing me any further advanced upon the problem I had set myself to solve than I was two weeks before. The subject of the murder had not even been broached; nor was Hannah spoken of, though I observed the papers were not allowed to languish an instant upon the stoop; mistress and servants betraying equal interest in their contents. All this was strange to me. It was as if you saw a group of human beings eating, drinking and sleeping upon the sides of a volcano hot with a late eruption and trembling with the birth of a new one. I longed to break this silence as we shiver glass, by shouting the name of Eleanore through those gilded rooms and satin-draped vestibules. I felt an insane impulse to tear up the very floors, and rend the walls, as if they could tell me, if they would, what I so yearned to know. But this Monday evening I was in a calmer mood. The day before, I had passed her house, and caught a glimpse of a face at a window, that was sweet and sad enough to nerve me for more than one week of disappointment. I determined to expect nothing from my visits to Mary Leavenworth's house, and entered it upon the eve in question with an equanimity such as I had not experienced since the first day I passed under its unhappy portals.

But when upon nearing the reception-room I saw Mary pacing the floor with the air of one who is restlessly awaiting something or somebody, I took a sudden resolution, and, advancing toward her, said: "Do I see you alone, Miss Leavenworth?"

She paused in her hurried action, blushed and bowed, but contrary to her usual custom did not bid me enter.

"Will it be too great an intrusion on my part if I venture to come in?" I asked.

Her glance flashed uneasily to the clock, and she seemed about to excuse herself, but suddenly yielded, and drawing up a chair before the fire, motioned me toward it. Though she endeavored to appear calm, I vaguely felt that I had chanced upon her in one of her most agitated moods, and that I had only to broach the subject I had in mind to behold that haughty aspect disappear before me like melting snow. I also felt that I had but few moments in which to do it. I accordingly plunged immediately into the subject.

"Miss Leavenworth," said I, "in obtruding upon you to-night, I have a purpose other than that of giving myself a pleasure. I have come to make an appeal."

Instantly I saw that in some way I had started wrong. "An appeal to make to me?" she asked, breathing coldness from every feature of her face.

"Yes," I went on with passionate recklessness. "Balked in every other endeavor to learn the truth, I have come to you whom I believe to be noble at the core for that help which seems likely to fail us in every other direction; for the word which, if it does not absolutely save your cousin, will at least put us upon the track of what will."

"I do not understand what you mean," returned she, slightly shrinking.

"Miss Leavenworth," pursued I, "it is needless for me to tell you in what position your cousin stands. You who remember both the form and drift of the questions put to her at the inquest, comprehend it all without any explanation from me. But what you may not know is this, that unless she is speedily relieved from the suspicion which justly or not has attached itself to her name, the consequences which such suspicion entails must fall upon her, and——"

"Good God!" she cried, "you do not mean that she will be——"

"Subject to arrest? Yes."

It was a blow. Shame, anguish and horror were in every line of her white face. "And all because of that key!" she murmured.

"Key? How did you know anything about a key?"

"Why," said she, flushing painfully, "I cannot say; didn't you tell me?"

"No," returned I.

"The papers, then."

"The papers have never mentioned it."

She grew more and more agitated. "I thought everyone knew. No, I did not, either," exclaimed she, in a sudden burst of shame and penitence. "I knew it was a secret but—oh, Mr. Raymond, it was Eleanore herself who told me."

"Eleanore?"

"Yes, that last evening she was here we were together in the drawing room."

"What did she tell?"

"That the key to the library had been seen in her possession."

I could scarcely conceal my incredulity. Eleanore, conscious of the suspicion with which her cousin regarded her, informed that cousin of a fact which seemed to give weight to her suspicion! I could not believe this.

"But you knew it?" Mary went on. "I have revealed nothing that I should have kept secret?"

"No," said I, "and, Miss Leavenworth, it is this thing which makes your cousin's position absolutely dangerous. It is a fact that, left unexplained, must ever link her name with infamy, a bit of circumstantial evidence no sophistry can smother, and no denial obliterate. Only her hitherto spotless reputation, and the efforts of one who, notwithstanding appearances, believes in her innocence, keeps her so long from the clutch of the officers of justice. That key and the silence preserved by her in regard to it is sinking her slowly into a pit from which the utmost endeavors of her best friends will soon be inadequate to extricate her."

"And you tell me this——"

"That you may have pity on the poor girl, who will not have pity on herself, and by the explanation of a few circumstances which cannot be mysteries to you, assist in bringing her from under the dreadful shadow that threatens to overwhelm her."

"And would you insinuate, sir," cried she, turning upon me with a look of great anger, "that I know any more than you do of this matter? that I possess any knowledge which I have not already made public, concerning the dreadful tragedy which has transformed our home into a desert, our existence into a lasting horror? Has the blight of suspicion fallen upon me, too, and have you come to accuse me in my own house——"

"Miss Leavenworth," I entreated, "calm yourself. I accuse you of nothing. I only desire you to enlighten me as to your cousin's probable motive for this criminating silence. You cannot be in ignorance of it. You are her cousin, almost her sister, have been at all events her daily companion for years, and must know for whom or for what she seals her lips, and conceals facts which, if known, would direct suspicion to the real criminal— that is, if you really believe what you have hitherto stated, that your cousin is an innocent woman."

She not making any answer to this, I rose and confronted her. "Miss Leavenworth, do you believe your cousin guiltless of this crime, or not?"

"Guiltless? Eleanore? Oh, my God, if all the world were only as innocent as she!"

"Then," said I, "you must likewise believe that if she refrains from speaking in regard to matters which to ordinary observers ought to be explained, she does it only from motives of kindness toward one less guiltless than herself."

"What? No, no, I do not say that. What made you think of any such explanation?"

"The action itself. With one of Eleanore's character, such conduct as hers admits of no other construction. Either she is mad, or she is shielding another at the expense of herself."

Mary's lip, which had trembled, slowly steadied itself. "And whom have you settled upon, as the person for whom Eleanore thus sacrifices herself?"

"Ah," said I, "there is where I seek assistance from you. With your knowledge of her history——"

But Mary Leavenworth, sinking haughtily back into her chair, stopped me with a quiet gesture. "I beg your pardon," said she, "but you make a mistake. I know little or nothing of Eleanore's personal feelings. The mystery must be solved by someone besides me."

I changed my tactics.

"When Eleanore confessed to you that the missing key had been seen in her possession, did she likewise inform you where she obtained it, and for what reason she was hiding it?"

"No."

"Merely told you the fact without any explanation?"

"Yes."

"Was not that a strange piece of gratuitous information for her to give one who, but a few hours before, had accused her to the face of committing a deadly crime?"

"What do you mean?" she asked, her voice suddenly sinking.

"You will not deny that you were once not only ready to believe her guilty, but that you actually charged her with having perpetrated this crime."

"Explain yourself," she cried.

"Miss Leavenworth, do you not remember what was said in that room upstairs, when you were alone with your cousin on the morning of the inquest, just before Mr. Gryce and myself entered your presence?"

Her eyes did not fall, but they filled with sudden terror. "You heard?" she whispered.

"I could not help it. I was just outside the door, and——"

"What did you hear?"

I told her.

"And Mr. Gryce?"

"He was at my side."

It seemed as if her eyes would devour my face. "Yet nothing was said when you came in?"

"No."

"You, however, have never forgotten it?"

"How could we, Miss Leavenworth?"

Her head fell forward in her hands, she seemed lost for one wild moment in a gulf of darkness. "And that is why you come here tonight," she suddenly exclaimed, desperately rousing herself and flashing full of indignation upon me. "With that sentence written upon your heart, you invade my presence, torture me with questions——"

"Pardon me," I broke in, "are my questions such as you, with reasonable regard for the honor of one you are accustomed to associate with, should hesitate to answer? Do I derogate from my manhood in asking you how and why you came to make an accusation of so grave a nature, at a time when all the circumstances of the case were freshly before you, only to insist fully as strongly upon your cousin's innocence when you found there was even more cause for your imputation than you had supposed?"

She did not seem to hear me. "Oh, my cruel fate!" she murmured. "Oh, my cruel fate!"

"Miss Leavenworth," said I, rising and taking my stand before her, "although there is a temporary estrangement between you and your cousin, you cannot wish to seem her enemy. Speak, then; let me at least know the name of him for whom she thus immolates herself. A hint from you——"

But rising, with a strange look, to her feet, she interrupted me with the stern remark: "If you do not know, I cannot inform you; do not ask me, Mr. Raymond." And she glanced at the clock for the second time.

I took another turn.

"Miss Leavenworth, you once asked me if a person who had

committed a wrong ought necessarily to confess it; and I replied no, unless by the confession reparation could be made. Do you remember?"

Her lips moved, but no words issued from them.

"I begin to think," I solemnly proceeded, following the lead of her emotion, "that confession is the only way out of this difficulty, that only by the words you can utter Eleanore can be saved from the doom that awaits her. Will you not, then, show yourself a true woman by responding to my earnest entreaties?"

I seemed to have touched the right chord, for she trembled, and a look of wistfulness filled her eyes. "Oh, if I could!" she murmured.

"And why can you not? You will never be happy till you do. Eleanore persists in silence, but that is no reason why you should emulate her example. You only make her position more doubtful by it."

"I know it, but I cannot help myself. Fate has got too strong a hold upon me; I cannot break away."

"That is not true. Anyone can escape from bonds imaginary as yours."

"No, no," cried she, "you do not understand."

"I understand this, that the path of rectitude is a straight one, and that he who steps into devious by-ways is going astray."

A flicker of light, pathetic beyond description, flashed for a moment across her face; her throat rose as, with one wild sob, her lips opened, she seemed yielding, when—a sharp ring at the front door bell!

"Oh," cried she, sharply turning, "tell him I cannot see him, tell him——"

"Miss Leavenworth," said I, taking her by both hands, "never mind the door, never mind anything but this; I have asked you a question which involves the mystery of this whole affair; answer me, then, for your soul's sake; tell me what the unhappy circumstances were which could induce you——"

But she tore her hands from mine. "The door!" cried she, "it will open, and——"

Stepping into the hall I met Thomas coming up the basement stairs. "Go back," said I, "I will call you when you are wanted."

With a bow he disappeared.

"You expect me to answer," exclaimed she, when I reentered, "now, in a moment? I cannot."

"But——"

"Impossible!" fastening her gaze upon the front door.

"Miss Leavenworth!"

She shuddered.

"I fear the time will never come if you do not speak now."

"Impossible," she reiterated.

Another twang at the bell.

"You hear!" said she.

I went into the hall and called Thomas. "You may open the door now," said I, and moved to return to her side.

But she pointed commandingly upstairs. "Leave me!" cried she, looking at Thomas as if to bid him wait.

"I will see you again before I go," said I, and hastened upstairs.

Thomas opened the door. "Is Miss Leavenworth in?" I heard a rich, tremulous voice inquire.

"Yes, sir," came in the butler's most respectful and measured accents, and leaning over the banisters I beheld, to my amazement, the form of Mr. Clavering enter the front hall and move toward the reception-room.

CHAPTER 5

On The Stairs

You cannot say I did it.
—MACBETH.

Excited, tremulous, filled with wonder at this unlooked-for event, I paused for a moment to collect my scattered senses, when, the sound of a low, monotonous voice breaking upon my ear from the direction of the library, I went toward it and found that it was Mr. Harwell reading aloud from his late employer's manuscript. It would be difficult for me to describe the effect which this simple discovery made upon me at this time. There, in that room of late death, withdrawn from the turmoil of the world, a hermit in his skeleton-lined cell, this man employed himself in reading and re-reading with passive interest the words of the dead, while above and below, human beings agonized in doubt and shame. Listening, I heard these words:

"By these means their native rulers will not only lose their jealous terror of our institutions, but acquire an actual curiosity in regard to them."

Opening the door I went in.

"Ah! you are late, sir," murmured he, rising and bringing forward a chair.

"Yes," replied I, with my thoughts on those two below.

"I am afraid you are not well," he went on.

I roused myself.

"I am not ill," I returned, and pulling the papers toward me, began looking them over. But the words danced before my eyes, and I was obliged to give up all attempt at work for that night.

"I fear that I shall not be able to assist you this evening, Mr. Harwell. The fact is, I find it difficult to give proper attention to this business, while the man who by a dastardly assassination has made it necessary goes unpunished."

The secretary in his turn pushed the papers aside, as if moved by a sudden distaste for them, but gave me no answer.

"You told me when you first came to me with news of this fearful tragedy, that it was a mystery; but it is one which must be solved, Mr. Harwell, it is wearing out the lives of too many that we love and respect."

The secretary gave me a look. "Miss Eleanore?" he murmured.

"And Miss Mary," I went on, "myself, you and many others."

"You have manifested much interest in the matter from the beginning," he said, methodically dipping his pen into the ink.

I stared at him in amazement.

"And you," said I, "do not take no interest in that which involves not only the safety, but the happiness and honor of the family in which you have dwelt so long?"

He looked at me with increased coldness. "I have requested, Mr. Raymond, that you would not converse with me upon this subject. It is not one which I am fond of discussing." And he arose.

"But fondness has nothing to do with it," I persisted. "If you know any facts connected with this affair, which have not yet been made public, it is manifestly your duty to state them. The position which Miss Eleanore occupies at this time is one which should arouse the sense of justice in every true breast, and if you——"

"If I knew anything which would serve to release her from this unhappy position, Mr. Raymond, I should have spoken long ago."

I bit my lip, weary of these continual bafflings, and rose also.

"If you have nothing more to say," he went on, "and feel utterly disinclined to work, why, I should be glad to excuse myself, as I have an engagement out."

"Do not let me keep you," I said bitterly. "I can take care of myself."

He turned upon me with a short stare as if this display of feeling was well-nigh incomprehensible to him, and then with a quiet, almost compassionate bow left the room. I heard him go upstairs, felt the jar when his room door closed, and, satisfied I was indeed to be left alone again, sat down to enjoy my solitude. But solitude in that room was unbearable. By the time Mr. Harwell again descended I felt that I could remain no longer, and stepping out into the hall told him that if he had no objection I would accompany him for a short stroll.

He bowed a stiff assent and hastened before me down the stairs. By the time I had closed the library door, he was half-way to the foot, and I was just remarking to myself upon the empliability of his figure and the awkwardness of his carriage as seen from my present standpoint, when suddenly I saw him stop, clutch the banister at his side, and hang there with a startled, deathly expression upon his half-turned countenance, that fixed me for an instant where I was in breathless astonishment and then caused me to rush down to his side, catch him by the arm, and cry:

"What is it? What is the matter?"

But thrusting out one powerful hand he pushed me upwards. "Go back," he whispered, in a voice shaking with intensest emotion, "go back." And catching me by the arm, he literally pulled me up the stairs. Arrived at the top he loosened his grasp and leaning, quivering from head to foot, over the banisters, glared below.

"Who is that?" he cried. "Who is that man? What is his name?"

Startled in my turn, I bent beside him and saw Henry Clavering come out of the reception-room and cross the hall.

"That is Mr. Clavering," I whispered, with all the self-possession I could muster. "Do you know him?"

Mr. Harwell fell back against the opposite wall. "Clavering, Clavering," he murmured with quaking lips; then suddenly bounding forward, clutched the railing before him, and fixing me with his eyes from which all the stoic calmness had gone down forever in flame and frenzy, gurgled into my ear—"You want to know who the assassin of Mr. Leavenworth is, do you? Look here, then, that is the man, Clavering!" And with a leap he bounded from my side, and swaying like a drunken man, disappeared from my gaze in the hall above.

My first impulse was to follow him. Rushing upstairs, I knocked at the door of his room, but no response came to my summons. I then called his name in the hall, but without avail; he was determined not to show himself. Resolved that he should not thus escape me, I returned to the library and wrote him a short note, in which I asked for an explanation of his tremendous accusation, saying that I would be in my rooms the next evening at six, when I should expect to see him. This done I descended to rejoin Mary.

But the evening was destined to be full of disappointments. She had retired to her room while I was in the library, and I had lost the interview from which I expected so much. "The woman is slippery as an eel," I inwardly commented, pacing the hall in my chagrin. "Wrapped in mystery, she expects me to feel for her the respect due to to an open and frank nature."

I was about to leave the house, when I saw Thomas descending the stairs with a letter in his hand.

"Miss Leavenworth's compliments, sir," said he, handing me the note, "and she is too fatigued to remain below this evening."

I moved aside to read it, feeling a little conscience-stricken as I traced the hurried, trembling handwriting through the following words:

> You ask more than I can give. Matters must be received as they are without explanation from me. It is the grief of my life to deny you, but I have no choice. God forgive us all and keep us from despair!
>
> M.

And below:

> . . . and we cannot meet now without embarrassment, it would be better for us to bear our burdens in silence and apart. Mr. Harwell will visit you. Farewell!'

As I was crossing Thirty-second Street I heard a quick footstep behind me, and turning, saw Thomas at my side. "Excuse me, sir," said he, "but I have something a little particular to say to you. When you asked me the other night what sort of a person the gentleman was who called on Miss Eleanore the evening of the murder, I didn't answer you as I should. The fact is, the detectives had been talking to me about that very thing and I felt shy; but, sir, I know you are a friend of the family, and I want to tell you now that that same gentleman, whoever he was—Mr. Robbins he called himself then—was at the house again tonight, sir, and the name he gave me this time to carry to Miss Leavenworth was Clavering. Yes, sir," he went on, seeing me start, "and as I told Molly, he acts queer for a stranger. When he came the other night, he hesitated a long time before asking for Miss Eleanore, and when I wanted his name, took out a card and wrote the one I told you of, sir, with a look on his face a little peculiar for a caller; besides——"

"Well?"

"Mr. Raymond," the butler went on, in a low, excited voice, edging up very closely to me in the darkness, "there is something I have never told any living being but Molly, sir, which may be of use to those as wishes to find out who committed this murder."

"A fact or a suspicion?" I inquired.

"A fact, sir; which I beg your pardon for troubling you with at this time, but Molly will give me no rest unless I speak of it to you or Mr. Gryce, her feelings being so worked up on Hannah's account, whom we all know is innocent, though folks do dare to say as how she must be guilty just because she is not to be found the minute they want her."

"But this fact?" I urged.

"Well, the fact is this. You see—I would tell Mr. Gryce," he resumed, unconscious of my anxiety, "but I have my fears of detectives, sir, they catch you up so quick at times, and seem to think you know so much more than you really do."

"But this fact——" I again broke in.

"Oh, yes, sir, the fact is, that that night, the one of the murder, you know, I saw Mr. Clavering, Robbins or whatever his name is, enter the house, but neither I nor anyone else saw him go out of it, nor do I know that he *did*."

"What do you mean?"

"Well, sir, what I mean is this. When I came down from Miss Eleanore and told Mr. Robbins, as he called himself at that time, that my mistress was ill and unable to see him (the word she gave me, sir, to deliver) Mr. Robbins instead of bowing and leaving the house as most gentlemen would have done, stepped into the reception-room and sat down. He may have felt sick, he looked pale enough; at any rate he asked me for a glass of water. Not knowing any reason then for suspicioning any-one's actions, I immediately went down to the kitchen for it, leaving him there in the reception-room alone. But before I could get it, I heard the front door close. 'What's that?' said Molly, who was helping me, sir. 'I don't know,' I said, 'unless it's the gentleman has got tired of waiting and gone.' 'If he's gone, he won't want the water,' she said. So down I set the pitcher and upstairs I come, and sure enough he was gone, or so I thought then. But who knows, sir, if he was not in that room or the drawing room, which was dark that night, all the time I was a-shutting up of the house?"

I made no reply to this; I was more startled than I cared to reveal.

"You see, sir, I wouldn't speak of such a thing about any person that comes to see the young ladies, but we all know someone who was in the house that night murdered my master, and as it was not Hannah——"

"You say that Miss Eleanore refused to see him," I inter-rupted in the hope that the simple suggestion would be enough to elicit further details of his interview with Eleanore.

"Yes, sir. When she first looked at the card she showed a lit-tle hesitation, but in a moment she grew very flushed in the face and bade me say what I told you. I should never have thought of it again if I had not seen him come blazoning and bold into the house this evening, with a new name on his tongue. Indeed, and I do not like to think any evil of him now, but Molly would have it I should speak to you, sir, and ease my mind—and that is all, sir."

When I arrived home that night, I entered into my memoran-dum book a new list of suspicious circumstances, but this time with the letter "C" at the top instead of "E."

CHAPTER 6

In My Office

Something between an hindrance and a help.
— WORDSWORTH.

The next day as, with nerves unstrung and an exhausted brain, I entered my office, I was greeted by the announcement:

"A gentleman, sir, in your private room—been waiting some time, very impatient."

Weary, and in no mood to hold consultation with clients new or old, I advanced with anything but an eager step toward my room, when upon opening the door I saw—Mr. Clavering.

Too much astounded for the moment to speak, I bowed to him silently, whereupon he approached me with the air and dignity of a highly-bred gentleman, and presented his card, on which I saw written, in free and handsome characters, his whole name, Henry Ritchie Clavering. After this introduction of himself, he apologized for making so unceremonious a call, saying, in excuse, that he was a stranger in town, that his business was one of great urgency, that he had casually heard honorable mention of me as a lawyer and a gentleman, and so had ventured to seek this interview on behalf of a friend who was so unfortunately situated as to require the opinion and advice of a lawyer upon a question that not only involved an extraordinary state of facts, but was of a nature peculiarily embarrassing to him, owing to his ignorance of American laws, and the legal bearing of these facts upon the same.

Having thus secured my attention and awakened my curiosity, he asked me if I would permit him to relate his story. Recovering in a measure from my astonishment, and subduing the extreme repulsion, almost horror, I felt for the man, I signified my assent, at which he drew from his pocket a memorandum book from which he read in substance as follows:

"An Englishman traveling in this country meets, at a fashionable watering-place, an American girl, with whom he falls deeply in love, and whom after a few days he desires to marry. Knowing his position to be good, his fortune ample, and his intentions highly honorable, he offers her his hand and is accepted. But a decided opposition arising in the family to the match, he is compelled to disguise his sentiments, though the engagement remained unbroken. While matters were in this uncertain condition, he received advices from England demanding his instant return, and alarmed at the prospect of a protracted absence from the object of his affections, he writes to the lady, informing her of the circumstances and proposing a secret marriage. She consents, with stipulations, the first of which is that he should leave her instantly upon the conclusion of the ceremony, and the second, that he should entrust the public declaration of the marriage to her. It was not precisely what he wished, but anything which served to make her his own was acceptable at such a crisis. He readily enters into the plans proposed. Meeting the lady at a parsonage some twenty miles from the watering-place at which she was staying, he stands up with her before a Methodist preacher, and the ceremony of marriage is performed. There were two witnesses, a hired man of the minister, called in for the purpose, and a lady friend who came with the bride; but there was no license, and the bride had not completed her twenty-first year. Now, was that marriage legal? If the lady, wedded in good faith upon that day by my friend, chooses to deny that she is his lawful wife, can he hold her to a compact entered into in so informal a manner? In short, Mr. Raymond, is my friend the lawful husband of that girl or not?"

While listening to this story, I found myself yielding to feelings greatly in contrast to those with which I greeted the relator but a moment before. I became so interested in his "friend's" case as to quite forget for the time being that I had ever seen or heard of Henry Clavering; and, after learning that the marriage ceremony took place in the State of New York, I replied to him, as near as I can remember, in the following words:

"In this State, and I believe it to be American law, marriage is a civil contract, requiring neither license, priest, ceremony nor certificate—and in some cases witnesses are not even necessary to give it validity. Of old, the modes of getting a wife were the same as those of acquiring any other species of property, and they are not materially changed at the present time. It is enough that the man and woman say to each other, 'From this time we are married,' or, 'You are now my wife,' or, 'my husband,' as the case may be. The mutual consent is all that is necessary. In fact, you may contract marriage as you contract to lend a sum of money, or to buy the merest trifle."

"Then your opinion is——"

"That, upon your statement, your friend is the lawful husband of the lady in question, presuming, of course, that no legal disabilities of either party existed to prevent such a union. As to the young lady's age, I will merely say that any fourteen-year-old girl can be a party to a marriage contract."

Mr. Clavering bowed, his countenance assuming a look of great satisfaction. "I am very glad to hear this," said he; "my friend's happiness is entirely involved in the establishment of his marriage."

He appeared so relieved, my curiosity was yet further aroused. I therefore said: "I have given you my opinion as to the legality of this marriage, but it may be quite another thing to prove it, should the same be contested."

He started, cast me an inquiring look, and murmured:

"True."

"Allow me to ask you a few questions. Was the lady married under her own name?"

"She was."

"The gentleman?"

"Yes, sir."

"Did the lady receive a certificate?"

"She did."

"Properly signed by the minister and witnesses?"

He bowed his head in assent.

"Did she keep this?"

"I cannot say; but I presume she did."

"The witnesses were——?"

"A hired man of the minister——"

"Who can be found?"

"Who cannot be found."

"Dead or disappeared?"

"The minister is dead, the man has disappeared."

"The minister dead!"

"Three months since."

"And the marriage took place when?"

"Last July."

"The other witness, the lady friend, where is she?"

"She can be found, but her action is not to be depended upon."

"Has the gentleman himself no proofs of this marriage?"

Mr. Clavering shook his head. "He cannot even prove he was in the town where it took place on that particular day."

"The marriage certificate was, however, filed with the clerk of the town?" said I.

"It was not, sir."

"How was that?"

"I cannot say; I only know that my friend has made inquiry, and that no such paper is to be found."

I leaned slowly back and looked at him. "I do not wonder that your friend is concerned in regard to his position if what you hint is true and the lady seems disposed to deny that any such ceremony ever took place. Still, if he wishes to go to law, the court may decide in his favor, though I doubt it. His sworn word is all he would have to go upon, and if she contradicts his testimony under oath, why, the sympathy of a jury is, as a rule, with the woman."

Mr. Clavering rose, looked at me with some earnestness, and finally asked in a tone which, though somewhat changed, lacked nothing of its former suavity, if I would be kind enough to give him, in writing, that portion of my opinion which directly bore upon the legality of the marriage; that such a paper would go far toward satisfying his friend that his case had been properly presented, as he was aware that no respectable lawyer would put his name to a legal opinion without first having carefully arrived at his conclusions by a thorough examination of the law bearing upon the facts submitted.

This request seeming so reasonable, I unhesitatingly complied with it, and handed him the opinion. He took it and, after reading it carefully over, deliberately copied it into his memorandum book. This done, he turned toward me, a strong though hitherto subdued emotion showing itself in his countenance.

"Now, sir," said he, rising upon me to the full height of his majestic figure, "I have but one more request to make; and that is, that you will receive back this opinion into your own possession, and in the day you think to lead a beautiful woman to the altar, pause, and ask yourself, 'Am I sure that the hand I clasp with such impassioned fervor is free? Have I any certainty for knowing that it has not already been given away like that of the lady whom, in this opinion of mine, I have declared to be a wedded wife according to the law of my country?'"

"Mr. Clavering!"

But he, with an urbane bow, laid his hand upon the knob of the door. "I thank you for your courtesy, Mr. Raymond, and I bid you good day. I hope you will have no need of consulting that paper before I see you again." And with another bow he passed out.

It was the most vital shock I had yet experienced, and for a moment I stood paralyzed. Me! Me! Why should he mix me up with the affair unless—but I would not contemplate that possibility. Eleanore married, and to this man? No, no; anything but that; and yet I found myself continually turning the supposition over in my mind until, to escape the torment of my own conjectures, I seized my hat and rushed into the street in the hope of finding him again and extorting from him an explanation of his mysterious conduct. But by the time I reached the sidewalk, he was nowhere to be seen. A thousand busy men with their various cares and purposes had pushed themselves between us, and I was obliged to return to my office with my doubts unsolved.

I think I never experienced a longer day; but it passed, and at five o'clock I had the satisfaction of inquiring for Mr. Clavering at the Hoffman House. Judge of my surprise when I learned that his visit to my office was his last action before taking passage upon the steamer leaving that day for Liverpool; that he was now on the high seas and all chance of another interview with him was at an end. I could scarcely believe the fact at first, but after a talk with the cabman who had driven him to my office and thence to the steamer, I became convinced. My first feeling was one of shame. I had been brought face to face with an accused man, had received an intimation from him that he was not expecting to see me again for some time, and had weakly gone on attending to my own affairs and allowed him to escape, like the simple tyro that I was; my next, the necessity of notifying Mr. Gryce of this man's departure. But it was now six o'clock, the hour set apart for my interview with Mr. Harwell. I could not afford to miss that, so, merely stopping to dispatch a line to Mr. Gryce, in which I promised to visit him that evening, I turned my steps toward home. I found Mr. Harwell there before me.

CHAPTER 7

"Trueman! Trueman! Trueman!"

Often do the spirits
Of great events stride on before the events,
And in today, already walks tomorrow.
—COLERIDGE.

Instantly a great dread seized me. What revelations might not this man be going to make? But I subdued the feeling and, greeting him with what cordiality I could, settled myself to listen to his explanations.

But Trueman Harwell had no explanations to give, it seemed; on the contrary, he had come to apologize for the very violent words he had used the evening before: words which, whatever their effect may have been upon me, he now felt bound to declare had been used without sufficient basis in fact to make their utterance of the least importance.

"But," cried I, "you must have thought you had grounds for so tremendous an accusation, or your act was that of a madman."

His brow wrinkled heavily, and his eyes assumed a very

gloomy expression. "It does not follow," returned he. "Under the pressure of surprise, I have known men utter convictions no better founded than mine, without running the risk of being called mad."

"Surprise? Mr. Clavering's face or form must, then, have been known to you. The mere fact of seeing a strange gentleman in the hall would have been insufficient to cause you astonishment, Mr. Harwell."

He uneasily fingered the back of the chair before which he stood, but made no reply.

"Sit down," I again urged, this time with a touch of command in my voice. "This is a serious matter, and I intend to deal with it as it deserves. You have said before that if you knew anything which might serve to exonerate Eleanore Leavenworth from the suspicion under which she stands, you would be ready to impart it."

"I said," he interrupted coldly, "that if I had known of anything which might serve to release her from her unhappy position, I should have spoken."

"Do not quibble," I returned. "You do know something, Mr. Harwell, and I ask you in the name of justice to tell me what it is."

"You are mistaken," he returned doggedly. "I know nothing. I have reasons, perhaps, for thinking certain things, but my conscience will not allow me in cold blood to give utterance to suspicions which may not only damage the reputation of an honest man, but place me in the unpleasant position of an accuser without substantial foundation for my accusations."

"You are there already," I retorted, with equal coldness. "Nothing can make me forget that in my presence you have denounced Henry Clavering as the murderer of Mr. Leavenworth. You had better explain yourself, Mr. Harwell."

He gave me a short look, but moved around and took the chair. "You have me at a disadvantage," he said in a lighter tone. "If you choose to profit by your position and press me to disclose the little I know, I can only regret the necessity under which I lie, and speak."

"Then you are deterred by conscientious scruples alone?"

"Yes, and by the meagerness of the facts at my command."

"I will judge of the facts when I have heard them."

He raised his eyes to mine, and I was astonished to observe a strange eagerness in their depths; evidently his convictions were stronger than his scruples. "Mr. Raymond," he began, "you are a lawyer and undoubtedly a practical man, but you may know what it is to scent danger before you see it, to feel influences working in the air over and about you, and yet be in ignorance of what it is that affects you so powerfully, till chance reveals that an enemy has been at your side, or a friend passed your window, or the shadow of death crossed your book as you read, or mingled with your breath as you slept?"

I shook my head, fascinated by the intensity of his gaze into some sort of response.

"Then you cannot understand me or what I have suffered these last three weeks." And he drew back with an icy reserve that seemed to promise but little to my now thoroughly awakened curiosity.

"I beg your pardon," I hastened to say, "but the fact of my never having experienced such sensations does not hinder me from comprehending the emotions of others more affected by spiritual influences than myself."

He drew himself slowly forward. "Then you will not ridicule me if I say, that upon the eve of Mr. Leavenworth's murder I experienced in a dream all that afterward occurred; saw him murdered; saw"—and he clasped his hands before him in an attitude inexpressibly convincing, while his voice sank to a horrified whisper—"saw the face of his murderer!"

I started, looked at him in amazement, a thrill as at the touch of a ghost running through me.

"And was that——" I began.

"My reason for denouncing the man I beheld before me in the hall of Miss Leavenworth's house last night? It was." And taking out his handkerchief he wiped his forehead, on which the perspiration was standing in large drops.

"You would, then, intimate that the face you saw in your dream and the face you saw in the hall last night were the same?"

He gravely nodded his head.

I drew my chair nearer to his. "Tell me your dream," said I.

"Well," replied he, in a low, awestruck tone, "it was the night before Mr. Leavenworth's murder. I had gone to bed feeling especially contented with myself and the world at large, for though my life is anything but a happy one"—and he heaved a short sigh—"some pleasant words had been said to me that day, and I was revelling in the happiness they had conferred, when suddenly a chill struck my heart, and the darkness which a moment before had appeared to me as the abode of peace thrilled to the sound of a supernatural cry, and I heard my name, 'Trueman! Trueman! Trueman!' repeated three times in a voice I did not recognize, and starting from my pillow beheld at my bedside a woman. Her face was strange to me," he went on solemnly, "but I can give you each and every detail of it, as bending above me, she stared into my eyes with a growing terror that seemed to implore help, though her lips were quiet and only the memory of that cry echoed in my ears."

"Describe the face," I interposed.

"It was a round, fair, lady's face. Very lovely in contour, but devoid of coloring; not beautiful, but winning from its childlike look of trust. The hair, banded upon the low, broad forehead, was brown; the eyes, which were very far apart, gray; the mouth, which was its most charming feature, delicate of make and very expressive. There was a dimple in the chin, but none in the cheeks. It was a face to be remembered."

"Go on," said I.

"Meeting the gaze of those imploring eyes, I started up. Instantly the face and all vanished, and I became conscious, as we do sometimes in dreams, of a certain movement in the hall below, and the next instant the gliding figure of a man of imposing size entered the library. I remember experiencing a certain thrill at this, half terror, half curiosity, though I seemed to know as if by intuition what he was going to do. Strange to say, I now seemed to change my personality and to be no longer a third party watching these proceedings, but Mr. Leavenworth himself, sitting at his library table and feeling his doom crawling upon him without capacity for speech or power of movement to avert it. Though my back was toward the man, I could feel his stealthy form traverse the passage, enter the room beyond, pass to that stand where the pistol was, try the drawer, find it locked, turn the key, procure the pistol, weigh it in an accustomed hand, and advance again. I could feel each foot-step he took as though his feet were in truth upon my heart, and I remember staring at the table before me, as if I expected every moment to see it run with my own blood. I can see now how the letters I had been writing danced upon the paper before me, appearing to my eyes to take the phantom shapes of persons and things long ago forgotten as I had thought; crowding my last moments with regrets and dead shames, wild longings and unspeakable agonies, through all of which that face, the face of my former dream, mingled, pale, sweet, and searching, while closer and closer behind me crept that noise-less foot till I could feel the glaring of the assassin's eyes across the narrow threshold separating me from death, and hear the click of his teeth as he set his lips for the final act. Ah!"—and the secretary's livid face showed the touch of awful horror— "what words can describe such an experience as that! In one moment all the agonies of hell in the heart and brain, the next a blank through which I seemed to see afar and, as if suddenly removed from all this, a crouching figure looking at its work with staring eyes and pallid back-drawn lips, and seeming to recognize no face that I had ever known, but one so hand-some, so remarkable, so unique in its formation and character, that it would be as easy for me to mistake the countenance of my father as the look and figure of the man revealed to me in my dream."

"And this face," said I, in a voice I failed to recognize as my own——

"Was that of him whom we saw leave Mary Leavenworth's presence last night and go down the hall to the front door."

CHAPTER 8

A Prejudice

> True, I talk of dreams,
> Which are the children of an idle brain
> Begot of nothing but vain phantasy.
> —ROMEO AND JULIET.

For one moment I sat a prey to superstitious horror, then my natural incredulity asserting itself, I looked up, and remarked:

"You say that all this took place the night previous to that of the actual occurrence?"

He bowed his head.

"For a warning," murmured he.

"But you did not seem to take it as such?"

"No; I am subject to horrible dreams; I thought but little of it in a superstitious way till I looked next day upon Mr. Leavenworth's dead body."

"I do not wonder you behaved strangely at the inquest; I should have thought you would."

"Ah, sir," returned he with a slow, sad smile, "no one knows what I suffered in my endeavors not to tell more than I actually knew, irrespective of my dream, of this murder and the manner of its accomplishment."

"You believe, then," said I, "that your dream foreshadowed the manner of the murder as well as the fact?"

"I do."

"It is a pity it did not go a little further, then, and tell us how the assassin escaped from, if not how he entered, a house secured as the Leavenworths' was."

His face flushed. "That would have been convenient," he said. "Also if I had been informed where Hannah was, and why a stranger and a gentleman should have stooped to the committal of such a crime."

Seeing that he was nettled, I dropped my bantering vein. "Why do you say a stranger?" I asked. "Are you so well acquainted with all who visit that house as to be able to say who are and who are not strangers to the family?"

"I am well acquainted with the faces of their friends, Mr. Raymond, and Henry Clavering is not amongst the number, but——"

"Were you ever with Mr. Leavenworth," I interrupted, "when he has been away from home, in the country, for instance, or upon his travels?"

"No," the secretary returned constrainedly.

"Yet I suppose he was in the habit of absenting himself from home?"

"Certainly."

"Can you tell me where he was last July, he and the ladies?"

"Yes, sir; they went to R——, if you mean that; spent some time there. The famous watering-place, you know. Ah!" he cried, seeing a change in my face, "do you think he could have met them there?"

I looked at him for a moment, then, rising in my turn, stood level with him, and exclaimed:

"You are keeping something back, Mr. Harwell; you have more knowledge of this man than you have hitherto given me to understand. What is it?"

He seemed astonished at my penetration, but replied: "I know no more of the man than I have already informed you, but"—and a burning flush crossed his face—"if you are determined to pursue this matter——" and he paused, with an inquiring look.

"I am resolved to find out all I can about Henry Clavering," I returned.

He lifted his head with a quick gesture. "Then," said he, "I can tell you this much. Henry Clavering wrote a letter to Mr. Leavenworth a few days before the murder, that, I have some reason to believe, produced a marked effect upon the household." And, folding his arms, the secretary stood quietly waiting for my next question.

"How do you know?" asked I.

"I opened it by mistake. I was in the habit of reading Mr. Leavenworth's business letters, and this being from one unaccustomed to write to him, lacked the mark which usually distinguish those of a private nature."

"And you saw the name of Clavering?"

"I did; Henry Ritchie Clavering."

"Did you read the letter?" I was trembling now.

The secretary did not reply.

"Mr. Harwell," I reiterated, "this is no time for false delicacy. Did you read that letter?"

"I did; but hastily and with an agitated conscience."

"You can, however, recall its general drift?"

"It was some complaint in regard to the treatment received by him at the hand of one of Mr. Leavenworth's nieces. I remember nothing more."

"Which niece?"

"There were no names mentioned."

"But you inferred——"

"No, sir; that is just what I did not do. I forced myself to forget the whole thing."

"And yet you say that it produced an effect upon the family?"

"I can see now that it did. None of them have ever appeared quite the same toward each other as before."

"Mr. Harwell," I now said; "when you were questioned as to the receipt of any letter by Mr. Leavenworth, which might seem in any manner to be connected with this tragedy, you denied having seen any such; how was that?"

"Mr. Raymond," he returned, "you are a gentleman; have a chivalrous regard for the ladies; do you think that you could have brought yourself (even if in your secret heart you considered some such result possible, which I am not ready to say I did) to mention at such a time as that the receipt of a letter complaining of the treatment received from one of Mr. Leavenworth's nieces, as a suspicious circumstance worthy to be taken into account by a coroner's jury?"

I shook my head. I could not but acknowledge the impossibility.

"What reason had I for thinking that letter was one of importance? I knew no Henry Ritchie Clavering."

"And yet you seemed to think it was," I murmured. "I remember you hesitated before replying."

"It is true, but not as I should hesitate now, if the question were put to me again."

Silence followed these words, during which I took two or three turns up and down the room.

"This is all very fanciful," I said, laughing in the vain endeavor to throw off the superstitious horror that unaccountably to myself still clung about me.

He bent his head in assent. "I know it," said he. "I am practical myself in broad daylight, and recognize the flimsiness of an accusation based upon a poor hard-working secretary's dream, as plainly as you do. That is the reason I desired to keep from speaking at all. Dreams are not things with which to confront a man in a court of justice; but, Mr. Raymond"— and his long thin hand fell upon my arm with a nervous intensity which gave me almost the sensation of an electric shock—"if the murderer of Mr. Leavenworth is ever brought to confess his deed, mark my words, he will prove to be the man of my dream."

I drew a long breath. For a moment his belief was mine; and a mingled sensation of relief and exquisite pain swept over me as I thought of the possibility of Eleanore being exonerated from crime only to be plunged into fresh humiliation and deeper abysses of suffering.

"He stalks the streets in freedom now," the secretary went on, as if to himself, "even dares to enter the house he has so woefully desecrated; but justice is justice, and sooner or later something will transpire which will prove to you that a premonition so wonderful as that I received had its significance; that the voice calling 'Trueman! Trueman!' was something more than the empty utterances of an excited brain; that it was Justice itself calling attention to the guilty."

I looked at him in wonder: did he know that the officers of justice were already upon the track of this same Clavering? I judged not from his look, but felt an inclination to make an effort and see.

"You speak with strange conviction," I said; "but in all

probability you are doomed to be disappointed. So far as we know, Mr. Clavering is a respectable man."

He lifted his hat from the table. "I do not propose to denounce him; I do not even propose to speak his name again. I am not a fool, Mr. Raymond. I have spoken thus plainly to you only in explanation of last night's most unfortunate betrayal; and while I trust that you will regard what I have told you as confidential, I also hope that you will give me credit for behaving on the whole as well as could be expected under the circumstances." And he held out his hand.

"Certainly," I replied as I took it. Then, with a sudden impulse to test the accuracy of this story of his, inquired if he had any means of verifying his statement of having had this dream at the time spoken of, that is before the murder and not afterward.

"No, sir; I know myself that I had it the night previous to that of Mr. Leavenworth's death; but I cannot prove the fact."

"You did not speak of it next morning to anyone?"

"Oh, no, sir; I was scarcely in a position to do so."

"Yet it must have had a great effect upon you, unfitting you for work——"

"Nothing unfits me for work," he murmured bitterly.

"I believe that is so," I returned, remembering his diligence for the last few days. "But you must at least have shown some traces of having passed an uncomfortable night, if no more. Have you, then, no recollection of anyone speaking to you in regard to your appearance the next morning?"

"Mr. Leavenworth may have done so; no one else would have been likely to have noticed," he returned, half-sadly.

"Mr. Harwell," I now said, "I shall not be at the house tonight; nor do I know when I shall return there. Personal considerations keep me from Miss Leavenworth's presence for a time, and I look to you to carry on the work we have undertaken, without my assistance, unless you can bring it here——"

"I can do that."

"I shall expect you, then, tomorrow evening."

"Very well, sir," and he was going, when a sudden thought seemed to strike him. "Sir," he said, "as we do not wish to return to this subject again, and as I have a natural curiosity in regard to the man whose countenance and figure are so well known to me while yet he retains his title of utter stranger, would you object to telling me what you know of him? You believe him to be a respectable man; are you acquainted with him, Mr. Raymond?"

"I know his name, and where he resides."

"And where is that?"

"In London; he is an Englishman."

"Ah!" he murmured with a strange intonation.

"Why do you say that?"

He bit his lip, looked down, then up, finally fixed his eyes on mine, and returned with marked emphasis: "I used an exclamation, sir, because I was startled."

"Startled?"

"Yes; you say he is an Englishman. Mr. Leavenworth had the most bitter antagonism to the English. It was one of his marked peculiarities. He would never be introduced to one if he could help it."

It was my turn to look thoughtful.

"You know," the secretary continued, "that Mr. Leavenworth was a man who carried his prejudices to the extreme. He had a hatred for the English race that almost amounted to mania. If he had known that letter he received was from an Englishman, I doubt if he would have read it. He used to say that he would sooner see a daughter of his dead before him than married to an Englishman."

I turned hastily aside to hide the effect which this announcement made upon me.

"You think I am exaggerating," he said. "Ask Mr. Veeley."

"No," I replied, "I have no reason for thinking so."

"He had doubtless some cause for hating the English, with which we are unacquainted," pursued the secretary. "He spent some time in Liverpool when young, and had, of course, many opportunities for studying their manners and character." And the secretary made another movement as if to leave.

But it was my turn to detain him now. "Mr. Harwell, excuse me," I said, "but you have been on familiar terms with Mr. Leavenworth for so long—do you think that in the case of one of his nieces, say, desiring to marry a gentleman of that nationality, his prejudice was sufficient to cause him absolutely to forbid the match?"

"I do."

I moved back. I had learned what I wished, and saw no further reason for prolonging the interview.

CHAPTER 9

Patchwork

Come, give us a taste of your quality.
—HAMLET.

Starting with the assumption that Mr. Clavering, in his conversation of the morning, had been giving me, with more or less accuracy, a detailed account of his own experience and position regarding Eleanore Leavenworth, I asked myself what particular facts it would be necessary for me to establish in order to prove the truth of this assumption, and found them to be:

I. That Mr. Clavering had not only been in this country at the time designated, viz., last July, but that he had been located for some little time at a watering-place in New York State.

II. That this watering-place should correspond to that in which Miss Eleanore Leavenworth was to be found at the same time.

III. That they had been seen while there to hold more or less communication together.

IV. That they had both been absent from town at some one time, long enough to have gone through the ceremony of marriage at a point twenty miles or so away.

V. That a Methodist clergyman, who has since died, lived at that time within a radius of twenty miles of the said watering-place.

I next asked myself how I was to establish these facts. Mr.

Clavering's life was, as yet, too little known to me to offer me any assistance; so leaving it for the present, I took up the thread of Eleanore's history, when upon tracing it back to the time given me, I found that she was known to have been in R——, a fashionable watering-place in this State. But if she was there, and my theory was correct, he must have been there also. To ascertain whether this was so, therefore, became my first business. I resolved to go to R—— on the morrow.

But before proceeding in an undertaking of such importance, I considered it expedient to make such inquiries and collect such facts as it should be possible for me to do in the few hours that lay before me. I went first to the house of Mr. Gryce.

I found him lying upon a hard sofa in the bare sitting room I have before mentioned, suffering from a severe attack of rheumatism; with his hands done up in bandages and his feet encased in multiplied folds of a dingy red shawl that looked as if it had been through the wars. Greeting me with a short nod that was both a welcome and an apology, he devoted a few words to an explanation of his unwonted position, and then, without further preliminaries, rushed into the subject that was uppermost in both our minds by inquiring in a slightly sarcastic way if I was very much surprised to find my bird flown when I returned to the Hoffman House that afternoon.

"I was astonished to find that you allowed him to fly at this time," replied I. "From the manner in which you requested me to make his acquaintance I supposed that you had reasons for considering him an important character in the tragedy which has just been enacted."

"And what makes you think I hadn't? Oh, the fact that I let him go off so easily? That's no proof. One does not put on the brakes till one is going downhill. But let that pass for the present; Mr. Clavering, then, did not explain himself before going?"

"That is a question," I returned, after due thought, "which I find it exceedingly difficult to answer. Constrained by circumstances, I cannot at present speak with the directness which is your due, but what I can say, I will. Know, then, that in my opinion, Mr. Clavering did explain himself in an interview with me this morning. But it was done in so blind a way that it will be necessary for me to make a few investigations before I shall feel sufficiently sure of my ground to take you into my confidence. He has given me a possible clue——"

"Wait," said Mr. Gryce. "Does he know this? Was it done intentionally and with sinister motive, or unconsciously and in plain good faith?"

"In good faith, I should say."

Mr. Gryce remained for a moment silent. "It is very unfortunate that you cannot explain yourself a little more definitely," he said at last. "I am almost afraid to trust you to make investigations, as you call them, on your own hook. You are not used to the business and will lose time, to say nothing of running upon false scents and using up your strength on unprofitable details."

"You should have thought of that when you admitted me into partnership."

"And you absolutely insist upon working this mine alone?"

"Mr. Gryce," said I, "the matter stands just here. Mr. Clavering, for all I know, is a gentleman of untarnished reputation. I am not even aware for what purpose you set me upon his trail. I only know that in thus following it, I have come upon certain facts that seem worthy of inquiry."

"Well, well," said he, "you know best. But the days are slipping by. Something must be done—and soon. The public are becoming clamorous."

"I know it, and for that reason I have come to you for such assistance as you can give me at this stage of the proceedings. You are in possession of certain facts relating to this man which it concerns me to know, or your conduct in reference to him has been purposeless. Now, frankly, will you make me master of those facts: in short, tell me all you know of Mr. Clavering without requiring an immediate return of confidence on my part?"

"That is asking a great deal of a professional detective."

"I know it, and under any other circumstances I should hesitate long before preferring such a request; but as things are, I don't see how I am to proceed in the matter, without some such concession on your part. At all events——"

"Wait a moment! Is not Mr. Clavering the lover of one of the young ladies?"

Anxious as I was to preserve the secret of my interest in that gentleman, I could not prevent the blush from rising to my face at the suddenness of this question.

"I thought as much," he went on. "Being neither a relative nor acknowledged friend, I took it for granted that he must occupy some such position as that in the family."

"I do not see why you should draw such an inference," said I, anxious to determine how much he knew about him. "Mr. Clavering is a stranger in town; has not even been in this country long; has, indeed, had no time to establish himself upon any such footing as you intimate."

"This is not the only time Mr. Clavering has been in New York. He was here a year ago to my certain knowledge."

"You know that?"

"Yes."

"How much more do you know? Can it be possible that I am groping blindly about for facts which are already in your possession? I pray you listen to my entreaties, Mr. Gryce, and acquaint me at once with what I want to know. You will not regret it. I have no selfish motive in this matter. If I succeed, the glory shall be yours; if I fail, the shame of the defeat shall be mine."

"That is fair," he muttered. "And how about the reward?"

"My reward will be to free an innocent woman from the imputation of crime which hangs over her."

This assurance seemed to satisfy him. His voice and appearance changed; for a moment he looked quite confidential. "Well, well," said he, "and what is it you want to know?"

"I would first learn how your suspicions came to light on him at all. What reason had you for thinking a gentleman of his bearing and position was in any way connected with this affair?"

"That is a question you ought not to be obliged to put," he returned.

"How so?"

"Simply because the opportunity of answering it was in your hands before ever it came into mine."

"What do you mean?"

"Don't you remember the letter mailed in your presence by

Miss Mary Leavenworth during your drive from her home to that of her friend in Thirty-seventh Street?"

"On the afternoon of the inquest?"

"Yes."

"Certainly, but——"

"You never thought to look at its superscription before it was dropped into the box."

"I had neither opportunity nor right to do so."

"Was it written in your presence?"

"It was."

"And you never regarded the affair as worth your attention?"

"However I may have regarded it, I did not see how, if Miss Leavenworth chose to drop a letter into a box with her own hands, I could in any way prevent her."

"That is because you are a *gentleman*. Well, it has its disadvantages," he muttered broodingly.

"But you," said I; "how came you to know of it? Ah, I see," remembering that the carriage in which we were riding at the time had been procured for us by him. "The man on the box was in your pay and 'informed,' as you call it."

Mr. Gryce winked at his muffled toes mysteriously. "That is not to the point," he said. "Enough that I heard that a letter which might reasonably prove to be of some interest to me was dropped at such an hour into the box on the corner of a certain street. That, coinciding in the opinion of my informant, I telegraphed to the station connected with that box, to take note of the address of a suspicious-looking letter about to pass through their hands on the way to the General Post Office, and following up the telegram in person, found that a curious epistle addressed in lead pencil and sealed with a stamp, had just arrived, the address of which I was allowed to see——"

"And which was?——"

"Henry R. Clavering, Hoffman House, New York."

I drew a deep breath. "And so that is how your attention first came to be directed to this man!"

"Yes."

"Strange. But go on—what next?"

"Why, next I followed up the clue, of course, by going to the Hoffman House and instituting inquiries. I learned that Mr.

Clavering was a regular guest of the hotel. That he had come there direct from the Liverpool steamer about three months since, and registering his name as Henry R. Clavering, Esq., London, had engaged a first class room which he had kept ever since. That, although nothing definite was known concerning him, he had been seen with various highly respectable people, both of his own nation and ours, by all of whom he was treated with respect. And lastly, that while not liberal, he had given many evidences of being a man of means. So much done, I entered the office and waited for him to come in, in the hopes of having an opportunity to observe his manner when the clerk handed him that strange-looking letter from Mary Leavenworth."

"And did you succeed?"

"No; an awkward gawk of a fellow stepped between us just at the critical moment, and I missed seeing what I wanted to. But I heard enough that evening from the clerk and servants of the agitation which had been observed in him ever since he received it to convince me I was upon a trail worth following. I accordingly put on my men, and for two days Mr. Clavering was subjected to the most rigid watch a man ever walked under. But nothing was gained by it; his interest in the murder, if interest at all, was a secret one, and though he walked the streets, studied the papers, and haunted the vicinity of the house in Fifth Avenue, he not only refrained from actually approaching it, but made no attempt to communicate with any of the family. Meanwhile, you crossed my path and, with your determination, incited me to renewed effort. Convinced from Mr. Clavering's bearing and the gossip I had by this time gathered in regard to him that no one short of a gentleman and a friend could succeed in getting at the clue of his connection with this family, I handed him over to you, and——"

"Found me rather an unmanageable colleague."

Mr. Gryce smiled very much as he might have done if a sour plum had been put in his mouth, but made no reply; and a momentary pause ensued.

"Did you think to inquire," I asked at last, "if anyone knew where Mr. Clavering had spent the evening of the murder?"

"Yes; but with no good result. That he was out during the

evening, they all agreed upon; also that he was in his bed in the morning when the servant came in to make his fire; but further than this no one seemed to know."

"So that, in fact, you gleaned nothing that would in any way connect this man with the murder, except his marked and agitated interest in it, and the fact that a niece of the murdered man had written a letter to him?"

"That is all."

"Another question: did you hear in what manner and at what time he procured a newspaper that evening?"

"No; I only learned that he was observed by more than one to hasten out of the dining room with the *Post* in his hand and go immediately to his room without touching his dinner."

"Humph! that does not look——"

"If Mr. Clavering had had a guilty knowledge of the crime, he would either never have ordered dinner before opening the paper or, having ordered it, he would have eaten it."

"Then you do not believe from what you have learned that Mr. Clavering is the guilty party?"

Mr. Gryce shifted uneasily, glanced at the papers protruding from my coat pocket, and exclaimed: "I am ready to be convinced from what you have learned that he is."

That sentence recalled me to the business in hand. Without appearing to notice the look he had given me, I recurred to my questions.

"How came you to know that Mr. Clavering was in this city last summer? Did you learn that, too, at the Hoffman House?"

"No; I ascertained that in quite another way. In short, I have had a communication from London in regard to the matter."

"From London?"

"Yes; I've a friend there in my own line of business, who sometimes assists me with a bit of information, when requested."

"But how? You have not had time to write to London and receive an answer since the murder."

"It is not necessary to write. It is enough for me to telegraph him the name of a person for him to understand that I want to know everything he can gather in a reasonable length of time about that person."

"And you sent the name of Mr. Clavering to him?"

"Yes, in cipher."

"And have received a reply?"

"This morning."

I looked toward his desk.

"It is not there," he said. "If you will be kind enough to feel in my breast-pocket you will find a letter——"

It was in my hand before he had finished his sentence.

"Excuse my eagerness," I said. "This kind of business is new to me, you know."

He smiled indulgently at a very old and faded picture that hung on the wall before him. "Eagerness is not a fault, only the betrayal of it. But read out what you have there. Let us hear what my friend Brown has to tell us of Mr. Henry Ritchie Clavering, of Portland Place, London."

I took the paper to the light and read as follows:

"Henry Ritchie Clavering, Gentleman, aged 43. Born in ——, Hertfordshire, England. His father was Chas. Clavering, for short time in the Army. Mother was Helen Ritchie, of Dumfriesshire, Scotland; she is still living. Home with H.R.C., in Portland Place, London. H.R.C. is a bachelor, 6 ft. high, squarely built, weight about 12 stone. Dark complexion, regular features. Eyes dark-brown; nose straight. Called a handsome man; walks erect and rapidly. In Society is considered a good fellow; rather a favorite, especially with ladies. Is liberal, not extravagant; reported to be worth about £5,000 per year, and appearances give color to this statement. Property consists of a small estate in Hertfordshire, and some funds, amount not known. Since writing this much, a correspondent sends the following in regard to his history. In '46 went from uncle's house to Eton. From Eton went to Oxford, graduating in '56. Scholarship good. In 1855 his uncle died and his father succeeded to the estates. Father died in '57 by a fall from his horse or a similar accident. Within a very short time H.R.C. took his mother to London, to the residence named, where they have lived to the present time.

"Traveled considerably in 1860; part of the time was with —— —— of Munich; also in party of Vandervorts from New York; went as far East as Cairo. Went to America in 1875 alone, but at end of three months returned on account of mother's illness. Nothing is known of his movements while in America.

"From servants, learn that he was always a favorite from a boy. More recently has become somewhat taciturn. Toward last of his stay, watched the post carefully, especially foreign ones. Posted scarcely anything but newspapers. Has written to Munich. Have seen from waste-paper basket, torn envelope directed to Amy Belden, no address. American correspondents mostly in Boston; two in New York. Names not known, but supposed to be bankers. Brought home considerable luggage and fitted up part of house as for a lady. This was closed soon afterward. Left for America two months since. Has been, I understand, traveling in the south. Has telegraphed twice to Portland Place. His friends hear from him but rarely. Letters rec'd recently, posted in New York. One by last steamer posted in F——, N.Y.

"Business here conducted by ——. In the country, —— of —— has charge of the property.

"BROWN."

The document fell from my hands.

F——, N.Y., was a small town near R——.

"Your friend is a trump," I declared. "He tells me just what I wanted most to know." And, taking out my book, I made a memorandum of the facts which had most forcibly struck me during my perusal of the communication before me.

"With the aid of what he tells me," I cried, "I shall ferret out the mystery of Henry Clavering in a week; see if I do not."

"And how soon," inquired Mr. Gryce, "may I expect to be allowed to take a hand in the game?"

"As soon as I am reasonably assured that I am upon the right tack."

"And what will it take to assure you of that?"

"Not much; a certain point settled and——"

"Hold on; who knows but what I can do that for you?" And looking toward the desk which stood in the corner, Mr. Gryce asked me if I would open the top drawer and bring him the bits of partly burned paper which I would find there.

Hastily complying, I brought three or four strips of ragged paper and laid them on the table at his side.

"Another result of Fobbs's researches under the coal on the first day of the inquest," shortly exclaimed Mr. Gryce. "You thought the key was all he found. Well, it wasn't. A second turning over of the coal brought these to light, and very interesting they are, too."

I immediately bent over the torn and discolored scraps with great anxiety. They were four in number, and appeared at first glance to be the mere remnants of a sheet of common writing-paper, torn lengthwise into strips and twisted up into lighters; but upon closer inspection they showed traces of writing upon one side, and what was more important still, the presence of one or more drops of spattered blood. This latter discovery was horrible to me, and so overcame me for the moment that I put the scraps down, and turning toward Mr. Gryce, inquired:

"What do you make of them?"

"That is just what I was about to inquire of you."

Swallowing my disgust, I took them up again. "They appear to be the remnants of some old letter," said I.

"They have that appearance," Mr. Gryce returned a little grimly.

"A letter which, from the drop of blood observable on the written side, must have been lying face up on Mr. Leavenworth's table at the time of the murder——"

"Just so."

"And from the uniformity in width of each of these pieces as well as their tendency to curl up when left alone, been first torn into even strips, and then severally rolled up, before being tossed into the grate where they were afterward found."

"That is all good," said Mr. Gryce, "go on."

"The writing, in so far as it is discernible, is that of a cultivated gentleman; it is not that of Mr. Leavenworth, for I have studied his chirography too much lately not to know it at a glance; but it may be—— Hold!" I suddenly exclaimed. "Have you any mucilage handy? I think that if I could paste these strips down upon a piece of paper, so that they would remain flat, I should be able to tell you what I think of them much more easily."

"There is mucilage on the desk," replied Mr. Gryce.

Procuring it, I proceeded to consult the scraps once more for evidence to guide me in their arrangement. These were more marked than I expected; the longer and best preserved strip with its "Mr. Hor" at the top showing itself at first blush to be the left-hand margin of the letter, while the machine-cut edge of the next in length presented tokens fully as conclusive of its being the right-hand margin of the same. Selecting these, then, I pasted them down on a piece of paper at just the distance they would occupy, if the sheet from which they were torn was of the ordinary commercial note size. Immediately it became apparent, first, that it would take two other strips of the same width to fill up the space left between them; and secondly, that the writing did not terminate at the foot of the sheet but was carried on to another page.

Taking up the third strip, I looked at its edge; it was machine-cut at the top and showed by the arrangement of its words that it was the margin strip of a second leaf. Pasting that down by itself, I scrutinized the fourth, and finding it also machine-cut at the top but not on the side, endeavored to fit it to the piece already pasted down, but the words would not match. Moving it along then to the position which it would hold if it were the third strip, I fastened it down.

"Well!" exclaimed Mr. Gryce, "that's business." Then, as I held it up before his eyes: "But don't show it to me. Study it yourself, and tell me what you think of it."

"Well," said I, "this much is certain, that it is a letter directed to Mr. Leavenworth from some 'House,' and dated—let's see; that is an *h*, isn't it?" And I pointed to the one letter just discernible on the line under the word 'House.'

"I should think so, but don't ask me."

"It must be an *h*. The year is 1875, and this is not the termination of either January or February. Dated then, March 1st, 1876, and signed——"

Mr. Gryce rolled his eyes in anticipatory ecstasy toward the ceiling.

"By Henry Clavering," I announced without hesitation.

Mr. Gryce's eyes returned to his swathed finger-ends. "Humph! how do you know that?"

"Wait a moment and I will show you!" And taking out of my pocket the card which Mr. Clavering had handed me as an introduction at our late interview, I laid it underneath the last line of writing on the second page. One glance was sufficient. Henry Ritchie Clavering on the card; H— —chie — in the same handwriting on the letter.

"Clavering it is," said he, "without a doubt." But I saw he was not surprised.

"And now," continued I, "for its general tenor and meaning." And commencing at the beginning, I read aloud the words as they came, with pauses at the breaks something as follows: "Mr. Hor — Dear — a niece whom yo —one too who see — the love and trus — any other man ca— autiful, so char——s she in face fo—— conversation. ery rose has its——rose is no exception—— ely as she is, char —— tender as she is, s—— pable of tramplin—— one who trusted —— heart —— him to —— he owes a —— honor —— ance.

If —— t believe —— her to —— cruel —— face, —— what is —— ble serv—— yours H—— tchie

"It reads like a complaint against one of Mr. Leavenworth's nieces." I said, and started at my own words.

"What is it?" cried Mr. Gryce. "What is the matter?"

"Why," said I, "the fact is I have heard this very letter spoken of. It *is* a complaint against one of Mr. Leavenworth's nieces, and was written by Mr. Clavering." And I told him of Mr. Harwell's communication in regard to the matter.

"Ah, then, Mr. Harwell has been talking, has he? I thought he was sworn off from gossip."

"Mr. Harwell and I have seen each other almost daily for the last two weeks," replied I; "it would be strange if he had nothing to tell me."

"And he says that he has read a letter written to Mr. Leavenworth by Mr. Clavering?"

"Yes; but whose particular words he has now forgotten."

"These few here may assist him in recalling the rest."

"I would rather not admit him to a knowledge of the existence of this piece of evidence. I don't believe in letting anyone into our confidence whom it is possible to keep out."

"I see you don't," dryly responded Mr. Gryce.

Not appearing to notice the fling conveyed by these words, I took up the letter once more, and began pointing out such half-formed words in it as I thought we might venture to complete, as the Hor —, yo —, see —autiful ——, char ——, for ——, tramplin ——, pable ——, serv ——.

This done, I next proposed the introduction of such others as seemed necessary to the sense, as *Leavenworth* after *Horatio*; *Sir* after *Dear*; *have* with a possible *you* before *a niece*; *thorn* after *its* in the phrase *rose has its*; *on* after *trampling*; *whom* after *to*; *debt* after *a*; *you* after *If*; *me ask* after *believe*; *beautiful* after *cruel*.

Between the columns of words thus furnished, I interposed a phrase or two here and there, the whole reading when done as follows:

—— *House. March 1st, 1876.*

Mr. Horatio Leavenworth
DEAR SIR—

(You) have a niece whom you one too who seems worthy the love and trust of any other man ca so beautiful, so charming is she in face form and conversation. But every rose has its thorn and (this) rose is no exception lovely as she is, charming (as she is), tender as she is, she is capable of trampling on one who trusted her heart a —— him to whom she owes a debt of honor a ance

If you don't believe me ask her to her cruel beautiful face what is (her) humble servant

YOURS:

HENRY RITCHIE CLAVERING.

"I think that will do," said Mr. Gryce, "we have got the general tenor of it, and that is all we want at this time."

"The whole tone of it is anything but complimentary to the lady it inveighs against," I returned. "He must have had, or imagined he had, some desperate grievance, to provoke him to the use of such plain language in regard to one he can still characterize as tender, charming, beautiful."

"Grievances are apt to lie back of mysterious crimes."

"I think I know what this one was," I said, "but"—seeing him look up—"must decline to communicate my suspicion to you for the present. My theory stands unshaken and in some degree confirmed, and that is all I can say."

"Then the letter does not supply the link you wanted?"

"No; it is a valuable bit of evidence, but it is not the link I am in search of just now."

"Yet it must be an important clue, or Eleanore Leavenworth would not have been to such pains, first to take it in the way she did from her uncle's table, and secondly——"

"Wait!" I said. "What makes you think this is the paper she took or was believed to have taken from Mr. Leavenworth's table on that fatal morning?"

"Why, the fact that it was found together with the key, which we know she dropped into the grate, and that there are drops of blood on it."

I shook my head; she had told me the paper which she had taken at that time was destroyed, though to be sure she might have so considered it.

"Why do you shake your head?" asked Mr. Gryce.

"Because I am not satisfied with your reason for believing this to be the paper taken by her from Mr. Leavenworth's table."

"And why?"

"Well," said I, "first, because Fobbs does not speak of seeing any paper in her hand, when she bent over the fire, leaving us to conclude that these pieces were in the scuttle of coal she threw upon it, which surely you must acknowledge to be a strange place for her to have put a paper she took such pains to gain possession of, and secondly, for the reason that these scraps were twisted as if they had been used for curl-papers or something of that kind; a fact hard to explain by your hypothesis."

The detective's eyes stole in the direction of my necktie, which was as near as he ever came to a face, with an expression of great interest. "You are a bright one," said he, "a very bright one; I quite admire you, Mr. Raymond."

A little surprised, and not altogether pleased with this unexpected compliment, I regarded him doubtfully for a moment and then asked:

"What is your opinion upon the matter?"

"Oh, you know I have no opinion. I gave up everything of that kind when I put the affair into your hands."

"Still——"

"That the letter of which these scraps are the remnant was on Mr. Leavenworth's table at the time of the murder is believed. That upon the body being removed, a paper was taken from the table by Miss Eleanore Leavenworth, is also believed. That when she found her action had been noticed and attention called to this paper and the key, she resorted to subterfuge in order to escape the vigilance of the watch that had been set over her, and partially succeeding in her endeavor, flung the key into the fire from which these same scraps were afterward recovered, is also known. The conclusion I leave to your judgment."

"Very well, then," said I, rising, "we will let conclusions go for the present. My mind must be settled in regard to the truth or falsity of a certain theory of mine, in order that my judgment may be worth much on this or any matter connected with the affair."

And only waiting to get the address of his subordinate, Q, in case I should need assistance in my investigations, I left Mr. Gryce and proceeded immediately to the house of Mr. Veeley.

CHAPTER 10

The Story of A Charming Woman

Fe, fi, fo, fum,
I smell the blood of an Englishman.
—Old Song.

I hold you as a thing enskied and sainted.
—Measure for Measure.

"You have never heard, then, any account of the circumstances which led to his marriage?"

It was my partner who spoke. I had been asking him to explain to me Mr. Leavenworth's well-known antipathy to the English race.

"No."

"If you had," returned he, rousing up in his bed—he was not yet entirely recovered from his illness—"you would not need to ask me for this explanation. But it is not strange you are ignorant of the matter. I doubt if there are half a dozen persons in existence who could tell you where Horatio Leavenworth found the lovely woman who afterward became his wife, much less give you any details of the circumstances which led to the marriage."

"I am very fortunate, then, in being in the confidence of one who can. What were those circumstances, Mr. Veeley?"

"It will aid you but little to hear; but since you desire it, you shall. Horatio Leavenworth when a young man was very ambitious; so much so, that at one time he aspired to marry a wealthy lady of Providence. But chancing to go to England, he there met a young woman whose grace and charm had such an effect upon him, that he relinquished all thought of the Providence lady, though it was some time before he could face the prospect of marrying the one who had so greatly interested him; as she was not only in the humblest circumstances, but was encumbered with a child concerning whose parentage the neighbors professed ignorance and she had nothing to say. But as is very apt to be the case in an affair like this, love and admiration soon got the better of worldly wisdom. Taking his future in his hands, he offered himself as her husband, when she immediately proved herself worthy of his regard, by entering at once into those explanations he was too much of a gentleman to demand.

"The story she told was very pitiful. It seems that she was an American by birth, her father having been a well-known merchant of Chicago. While he lived, her home was one of luxury, but just as she was emerging into womanhood, he died. It was at his funeral she met the man destined to be her ruin. How he came there she never knew; he was not a friend of her father's. It is enough he was there and saw her, and that in three weeks—don't shudder, she was such a child—they were married. In twenty-four hours she knew what that word meant for her; it meant blows. Everett, I am telling no fanciful story. In twenty-four hours after that girl was married, her husband coming home drunk into the house, found her in his way and knocked her down. It was but the beginning. Her father's estate, on being settled up, proving to be less than expected, he carried her off to England, where he did not wait to be drunk in order to maltreat her. She was not free from his cruelty night or day. Before she was sixteen she had run the whole gamut of human suffering, and that, not at the hands of a coarse, common ruffian, but from an elegant, handsome, luxury-loving gentleman, whose taste in dress was so nice, he would sooner fling a garment of hers into the fire than see her go into company clad in a manner he did not consider becoming. She bore it till her child was born, then she fled. Two days after the little one saw the light, she rose up from her bed and taking her baby in her arms ran out of the house. The few jewels she had put into her pocket supported her till she could set up a little shop. After that, she lived as one born and bred as she had been might be supposed to do, in a situation so at war with her earlier training and natural instincts. As for her husband, she neither saw him nor heard from him from the day she left him till about two weeks before Horatio Leavenworth first met her, when she learned from the papers that he was dead. She was therefore free, but though she loved Horatio Leavenworth with all her heart, she would not marry him. She felt herself forever stained and soiled by that one awful year of abuse and contamination. Nor could he persuade her. Not till the death of her child, a month or so after his proposal, did she consent to give him her hand and what remained of her unhappy life. He brought her to New York, surrounded her with luxury and every tender care, but the arrow had gone too deep; two years from the day her child breathed its last, she, too, died. It was the blow of his life to Horatio Leavenworth; he was never the same man again. Though Mary and Eleanore shortly after entered his home, he never recovered his old light-heartedness. Money became his idol, and the ambition to make and leave a great fortune behind him modified all his views of life. But one proof remained that he never forgot the wife of his youth, and that was, he could not bear to have the word 'Englishman' uttered in his hearing."

Mr. Veeley paused, and I rose to go. "Do you remember how Mrs. Leavenworth looked?" I asked. "Could you describe her to me?"

He seemed a little astonished at my request, but immediately said: "She was a very pale woman; not strictly beautiful, but of a contour and expression of great charm. Her hair was brown, her eyes gray——"

"And very wide apart?"

He nodded, looking still more astonished. "How came you to know? Have you seen her picture?"

I did not answer that question.

On my way downstairs I bethought me of a letter which I had in my pocket for Mr. Veeley's son Fred, and knowing of no surer way of getting to him that night than by leaving it on the library table, I stepped to the door of that room which in this house was at the rear of the parlors, and receiving no reply to my knock, opened it and looked in.

The room was unlighted, but a cheerful fire was burning in the grate, and by its glow I espied a lady crouching on the hearth, whom at first glance I took for Mrs. Veeley. But upon advancing and addressing her by that name, I saw my mistake; for the person before me not only refrained from replying, but rising at the sound of my voice, revealed a form so noble in its height and conspicuous in its grace, that all possibility of its being that of the dainty wife of my partner fled.

"I see that I have made a mistake," said I. "I beg your pardon," and would have left the room, but something in the general attitude of the lady before me restrained me, and believing it to be Mary Leavenworth, I inquired:

"Can it be this is Miss Leavenworth?"

The noble figure appeared to droop, the gently lifted head to fall, and for a moment I doubted if I had been correct in my supposition. Then form and head slowly erected themselves, a soft voice spoke and I heard a low "yes," and hurriedly advancing, confronted, not Mary with her glancing, feverish gaze and scarlet, trembling lips, but Eleanore, the woman whose faintest look had moved me from the first, the woman whose husband I believed myself to be even then pursuing to his doom.

The surprise was too great; I could neither sustain nor conceal it. Stumbling slowly back, I murmured something about having believed it to be her cousin; and then, conscious only of the one wish to fly a presence I dared not encounter in my present mood, turned, when her rich, heart-full voice rose once more and I heard:

"You will not leave me without a word, Mr. Raymond, now that chance has thrown us together?" Then as I came slowly forward: "Were you so very much astonished to find me here?"

"I do not know—I did not expect——" was my incoherent reply. "I had heard that you were ill; that you went nowhere; that you had no wish to see your friends."

"I have been ill," she said, "but I am better now, and have come to spend the night with Mrs. Veeley because I could not endure the stare of the four walls of my room any longer."

This was said without any effort at plaintiveness, but rather as if she thought it necessary to excuse herself for being where she was.

"I am glad that you have done so," said I. "You ought to be here all the while. That dreary, lonesome boarding-house is no place for you, Miss Leavenworth. It distresses us all to feel that you are exiling yourself at this time."

"I do not wish anybody to be distressed," she returned. "It is best for me to be where I am. It is not exile, nor am I all alone. A little girl is there, a child, one whose innocent eyes see nothing but innocence in mine. She will keep me from too great a despair. Do not let my friends be anxious; I can bear it." Then in a lower tone: "There is but one thing that utterly disturbs me, and that is my ignorance of what is going on at home. Sorrow I can bear, but suspense is killing me. Will you not tell me, then, something of Mary and home? I cannot ask Mrs. Veeley; she is kind, but has no real knowledge of Mary or me, nor does she know anything of our estrangement. She thinks me obstinate, and blames me for leaving my cousin in her trouble. But you know that I could not do otherwise. You know——" Her voice wavered off into a tremble and she did not conclude.

"I cannot tell you much," I hastened to reply, "but whatever knowledge is at my command is certainly yours. Is there anything in particular you would like to ask?"

"I would like to know how Mary is, whether she is well and—and composed."

"Your cousin is not ill," I returned, "but I fear that I can hardly say she is composed. She is in great anguish, Miss Leavenworth. She is not only overwhelmed at the loss which has befallen her, but overcome with anxiety for you. You must not think of her as being otherwise than troubled."

"You see her often, then?" said she.

"I am assisting Mr. Harwell in preparing your uncle's book for the Press and necessarily am there much of the time," replied I.

"My uncle's book!" The words came in a tone of low horror.

"Yes, Miss Leavenworth. It has been thought best to bring it before the world, and——"

"And Mary has set you at the task?"

"Yes."

It seemed as if she could not escape from the horror which had overtaken her. "How could she? Oh, how could she?"

"She considers herself as doing what her uncle would approve. He was very anxious, as you know, to have the book out by July; she is but fulfilling his wishes——"

"Do not speak of it," cried she, falling a step back, "I cannot bear it." Then as if she feared she had hurt my feelings by her abruptness, lowered her voice and said: "I do not, however, know of anyone I should be better pleased to have charged with the task than yourself. With you it will be a work of respect and reverence; but a stranger—oh, I could not have endured a stranger touching it."

She was fast falling into her old horror, but rousing herself, murmured: "I wanted to ask you something; ah, I know"— and she moved a little so as to face me, "I wish to inquire if everything is as before in the house; the servants the same and—and other things?"

"There is a Mrs. Darrell there; I do not know of any other change."

"Mary does not talk of going away?"

"I think not."

"But she has visitors? Someone besides Mrs. Darrell to help her bear her loneliness?"

I felt a deathly chill strike me. "Yes," I replied, "a few."

"Would you mind naming them?" She asked in a low, distinct voice.

"Certainly not," I returned, looking away from her face. "Mrs. Veeley, of course, Mrs. Gilbert, Miss Martin, and a—a——"

"Go on," she whispered.

"A gentleman by the name of Clavering."

"You speak that name with evident embarrassment," she said after a moment of intense anxiety on my part. "May I inquire why?"

Astounded, I raised my eyes to her face. It was very pale and flashed like marble in the firelight, and wore the old look of self-repressed calm I remembered so well. I immediately dropped my gaze.

"Why? Because there are some circumstances surrounding him which have struck me as peculiar."

"How so?" she asked.

"He appears under two names. Today it is Clavering; a short time ago it was——"

"Go on."

"Robbins."

Her dress rustled on the hearth; there was a sound of desolation in it, but her voice when she spoke was expressionless as that of an automaton.

"How many times has this person, of whose name you do not appear to be certain, been to see Mary?"

"Once."

"When was it?"

"Last night."

"Did he stay long?"

"About twenty minutes, I should say."

"And do you think he will come again?"

"No."

"Why?"

"He has left the country."

A short silence followed this. I felt her eyes searching my face, but doubt whether if I had known that she held a loaded pistol in her hand, I could have looked up at that moment.

"Mr. Raymond," she said at length in a changed tone, "the last time I saw you you told me that you were going to make some endeavor to restore me to my former position before the world. I did not wish you to do so then, nor do I wish you to do so now. Can you not make me comparatively happy, then, by assuring me that you have abandoned or will abandon a project so hopeless?"

"It is impossible," said I; "I cannot abandon it. Much as I grieve to be a source of sorrow to you, it is best you should know that I can never give up the hope of righting you while I live."

She put out one quick hand in a sort of hopeless deprecation inexpressibly touching to behold in the fast-waning firelight. But I was relentless.

"I should never be able to lie quietly in my grave if through any weakness I should miss the blessed privilege of setting the wrong right, and saving a noble woman from unmerited disgrace." And then seeing that she was not likely to reply to this, drew a step nearer and said: "Is there not some little kindness I can show you, Miss Leavenworth, which you can mention before we part? Some message you would like taken, or some action performed which only a friend could do?"

She stopped to think. "No," she said; "I have only one request to make, and that you refuse to grant."

"For the most unselfish reasons," I urged.

She slowly shook her head. "You think so," murmured she; then before I could reply: "I could desire one little favor shown me, however."

"What is that?"

"That if anything should transpire; if Hannah should be found, or—or my presence required in any way, you will not keep me in ignorance. That you will let me know the worst when it comes, without fail."

"I will."

"And now good night; Mrs. Veeley is coming back and you would scarcely wish to be found here by her."

"No," said I.

And yet I did not go, but stood watching the firelight flicker on her black dress till the thought of Clavering and the duty I had for the morrow came like cold steel to my heart, and I turned away toward the door. But at the threshold I paused again and looked back. Oh, the flickering, dying fire flame! Oh, the crowding, clustering shadows! Oh, that drooping figure in their midst, with its clasped hands and its hidden face! I see it all again; I see it as in a dream; then darkness falls, and in the glare of the gas-lighted streets I am hastening along, solitary and sad, to my lonely home.

CHAPTER 11

A Report Followed By Smoke

> Oft expectation fails, and most oft there
> Where most it promises; and oft it hits,
> Where Hope is coldest, and Despair most sits.
>   —ALL'S WELL THAT ENDS WELL.

When I told Mr. Gryce that I only waited for the determination of one fact, to feel justified in throwing the case unreserv-
edly into his hands, I alluded to the proving or disproving of
the supposition that Henry Clavering had been a guest at the
same watering-place with Eleanore Leavenworth the summer before.

When, therefore, I found myself the next morning with the
visitors' book of the Hotel Union at R—— in my hands, it was
only by the strongest effort of will that I could restrain my impatience. The suspense, however, was short. Almost immediately I encountered his name written not half a page below
those of Mr. Leavenworth and his nieces, and whatever may
have been my emotion at finding my suspicions thus confirmed,
I recognized the fact that I was in the possession of a clue which
would yet lead to the solving of the fearful problem which had
been imposed upon me.

Hastening to the telegraph-office I sent a message for the
man promised me by Mr. Gryce, and receiving for answer
that he could not be with me before three o'clock, started for
the house of Mr. Monell, a client of ours, living in R——. I
found him at home, and during our interview of two hours suffered the ordeal of appearing at ease and interested in what he
had to say, while my heart was heavy with its first disappointment and my brain on fire with the excitement of the work
then on my hands.

I arrived at the station just as the train came in. There was
but one passenger for R——, a brisk young man, whose whole
appearance was so different from what I expected Q's to be

that I at once made up my mind he could not be the man I was looking for, and was therefore turning away disappointed, when he approached and handed me a card on which was inscribed the single character "?" Even then I could not bring myself to believe that the slyest and most successful agent in Mr. Gryce's employ was before me till, catching his eye, I saw such a keen, enjoyable twinkle sparkle for a moment from its depths, that all doubt fled, and returning his bow with a show of satisfaction, I remarked:

"You are very punctual; I like that."

He gave another short, quick nod. "Glad, sir, to please you. Punctuality is too cheap a virtue not to be practiced by a man on the look-out for a rise. But what orders, sir? Down train due in ten minutes; no time to spare."

"Down train? What have we to do with that?"

"I thought you might wish to take it, sir. Mr. Brown"—winking expressively at the name—"always checks his carpet-bag for home when he sees me coming. But that is your affair; I am not particular."

"I wish to do what is wisest."

"Go home, then, as speedily as possible." And he gave a third sharp nod exceedingly business-like and determined.

"If I leave you, it is with the understanding that you come first to me with your information. That you are in my employ and in that of no one else for the time being, and that mum is the word till I give you liberty to speak."

"Yes, sir. When I work for Brown & Co., I work for them; and when I work for Smith & Co., I work for them."

"Very well, then," said I, giving him a memorandum I had made before leaving Mr. Monell's, "here are your instructions."

He looked it over with a certain degree of care, then stepped into the waiting-room and threw it into the stove, saying in a low tone: "So much in case I should meet with some accident; have an apoplectic fit or anything of that sort."

"But——"

"Oh, don't worry; I shan't forget. I've a memory, sir. No need of anybody using pen and paper with me." And laughing in the short, quick way one would expect from a person of his appearance and conversation, he added: "You will probably hear from me in a day or so," and bowing, took his brisk, free way down the street just as the train came rushing up to the station where I was.

My instructions to Q were as follows:

1. To find out on what day and in whose company the Misses Leavenworth arrived at R—— the year before. What their movements were while there, and with whom they most consorted. Also the date of their departure and such facts as could be gathered in regard to their habits, etc.

2. Ditto in respect to a Mr. Henry Clavering, fellow guest and probable friend of said ladies.

3. Name of individual fulfilling the following requirements. Clergyman, Methodist, deceased since last December or thereabouts, who in July of 'Seventy-five was located in some town not over twenty miles from R——.

4. Also name and present whereabouts of a man at that time in service of the above.

To say that I passed the interval of time necessary to a proper inquiry into these matters in any reasonable frame of mind, would be to give myself credit for an equanimity of temper which I unfortunately do not possess. Never have days seemed so long as the two which interposed between my return from R—— and the receipt of the following letter:

SIR:

1. Individuals mentioned arrived in R—— July 3, 1875. Party consisted of four; themselves, uncle, and the girl named Hannah. Uncle remained three days and then left for a short tour through Massachusetts. Gone two weeks, during which ladies were seen more or less with the gentleman named between us, but not to an extent sufficient to excite gossip or occasion remark, when said gentleman left R—— abruptly, two days after uncle's return. Date July 19. As to habits of ladies, more or less social. They were always to be seen at picnics, rides, etc., and in the ballroom. M—— liked best. E—— considered grave, and toward the last of her stay, moody. It is remembered now, that her manner was al-

ways peculiar, and that she was more or less shunned by her cousin. A servant-girl now in the hotel says, however, she was the sweetest lady ever breathed. No particular reason for this opinion. Uncle, ladies and servant left R—— for New York, August 7, 1875.

2. H. C. arrived at the hotel in R—— July 6, 1875, in company with Mr. and Mrs. Vandervort, friends of the above. Left July 19, two weeks from day of arrival. Little to be learned in regard to him. Remembered as the handsome gentleman who was in the party with the L. girls, and that is all.

3. F——, a small town, some sixteen or seventeen miles from R——, had for its Methodist minister in July of last year a man who has since died, Samuel Stebbins by name. Date of decease January 7 of this year.

4. Name of man in employ of S. S. at that time, is Timothy Cook. He has been absent, but returned to F—— two days ago. Can be seen if required.

"Ah, ha!" I cried aloud at this point in my sudden surprise and satisfaction; "now we have something to work with!" And sitting down I penned the following reply:

T. C. wanted by all means. Also any evidence going to prove that H. C. and E. L. were married at the house of Mr. S. on any day of July or August last.

Next morning came the following telegram:

T. C. on the road. Remembers a marriage. Will be with you by 2 p.m.

At three o'clock of that same day, I stood before Mr. Gryce. "I am here to make my report," said I.

The flicker of a smile passed over his face, and he gazed for the first time at his bound-up finger-ends with a softening aspect that must have done them good. "I'm ready," said he.

"Mr. Gryce," I began, "do you remember the conclusion we came to at our first interview in this house?"

"I remember the one *you* came to."

"Well, well," returned I a little peevishly, "the one I came to, then. It was this: that if we could find to whom Eleanore Leavenworth felt she owed her best duty and love, we should discover who it was that murdered her uncle."

"And do you imagine you have ascertained this?"

"I do."

His eyes stole a little nearer my face. "Well!" exclaimed he, "that is good; go on."

"When I undertook this business of clearing Eleanore Leavenworth from suspicion," resumed I, "it was with the premonition that this person would prove to be her lover, but I had no idea he would prove to be her husband."

Mr. Gryce's gaze flashed like lightning to the ceiling. "What?" said he with a frown.

"The lover of Eleanore Leavenworth is likewise her husband," I repeated. "Mr. Clavering holds no lesser connection to her than that."

"How have you found that out?" demanded Mr. Gryce in a harsh tone that argued disappointment or displeasure.

"That, it is not necessary for me to state. The question is not how I became acquainted with a certain thing, but is what I assert in regard to it true? I believe that it is, and if you will cast your eye over this summary of events gleaned by me from the lives of these two individuals, I think you will agree with me." And I held up before his eyes the following:

"During two weeks commencing July 6, of the year 1875, and ending July 19, of the same year, Henry R. Clavering of London, and Eleanore Leavenworth of New York, were guests in the same hotel. *Fact proved by visitors' book of the Hotel Union at R——, New York.*

"They were not only guests in the same hotel, but are known to have held more or less communication with each other. *Fact proved by such servants now employed in R—— as were in the hotel at that time.*

"July 19. Mr. Clavering left R—— abruptly, a circumstance that would not be considered remarkable if Mr. Leavenworth, whose violent antipathy to Englishmen as husbands is publicly known, had not just returned from a journey.

"July 30. Mr. Clavering was seen in the parlor of Mr. Stebbins, the Methodist minister at F——, a town about sixteen miles from R——, where he was married to a lady of great beauty. *Proved by Timothy Cook, a man in the employ of Mr. Stebbins, who was called in from the garden to witness the ceremony and sign a paper supposed to be a certificate.*

"July 31. Mr. Clavering takes steamer for Liverpool. *Proved by newspapers of that date.*

"September. Eleanore Leavenworth in her uncle's house in New York, conducting herself as usual, but pale of face and preoccupied in manner. *Proved by servants then in her service.* Mr. Clavering in London; watches the States mails with eagerness, but receives no letters. Fits up room elegantly as for a lady. *Proved by Secret Communication from London.*

"November. Miss Leavenworth still in uncle's house. No publication of her marriage ever made. Mr. Clavering in London; shows signs of uneasiness; the room prepared for lady closed. *Proved as above.*

"January 17, 1876. Mr. Clavering having returned to America, engages room at Hoffman House, New York.

"March 1, or 2. Mr. Leavenworth receives a letter signed by Henry Clavering, in which he complains of having been ill-used by one of that gentleman's nieces. A manifest shade falls over the family at this time.

"March 4. Mr. Clavering under a false name inquires at the door of Mr. Leavenworth's house, for Miss Eleanore Leavenworth. *Proved by Thomas.*"

"March fourth?" exclaimed Mr. Gryce at this point. "That was the night of the murder."

"Yes; the Mr. Le Roy Robbins said to have called that evening was none other than Mr. Clavering."

"March 19. Miss Mary Leavenworth, in a conversation with me, acknowledges that there is a secret in the family, and is just upon the point of revealing its nature, when Mr. Clavering enters the house. Upon his departure, she declares her unwillingness ever to mention the subject again."

Mr. Gryce slowly waved the paper aside. "And from these facts you draw the inference that Eleanore Leavenworth is the wife of Mr. Clavering?"

"I do."

"And that being his wife——"

"It would be natural for her to make what endeavor she could, to conceal anything she knew serving to incriminate him."

"Always supposing Clavering himself had done anything criminal!"

"Of course."

"Which latter supposition you now propose to justify!"

"Which latter supposition *we* must now endeavor to prove justifiable."

A peculiar gleam shot over Mr. Gryce's somewhat abstracted face. "Then you have no new evidence against Mr. Clavering?"

"I should think the fact just given, of his standing in the relation of unacknowledged husband to the suspected party, was something."

"No positive evidence as to his being the assassin of Mr. Leavenworth, I mean?"

I was obliged to tell him no; none which he would call of a positive nature. "But I can show the existence of motive, and I can likewise show that it was not only possible but probable that he was in the house at the time of the murder."

"Ah, you can!" cried Mr. Gryce, rousing a little from his abstraction.

"The motive was the usual one of self-interest. Mr. Leavenworth stood in the way of Eleanore's acknowledging him as a husband, and he must therefore be put out of the way."

"Weak!"

"Motives for murders are sometimes weak."

"The motive for this was not. There is not only too much calculation observable in the whole thing, but the manner of it was too cold, for the arm to have been nerved by anything

short of the most deliberate intention, founded upon the dead-
liest necessity of passion or avarice."

"Avarice?"

"One should never deliberate upon the causes which lead to
the destruction of a rich man, without taking into account that
most common passion of the human race."

"But——"

"Let us hear what you have to say of Mr. Clavering's presence in the house at the time of the murder."

"Well," said I, "if the motive was weak, I fear that you will
find this more so." And I related what Thomas, the butler, had
told me in regard to Mr. Clavering's call upon Miss Leavenworth that night, and the lack of proof which existed as to his
having left the house when supposed to do so.

"That is worth remembering," said Mr. Gryce at the conclusion. "Valueless as direct evidence that he was implicated in
this crime, it would be very important as circumstantial." Then
in a graver tone than any which he had yet used in his conver-
sations with me, he went on to say: "Mr. Raymond, are you
aware that in all this you have been strengthening the case
against Eleanore Leavenworth instead of weakening it?"

I could only ejaculate in my sudden wonder and horror.

"You have shown her to be secret, sly and unprincipled, capable of wronging those to whom she was most bound, her
uncle and her husband."

"You put it very strongly," said I, conscious of a shocking
discrepancy between this description of Eleanore's character
and all that I had preconceived in regard to it.

"No more so than your own conclusions from this story
warrant me in doing." Then as I sat silent, murmured low, and
as if to himself: "If the case was dark against her before, it is
doubly so with this supposition established of her being the
woman secretly married to Mr. Clavering."

"And yet," cried I, unable to give up without a struggle
the hope I had been cherishing for so long, "you do not, cannot believe the noble-looking Eleanore guilty of this horrible crime?"

"No," said he, slowly, "you might as well know right here

what I think about that. I believe Eleanore Leavenworth to be an innocent woman."

"You do? Then what," cried I, swaying between joy at this admission and doubt as to the meaning of his former expressions, "remains to be done?"

Mr. Gryce quietly responded: "Why, nothing but to prove that your supposition is not true."

CHAPTER 12

Timothy Cook

Look here upon this picture and upon this.
—HAMLET.

I stared at him in amazement.

"I doubt if it will be so very difficult," said he. Then in a sudden burst: "Where is the man Cook?"

"He is below," returned I; "he and Q. I brought them with me."

"That was wise; let us see the boys; have them up."

Stepping to the door I called them.

"I expected, of course, you would want to question them," said I, coming back.

In another moment the spruce Q and the shock-headed Cook entered the room.

"Ah," said Mr. Gryce, looking toward the latter if not directly at him; "this is the deceased Mr. Stebbins's hired man, is it? Well, you look as though you could tell the truth."

"I usually calculate to do that thing, sir; at all events I was never called a liar that I can remember."

"Of course not, of course not," returned the detective, very affably for him. Then without any further introduction: "What was the first name of the lady you saw married in your master's house last summer?"

"Bless me if I know! I don't think I heard, sir."

"But you recollect how she looked?"

"As well as if she was my own mother. No disrespect to the lady, sir, if you know her," he made haste to add, glancing hurriedly at me. "What I mean is, that she was so handsome, I could never forget the look of her sweet face if I lived a hundred years."

"Can you describe her?"

"I don't know, sirs; she was tall and grand-looking, had the brightest eyes and the whitest hand and smiled in a way to make even a common man like me wish he had never seen her."

"Would you know her in a crowd?"

"I would know her anywhere."

"Very well, now tell us all you can about that marriage."

"Well, sirs, it was something like this. I had been in Mr. Stebbins's employ I should say about a year, when one morning as I was hoeing in the garden that runs along by the road, I saw a gentleman step from the platform of the station, look up and down the road for a minute, and then walk rapidly to our gate and come in. I noticed him particularly, because he was so fine-looking, unlike anybody in F——, and, indeed, unlike anybody I had ever seen, for that matter; but I shouldn't have thought much about it if there hadn't come along, not five minutes after, a buggy with two ladies in it, which stopped at our gate, too. I saw they wanted to get out, so I went and held their horse for them and they got down and went into the house."

"Did you see their faces?"

"No, sir; not then. They had veils on."

"Very well, go on."

"I hadn't been to work long before I heard someone calling my name, and looking up saw Mr. Stebbins standing in the door, beckoning. I went to him, and he said: 'I want you, Tim; wash your hands and come into the parlor.' I had never been asked to do that before, and it struck me all of a heap, but I did what he asked, and was so taken aback at the looks of the lady I saw standing up on the floor with the handsome gentleman, that I stumbled over a stool and made a great racket, and didn't know much where I was or what was going on, till I heard Mr. Stebbins say 'man and wife,' and then it came over me in a hot kind of way that it was a marriage I was seeing."

Timothy Cook stopped to wipe his forehead as if overcome with the very recollection, and Mr. Gryce took the opportunity to remark:

"You say there were two ladies; now where was the other one at this time?"

"She was there, sir, but I didn't mind much about her, I was so taken up with the handsome one and the way she had of smiling, when anyone looked at her. I never saw the beat."

I felt a quick thrill go through me, but why or for what I could not at that moment have determined.

"Can you remember the color of her hair or eyes?"

"No, sir; I had a feeling as if she wasn't dark, and that is all I know."

"But you remember her face?"

"Yes, sir."

Mr. Gryce here whispered me to procure the two pictures which I would find in a certain drawer in his desk, and set them up in different parts of the room unbeknown to the man.

"You have before said," pursued Mr. Gryce, "that you have no remembrance of her name. Now, how was that? Weren't you called upon to sign the certificate?"

"Yes, sir; but I am most ashamed to say it, I was in a sort of maze and didn't hear much, and only remember that it was a Mr. Clavering she was married to, and that someone called someone else Elner, or something like that. I wish I hadn't been so stupid, sir, if it would have done you any good."

"Tell us about the signing of the certificate," said Mr. Gryce.

"Well, sir, there isn't much to tell. Mr. Stebbins asked me to put my name down in a certain place on a piece of paper he pushed toward me, and I put it down there, that is all."

"Was there no other name there when you wrote yours?"

"No, sir. Afterward Mr. Stebbins turned toward the other lady who now came forward, and asked her if she wouldn't please sign it, and she said 'yes,' and came very quickly and did so."

"And didn't you see her face then?"

"No, sir; her back was to me when she threw by her veil,

and I only saw Mr. Stebbins staring at her as she stooped with a kind of wonder on his face, which made me think that she might have been something worth looking at, too, but I didn't see her myself."

"Well, what happened then?"

"I don't know, sir. I went stumbling out of the room and didn't see anything more."

"Where were you when the ladies went away?"

"In the garden, sir; I had gone back to my work."

"You saw them, then; was the gentleman with them?"

"No, sir; that was the queer part of it all. They went back as they came, and so did he; and in a few minutes Mr. Stebbins came out where I was and told me I was to say nothing about what I had seen, for it was a secret."

"Were you the only one in the house who knew anything about it? Weren't there any women around?"

"No, sir; Miss Stebbins had gone to the sewing circle."

I had by this time some faint impression of what Mr. Gryce's suspicions were, and in arranging the pictures had placed one, that of Eleanore—and an exquisite portrait it was, too—on the mantelpiece, and the other, which was an uncommonly fine photograph of Mary, in plain view on the desk. But Mr. Cook's back was as yet toward that part of the room, and taking advantage of the moment; I returned and asked him if that was all he had to tell us about this matter.

"Yes, sir."

"Then," said Mr. Gryce with a glance at Q, "isn't there something here you can give Mr. Cook in payment for his story? Look around, will you?"

Q nodded and moved toward a cupboard in the wall which was at the side of the mantelpiece, Mr. Cook following him with his eyes as was natural, when with a sudden start he crossed the room and, pausing before the mantelpiece, looked at the picture of Eleanore which I had put there, gave a low grunt of satisfaction or pleasure, looked at it again and walked away. I felt my heart leap up into my throat, and moved by what impulse of dread or hope I cannot say, turned my back, when suddenly I heard him give vent to a startled exclamation, followed by the words: "Why, here she is, this is her, sirs," and turning around, saw him hurrying toward us with Mary's picture in his hands.

I do not know as I was greatly surprised. I was powerfully excited as well as conscious of a certain whirl of thought and an unsettling of old conclusions that was very confusing; but surprised? No. It seemed as if the manner of Mr. Gryce had too well prepared me.

"This the lady who was married to Mr. Clavering, my good man? I guess you are mistaken," cried Mr. Gryce in a very incredulous tone.

"Mistaken? Didn't I say I would know her anywhere? This is the lady, if she is the President's wife herself." And Mr. Cook leaned over it with a devouring look that was not without its element of homage.

"I am very much astonished," Mr. Gryce went on, winking at me in a slow diabolical way that in another mood would have aroused my fiercest anger.

"Now, if you had said the other lady was the one"—pointing to the picture on the mantelpiece—"I shouldn't have wondered."

"She? I never saw that lady before; but this one—would you mind telling me her name, sirs?"

"If what you say is true, her name is Mrs. Clavering."

"Clavering? Yes, that was his name."

"And a very lovely lady," said Mr. Gryce. "Morris, haven't you found anything yet?"

"Yes, sir," replied Q, bringing forward glasses and a bottle.

But Mr. Cook was in no mood for liquor. I think he was struck by remorse; for, looking from the picture to Q, and from Q to the picture, he said:

"If I have done this lady wrong by my talk, I'll never forgive myself. You told me I would be helping her to get her rights; if you have deceived me——"

"Oh, I haven't deceived you," broke in Q in his short sharp way. "Ask that gentleman there if we are not all interested in Mrs. Clavering getting her due."

He had designated me, but I was in no mood to reply. I longed to have the man dismissed, that I might inquire the reason of the great complacency which I now saw overspreading Mr. Gryce's frame to his very finger ends.

"Mr. Cook needn't be concerned," remarked Mr. Gryce. "If he will take a glass of warm drink, to fortify him for his walk, I think he may go to the lodgings Mr. Morris has provided for him, without fear. Give the gent a glass, and let him mix for himself."

But it was a full ten minutes before we were delivered of the man and his vain regrets. Mary's image had seemed to call up every latent feeling in his heart, and I could but wonder over a loveliness that was capable of swaying even such as he. But at last he yielded to the seductions of the now wily Q, and departed.

Left alone with Mr. Gryce, I must have allowed some of the confused emotions which filled my breast to become apparent on my countenance, for after a few minutes of ominous silence, he exclaimed very grimly, and yet with a latent touch of that complacency I had before noticed:

"This discovery rather upsets you, doesn't it? Well, it don't me," shutting his mouth like a trap. "I expected it."

"You must have formed very different conclusions from what I have done," I returned, "or you would see that this discovery alters the complexion of the whole affair."

"It does not alter the truth."

"What is the truth?"

Mr. Gryce's very legs grew thoughtful; his voice sank to its deepest tone. "Do you very much want to know?"

"Want to know the truth? What else are we after?"

"Then," said he, "to my notion, the complexion of things has altered, but very much for the better. As long as Eleanore was believed to be the wife her action in this matter was accounted for, but the tragedy itself was not. Why should Eleanore or Eleanore's husband wish the death of a man whose bounty was believed by them to cease with his life? But with Mary, the heiress, proved the wife!—I tell you, Mr. Raymond, it all hangs together now. You must never, in reckoning up an affair of murder like this, forget who it is that most profits by the deceased man's death."

"But Eleanore's silence? Her concealment of certain proofs and evidences in her own breast—how will you account for that? I can imagine a woman devoting herself to the shielding of a husband from the consequences of crime, but a cousin's husband, never."

Mr. Gryce put his feet very close together and softly grunted. "Then you still think Mr. Clavering the assassin of Mr. Leavenworth?"

I could only stare at him in my sudden doubt and dread. "Still think?" I repeated.

"Mr. Clavering, the murderer of Mr. Leavenworth?"

"Why, what else is there to think? You don't—you can't suspect Eleanore of having deliberately undertaken to help her cousin out of a difficulty by taking the life of their mutual benefactor?"

"No," said Mr. Gryce, "no, I do not think Eleanore Leavenworth had any hand in the business."

"Then who——" I began, and stopped, lost in the dreadful vista that was opening before me.

"Who? Why, who but the one whose past deceit and present necessity demanded his death as a relief? Who, but the beautiful, gorgeous, money-loving, man-deceiving goddess——"

I leaped to my feet in my sudden horror and repugnance. "Do not mention the name," cried I; "you are wrong, but do not speak the name."

"Excuse me," said he, "but it will have to be spoken many times, and we may as well begin—Mary Leavenworth, or if you like it better, Mrs. Henry Clavering. Are you so much surprised? It has been my thought from the beginning."

CHAPTER 13

Mr. Gryce Explains Himself

Sits the wind in that corner?
—MUCH ADO ABOUT NOTHING.

I do not propose to enter into a description of the mingled feelings that overwhelmed me at this announcement. As a drowning man is said to live over in one terrible instant the events of a lifetime, so each word that had been uttered in my hearing by Mary, from her first introduction to me in her own room on the morning of the inquest, to our final conversation on the night of Mr. Clavering's call, swept in one wild phantasmagoria through my brain, leaving me aghast at the signification which her whole conduct seemed to acquire from the lurid light which now fell upon it.

"I see that I have pulled down an avalanche of doubts about your ears!" exclaimed my companion from the height of his calm superiority. "You never thought of this possibility, then, yourself?"

"Do not ask me what I have thought. I only know one thing, and that is that I will never believe your suspicions true. That, however much Mary may have been benefited by her uncle's death, she never had a hand in it; actual hand, I mean," added I with an attempt to be honest.

"And what makes you think not?"

"And what makes you think she had? It is for you to prove that she had, not for me to prove she had not!"

"Ah," said Mr. Gryce, in his slow sarcastic way, "you recollect that principle of law, do you? If I remember right, you have not always been so punctilious in regarding it or wishing to have it regarded, when the question was whether Mr. Clavering was the assassin or not."

"But he is a man. It does not seem so dreadful to accuse a man of crime. But a woman—and such a woman! I cannot listen to it; it is horrible. Nothing short of absolute confession on her part will ever make me believe Mary Leavenworth or any other woman committed this deed. It was too cruel, too deliberate, too——"

"Read the criminal records," broke in Mr. Gryce.

But I was obstinate. "I do not care for the criminal records. All the criminal records in the world would never make me believe Eleanore perpetrated this crime, nor will I be less generous toward her cousin. Mary Leavenworth is a faulty woman, but not a guilty one."

"You are more lenient in your judgment of her than her cousin was, it appears.'"

"I do not understand you," murmured I, feeling a new and yet more fearful light breaking upon me.

"What, have you forgotten, in the hurry of these late events, the sentence of accusation which we overheard uttered between these ladies on the morning of the inquest?"

"No, but——"

"You believed it to have been spoken by Mary to Eleanore?"

"Of course; didn't you?"

Oh, the smile that crossed Mr. Gryce's face! "Scarcely. I left that baby play for you. I thought one was enough to follow on that track."

The light, the light that was breaking upon me! "And do you mean to say," cried I, "that it was Eleanore who was speaking at that time? That I have been laboring all these weeks under a terrible mistake, and that you could have righted me with a word and did not?"

"Well," said he, "as to that, I had a purpose in letting you follow your own lead for awhile. In the first place, I was not myself sure which spoke; though I had but little doubt about the matter. The voices are, as you must have noticed, very much alike, while the attitudes in which we found them upon entering were such as to be explainable equally by the supposition that Mary was in the act of launching a denunciation, or in that of repelling one. So that while I did not hesitate myself as to what was the true explanation of the scene before me, I was pleased to find that you accepted a contrary one; as in this way both theories would have the chance of being tested; as was right in a case of so much mystery. You accordingly took up the affair with one idea for your starting-point, and I with another. You saw every fact as it developed through the medium of Mary's belief in Eleanore's guilt, and I through the contrary. And what has been the result? With you, doubt, contradiction, constant unsettlement, and unwarranted resorts to strange sources of reconcilement between appearances and your own convictions; with me, growing assurance and a belief which each and every development, so far, has but served to strengthen and make more probable."

Again that wild panorama of events, looks and words swept before me. Mary's reiterated assertions of her cousin's innocence; Eleanore's attitude of lofty silence in regard to certain matters which might be considered by her as pointing toward the murderer.

"Your theory must be the correct one," said I at last, "it was undoubtedly Eleanore who spoke. She believes in Mary's guilt, and I have been blind indeed not to have seen it from the first."

"If Eleanore Leavenworth believes in her cousin's criminality, she must have some good reason for doing so."

I was obliged to admit that, too.

"She did not conceal in her bosom that telltale key—found who knows where—and destroy, or seek to destroy, it and the letter which introduced her cousin to the public as the cruel unprincipled destroyer of a trusting man's peace, for nothing."

"No, no."

"And yet, you, a stranger, a young man who have never seen Mary Leavenworth in any other light than that in which her coquettish nature sought to display itself, presume to say she is innocent in the face of the attitude maintained by Eleanore Leavenworth from the first."

"But," said I, in my great unwillingness to accept his conclusions, "Eleanore Leavenworth is but mortal. She may have been mistaken in her inferences. She has never stated what her suspicion was founded upon, nor can we know what basis she has for maintaining the attitude you speak of. Clavering is as likely to be the assassin as Mary, for all we know, and possibly for all she knows."

"You seem to be almost superstitious in your belief in Clavering's guilt."

I recoiled. Was I? Could it be that Mr. Harwell's fanciful conviction in regard to this man had in any way influenced me to the detriment of my better judgment?

"And you may be right," Mr. Gryce went on; "I do not pretend to be set in my notions. Future investigation may succeed in fixing something upon him, though I hardly think it likely. His behavior as the secret husband of a woman possessing motives for the commission of a crime has been too consistent throughout."

"All except his leaving her."

"No exception at all, for he hasn't left her."

"What do you mean?"

"I mean that instead of leaving the country, Mr. Clavering has only made pretense of doing so. That in place of dragging himself off to Europe at her command, he has only changed his lodgings, and can now be found, not only in a house opposite hers, but in the window of that house, where he sits day after day watching who goes in and out of her front door."

I remembered his parting injunction to me in that memorable interview we had in my office, and saw myself compelled to put a new construction upon it.

"But I was assured at the Hoffman House that he had sailed for Europe, and myself saw the man who professes to have driven him to the steamer."

"Just so."

"And Mr. Clavering returned to the city after that?"

"In another carriage, and to another house."

"And you tell me that man is all right?" said I.

"No," returned he, "I only say there isn't the shadow of evidence against him as the person who shot Mr. Leavenworth."

Rising, I paced the floor, and for a few minutes silence fell between us. But the clock striking recalled me to the necessity of the hour and, turning, I asked Mr. Gryce what he proposed to do now.

"There is but one thing I can do," returned he.

"And that is?"

"To go upon such lights as I have, and cause the arrest of Miss Leavenworth."

I had by this time schooled myself to endurance and was

able to hear this without uttering an exclamation. But I could not let it pass without making one effort to combat his determination.

"But," said I, "I do not see what evidence you have positive enough in its character to warrant you in such action. You have yourself intimated that the existence of motive is not enough, even though taken with the fact of the suspected party being in the house at the time of the murder, and what more have you to urge against Miss Leavenworth?"

"Pardon me," he interrupted. "I said, 'Miss Leavenworth.' I should have said 'Eleanore Leavenworth.'"

"Eleanore? What, when you and all unite in thinking that she alone of all these parties to the crime is utterly guiltless of wrong?"

"And yet who is the only one upon whom anything has, as yet, been fixed."

I could but acknowledge that.

"Mr. Raymond," he remarked very gravely, "the public is becoming clamorous; something must be done to satisfy it, if only for the moment. Eleanore has laid herself open to the suspicion of the police and must take the consequences of her action. I am sorry; she is a noble creature, I admire her; but justice is justice, and though I think her innocent I shall be forced to put her under arrest unless——"

"But I cannot be reconciled to it," cried I. "It is doing an irretrievable injury to one whose only fault is an undue and mistaken devotion to an unworthy cousin. If Mary is the——"

"Unless something occurs between now and tomorrow morning," Mr. Gryce went on, as if I had not spoken.

"Tomorrow morning?"

"Yes."

I tried to realize it, tried to face the fact that all my efforts had been for nothing, and failed.

"Will you not grant me one more day?" I asked in my desperation.

"What to do?"

Alas, I did not know. "To confront Mr. Clavering and force from him the truth."

"To make a mess of the whole affair," cried he. "No, sir; the die is cast. Eleanore Leavenworth knows the one point which fixes this crime upon her cousin, and she must tell us that point or suffer the consequences of her refusal."

I made one more effort.

"But why tomorrow? Having exhausted so much time already in our inquiries, why not take a little more; especially as we are constantly growing warmer upon the trail? A little more moleing——"

"A little more folderol!" exclaimed Mr. Gryce, losing his temper. "No, sir; the hour for moleing has passed; something decisive has got to be done now; though to be sure if I could find the one missing link I want——"

"Missing link? What is that?"

"The immediate motive of the tragedy; a bit of proof that Mr. Leavenworth threatened his niece with his displeasure or Mr. Clavering with his revenge, would lift me right up on to the spot I want to be; no arresting of Eleanore then. No, my lady, I would walk right into your own gilded parlors, and when you asked me if I had found the murderer yet, say, 'Yes,' and show you a bit of paper that would surprise you, I'm thinking. But missing links are not so easily found. This has been moled for, and moled for, as you are pleased to call our system of investigation, and totally without result. Nothing but the confession of some one of these several parties to the crime will give us what we want. I will tell you what I will do," he suddenly cried "Miss Leavenworth has desired me to report to her; she is very anxious for the detection of the murderer, you know, and offers an immense reward. Well, I will gratify this desire of hers. The suspicions I have, together with my reasons for them, will make an interesting disclosure. I should not greatly wonder if they produced an equally interesting confession."

I could only jump to my feet in my horror.

"At all events I propose to try it. Eleanore is worth that much risk, anyway."

"It will do no good," said I. "If Mary is guilty, she will never confess it. If not——"

"She will tell us who is."

"No," said I, "not if it is Clavering, her husband."

"Yes," returned he, "even if it is Clavering, her husband. She has not the devotion of Eleanore."

That I could but acknowledge. She would hide no keys for the sake of shielding another; no, if Mary were accused she would speak. The future opening before us looked somber enough. And yet, when in a short time from that I found myself alone in the busy street, the thought that Eleanore was free rose above all others, filling and moving me till my walk home in the rain that day has become a marked memory of my life. It was only with nightfall that I began to realize the truly critical position in which Mary stood if Mr. Gryce's theory was correct. But once seized with this thought, nothing could drive it from my mind. Shrink as I would, it was ever before me, haunting me with the direst forebodings. Nor, though I retired early, could I succeed in getting either sleep or rest. All night I tossed on my pillow, saying over to myself with dreary iteration: "Something must happen, something will happen to prevent Mr. Gryce doing this dreadful thing." Then I would start up and ask what there was that could happen, and my mind would run over the various contingencies which might occur, as—Mr. Clavering might confess; Hannah might come back; Mary herself wake up to her position and speak the word I had seen trembling on her lips for so long. But further thought showed me how unlikely any of these things were to happen, and it was with a brain utterly exhausted that I fell asleep in the early dawn, to dream I saw Mary standing above Mr. Gryce with a pistol in her hand. I was awakened from this pleasing vision by a heavy knock at the door. Hastily rising, I asked who was there. The answer came in the shape of an envelope thrust under the door. Raising it, I found it to be a note. It was from Mr. Gryce, and ran thus:

Come at once; Hannah Chester is found.

"Hannah found?"

"So we have reason to think."

"When? Where? By whom?"

"Sit down, and I will tell you."

Drawing up a chair in a flurry of hope and fear, I sat down by Mr. Gryce's side.

"She is not in the cupboard," that personage exclaimed, observing without doubt how my eyes went traveling about the room in my anxiety and impatience. "We are not absolutely sure that she's anywhere. But word has come to us that a girl's face, believed to be Hannah's, has been seen at the upper window of a certain house in—don't start—R——, where a year ago she was in the habit of visiting while at the hotel with the Misses Leavenworth. Now, as it has already been determined that she left New York the night of the murder, by the —— —— railroad, though for what point we have been unable to ascertain, we consider the matter worth inquiring into."

"But——"

"If she is there," went on Mr. Gryce, "she is secreted; kept very close. No one except the informant has ever seen her, nor is there any suspicion among the neighbors of her being in town."

"Hannah secreted at a certain house in R——? Whose house?"

Mr. Gryce dowered me with one of his grimmest smiles. "The name of the lady she's with is given in the communication as Belden; Mrs. Amy Belden."

"Amy Belden! The name found written on a torn envelope by Mr. Clavering's servant girl in London?"

"Yes."

I made no attempt to conceal my satisfaction. "Then we are upon the verge of some discovery; Providence has interfered and Eleanore will be saved. But when did you get this word?"

"Last night, or rather, this morning; Q brought it."

"It was a message, then, to Q?"

"Yes, the result of his moleings while in R——, I suppose."

"Who was it signed by?"

"A respectable tinsmith who lives next door to Mrs. B——."

"And is this the first you knew of an Amy Belden living in R——?"

"Yes."

"Widow or wife?"

"Don't know; don't know anything about her but her name."

"But you have already sent Q to make inquiries?"

"No; the affair is a little too serious for him to manage; that is, I hesitate trusting him alone. A contingency might arise when brains would be useful, and though Q has enough of the prying sort, he is not equal to great occasions, and might fail just for the lack of a keen mind to direct him."

"In short——"

"I wish you to go. Since I cannot be there myself, I know of no one else sufficiently up to the affair to conduct the enterprise to a successful issue. You see, it is not enough to find and identify the girl. The present condition of things demands that the arrest of so important a witness as this should be kept secret if possible. Now, for a man to walk into a strange house in a distant village, find a girl who is secreted there, frighten her, cajole her, force her, as the case may be, from her hiding-place to a detective's office in New York, and all without the knowledge of the next-door neighbor, if possible, requires judgment, brains, genius. Then the woman who conceals her! She must have her reasons for doing so, and they must be known. Altogether the affair is a delicate one. Do you think you can manage it?"

"I would at least like to try."

Mr. Gryce settled himself on the sofa. "To think what pleasure I am losing on your account!" he murmured, gazing reproachfully at his helpless limbs. "But to business. How soon can you start?"

"Immediately."

"Good! There is a train leaves the station at twelve-fifteen. Take that. Once in R—— it will be for you to determine upon some means for making Mrs. Belden's acquaintance without arousing her suspicions. Q, who will follow you, will hold himself in readiness to render you any assistance you may require, only this thing is to be understood: as he will doubtless go in disguise, you are not to recognize him, much less interfere with him and his plans, till he gives you leave to do so by some preconcerted signal. You are to work in your way, and he in his, till circumstances seem to require mutual support and countenance. I cannot even say whether you will see him or not; he may find it necessary to keep out of the way; but you may be sure of one thing, that he will know where you are, and that the display of—well, let us say a red silk handkerchief—have you such a thing?"

"I will get one."

"Will be regarded by him as a sign that you desire his presence or assistance, whether it be shown about your person or at the window of your room."

"And these are all the instructions you can give me?" I said as he paused.

"Yes, I don't know of anything else. You must depend largely upon your own discretion, and the exigencies of the moment. I cannot tell you now what to do. Your own wit will be the best guide. Only, if possible, let me either hear from you or see you by tomorrow at this time."

And he handed me a cipher in case I should wish to telegraph.

BOOK III

HANNAH

CHAPTER I

Amy Belden

A merrier man
Within the limits of becoming mirth,
I never spent an hour's talk withal.
—LOVE'S LABOR'S LOST.

It was a bleak day in April that I stepped, for the second time in my life, from the cars at R—— and took my way down the broad, well-populated street leading to the hotel and its sur-rounding villas. Not that I had any intention this time of mak-ing even a casual stop at that attractive refuge for New York pleasure-seekers. My intention was rather to seek out our cli-ent, Mr. Monell, and from him learn the best manner of ap-proaching Mrs. Belden. To his hospitable mansion, then, on the road to F——, I hastened, and was so fortunate as to meet him driving into town behind his famous trotter Alfred; an en-counter, if I may so call it, which struck me as peculiarly fortu-nate, giving me, as it did, ample opportunity for a *tête-à-tête* conversation with him without imposing upon me the delay which a visit to his house must have necessarily occasioned.

"Well, and how goes the day?" was the exclamation of my friend as, the first greetings passed, we drove rapidly into town.

"Your part in it goes pretty smoothly," returned I; and, thinking I could never hope to win his attention to my affairs till I had satisfied him in regard to his own, I told him what I knew concerning his case then pending; a subject so prolific of question and answer that we had driven twice around the town before he remembered that he had a letter to post. As it was an important one admitting of no delay, we hastened at once to the post office, where he went in, leaving me outside to watch the rather meager stream of goers and comers who at that time of day make the post office of a country town their place of rendezvous. Among these, for some reason, I specially noted

one middle-aged woman; why, I cannot say; her appearance
was anything but remarkable. And, yet when she came out
with two letters in her hand, one in a large and one in a small
envelope, and meeting my eye hastily drew them under her
shawl, I found myself wondering what was in her letters and
who she could be, that the casual glance of a stranger should
unconsciously move her to an action so suspicious. But Mr.
Monell's reappearance at the same moment diverted my attention, and in the interest of the conversation that followed I
soon forgot both the woman and her letters. For, determined
that he should have no opportunity to revert to that end-
less topic, a law case, I exclaimed with the first crack of the
whip: "There, I knew there was something I wanted to ask
you. It is this: are you acquainted with anyone in this town by
the name of Belden?"

"There is a widow Belden in town; I don't know of
any other."

"Is her first name Amy?"

"Yes, Mrs. Amy Belden."

"That is the one," said I. "Who is she? What is she? And
what is the extent of your acquaintance with her?"

"Well," said he, "I cannot conceive why you should be interested in such an antiquated piece of commonplace goodness as
she is, but seeing you ask, I have no objection to telling you
that she is the very respectable relict of a deceased cabinet-maker
of this town; that she lives in a little house down the street
there; and that if you have any forlorn old tramp to be lodged
overnight, or any destitute family of little ones to be looked
after, she is the one to go to. As to knowing her, I know her as
I do a dozen other members of our church there up over the
hill. When I see her, I speak to her, and that is all."

"A respectable widow, you say. Any family?"

"No; lives alone; has a little income, I believe; must have, to
put the money on the plate she always does; but spends her
time in plain sewing and such deeds of charity as one with small
means but willing heart can find the opportunity of doing in a
town like this. But why, in the name of wonders, do you ask?"

"Business," said I, "business. Mrs. Belden—don't mention
it, by the way—has got mixed up in a case of mine, and I felt it

due to my curiosity, if not to my purse, to find out something about her. And I am not satisfied yet. The fact is, I would give something, Monell, for the opportunity of studying this woman's character. Now, couldn't you manage to get me introduced into her house in some way that would make it possible and proper for me to converse with her at my leisure? Business would thank you if you could."

"Well, I don't know; I suppose it could be done. She used to take lodgers in the summer when the hotel was full, and might be induced to give a bed to a friend of mine who is very anxious to be near the post office on account of a business telegram he is expecting, and which, when it comes, will demand his immediate attention." And Mr. Monell gave me a sly wink of his eye, little imagining how near the mark he had really struck.

"You need not say that. Tell her that I have a peculiar dislike to sleeping in a public-house, and that you knew of no one who could better accommodate me for the short time I desire to be in town, than herself."

"And what will be said of my hospitality in allowing you under those circumstances to remain in any other house than my own?"

"I don't know," returned I; "very hard things, I doubt, but I guess your hospitality can stand it."

"Well, if you persist, we will see what can be done." And, driving up to a neat white cottage of homely but sufficiently attractive appearance, he stopped.

"This is her house," said he, jumping to the ground. "Let's go in and see what we can do."

Glancing up at the windows which were all closed save the two on the veranda overlooking the street, I thought to myself: "If she has anybody in hiding here, whose presence in the house she desires to keep secret, it is folly to hope she will take me in, however well recommended I may come." But yielding to the example of my friend, I alighted, in my turn, and followed him up the short grass-bordered walk to the front door.

"As she has no servant, she will come to the door herself, so be ready," said he as he knocked.

I had barely time to observe that the curtains to the window at my left suddenly dropped, when a hasty step made itself heard within, and a quick hand threw open the door, and I saw before me the woman whom I had observed at the post office, and whose action with the letters had struck me as being peculiar. I recognized her at first glance, though she was differently dressed and had evidently passed through some worry or excitement that had altered the expression of her countenance and made her manner what it was not at that time, strained and a trifle uncertain. But I saw no reason for thinking that she remembered me. On the contrary, the look she directed toward me had nothing but inquiry in it, and when Mr. Monell pushed me forward with the remark: "A friend of mine; in fact, my lawyer from New York," she dropped a hurried old-fashioned curtsey, whose only expression was a manifest desire to appear sensible of the honor conferred upon her, through the mist of a certain trouble that confused everything about her.

"We have come to ask a favor, Mrs. Belden; but may we not come in?" said my client in a round, hearty voice, well calculated to recall a person's thoughts into their proper channel. "I have heard many a time of your cozy home and would like an opportunity to see it." And, with a blind disregard to the look of surprised resistance that rose involuntarily into her eyes, he stepped gallantly into the little room whose cheery red carpet and bright picture-hung walls showed invitingly through the half-open door at our left.

Finding her premises thus invaded by a sort of French *coup d'état,* Mrs. Belden made the best of the situation and, pressing me to enter also, devoted herself to hospitality. As for Mr. Monell, he quite blossomed out in his endeavors to make himself agreeable; so much so, that I shortly found myself laughing at his sallies, though my heart was full of anxiety lest, after all, our efforts should fail of the success they certainly merited. Meanwhile, Mrs. Belden softened more and more, joining in the conversation with an ease hardly to be expected from one in her humble circumstances. Indeed, I soon saw that she was no common woman. There was a refinement in her speech and manner that, combined with her motherly presence and gentle air, was very pleasing. The last woman in the world I should ever have suspected of any underhanded proceeding, if I had not marked the peculiar look of hesitation that crossed her face when Mr. Monell broached the subject of my entertainment there.

"I don't know, sir; I would be glad, but," and she turned a very scrutinizing look upon me, "the fact is, I have not taken lodgers of late, and I have got out of the way of the whole thing, and am afraid I cannot make him comfortable. In short, you will have to excuse me."

"But we can't," returned Mr. Monell. "What, entice a fellow into a room like this"—and he cast a hearty admiring glance round the apartment, which for all its simplicity, both its warm coloring and general air of cosiness amply merited, "and then turn a cold shoulder upon him when he humbly entreats the honor of staying one poor, little, pitiful night in the enjoyment of its attractions? No, no, Mrs. Belden, I know you too well for that. Lazarus himself couldn't come to your door and be turned away, much less a good-hearted, clever-headed gentleman like my friend here."

"You are very good," she began, an almost weak love of praise showing itself for a moment in her eyes, "but I have no room prepared: I have been house-cleaning and everything is topsy-turvy. Mrs. Wright, now, over the way——"

"My young friend is going to stop here," Mr. Monell broke in with frank positiveness. "If I cannot have him at my own house, and for certain reasons it seems that I cannot, I shall at least have the satisfaction of knowing he is in the charge of the best housekeeper in R——"

"Yes," I put in, but without too great a show of interest, "I should be sorry, once introduced here, to be obliged to go elsewhere."

The troubled eye wavered away from us to the door.

"I was never called inhospitable," she commenced, "but everything in such disorder—— What time would you like to come?" she suddenly asked.

"I was in hopes I might remain now," replied I; "I have some letters to write and would ask nothing better than for leave to sit here and write them."

At the word letters I saw her hand go to her pocket in a movement which must have been involuntary, for her countenance did not change, and she made the quick reply:

"Well, you may. If you can put up with what I can give you, why, it shall not be said that I refused you what Mr. Monell is pleased to call a favor." And, complete in her reception as she had been in her resistance, she gave us a pleasant smile and, ignoring my thanks, bustled out with Mr. Monell to the buggy, where she received my bag and, what was doubtless more to her taste, the compliments he was now more than ever ready to bestow upon her.

"I will see that some room is got ready for you in a very short space of time," she said upon re-entering. "Meanwhile, make yourself at home here and, if you wish to write, why, I think you will find everything for the purpose in these drawers." And, wheeling up a table to the easy chair in which I sat, she pointed to the small compartments beneath with an air of such manifest desire that I should make use of anything and everything she had, that I found myself wondering over my position with a sort of startled embarrassment that was not remote from shame.

"Thank you," said I; "I have materials of my own." And I hastened to open my bag and bring out the writing-case which I always carried with me.

"Then I will leave you," said she; and with a quick bend and a short hurried look out of the window she hastily quitted the room.

I could hear her steps cross the hall, go up two or three stairs, pause, go up the rest of the flight, pause again, and then pass on. I was left on the first floor alone.

CHAPTER 2

A Weird Experience

Flat burglary as ever was committed.
—MUCH ADO ABOUT NOTHING.

The first thing I did was to inspect the room in which I was.

It was a pleasant apartment, as I have said before, square, sunny, and well furnished, impressing one as he entered with a general air of welcome and home likeness. On the floor was a crimson carpet, on the walls several pictures, at the windows cheerful curtains of white, tastefully ornamented with ferns and autumn leaves, in one corner an old melodeon, and in the center of the room a table draped with a bright cloth, on which were various little knick-knacks which, without being rich or expensive, were both pretty and, to a certain extent, ornamental. But it was not these things, which I had seen repeated in so many other country homes, that especially attracted my attention, or drew me forward in the slow march which I undertook around the room. It was something underneath all these, the evidences which I found, or sought to find, not only in the general aspect of the whole, but in each trivial object itself, of the character, disposition, and history of the woman with whom I now had to deal. It was for this reason I studied the daguerreotypes on the mantelpiece, the books on the shelf, and the music on the rack; for this and the still further purpose of noting if any indications were to be found of there being in the house any such person as Hannah.

First, then, for the little library, which I was pleased to see occupied one corner of the room. Composed of a few well-chosen books, poetical, historical, and narrative, it was of itself sufficient to account for the evidences of latent culture observable in Mrs. Belden's conversation. Taking out a well-worn copy of Byron, I opened it. There were many passages marked, and replacing the book with a mental comment upon her evident impressibility to the softer emotions, I turned toward the melodeon that fronted me from the opposite wall. It was closed, but on its neatly covered top lay one or two hymn-books, a basket of russet apples, and a piece of half-completed knitting-work.

I took up the latter, but was forced to lay it down again without coming to the remotest idea of what it was intended to be. Proceeding on, I next stopped before a window opening upon the small yard that ran about the house, and separated it from the one adjoining. Looking out, I thought of the many glances of curiosity, dismay, anger, joy, sorrow, disappointment that had pierced their way from that spot to the street beyond since the building was tenanted, and that especial window set apart for the rocking-chair and worktable, when suddenly I espied, written on the glass with a diamond-point, a row of letters which, as nearly as I could make out, were meant for some word or words, but which utterly failed in sense or apparent connection. Passing it by as the work of some schoolgirl, I glanced down at the workbasket standing on a table at my side. It was full of various kinds of work, among which I spied a pair of stockings, which were much too small, as well as in too great a state of disrepair, to belong to Mrs. Belden, or so I thought; and drawing them carefully out, I examined them to see if I could find any name marked on them. Do not start when I say that I saw the letter H plainly printed upon them. Thrusting them back, I drew a deep breath of relief, gazing, as I did so, out of the window, when those letters again attracted my attention.

Gnirevalc Yram

What could they mean? Idly I began to read them backward, when—But try for yourself, reader, and judge what my surprise must have been at the result! Elated at the discovery thus made, I sat down to write my letters. I had barely finished them, when Mrs. Belden came in with the announcement that supper was ready. "As for your room," said she, "I have prepared my own for your use, thinking it would be more convenient for you to be on the first floor." And throwing open a door at my side, she displayed a small but comfortable room, in which I could dimly see a bed, an immense bureau, and a shadowy looking-glass in a dark old-fashioned frame.

"I live in very primitive fashion," resumed she, leading the way into the dining room, "but I mean to be comfortable, and make others so."

"I should say that you amply succeeded," I rejoined with an appreciative glance at her well-spread board.

She smiled, and I felt that I had paved the way to her good graces, in a way that would yet redound to my advantage.

Shall I ever forget that supper! its dainties, its pleasant freedom, its mysterious, pervading atmosphere of unreality, and the constant sense which every bountiful dish she pressed upon me brought of the shame of eating this woman's food, with such feelings of suspicion in my heart! Shall I ever forget the emotion I experienced, when I first perceived she had something on her mind, which she longed, yet hesitated to give utterance to! Or how she started when a cat jumped down from the sloping roof of the kitchen on to the grass-plot at the back of the house, or how my heart throbbed when I heard, or thought I heard, a board creak overhead! We were in a little room, long and narrow, which seemed, curiously enough, to run cross-wise of the house, opening on one side into the parlor, whose gloomy, half-lighted interior did not add much to the cheerfulness of the hour, and on the other into the small bedroom, which had been allotted to my use.

"You live in this house alone, without fear?" I asked, as Mrs. Belden, contrary to my desire, put another bit of cold chicken on my plate. "Have you no marauders in this town, no tramps, of whom a solitary woman like you might reasonably be afraid?"

"No one will hurt me," said she, "and no one ever came here for food or shelter, but got it."

"I should think, then, that living, as you do, upon a railroad, you would be constantly overrun with worthless beings, whose only trade is to take all they can get, without giving a return."

"I cannot turn them away," she said; "it is the only luxury I have, to feed the poor."

"But the idle, restless ones, who neither will work, nor let others work——"

"Are still the poor."

Mentally remarking, here is the woman to shield an unfortunate who has somehow become entangled in the meshes of a
great crime, I drew back from the table. As I did so, the thought
crossed me, that in case there was any such person in the house
as Hannah, she would take the opportunity of going upstairs
with something for her to eat; and I cast a calculating glance at
the plates of bread and cold chicken before me, in the hope of
being able to tell if anything should be hereafter subtracted
from them.

"I will smoke my cigar on the veranda," said I; "after
which I hope you will be at leisure to sit down with me for a
short chat."

"Thank you," returned she, almost eagerly, the desire of making some avowal showing itself plainer than ever in her manner.
"But do not go out on the veranda, unless you wish. I have no
morbid dread of smoke, if I am a housekeeper."

"I prefer the veranda," said I; "a whiff of fresh air is just
what I want."

The truth was, I was becoming anxious about Q. I felt that
the least token of his presence in town would be very encouraging. But it seemed that I was not to be afforded even that small
satisfaction. In vain I tramped the veranda from end to end; I
neither saw nor heard the short, quick laugh I half-expected to
fall upon my ears from some unknown quarter. If Q was anywhere near, he was lying very low.

Once again seated with Mrs. Belden (who I know came
downstairs with an empty plate, for going into the kitchen for
a drink, I caught her in the act of setting it down on the table)
I made up my mind to wait a reasonable length of time for
what she had to say, and then, if she did not speak, make an
endeavor on my own part to get at her secret.

But the avowal was nearer than I expected, and different,
and brought its own train of consequences with it.

"You are a lawyer, I believe," she began, taking down her
knitting work, with a forced display of industry.

"Yes," said I, "that is my profession."

She remained for a moment silent, creating great havoc in

her work I am sure, from the glance of surprise and vexation she afterward threw it. Then in a hesitating voice, remarked:

"Perhaps you may be willing, then, to give me some advice. The truth is, I am in a very curious predicament; one from which I don't know how to escape, and yet which demands immediate action. I should like to tell you about it, may I?"

"You may; I shall be only too happy to give you any advice in my power."

She drew in her breath with a sort of vague relief, though her forehead did not lose its frown.

"It can all be said in a few words. I have in my possession a packet of papers which were entrusted to me by two ladies, with the understanding that I should neither return nor destroy them, without the full cognizance and expressed desire of both parties, given in person or writing. That they were to remain in my hands till then, and that nothing or nobody should extort them from me."

"That is easily understood," said I, for she stopped.

"But now comes word from one of the ladies, the one, too, most interested in the matter, that for certain reasons, the immediate destruction of those papers is necessary to her peace and safety."

"And do you want to know what your duty is in that case?"

"Yes," replied she tremulously.

I rose, I could not help it, a flood of conjectures rushing in tumult over me.

"It is to hold on to the papers like grim death, till released from your guardianship, by the means to which you have pledged yourself."

"Is that your opinion, as a lawyer?"

"Yes, and as a man. Once pledged in that way, you have no choice. It would be a betrayal of trust, to yield to the solicitations of one party, what you have undertaken to return to both. The fact that grief or loss might follow your retention of these papers does not release you from your bond. You have nothing to do with that; besides, you are by no means sure that the representations of the so-called interested party are true. You might be doing a greater wrong by destroying in this way what is manifestly considered of value to them both, than by preserving the papers intact, according to compact."

"But the circumstances? Circumstances alter cases, and in short, it seems to me that the wishes of the one most interested ought to be regarded, especially as there is an estrangement between these ladies, which may hinder the other's consent from ever being obtained."

"No," said I, "two wrongs never make a right; nor are we at liberty to do an act of justice, at the expense of an injustice. The papers must be preserved, Mrs. Belden."

Her head sank very despondingly; evidently it had been her wish to please the interested party. "Law is very hard," she said, "very hard."

"This is not only law, but plain duty," I remarked. "Suppose a case different, suppose the honor and happiness of the other party depended upon the preservation of the papers, where would your duty be then?"

"But——"

"A contract is a contract," said I, "and cannot be tampered with. Having accepted the trust and given your word, you are obliged to fulfill to the letter all its conditions. It would be a breach of trust for you to return or destroy the papers without the mutual consent necessary."

An expression of great gloom settled slowly over her features. "I suppose you are right," said she and became silent.

Watching her, I thought to myself: "If I were Mr. Gryce or even Q, I would never leave this seat till I had probed this matter to the bottom, learned who the parties are, and where those precious papers are hidden, that seem to be of so much importance." But being neither, I could only keep her talking upon the subject until she should let fall some word that might serve as a guide to my further enlightenment; I therefore turned with the intention of asking her some question, when my attention was attracted by the figure of a woman coming out of the back door of the neighboring house, who for general dilapidation, and uncouthness of bearing, was a perfect type of the style of tramp of whom we had been talking at the supper-table. Gnawing a crust which she threw away as she reached the street, she trudged down the path, her scanty dress, piteous in its rags and soil, flapping in the keen spring wind, and revealing ragged shoes red with the mud of the highway.

"There is a customer," said I, "that may interest you."

Mrs. Belden seemed to awake from a trance. Rising slowly she looked out, and with a rapidly softening gaze surveyed the forlorn creature before her.

"Poor thing!" she muttered; "there is a case for charity, to be sure. But I cannot do much for her tonight," she cried as the woman stopped at the gate. "A good supper is all I can give her."

And going to the front door she bade her step round the house to the kitchen, where in another moment I heard the rough creature's voice rise in one long "Bless you!" that could only have been produced by the setting before her of the good things with which Mrs. Belden's larder seemed to be teeming.

But supper was not all she wanted. After a decent length of time employed as I should judge in mastication, I heard her voice rise once more in a plea for shelter.

"The barn, ma'am," I heard her say, "or the wood-house, any place where I can lie out of the wind." And she commenced a long tale of want and disease, so piteous to hear, that I was not at all surprised when Mrs. Belden told me, upon reentering, that she had consented, notwithstanding her previous determination, to allow the woman to lie before the kitchen fire for the night.

"She has such an honest eye," said she, "and charity is my only luxury, you know."

The interruption of this incident effectually broke up our conversation. Mrs. Belden went upstairs and for some time I was left alone to ponder over what I had heard, and determine upon my future course of action. I had just reached the conclusion that she would be fully as liable to be carried away by her feelings to the destruction of the papers in her charge, as to be governed by the rules of equity I had laid down for her, when I heard her stealthily descend the stairs and go out of the front door. Distrustful of her intentions, I took my hat and hastily followed her. She was on her way down the main street, and my first thought was that she was bound for some neighbor's house or perhaps for the hotel itself; but the settled swing into which she soon altered her restless pace satisfied me that she had some more distant goal in prospect; and before long I found myself passing the hotel with its appurtenances, even the little school-house that was the last building at this end of the village, and stepping out into the country beyond. What could it mean?

But still her fluttering figure hastened on, the outlines of her form with its close shawl and neat bonnet growing fainter and fainter in the now settled darkness of an April night, and still I followed, walking on the turf at the side of the road lest she should hear my footsteps and look round. At last we reached a bridge. Over this I could hear her pass, and then every sound ceased. She had paused and was evidently listening. It would not do for me to pause, too, so gathering myself into as awkward a shape as possible, I sauntered by her down the road; but arrived at a certain point, stopped and began retracing my steps with a sharp look-out for her advancing figure, till I had arrived once more at the bridge. She was not there.

Convinced now that she had discovered my motive for being in her house, and by leading me from it, had undertaken to supply Hannah with an opportunity to escape, I was about to hasten back to the charge I had so incautiously left, when a strange sound heard at my left arrested me. It came from the banks of the puny stream which ran under the bridge, and was like the creaking of an old door on worn-out hinges.

Leaping the fence I made my way as best I could down the sloping field in the direction from which the sound had come. It was quite dark, and my progress was slow; so much so, that I began to fear I had ventured upon a wild-goose chase, when an unexpected streak of lightning shot across the sky, and by its glare I saw before me what seemed, in the momentary glimpse I had of it, to be an old barn. From the rush of waters near at hand, I judged that it was built on the edge of the stream, and consequently hesitated to advance, when I heard the sound of heavy breathing near me, followed by a stir as of someone feeling his way over a pile of loose boards, and presently while I stood there, a faint blue light flashed up from the interior of the barn, and I saw through the tumbled-down door that faced me the form of Mrs. Belden standing with a lighted

match in her hand, gazing round on the four walls that encom-
passed her. Hardly daring to breathe lest I should alarm her, I
watched her while she turned and peered at the roof above her,
which was so old as to be more than half-open to the sky, at
the flooring beneath which was in a state of equal dilapidation,
and finally at a small tin box which she drew from under her
shawl and laid on the ground at her feet. The sight of that box
at once satisfied me as to the nature of her errand. She was
going to hide what she dared not destroy; and relieved upon
this point, I was about to take a step forward, when the match
went out in her hand. While she was engaged in lighting another, I considered that perhaps it would be better for me not
to arouse her apprehensions by accosting her at this time and
thus endanger the success of my main scheme, but to wait till
she was gone, before I endeavored to secure the box. Accordingly I edged my way up to the side of the barn and waited till
she should leave it, knowing that if I attempted to peer in at
the door, I ran great risk of being seen, owing to the frequent streaks of lightning which now flashed about us on
every side. Minute after minute went by with its weird alternations of heavy darkness and sudden glare; and still she did not
come. At last, just as I was about to start impatiently from my
hiding-place, she reappeared and began to withdraw with fal-
tering steps toward the bridge. When I thought her quite out of
hearing, I stole from my retreat and entered the barn. It was, of
course, as dark as Erebus, but thanks to being a smoker I was
as well provided with matches as she had been, and having
struck one, I held it up; but the light it gave was very feeble,
and as I did not know just where to look, it went out before I
had obtained more than a cursory glimpse of the spot where I
was. I thereupon lit another, but though I confined my attention to one place, namely, the floor at my feet, it too went out
before I could conjecture, by means of any sign seen there,
where she had hidden the box. I now for the first time realized
the difficulty before me. She had probably made up her mind
before she left home, in just what portion of this old barn
she would conceal her treasure; but I had nothing to guide me:
I could only waste matches. And I did waste them. A dozen
had been lit and extinguished before I was so much as sure the

box was not under a pile of debris that lay in one corner, and I had taken the last in my hand, before I became aware that one of the broken boards of the floor was pushed a little out of its proper position. One match! and that board was to be raised, the space beneath examined, and the box, if there, lifted safely out.

I concluded not to waste my resources, so kneeling down in the darkness, I groped for the board, tried it and found it to be loose. Wrenching at it with all my strength, I tore it free and cast it aside: then lighting my match looked into the hole thus made. Something, I could not tell what, stone or box, met my eye, but while I reached for it, the match flew out of my hand. Deploring my carelessness, but determined at all hazards to secure what I had seen, I dived down deep into the hole, and in another moment had the object of my curiosity in my hands. It was the box.

Satisfied at this result of my efforts, I turned to depart, my one wish now being to arrive home before Mrs. Belden. Was it possible? She had several minutes the start of me; I would have to pass her on the road and in so doing might be recognized. Was the end worth the risk? I decided that it was.

Regaining the highway I started at a brisk pace. For some little distance I kept it up, neither overtaking nor meeting anyone. But suddenly at a turn in the road I came unexpectedly upon Mrs. Belden standing in the middle of the path, looking back. Somewhat disconcerted, I hastened swiftly by her, expecting, of course, that she would make some effort to stop me. But she let me pass without a word. Indeed, I doubt now if she even saw or heard me. Astonished at this treatment, and still more surprised that she made no attempt to follow me, I looked back, when I saw what it was that enchained her to the spot, and made her so unmindful of my presence. The barn behind us was on fire!

Instantly I realized that it was the work of my hands; I had dropped a half-extinguished match, and it had fallen upon some inflammable substance.

Aghast at the sight, I paused in my turn and stood staring. Higher and higher the red flames mounted, brighter and brighter glowed the clouds above the stream beneath; and in the fascination of watching it all, I forgot Mrs. Belden. But a short agitated gasp from her soon recalled her presence to mind, and drawing nearer, I heard her exclaim like a person speaking in a dream: "Well, I didn't mean to do it," then lower, and with a certain satisfaction in her tone, "but it's all right anyway; the thing is now lost for good, and Mary will be satisfied without anyone being to blame."

I did not linger to hear more; if that was the conclusion she had come to, she would not wait there long, especially as the sound of distant shouts and running feet announced that a crowd of village boys was on its way to the scene of conflagration.

The first thing I did upon my arrival at the house was to assure myself that no evil effects had followed my inconsiderate desertion of it to the mercies of the tramp she had taken in; the next to retire to my room and take a peep at the box. I found it to be a neat, tin coffer, fastened with a lock. Satisfied from its weight that it contained nothing heavier than the papers of which Mrs. Belden had spoken, I hid it under the bed and returned to the sitting room. I had barely taken a seat and lifted a book when Mrs. Belden came in.

"Well!" cried she, taking off her bonnet and revealing a face much flushed with exercise but greatly relieved in expression; "this *is* a night! It lightens, and there is a fire somewhere down street, and altogether it is perfectly dreadful out. I hope you have not been lonesome," continued she with a keen look at my face, which I bore in the best way I could. "I had an errand to attend to, but didn't expect to stay so long."

I returned some nonchalant reply, and she hastened from the room to fasten up the house.

I waited, but she did not come back; fearful perhaps of betraying herself, she had retired to her own apartment, leaving me to take care of myself as best I might. I own that I was rather relieved at this. The fact is, I did not feel equal to any more excitement that night, and was glad to put off further action until the next day. As soon, then, as the storm was over I myself went to bed, and after several ineffectual efforts, succeeded in getting asleep.

CHAPTER 3

The Missing Witness

I fled and cried out death.
—Milton.

"Mr. Raymond!"

The voice was low and searching, it reached me in my dreams, waked me and caused me to look up. Morning had begun to break, and by its light I saw standing in the open door leading into the dining room the forlorn figure of the tramp who had been admitted into the house the night before. Angry and perplexed, I was about to bid her begone, when to my great surprise she pulled out a red handkerchief from her pocket and I recognized Q.

"Read that," said he, hastily advancing and putting a slip of paper into my hand. And without another word or look he left the room, closing the door behind him.

Rising in considerable agitation I took it to the window, and by the rapidly increasing light succeeded in making out the rudely scrawled lines as follows:

"She is here; I have seen her; in the room marked with a cross in the accompanying plan. Wait till eight o'clock, then go up. I will contrive some means of getting Mrs. B—— out of the house."

Sketched below this was the following plan of the upper floor.

Hannah, then, was in the small back room over the dining room and I had not been deceived when I imagined that I heard steps overhead the evening before. Greatly relieved and yet at the same time much moved at the near prospect of being brought face to face with the one who there was every reason to believe was acquainted with the dreadful secret involved in the Leavenworth murder, I lay down once more and endeavored to catch another hour's rest. But one might as well try to sleep watching the approach of an enemy with his hand on the trigger of a pistol! I soon gave up the effort in despair and contented myself with listening to the sounds of awakening life which now began to make themselves heard in the house and neighborhood.

As Q had closed the door after him, I could only faintly hear Mrs. Belden when she came downstairs. But the short surprised exclamation which she uttered upon reaching the kitchen and finding the tramp gone and the back door wide open came plainly enough to my ears, and for a moment I was not sure but that Q had made a mistake in thus leaving so unceremoniously. But he had not studied Mrs. Belden's character in vain the night before. As she came in the course of her preparation for breakfast into the room adjoining mine, I could hear her murmur to herself:

"Poor thing! she has lived so long in the fields and at the roadside, she finds it unnatural to be cooped up in the house all night."

The trial of that breakfast! The effort to eat and appear unconcerned, to chat and make no mistake. May I never be called upon to go through such another. But at last it was over and I was left free to await in my own room the time for the dreaded though much to be desired interview. Slowly the minutes passed, eight o'clock struck, when just as the last vibration ceased, there came a loud knock at the back door, and a little boy burst into the kitchen crying at the top of his voice: "Papa's got a fit! Oh, Mrs. Belden, papa's got a fit, do come."

Rising as was natural, I hastened toward the kitchen, meeting Mrs. Belden's serious face in the doorway.

"A poor wood-chopper down the street has fallen in a fit," she said, "and they have sent for me. Will you please watch over the house while I am gone? I won't be absent any longer than I can help."

And almost without waiting for my reply, she caught up a shawl from off the chair, threw it over her head and followed the urchin, who was in a state of great excitement, out into the street.

Instantly the silence of death seemed to fill the house, and a dread, the greatest I had ever experienced, settled upon me. To leave the kitchen, go up those stairs and confront that girl, seemed for the moment beyond my power. I could not have hesitated more had I been about to lift a curtain that enshrouded the corpse of all I held dearest upon earth. And yet I was conscious of eagerly longing to know the worst, and of an emotion strong as either, of utter thankfulness for Eleanore's sake that all had come around so easily and well. It was some seconds before I could muster up courage to face the duty before me, but once on the stair, I found myself relieved from the especial dread which had overwhelmed me, and possessed instead a sort of combative curiosity that led me to throw open the door which I saw at the top with a certain fierceness new to my nature and not altogether suitable, perhaps, to the occasion.

I found myself in a large bedroom, evidently the one occupied by Mrs. Belden the night before. Barely stopping to note certain evidences which were apparent of her having passed a restless night, I passed on to the door leading into the room marked with a cross in the plan drawn for me by Q. It was a rough affair, made of pine boards and rudely painted, as though it had been put up in a hurry long after the rest of the house was finished. Pausing before it, I listened. All was still. Raising the latch I endeavored to enter. The door was locked. Pausing again, I bent my ear to the keyhole. Not a sound came from within; the grave itself could not have been stiller. Awe-struck and irresolute, I looked about me and questioned what I had best do. Suddenly I remembered that in the plan Q had given me, I had seen an intimation of another door leading into this same room from the one on the opposite side of the hall. Going hastily around to it, I tried it with my hand as I had the one before. But this was also fastened. Convinced at last that nothing was left but force, I spoke for the first time and calling the girl by name, commanded her to open the door. Receiving no response, I said aloud with an accent of severity:

"Hannah Chester, you are discovered; if you do not open the door, we shall be obliged to break it down; save us the trouble, then, and open immediately." Still no reply.

Going back a step I threw my whole weight against the door. It creaked ominously but still resisted. Stopping only long enough to be sure no movement had taken place within, I pressed against it once more, this time with all my strength, when it flew from its hinges and I fell forward into a room so stifling, chill, and dark that I paused for a moment to collect my scattered senses before venturing to look around me. It was well I did so. In another moment the pallor and fixity of the pretty Irish face staring upon me from amidst the tumbled clothes of a bed drawn up against the wall at my side struck me with so deathlike a chill, that had it not been for that one instant of preparation, I should have been seriously dismayed. As it was, I could not prevent a feeling of sickly apprehension from seizing me, as I turned toward the silent figure stretched so near, and observed with what marble-like repose it lay beneath the patchwork quilt drawn across it, asking myself if sleep could be indeed so like death in its appearance. For that it was a sleeping woman I beheld I did not seriously doubt. There were too many evidences of careless life in the room for any other inference. The clothes left just as she had stepped from them in a circle on the floor; the liberal plate of food placed in waiting for her on the chair by the door— food amongst which I recognized, even in this first casual glance, the same dish which we had had for breakfast—all and everything in the room spoke of robust life and reckless belief in the morrow.

And yet so white was the brow turned up to the bare beams of the unfinished wall above her, so glassy the look of the half-opened eyes, so motionless the arm lying half-under, half-over the edge of the coverlid, that it was impossible not to shrink from contact with a creature so dire in her unconsciousness. But contact seemed to be necessary; any cry which I could raise at that moment would be ineffectual enough to pierce those dull ears. Nerving myself, therefore, I stooped and lifted the hand which lay with its telltale scar mockingly uppermost, intending to speak, call, do something, anything to arouse her. But at the first touch of her hand on mine, an unspeakable horror thrilled me. It was not only icy cold but stiff. Dropping it in my agitation I started back and again surveyed the face. Great God, when did life ever look like that? What sleep ever wore such pallid hues, such accusing fixedness? Bending once more, I listened at the lips. Not a breath, nor a stir. Shocked to the core of my being, I made one final effort. Tearing down the clothes I laid my hand upon her heart. It was pulseless as stone.

CHAPTER 4

Burned Paper

I could have better spared a better man.
—HENRY IV.

I do not think I called immediately for help. The awful shock of this discovery coming as it did at the very moment when life and hope were strongest within me; the sudden downfall which it brought of all the plans based upon this woman's unexpected testimony; and worst and most terrific of all, the dread coincidence of this sudden death with the exigency in which the guilty party, whoever it was, was supposed to be at that hour, were much too appalling for instant action. I could only stand and stare at the quiet face before me, smiling in its peaceful rest as if death were pleasanter than we think, and marvel over the providence which had brought us renewed fear instead of relief, complication instead of enlightenment, disappointment instead of realization. For eloquent as is death even on the faces of those unknown and unloved by us, the causes and consequences of this one were much too important to allow the mind to dwell upon the pathos of the scene itself. Hannah the girl was lost in Hannah the witness.

But gradually as I gazed, the look of expectation which I perceived hovering about the wistful mouth and half-open lids attracted me, and I bent above her as a friend might do, asking myself if she were quite dead and whether or not immediate medical assistance would be of any avail. But the more closely I looked, the more certain I became that she had been dead for some hours, and the dismay occasioned by this thought, taken with regrets which I must ever feel, that I had not adopted the bold course the evening before, and by forcing my way to the hiding-place of this poor creature, interrupted, if not prevented the consummation of her fate, startled me into a realization of my present situation, and leaving her side I went into the next room, threw up the window, and fastened to the blind the red handkerchief which I had taken the precaution to bring with me.

Instantly a young man, whom I was fain to believe Q, though he bore not the least resemblance either in dress or facial expression to any renderings of that youth which I had yet seen, emerged from the tinsmith's house, and approached that in which I was.

Observing him cast a hurried glance in my direction, I crossed the floor and stood awaiting him at the head of the stairs.

"Well?" he whispered upon entering the house and meeting my glance from below, "have you seen her?"

"Yes," I returned bitterly, "I have seen her."

He hurriedly mounted to my side. "And she has confessed?"

"No; I have had no talk with her." Then as I perceived him growing alarmed at my voice and manner, drew him into Mrs. Belden's room and hastily inquired: "What did you mean this morning when you informed me that you had seen this girl? that she was in a certain room where I might find her?"

"What I said."

"You have, then, been to her room?"

"No; I have only been on the outside of it. Seeing a light, I crawled up on to the ledge of the slanting roof last night while both you and Mrs. Belden were out, and looking through a window, saw her moving round the room." He must have observed my countenance change, for he stopped. "What is to pay?" he cried.

I could restrain myself no longer. "Come," I said, "and see for yourself!" And leading him to the little room I had just left, I pointed to the silent form lying within. "You told me I should find Hannah here; but you did not tell me I should find her thus."

"Great Heavens!" he cried with a start, "not dead?"

"Yes," I said, "dead."

It seemed as if he could not realize it. "But it is impossible!" he returned. "She is in a heavy sleep, has taken a narcotic——"

"It is not sleep," I said, "or if it is she will never wake. Look!" And taking the hand once more in mine, I let it fall in its stone weight upon the bed.

The sight seemed to convince him. Calming down, he stood gazing at her with a very strange expression upon his face. Suddenly he moved and began quietly turning over the clothes that were lying on the floor.

"What are you doing?" I asked. "What are you looking for?"

"I am looking for the bit of paper from which I saw her take what I supposed to be a dose of medicine last night. Oh, here it is," he cried, lifting a morsel of paper that, lying on the floor under the edge of the bed, had hitherto escaped his notice.

"Let me see!" I anxiously exclaimed.

He handed me the paper, on the inner surface of which I could dimly discern the traces of an impalpable white powder.

"This is important," I declared, carefully folding the paper together. "If there is enough of this powder remaining to show that the contents of this paper were poisonous, the manner and means of the girl's death are accounted for, and a case of deliberate suicide made evident."

"I am not so sure of that," he retorted. "If I am any judge of countenances, and I rather flatter myself that I am, this girl had no more idea she was taking poison than I had. She looked not only bright but gay; and when she tipped up the paper, a smile of almost silly triumph crossed her face. If Mrs. Belden gave her that dose to take, telling her it was medicine——"

"That is something which yet remains to be learned, also

whether the dose as you call it was poison or not. It may be she died of heart disease."

He simply shrugged his shoulders and pointed first at the plate of breakfast left on the chair, and secondly at the broken-down door.

"Yes," I said, answering his look, "Mrs. Belden has been in here this morning and Mrs. Belden locked the door when she went out, but that proves nothing beyond her belief in the girl's hearty condition."

"A belief which that white face on its tumbled pillow did not seem to shake?"

"Perhaps in her haste she may not have looked at the girl, but have set the dishes down without more than a casual glance in her direction?"

"I don't want to suspect anything wrong, but it is such a coincidence!"

This was touching me on a sore point, and I stepped back. "Well," said I, "there is no use in our standing here busying ourselves with conjectures. There is too much to be done. Come!" and I moved hurriedly toward the door.

"What are you going to do?" asked he. "Have you forgotten this is but an episode in the one great mystery we are sent here to unravel? If this girl did come to her death by some foul play, it is our business to find it out."

"That must be left for the coroner to do. It has now passed out of our hands."

"I know; but we can at least take full note of the room and everything in it before throwing the affair into the hands of strangers. Mr. Gryce will expect that much of us, I am sure."

"I have looked at the room. The whole is photographed on my mind. I am only afraid I can never forget it."

"And the body? Have you noticed its position? the lay of the bedclothes around it? the lack there is of all signs of struggle or fear? the repose of the countenance? the easy fall of the hands?"

"Yes, yes; don't make me look at it any more."

"Then the clothes hanging on the wall?" rapidly pointing out each object as he spoke. "Do you see? a calico dress, a shawl—not the one in which she was believed to have run away, but an

old black one, probably Mrs. Belden's. Then this chest"—
opening it—"containing a few underclothes marked—let us
see, ah, with the name of the lady of the house, but smaller than
any she ever wore; made for Hannah, you observe, and marked
with her own name to prevent suspicion. And then these other
clothes lying on the floor, all new, all marked in the same way.
Then this—Halloo! look here," he suddenly cried.

Going over to where he stood I stooped down, when a washbowl half-full of burned paper met my eye.

"I saw her bending over something in this corner, and could
not think what it was. Can it be that it was a suicide after all?
She has evidently destroyed something here which she didn't
wish anyone to see."

"I do not know," I said. "I could almost hope it to be so."

"Not a scrap, not a morsel left to show what it was; how
unfortunate!"

"Mrs. Belden must solve this riddle," I cried.

"Mrs. Belden must solve the whole riddle," he replied, "the
secret of the Leavenworth murder hangs upon it." Then with a
lingering look toward the mass of burned paper; "Who knows
but what that was a confession?"

The conjecture seemed only too probable.

"Whatever it was," said I, "it is now ashes, and we have got
to accept the fact and make the best of it."

"Yes," said he with a deep sigh; "that's so, but Mr. Gryce will
never forgive me for it, never. He will say I ought to have known
that it was a suspicious circumstance, this taking of a dose of
medicine at the very moment detection stood at her back."

"But she did not know that; she did not see you."

"We don't know what she saw nor what Mrs. Belden saw.
Women are a mystery, and though I flatter myself that ordinarily I am a match for the keenest bit of female flesh that ever
walked, I must say that in this case I feel myself thoroughly
and shamefully worsted."

"Well, well," said I, "the end has not come yet; who knows
what a talk with Mrs. Belden will evoke? And by the way, she
will be coming back soon and I must be ready to meet her. Everything depends upon finding out, if I can, whether she is

aware of this tragedy or not. It is just possible she knows nothing of it."

And hurrying him from the room, I pulled the door to behind me, and led the way downstairs.

"Now," said I, "there is one thing which must be immediately attended to, and that is, a telegram must be sent to Mr. Gryce acquainting him with this unlooked-for occurrence."

"All right, sir," and Q started for the door.

"Wait one moment," said I. "I may not have another opportunity to mention it. Mrs. Belden received two letters from the postmaster yesterday; one in a large and one in a small envelope; if you could find out where they were postmarked——"

Q put his hand in his pocket. "I think I will not have to go far to find out where one of them came from. Good George, I have lost it!" And before I knew it, he had returned upstairs.

That moment I heard the gate click.

CHAPTER 5

Q

Thereby hangs a tale.
—Taming of the Shrew.

"It was all a hoax; nobody was ill; I have been imposed upon, meanly imposed upon." And Mrs. Belden, flushed and panting, entered the room where I was, and proceeded to take off her bonnet. But whilst doing so she paused and suddenly exclaimed, "What is the matter? How you look at me! Has anything happened?"

"Something very serious has occurred," I replied; "you have been gone but a little while, but in that time a discovery has been made——" I purposely paused here that the suspense might elicit from her some betrayal; but though she turned pale,

she manifested less emotion than I expected, and I went on—
"which is likely to produce very important consequences."

To my surprise she burst violently into tears. "I knew it, I
knew it!" she murmured. "I always said it would be impossible
to keep it secret if I let anybody into the house; she is so restless. But I forget," she suddenly said with a frightened look;
"you haven't told me what the discovery was. Perhaps it isn't
what I thought; perhaps——"

I did not hesitate to interrupt her. "Mrs. Belden," I said, "I
shall not try to mitigate the blow. A woman who, in the face of
the most urgent call from law and justice, can receive into her
house and harbor there a witness of such importance as Hannah, cannot stand in need of any great preparation for hearing
that her efforts have been too successful, that she has accomplished her design of suppressing valuable testimony, that law
and justice are outraged, and that the innocent woman whom
this girl's evidence might have saved stands forever compromised in the eyes of the world, if not in those of the officers of
the law."

Her eyes, which had never left me during this address, flashed
wide with dismay.

"What do you mean?" she cried. "I have intended no wrong,
I have only tried to save people. I—I—— But who are you?
What have you got to do with all this? What is it to you what I
do or don't do? You said you were a lawyer. Can it be you are
come from Mary Leavenworth to see how I am fulfilling her
commands, and——"

"Mrs. Belden," I said, "it is of small importance now as to
who I am or for what purpose I am here. But that my words
may have the more effect, I will say, that whereas I have not
deceived you either as to my name or position, it is true that I
am the friend of the Misses Leavenworth, and that anything
which is likely to affect them is of interest to me. When, therefore, I say that Eleanore Leavenworth is irretrievably injured
by this girl's death——"

"Death? what do you mean? death?"

The burst was too natural, the tone too horror-stricken for
me to doubt for another moment as to this woman's ignorance
of the true state of affairs.

"Yes," I repeated, "the girl you have been hiding so long and so well is now beyond your control. Only her dead body remains, Mrs. Belden."

I shall never lose from my ears the shriek which she uttered nor the wild: "I don't believe it! I don't believe it!" with which she dashed from the room and rushed upstairs.

Nor that after-scene when in the presence of the dead she stood wringing her hands and protesting, amid sobs of the sincerest grief and terror, that she knew nothing of it; that she had left the girl in the best of spirits the night before; that it was true she had locked her in, but that was what she always did when anyone was in the house; and that if she died of any sudden attack, it must have been quietly, for she had heard no stir all night, though she had listened more than once, being naturally anxious lest the girl should make some disturbance that would arouse me.

"But you were in here this morning?" said I.

"Yes; but I didn't notice. I was in a hurry and thought she was asleep; so I set the things down where she could get them and came right away, locking the door as usual."

"It is strange," said I, "that she should have died this night of all others. Was she ill yesterday?"

"No, sir; she was even brighter than common, more lively. I never thought of her being sick then or ever. If I had——"

"You never thought of her being sick?" a voice here interrupted. "Why, then, did you take such pains to give her a dose of medicine last night?" And Q entered from the room beyond.

"I didn't," said she, evidently under the supposition that it was I who had spoken. "Did I, Hannah, did I, poor girl?" stroking the hand that lay in hers with what appeared to be genuine sorrow and regret.

"How came she by it, then? Where did she get it if you didn't give it to her?"

This time she seemed to be aware that someone besides myself was talking to her, for hurriedly rising, she looked at the man with a wondering stare, before replying:

"I don't know who you are, sir, but I can tell you this, the girl had no medicine; took no dose; she wasn't sick last night that I know of."

"Yet I saw her swallow a powder."

"Saw her—the world is crazy or I am—saw her swallow a powder? How could you see her do that or anything else? Hasn't she been shut up in this room for twenty-four hours?"

"Yes; but with a window like that in the roof, it isn't so very difficult to see into a room, madam."

"Oh," she cried, shrinking, "I have a spy in the house, have I? But I deserve it; I kept her imprisoned in four close walls and never came to look at her once all night. I don't complain, but what was it you said that you saw her take? medicine? poison?"

"I didn't say poison."

"But you meant it. You think she has poisoned herself and that I had a hand in it?"

"No," I hastened to remark, "he does not think you had a hand in it. He says he saw the girl herself swallow something which he believes to have been the occasion of her death, and only asks you now where she obtained it."

"How can I tell? I never gave her anything; didn't know she had anything."

Somehow I believed her, and so felt unwilling to prolong the present interview, especially as each moment delayed the action which I felt it incumbent upon us to take. So, motioning Q to depart upon his errand, I took Mrs. Belden by the hand and endeavored to lead her from the room. But she resisted, sitting down by the side of the bed with the expression, "I will not leave her again; do not ask it; here is my place, and here will I stay," while Q, obdurate for the first time, stood staring severely upon us both, and would not move though I urged him again to make haste, saying that the morning was slipping away, and that the telegram to Mr. Gryce ought to be sent.

"Till that woman leaves the room, I don't; and unless you promise to take my place in watching her, I don't quit the house."

Astonished, I left her side and crossed to him. "You carry your suspicions too far," I whispered, "and I think you are too rude. We have seen nothing, I am sure, to warrant us in any such action; besides, she can do no harm here; though as for watching her, I promise to do that much if it will relieve your mind."

"I don't want her watched here; take her below. I cannot leave while she remains."

"Are you not assuming a trifle the master?"

"I don't know, perhaps. If I am, it is because I have something in my possession which excuses my conduct."

"What is that, the letter?"

"Yes."

Agitated now in my turn, I held out my hand. "Let me see," I said.

"Not while that woman remains in the room."

Seeing him implacable, I returned to Mrs. Belden.

"I must entreat you to come with me," said I. "This is not a common death; we shall be obliged to have the coroner here, and other. You had better leave the room and go below."

"I don't mind the coroner; he is a neighbor of mine; his coming won't prevent my watching over the poor girl until he arrives."

"Mrs. Belden," I said, "your position as the only one conscious of the presence of this girl in your house makes it wiser for you not to invite suspicion by lingering any longer than is necessary in the room where her dead body lies."

"As if my neglect of her now were the best surety of my good intentions toward her in time past!"

"It will not be neglect for you to go below with me at my earnest request. You can do no good here by staying; will, in fact, be doing harm. So listen to me, or I shall be obliged to leave you in charge of this man and go myself to inform the authorities."

This last argument seemed to affect her, for with one look of shuddering abhorrence at Q, she rose, saying: "You have me in your power," and then, without another word, threw her handkerchief over the girl's face and left the room. In two minutes more I had the letter of which Q had spoken in my hands.

"It is the only one I could find, sir. It was in the pocket of the dress Mrs. Belden had on last night. The other must be lying around somewhere, but I haven't had time to find it. This will do though, I think. You will not ask for the other."

Scarcely noticing at the time with what deep significance he spoke, I opened the letter. It was the smaller of the two I had seen her draw under her shawl the day before at the post office, and read as follows:

DEAR, DEAR FRIEND,

I am in awful trouble. You who love me must know it. I cannot explain, I can only make one prayer. Destroy what you have, today, instantly, without question or hesitation. The consent of anyone else has nothing to do with it. You must obey. I am lost if you refuse. Do then what I ask and save

ONE WHO LOVES YOU.

It was addressed to Mrs. Belden; there was no signature or date, only the post-mark New York; but I knew the handwriting. It was Mary Leavenworth's.

"A damning letter!" came in the dry tones which Q seemed to think fit to adopt on this occasion. "And a damning bit of evidence against the one who wrote it, and the woman who received it!"

"A terrible piece of evidence indeed!" said I, "if I did not happen to know that this letter refers to the destruction of something radically different from what you suspect. It alludes to some papers in Mrs. Belden's charge; nothing else."

"Are you sure, sir?"

"Quite; but we will talk of this hereafter. It is time you sent your telegram and went for the coroner."

"Very well, sir." And with that we parted, he to perform his role and I mine.

I found Mrs. Belden walking the floor below, bewailing her situation and uttering wild sentences as to what the neighbors would say of her, what the minister would think, what Clara, whoever that was, would do, and how she wished she had died before ever she had meddled with the affair.

Succeeding in calming her after a while, I induced her to sit down and listen to what I had to say. "You will only injure yourself by this display of feeling," I remarked, "besides unfitting yourself for what you will presently be called upon to go through." And laying myself out to comfort the unhappy woman, I first explained the necessities of the case, and next inquired if she had no friend upon whom she could call in this emergency.

To my great surprise she replied no; that while she had kind neighbors and good friends, there was no one upon whom she could call in a case like this, either for assistance or sympathy, and that unless I would take pity on her, she would have to meet it alone. "As I have met everything," she said, "from Mr. Belden's death to the loss of most of my little savings in a town fire last year."

I was touched by this; that she who, in spite of her weakness and inconsistencies of character, possessed at least the one virtue of sympathy with her kind should feel any lack of friends. Unhesitatingly I offered to do what I could for her, providing she would treat me with the perfect frankness which the case demanded. To my great relief she expressed not only her willingness but her strong desire to tell all she knew. "I have had," said she, "enough of secrecy for my whole life." And indeed I do believe she was so thoroughly frightened, that if a police-officer had come into the house and asked her to reveal secrets compromising the good name of her own son, she would have done so without cavil or question. "I feel as if I wanted to take my stand out on the common, and in the face of the whole world declare what I have done for Mary Leavenworth. But first," she whispered, "tell me for God's sake how those girls are situated. I have not dared to ask or write. The papers say a good deal about Eleanore, but nothing about Mary; and yet Mary herself writes only of her own peril, and of the danger she would be in if certain facts were known. What is the truth? I don't want to injure them, only to take care of myself."

"Mrs. Belden," I said, "Eleanore Leavenworth has got into her present difficulty by not telling all that was required of her. Mary Leavenworth—but I cannot speak of her till I know what you have to divulge. Her position, as well as that of her cousin, is too anomalous for either you or me to discuss. What we want to learn from you is how you became connected with this affair, and what it was that Hannah knew which caused her to leave New York and take refuge here."

But Mrs. Belden, clasping and unclasping her hands, met my gaze with one full of the most apprehensive doubt. "You will never believe me," she cried, "but I don't know what Hannah knew. I am in utter ignorance of what she saw or heard on that fatal night; she never told and I never asked. She merely said that Miss Leavenworth wished me to secrete her for a short time, and I, because I loved Mary Leavenworth and admired her beyond anyone I ever saw, weakly consented, and——"

"Do you mean to say," I interrupted, "that after you knew of the murder, you at the mere expression of Miss Leavenworth's wishes, continued to keep this girl concealed, without asking her any questions or demanding any explanations?"

"Yes, sir; you will never believe me, but it is so. I thought that since Mary had sent her here, she must have her reasons, and—and—I cannot explain it now, it all looks so differently, but I did do as I have said."

"But that was very strange conduct. You must have had strong reasons for obeying Mary Leavenworth so blindly."

"Oh, sir," she gasped, "I thought I understood it all; that Mary, the bright young creature, who had stooped from her lofty position to make use of me and to love me, was in some way linked to the criminal, and that it would be better for me not to know any more, only to do what I was bid, and trust it would prove all right. I did not reason about it; I only followed my impulse. I couldn't do otherwise, it isn't my nature. When I am requested to do anything by a person I love, I cannot refuse."

"And you love Mary Leavenworth, a woman whom you yourself seem to consider capable of a great crime?"

"Oh, I didn't say that; I don't know as I thought that. She might be in some way connected with it, without being the actual perpetrator. She could never be that, she is too dainty."

"Mrs. Belden," I said, "what do you know of Mary Leavenworth which makes even that supposition possible?"

The white face of the woman before me flushed. "I scarcely know what to reply," she cried. "It is a long story, and——"

"Never mind the long story," I interrupted. "Let me hear the one vital reason."

"Well," said she, "it is this, that Mary was in an emergency from which nothing but her uncle's death could release her."

"Ah, how's that?"

But here we were interrupted by the sound of steps on the porch, and looking out, I saw Q entering the house alone. Leaving Mrs. Belden where she was, I stepped into the hall. "Well!" said I, "what is the matter? Haven't you found the coroner? Isn't he at home?"

"No, gone away; off in a buggy to look after a man that was found some ten miles from here, lying in a ditch beside a yoke of oxen." Then, as he saw my look of relief, for I was glad of this temporary delay, said with an expressive wink: "It would take a fellow a long time to go to him—if he wasn't in a hurry—hours, I think."

"Indeed!" I returned, amused at his manner. "Rough road?"

"Very; no horse *I* could get would travel it faster than a walk."

"Well," said I, "so much the better for us. Mrs. Belden has a long story to tell, and——"

"Doesn't wish to be interrupted. I understand."

I nodded and he turned toward the door.

"Have you telegraphed to Mr. Gryce?" I asked.

"Yes, sir."

"Do you think he will come?"

"Yes, sir, if he has to hobble on two sticks."

"At what time do you look for him?"

"*You* will look for him as early as three o'clock. *I* shall be among the mountains, ruefully eyeing a broken-down team or some such thing." And leisurely donning his hat, he strolled away down the street, like one who has the whole day on his hands and doesn't know what to do with it.

Going back to Mrs. Belden, I explained that the coroner was out of town, and would not be back for some time; that we had, therefore, some hours before us which could not be better employed than by her giving me some account of what she knew concerning the matter in hand. She expressed herself as willing to do so, and immediately composed herself to her task. As what she told involves a long story, I will devote a chapter to it and christen it Mrs. Belden's narrative.

CHAPTER 6

Mrs. Belden's Narrative

Cursed, destructive Avarice,
Thou everlasting foe to Love and Honor.
—TRAP'S ABRAM.

——Mischief never thrives
Without the help of Woman.
—THE SAME.

It will be a year next July since I first saw Mary Leavenworth. I was living at that time a most monotonous existence. Loving what was beautiful, hating what was sordid, drawn by Nature toward all that was romantic and uncommon, but doomed by my straitened position and the loneliness of my widowhood to spend my days in the weary round of plain sewing, I had begun to think that the shadow of a humdrum old age was settling down upon me, when one morning, in the full tide of my dissatisfaction, Mary Leavenworth stepped across the threshold of my door, and with one smile, changed the whole tenor of my life.

This may seem exaggeration to you, especially when I tell you that her errand was simply one of business, she having heard I was handy with my needle; but if you could have seen her as she appeared that day, marked the look with which she approached me, and the smile with which she left, you would pardon the folly of a romantic old woman who beheld a fairy queen, where others saw a lovely young lady. The fact is, I was dazzled by her beauty and her charms. And when a few days after she came again and, crouching down on the stool at my feet, asked leave to sit with me awhile and rest, saying she was so tired of the gossip and tumult down at the hotel, and so longed at times to run away and hide with someone who would let her act like the child she was, I experienced for the moment, I believe, the truest happiness of my life. Feeling so, it was impossible for me not to show it. Something of all that which I had kept repressed till now awoke in response to her persuasive glance, and before long I found her looking up into my face with manifest pleasure, listening eagerly while I told her, almost without my own volition, the story of my past life in the form of a tender allegory.

The next day saw her in the same place, and the next; always with the eager, laughing eyes, and the fluttering, uneasy hands, that grasped everything they touched, and broke everything they grasped.

But the fourth day she was not there, nor the fifth, nor the sixth, and I was beginning to feel the old shadow settling back upon me, when one night, just as the dusk of twilight was merging into evening gloom, she came stealing in at the front door, and creeping up to my side, put her hands over my eyes with such a low, ringing laugh, that I started.

"You don't know what to make of me!" cried she, throwing aside her cloak, and revealing herself in the full splendor of evening attire. "I don't know what to make of myself; only," she whispered, "I felt that I must run away and tell someone that, for the first time in my life, I am fully alive; that a certain pair of eyes have been looking into mine, and that not Mary of Scots, with all her beauty and queenliness, ever felt herself more of the sovereign or more the woman than I do tonight."

And with a turn of her head, that must have rivaled any gesture of that beautiful queen, she gathered up her cloak around her, and laughingly cried:

"Have you had a visit from a flying sprite? Has one little ray of moonlight found its way into your prison for a wee moment, with Mary's laugh and Mary's snowy silk and flashing diamonds? Say!" and she patted my cheek and smiled so bewilderingly, that even now with all the dull horror of these afterevents crowding upon me, I cannot but feel something like tears spring to my eyes at the thought of it.

"And so the Prince has come for you?" I whispered, alluding to a story I had told her the last time she had visited me; a story in which a girl, who had waited all her life in rags and degradation for the lordly knight who was to raise her from a hovel to a throne, died just as her one lover, an honest peasant-lad whom she had discarded in her pride, arrived at her door with the fortune in his hand he had spent all his days in amassing for her sake.

But at that she flushed and drew back toward the door.

"I don't know, I am afraid not. I—I don't think anything about that. Princes are not so easily won," she murmured.

"What, are you going?" I said, "and alone? Let me accompany you."

But she only shook her fairy head, and replied: "No, no, that would be spoiling the romance indeed. I have come upon you like a sprite and like a sprite will I go." And flashing like the moonbeam she was, she glided out into the night, and floated away down the street.

When she next came, I observed a feverish excitement in her manner that assured me even plainer than the coy sweetness displayed in our last interview that her heart had been touched by her lover's attentions. Indeed, she hinted as much before she left, saying in a melancholy tone, when I had ended my story in the usual happy way with kisses and marriage—"I shall never marry!" finishing the exclamation with a long-drawn sigh, that somehow emboldened me to say, perhaps because I knew she had no mother:

"And why? What reason can there be for such rosy lips saying their possessor will never marry?"

She gave me one quick look, and then dropped her eyes. I feared I had offended her, and was feeling very humble, when she suddenly replied in an even but low tone, "I said I should never marry, because the one man who pleases me is the last whom Fate will allow me for a husband."

"Fate?" repeated I, all the hidden romance of my nature starting into sudden life.

"Yes."

"What do you mean? Tell me."

"There is nothing to tell," said she, "only I have been so weak as to"—she would not say fall in love, she was a proud woman—"admire a man whom my uncle will never allow me to marry."

And she rose as if to go, but I drew her back. "Whom your

uncle will not allow you to marry?" I repeated. "Why, because he is poor?"

"No; uncle loves money, but not to such an extent as that. Besides, Mr. Clavering is not poor. He is the owner of a beautiful place in his own country——"

"Own country," I interrupted. "Is he not an American?"

"No," she returned, "he is an Englishman."

I did not see why she need say that in just the way she did, but supposing she was aggravated by some secret memory, went on to inquire—"Then what difficulty can there be? Isn't he——" I was going to say steady, but refrained.

"He is an Englishman," cried she, in the same bitter tone as before. "In saying that, I say it all. Uncle will never let me marry an Englishman."

I looked at her in amazement. Such a puerile reason as that had never entered my mind.

"He has an absolute mania on the subject," resumed she. "I might as well ask him to allow me to drown myself as to marry an Englishman."

A woman of truer judgment than myself would have said: "Then if that is so, why not discard from your breast all thought of him? Why dance with him, and talk to him, and let your admiration develop into love?" But I was all romance then, and angry at a prejudice I could neither understand nor appreciate. I said:

"But that is mere tyranny! Why should he hate the English so? And why, if he does, should you feel yourself obliged to gratify him in a whim so unreasonable?"

"Why? Shall I tell you, Auntie?" she said, flushing and looking away.

"Yes," I returned; "tell me everything."

"Well, then, if you want to know the worst of me, as you already know the best, I hate to incur my uncle's displeasure, because—because—I have always been brought up to regard myself as his heiress, and I know that if I should marry contrary to his wishes, he would instantly change his mind, and leave me penniless."

"But," I cried, my romance a little dampened by this admission, "you tell me Mr. Clavering has enough to live upon, so you would not want; and if you love——"

Her violet eyes fairly flashed in her amazement.

"You don't understand," she said; "Mr. Clavering is not poor, but uncle is rich. I shall be a queen——" There she paused, trembling and falling on my breast. "Oh, it sounds mercenary, I know," she sobbed, "but it is the fault of my bringing up. I have been taught to worship money. I would be utterly lost without it. And yet"—her whole face softening with the light of another emotion, "I cannot say to Henry Clavering: 'Go! I love my riches better than you!' I cannot, oh, I cannot."

"You love him, then," said I, determined to get at the truth of the matter if possible.

She rose restlessly. "Isn't that a proof of love? If you knew me you would say it was." And, turning, she took her stand before a picture that hung on the wall of my sitting room.

"That looks like me," she said.

It was one of a good pair of photographs I possessed.

"Yes," I remarked, "that is why I prize it."

She did not seem to hear me; she was absorbed in gazing at the exquisite face before her. "That is a winning face," I heard her say. "Sweeter than mine. I wonder if she would ever hesitate between love and money. I do not believe she would," her own countenance growing gloomy and sad as she said so, "she would think only of the happiness she would confer; she is not hard like me; Eleanore herself would love this girl."

I think she had forgotten my presence, for at the mention of her cousin's name, she turned quickly round with a half-suspicious look, saying lightly:

"My dear old Mamma Hubbard looks horrified. She did not know she had such a very unromantic little wretch for a listener, when she was telling all those wonderful stories of Love slaying dragons, and living in caves, and walking over burning plowshares as if they were tufts of spring grass, did she?"

"No," I said, taking her by an irresistible impulse of admiring affection into my arms, "but if I had, it would have made no difference. I should still have talked about love, and of all it can do to make this weary workaday world sweet and delightful."

"Would you? Then you do not think me such a wretch?"

What could I say? I thought her the winsomest being in the world, and frankly told her so. Instantly she brightened into her very gayest self. Not that I thought then, much less do I think now, that she particularly cared for my good opinion; but her nature demanded admiration and unconsciously blossomed under it, as a flower under the sunshine.

"And you will still let me come and tell you how bad I am— that is, if I go on being bad, as I doubtless shall to the end of the chapter? You will not turn me off?"

"I will never turn you off"

"Not if I should do a dreadful thing? Not if I should run away with my lover some fine night, and leave Uncle to discover how ill his affectionate partiality had been requited?"

It was lightly said, and lightly meant, for she did not even wait for my reply. But its seed sank deep into our two hearts for all that. And for two days I spent my time in planning how I should manage if it should ever fall to my lot to conduct to a successful issue so enthralling a piece of business as an elopement. You may imagine, then, how delighted I was, when one evening Hannah, this unhappy girl who is now lying dead under my roof, and who was occupying the position of lady's maid to Miss Mary Leavenworth at that time, came to my door with a note from her mistress, running thus:

Have the loveliest story of the season ready for me tomorrow; and let the prince be as handsome as—as someone you have heard of, and the princess as foolish as your little yielding pet,

MARY.

Which short note could only mean that she was engaged. But morning-light did not bring my Mary, nor noontide, nor evening. The next day came and went, but beyond hearing that Mr. Leavenworth had returned—he had been away traveling—I received neither word nor token. Two more days dragged by, when just as twilight set in she came. It had been a week since I had seen her, but it might have been a year by the change I observed in her countenance and expression. I could scarcely greet her, with any show of pleasure, she was so unlike her former self.

"You are disappointed, are you not?" said she, looking at me. "You expected revelations, whispered hopes, and all manner of sweet confidences, and you see, instead, a cold, bitter woman, who, for the first time in your presence, feels inclined to be reserved and uncommunicative."

"That is because you have had more to trouble than encourage you in your love," I returned, though not without a certain shrinking caused more by her manner than words.

She did not reply to this, but rose and paced the floor; coldly at first, but afterward with a certain degree of excitement that proved to be the prelude to a change in her manner, for suddenly pausing she turned to me and said: "Mr. Clavering has left R——, Mrs. Belden."

"Left!"

"Yes, my uncle commanded me to dismiss him, and I obeyed."

The work dropped from my hands, in my heartfelt disappointment. "Ah! then he knows of your engagement to Mr. Clavering?"

"Yes; he had not been in the house five minutes before Eleanore told him."

"Then *she* knew?"

"Yes"; with a half-sigh. "She could hardly help it. I was foolish enough to give her the cue in my first moment of joy and weakness. I did not think of the consequences; but I might have known. She is so conscientious."

"I do not call it conscientiousness to tell another's secrets," I returned.

"That is because you are not Eleanore."

Not having a reply for this, I said: "And so your uncle did not regard your engagement with favor?"

"Favor? Did I not tell you he would never allow me to marry an Englishman? He said he would sooner see me buried."

"And you yielded? Made no struggle? Let the hard, cruel man have his way?"

She was walking off to look again at that picture which had attracted her attention the time before, but at this word gave me one little sidelong look that was inexpressibly suggestive.

"I obeyed him when he commanded, if that is what you mean."

"And dismissed Mr. Clavering after having given him your word of honor to be his wife?"

"Why not, when I found I could not keep my word?"

"Then you have decided not to marry him?"

She did not reply at once, but lifted her face mechanically to the picture.

"My uncle would tell you that I had decided to be governed wholly by his wishes," she responded at last with what I felt was self-scornful bitterness.

Greatly disappointed, I burst into tears: "Oh, Mary!" I cried, "Oh, Mary!" and instantly blushed, startled that I had called her by her first name.

But she did not appear to notice.

"Have you any complaint to make?" she asked. "Is it not my manifest duty to be governed by my uncle's wishes? Has he not brought me up from childhood? lavished every luxury upon me? made me all I am, even to the love of riches which he has instilled into my soul with every gift he has thrown into my lap, every word he has dropped in my ear, since I was old enough to know what riches meant? Is it for me now to turn my back upon fostering care so wise, beneficent, and free, just because a man whom I have known some two weeks chances to offer me in exchange what he pleases to call his love?"

"But," I feebly essayed, convinced perhaps by the tone of sarcasm in which this was uttered that she was not far from my way of thinking after all, "if in two weeks you have learned to love this man more than everything else, even the riches which make your uncle's favor a thing of such moment——"

"Well?" said she, "what then?"

"Why, then I would say, secure your happiness with the man of your choice if you have to marry him in secret, trusting to your influence over your uncle to win the forgiveness he never can persistently deny."

You should have seen the arch expression which stole across her face at that. "Would it not be better," she asked, creeping to my arms and laying her head on my shoulder; "would it not be better for me to make sure of that uncle's favor first, before undertaking the hazardous experiment of running away with a too ardent lover?" Struck by her manner, I lifted her face and looked at it. It was one amused smile.

"Oh, my darling," said I, "you have not, then, dismissed Mr. Clavering?"

"I have sent him away," she whispered demurely.

"But not without hope?"

She burst into a ringing laugh. "Oh, you dear old Mamma Hubbard, what a matchmaker you are to be sure! You appear as much interested as if you were the lover himself."

"But tell me," I urged.

In a moment her serious mood returned. "He will wait for me," said she.

The next day I submitted to her the plan I had formed for her clandestine intercourse with Mr. Clavering. It was for them both to assume names, she taking mine as one less liable to provoke conjecture than a strange name, and he that of Le Roy Robbins. The plan pleased her, and with the slight modification of a secret sign being used on the envelope to distinguish her letters from mine, was at once adopted.

And so it was I took the fatal step that has involved me in all this trouble. With the gift of my name to this young girl to use as she would and sign what she would, I seemed to part with what was left me of judgment and discretion. Henceforth I was only her scheming, planning, devoted slave, now copying the letters which she brought me and enclosing them to the false name we had agreed upon, and now busying myself in devising ways to forward to her those which I received from him, without risk of discovery. Hannah was usually the medium we employed for this, as Mary felt that it would not be wise in her to come too often to my house. To this girl's charge, then, I gave such notes as I could not forward in any other way, secure in the reticence of her nature as well as in her inability to read, that these letters addressed to Mrs. Amy Belden would arrive at their proper destination without mishap. And I believe they always did. At all events no difficulty that I ever heard of arose out of the use of this girl as a go-between.

But a change was at hand. Mr. Clavering, who had left an

invalid mother in England, suddenly received notice that she was very ill and requested his immediate return. He prepared to obey the summons, but flushed with love, distracted by doubts, smitten with the fear that once withdrawn from the neighborhood of a woman so universally courted as Mary, he would stand small chance of retaining his position in her regard, he wrote to her, telling his fears and asking her to marry him before he went.

"Make me once your husband and I will follow your wishes in all things," he wrote. "The certainty that you are mine will make parting possible; without it I cannot go, no, not if my mother should die without the comfort of saying good-bye to her only child."

By some chance she was in my house when I brought this letter from the post office, and I shall never forget how she started when she read it. But from looking as if she had received an insult, she speedily settled down into a calm consideration of the subject, writing and delivering into my charge for copying a few lines in which she promised to accede to his request, if he would agree to leave the public declaration of the marriage to her discretion and consent to bid her farewell at the door of the church or wherever the ceremony of marriage should take place, never to come into her presence again till such declaration had been made. Of course this brought in a couple of days the sure response. "Anything so you will be mine." And Amy Belden's wits and powers of planning were all summoned into requisition for the second time, to devise how this matter could be arranged without subjecting the parties to the chance of detection. I found the thing very difficult. In the first place it was essential that the marriage should come off within three days, Mr. Clavering having upon the receipt of her letter secured his passage upon a steamer that sailed on the following Saturday; and next both he and Miss Leavenworth were too conspicuous in their personal appearance to make it at all possible for them to be married without remark, anywhere within gossiping distance of this place. And yet it was desirable that the scene of the ceremony should not be too far away, or the time occupied in effecting the journey to and from the place would necessitate an absence from the hotel on the part of Miss Leavenworth long enough to arouse the suspicions of Eleanore; something which Mary felt it wiser to avoid. Her uncle, I have forgotten to say, was not here—having gone off traveling again, shortly after the apparent dismissal of Mr. Clavering. F——, then, was the only town I could think of which combined the two advantages of distance and accessibility. Although upon railroad, it was an insignificant place, and had what was better yet, a very obscure man for its clergyman, living, which was best of all, not ten rods from the station. If they could meet there? Making inquiries, I found that it could be done, and all alive to the romance of the occasion, proceeded to plan the details.

And now I am coming to what might have caused the overthrow of the whole scheme; I allude to the detection on the part of Eleanore of the correspondence between Mary and Mr. Clavering. It happened thus. Hannah, who in her goings back and forth had grown very fond of my society, had come in to sit with me for a while one evening. She had not been in the house, however, more than three minutes before there came a knock at the front door, and going to it I saw, as I supposed, Mary, from the long cloak she wore, standing before me. Thinking she had come with a letter for Mr. Clavering, I grasped her arm and drew her into the hall, saying: "Have you got it? I must post it tonight or he will not receive it in time." There I paused, for the panting creature I had by the arm turning upon me, I saw that it was a stranger.

"You have made a mistake," she cried. "I am Eleanore Leavenworth, and I have come for my girl Hannah. Is she here?"

I could only raise my hand in apprehension and point to the girl sitting in the corner of the room before her. Miss Leavenworth immediately turned back.

"Hannah, I want you," said she, and would have left the house without another word, but I caught her by the arm.

"Oh, miss——" I began, but she gave me such a look, I dropped her arm as if it had been hot steel.

"I have nothing to say to you," she cried in a low, thrilling voice. "Do not detain me." And with a glance to see if Hannah were following her, she went out.

For an hour I sat crouched on the stair just where she had

left me. Then I went to bed, but I did not sleep a wink that night. You can imagine, then, my wonder, when with the first glow of the early morning light, Mary, looking more beautiful than ever, came running up the steps and into the room where I was with the letter for Mr. Clavering trembling in her hand.

"Oh!" I cried in my joy and relief, "didn't she understand me, then?"

The gay look on Mary's face turned to one of reckless scorn. "If you mean Eleanore, yes. She is duly initiated, Mamma Hubbard; knows that I love Mr. Clavering and write to him. I couldn't keep it secret after the mistake you made last evening, so I did the next best thing, told her the truth."

"Not that you were about to be married?"

"Certainly not. I don't believe in unnecessary communications."

"And you did not find her as angry as you expected?"

"I will not say that; she was angry enough. And yet"—continued Mary with a burst of self-scornful penitence, "I will not call Eleanore's loftly indignation, anger. She was grieved, Mamma Hubbard, grieved." And with a laugh that I believe was rather the result of her own relief than of any wish to reflect on her cousin, she threw her head on one side and eyed me with a look which seemed to say: "Do I plague you so very much, you dear old Mamma Hubbard?"

She did plague me and I could not conceal it. "And will she not tell your uncle?" I gasped.

The naïve expression on Mary's face quickly changed. "No," said she.

I felt a heavy hand hot with fever lifted from my heart. "And we can still go on?"

She held out the letter for reply.

The plan agreed upon between us for the carrying out of our intentions was this. At the time appointed, Mary was to excuse herself to her cousin upon the plea that she had promised to take me to see a friend in the next town. She was then to enter a buggy previously ordered and drive here, where I was to join her. We were then to proceed immediately to the minister's house in F——, where we had reason to believe we should find everything prepared for us. But in this plan, simple as it was,

one thing was forgotten, and that was the character of Eleanore's love for her cousin. That she would suspect something
was wrong we did not doubt, but that she would actually follow her up and demand an explanation of her conduct was
what neither she who knew her so well, nor I who knew her so
little, ever imagined possible. And yet that was just what occurred. But let me explain. Mary, who had followed out the
program to the point of leaving a little note of excuse on Eleanore's dressing-table, had come to my house and was just taking off her long cloak to show me her dress, when there came a
commanding knock at the front door. Hastily pulling her cloak
about her I ran to open it, intending, you may be sure, to dismiss my visitor with short ceremony, when I heard a voice behind me say, "Good Heavens, it is Eleanore!" and glancing
back, saw Mary looking through the window-blind upon the
porch without.

"What shall I do!" cried I, shrinking back.

"Do? why, open the door and let her in; I am not afraid of
Eleanore."

I immediately did so, and Eleanore Leavenworth, very pale
but with a resolute countenance, walked into the house and
into this room, confronting Mary in very nearly the same spot
where you are now sitting. "I have come," said she, lifting a
face whose expression of mingled sweetness and power I could
not but admire even in that moment of apprehension, "to ask
you, without any excuse for my request, if you will allow me to
accompany you upon your drive this morning?"

Mary, who had drawn herself up to meet some word of
accusation or appeal, turned carelessly away to the glass. "I am
very sorry," she said, "but the buggy holds only two, and I
shall be obliged to refuse."

"I will order a carriage."

"But I do not wish your company, Eleanore. We are off on a
pleasure trip and desire to go as we have planned by ourselves."

"And you will not allow me to accompany you?"

"I cannot prevent your going in another carriage."

Eleanore's face grew yet more earnest in its expression.
"Mary," said she, "we have been brought up together. I am
your sister in affection if not in blood, and I cannot see you

start upon this adventure with no other companion than this woman. Neither conscience, love, nor the gratitude I feel for our absent uncle will allow me. If you go where you propose, I must accompany you. Then tell me, shall it be at your side as a sister, or on the road behind you as the enforced guardian of your honor against your will?"

"My honor?"

"You are going to meet Mr. Clavering."

"Well?"

"Twenty miles from home."

"Well?"

"Now is it discreet or honorable for you to do this? If it is, discretion and honor are not the virtues which I have been brought up to think them."

Mary's haughty lip took an ominous curve. "The same hand that raised you has raised me," she cried bitterly.

"This is no time to speak of that," returned Eleanore.

Mary's countenance flushed. All the antagonism of her nature was aroused. She looked absolutely Juno-like in her wrath and reckless menace. "Eleanore," cried she, "I am going to F—— to marry Mr. Clavering. *Now* do you wish to accompany me?"

"I do."

Mary's whole manner changed. Leaping forward she grasped her cousin's arm and shook it. "Why?" cried she. "What do you intend to do?"

"To witness the marriage if it be a true one, to step between you and shame if any element of falsehood should come in to affect its legality."

Mary's hand fell from her cousin's arm. "I do not understand you," said she, "I thought you never gave countenance to what you considered wrong."

"Nor do I. Anyone who knows me will understand that I do not give my approval to this marriage just because I attend its ceremonial in the capacity of an unwilling witness."

"Then why go?"

"Because I value your honor above my own peace. Because I love our common benefactor and know that he would never pardon me if I let his darling be married, however contrary her union might be to his wishes, without lending the support of my presence to make the transaction at least a respectable one."

"But in so doing you will be involved in a world of deception—which you hate."

"Any more so than now?"

"Mr. Clavering does not return with me, Eleanore."

"No, I supposed not."

"I leave him immediately after the ceremony."

Eleanore bowed her head.

"He goes to Europe."

A pause.

"And I return home."

"There to wait for what, Mary?"

Mary's face crimsoned and she turned slowly away.

"What every other girl does under such circumstances, I suppose. The development of more reasonable feelings in an obdurate parent's heart."

Eleanore sighed and a short silence ensued, broken by Eleanore's suddenly falling upon her knees and clasping her cousin's hand. "Oh, Mary," she sobbed, her haughtiness all disappearing in a gush of wild entreaty, "consider what you are doing! think, before it is too late, of the consequences which must follow such an act as this. Marriage founded upon deception can never lead to happiness. Love—but it is not that. Love would have led you either to have dismissed Mr. Clavering at once or to have openly accepted the fate which a union with him would bring. Only passion stoops to subterfuge like this. And you," continued she, rising and turning toward me in a sort of forlorn hope very touching to see, "you who have borne and brought up children, will you see this young motherless girl, driven by caprice and acknowledging no moral restraint, enter upon the dark and crooked path she is planning for herself, without one word of warning and appeal? Tell me, mother of children, dead and buried, what excuse you will have for your own part in this day's work, when she, with her face marred by the sorrows which must follow this deception, comes to you——"

"The same excuse, probably," Mary's voice broke in chill and strained, "which you will have when uncle inquires how you came to allow such a very wicked piece of business to be accomplished in his absence; that she could not help herself, that Mary would gang her aim gait, and everyone around must accommodate themselves to it."

It was like a draft of icy air suddenly let loose in a room heated up to fever point. Eleanore stiffened immediately, and drawing back pale and composed turned upon her cousin with the remark:

"Then nothing can move you?"

The curling of Mary's lips was her only reply.

Mr. Raymond, I do not wish to weary you with my feelings, but the first great distrust I ever felt of my wisdom in pushing this matter so far came with that curl of Mary's lip. Plainer than Eleanore's words it showed me the temper with which she was entering upon this undertaking, and struck with momentary dismay, I advanced to speak when Mary stopped me.

"There now, Mamma Hubbard, don't you go and acknowledge that you are frightened, for I won't hear it. I have promised to marry Henry Clavering today and I am going to keep my word—if I don't love him," she added with bitter emphasis. Then smiling upon me in a way that caused me to forget everything save the fact that she was going to her bridal, she handed me her veil to fasten. As I was doing it with very trembling fingers, she said, looking straight at Eleanore:

"You have shown yourself more interested in my fate than I have ever thought possible. Will you continue to display that concern all the way to F——, or may I hope that I shall be allowed to dream in peace upon the step which, according to you, is about to hurl upon me such dreadful consequences?"

"If I go with you to F——," Eleanore returned, "it is as a witness, no more. My sisterly duty is done."

"Very well, then," Mary said, dimpling with sudden gaiety, "I suppose I shall have to accept the situation. Mamma Hubbard, I am so sorry to disappoint you, but the buggy *won't* hold three. If you are good, you shall be the first to congratulate me," she whispered, "when I come home tonight." And almost before I knew it, the two had taken their seats in the buggy that was waiting at the door. "Good-bye," cried Mary, waving her hand from the back, "wish me much joy—of my ride."

I tried to do so, but the words wouldn't come. I could only wave my hand in response and rush sobbing into the house.

Of that day and its long hours of alternate remorse and anxiety, I cannot trust myself to speak. Let me come at once to the time when seated alone in my lamp-lighted room, I waited and watched for the token of their return which Mary had promised me. It came in the shape of Mary herself, who, wrapped in her long cloak and with her beautiful face aglow with blushes, came stealing into the house just as I was beginning to despair.

A strain of wild music from the hotel porch where they were having a dance entered with her, producing such a weird effect upon my fancy that I was not at all surprised when, in flinging off her cloak, she displayed garments of bridal white and a head crowned with snowy roses.

"Oh, Mary!" cried I, bursting into tears, "you are then——"

"Mrs. Henry Clavering, at your service. I'm a bride, Auntie."

"Without a bridal," I murmured, taking her passionately into my embrace.

She was not insensible to my emotion. Nestling close to me, she gave herself up for one wild moment to a genuine burst of tears, saying between her sobs all manner of tender things, telling me how she loved me, and how I was the only one in all the world to whom she dare come on this, her wedding night, for comfort or congratulation, and of how frightened she felt now it was all over, as if with her name she had parted with something of inestimable value.

"And does not the thought that you have made someone the proudest of men solace you?" I asked, more than dismayed at this failure of mine to make these lovers happy.

"I don't know," she sobbed. "What satisfaction can it be for him to feel himself tied for life to a girl who sooner than lose a prospective fortune, subjected him to such a parting?"

"Tell me about it," said I.

But she was not in the mood at that moment. The excitement of the day had been too much for her. A thousand fears seemed to beset her mind. Crouching down on the stool at my feet, she sat with her hands folded and a glare on her face that lent an aspect of strange unreality to her brilliant attire. "How shall I keep it secret! The thought haunts me every moment; how can I keep it secret!"

"Why, is there any danger of its being known?" I inquired. "Were you seen or followed?"

"No," she murmured. "It all went off well, but——"

"Where is the danger, then?"

"I cannot say; but some deeds are like ghosts. They will not be laid; they reappear; they gibber; they make themselves known whether we will or not. I did not think of this before. I was mad, reckless, what you will. But ever since the night has come, I have felt it crushing upon me like a pall that smothers life and youth and love out of my heart. While the sunlight remained I could endure it, but now—oh, Auntie, I have done something that will keep me in constant fear. I have allied myself to a living apprehension. I have destroyed my happiness."

I was too aghast to speak.

"I have tried to play gaiety for two hours. I have stood up in the parlors below, dressed in my bridal white and crowned with my wreath of roses, making believe to myself that I was receiving wedding-guests and that all the compliments bestowed upon me—and they were only too numerous—were just so many congratulations upon my marriage. But it was no use; Eleanore knew it was no use. She has gone to her room to pray, while I—I have come here for the first time, perhaps for the last, to fall at someone's feet and cry—'God have mercy upon me!'"

I looked at her in uncontrollable emotion. "Oh, Mary," said I, "have I only succeeded, then, in making you miserable!"

She did not answer, she was engaged in picking up the crown of roses which had fallen from her hair to the floor.

"If I had not been taught to love money so!" she said at length. "If like Eleanore I could look upon the splendor which has been ours from childhood as a mere accessory of life, easy to be dropped at the call of duty or affection! If prestige, adulation, and elegant belongings were not so much to me, or love, friendship, and domestic happiness more! If only I could walk a step without dragging the chain of a thousand luxurious

longings after me! Eleanore can. Lordly as she is in her beautiful womanhood, haughty as she can be when the delicate quick
of her personality is touched too rudely, I have known her to
sit by the hour in a low, chilly, ill-lighted, and ill-smelling garret, cradling a dirty child on her knee, and feeding with her own
hand an impatient old woman whom no one else would consent to touch. Oh, oh, they talk about repentance and a change
of heart! If someone or something would only change mine!
But there is no hope of that! no hope of my ever being anything
else than what I am, a selfish, willful, mercenary girl."

Nor was this mood a mere transitory one. That same night
she made a discovery which increased her apprehension almost
to terror. This was nothing less than the fact that Eleanore had
been keeping a diary of the last few weeks. "Oh," she cried in
relating this to me the next day, "what security shall I ever feel
as long as this diary of hers remains to confront me every time
I go into her room! And she will not consent to destroy it,
though I have done my best to show her that it is a betrayal of
the trust I reposed in her. She says that it is all there is to show
her reasons for doing as she has, and that without it she would
lack means of defense, if uncle should ever accuse her of treach-
ery to him and his happiness. She promises to keep it locked
up, but what good will that do? A thousand accidents might
happen, any of them sufficient to throw it into uncle's hands. I
shall never feel safe for a moment while it exists."

I endeavored to calm her by saying that if Eleanore was
without malice, such fears were groundless. But she would not
be comforted, and seeing her so wrought up, I suggested that
she should ask Eleanore to deliver it into my keeping till such
time as she should feel the necessity of using it. The idea struck
Mary favorably. "Oh, yes," cried she, "and I will put my certificate with it and so get rid of all my care at once." And before the afternoon was over she had seen Eleanore and made
her request.

It was acceded to with this proviso, that I was neither to destroy nor give up all or any of the papers except upon their
united demand. A small tin box was accordingly procured, into
which were put all the proofs of Mary's marriage then existing,
viz.: the certificate, Mr. Clavering's letters, and such leaves

from Eleanore's diary as referred to this matter. It was then handed over to me with the stipulation I have already mentioned, and I stowed it away in a certain closet upstairs, where it has lain undisturbed till last night.

Here Mrs. Belden paused, and blushing painfully, raised her eyes to mine with a look in which anxiety and entreaty were curiously blended.

"I don't know what you will say," she began, "but led away by my fears, I took that box out of its hiding-place last evening, and notwithstanding your advice, carried it from the house and it is now——"

"In my possession," said I quietly.

I don't think I ever saw her look more astounded, not even when I told her of Hannah's death. "Impossible!" she exclaimed. "I left it last night in the old barn that was burned down. I merely meant to hide it for the present and could think of no better place in my hurry; for the barn is said to be haunted—a man hung himself there once—and no one ever goes there. I—I—you cannot have it," cried she, "unless——"

"Unless I found and brought it away before the barn was destroyed," I suggested.

Her face flushed deeper: "Then you followed me?"

"Yes," said I. Then as I felt my own countenance redden, hastened to add: "We have been playing strange and unaccustomed parts, you and I. Some time when all these dreadful events shall be a mere dream of the past, we will ask each other's pardon. But never mind all this now. The box is safe, and I am anxious to hear the rest of your story."

This seemed to compose her, and after a minute she continued:

Mary seemed more like herself after this. And though owing to Mr. Leavenworth's return and their subsequent preparations for departure, I saw but little more of her, what I did see was enough to make me fear that with the locking up of the proofs of her marriage she was indulging the idea that the marriage itself had become void. But I may have wronged her in this.

The story of those few weeks is almost finished. On the eve of the day before she left, Mary came to my house to bid me good-bye. She had a present in her hand, the value of which I will not state, as I did not take it, though she coaxed me with all her prettiest wiles. But she said something that night that I have never been able to forget. It was this. I had been speaking of my hope that before two months had elapsed she would so win upon Mr. Leavenworth that she would be able to send for Mr. Clavering, and that when that day came, I should wish to be advised of it, when she suddenly interrupted me by saying:

"Uncle will never be won upon, as you call it, while he lives. If I was convinced of it before, I am sure of it now. Nothing but his death will ever make it possible for me to send for Mr. Clavering." Then seeing me look aghast at the long period of separation which this seemed to betoken, blushed a little and whispered: "The prospect looks somewhat dubious, doesn't it? But if Mr. Clavering loves me, he can wait."

"But," said I, "your uncle is only little past the prime of life and appears to be in robust health; it will be years of waiting, Mary."

"I don't know," murmured she. "I think not. Uncle is not as strong as he looks and——" She did not say any more, horrified perhaps at the turn the conversation was taking. But there was an expression on her countenance that set me thinking at the time and has kept me thinking ever since.

Not that any actual dread of such an occurrence as has since happened came to me then to make the long months which now intervened worse than they were. I was as yet too much under the spell of her charm to allow anything calculated to throw a shadow over her image to remain long in my thoughts. But when some time in the autumn a letter came to me personally from Mr. Clavering, filled with a vivid appeal to tell him something of the woman who in spite of her vows doomed him to a suspense so cruel, and when on the evening of the same day a friend of mine who had just returned from New York spoke of meeting Mary Leavenworth at some gathering, surrounded by manifest admirers, I began to realize the alarming features of the affair as it then existed, and sitting down I wrote her a letter. Not in the strain in which I had been accustomed to talk to her—I had not her pleading eyes and trembling, caressing hands ever before me to beguile my judgment from its proper exercise—but honestly and earnestly telling her how Mr. Clavering felt and what was the risk she ran in keeping so ardent a lover from his rights. The reply she sent rather startled me.

"I have put Mr. Robbins out of my calculations for the present, and advise you to do the same, disappointing as it may be to you. As for the gentleman himself, I have told him that when I could receive him I would be careful to notify him. That day has not yet come.

"But do not let him be discouraged," she added in a postscript. "When he does receive his happiness, it will be a satisfying one."

When, I thought. Ah, it is that *when* which is likely to ruin all! But intent only upon fulfilling her will, I sat down and wrote a letter to Mr. Clavering, in which I stated what she had said and begged him to have patience, adding that I would surely let him know if any change took place in Mary or her circumstances. And having dispatched it to his address in London, awaited the development of events.

They were not slow in transpiring. In two weeks from that time I heard of the sudden death of Mr. Stebbins, the minister who had married them; and while yet laboring under the agitation produced by this shock, was further startled by seeing in a New York paper the name of Mr. Clavering among the list of arrivals at the Hoffman House; showing that my letter to him had failed in its intended effect, and that the patience Mary had calculated upon so blindly was verging to its end. I was consequently far from being surprised when, in a couple of weeks or so afterward, a letter came from him to my address, which, owing to the careless omission of the private mark upon the envelope, I opened, and read enough to learn that, driven to desperation by the constant failures which he had experienced in all his endeavors to gain access to her in public or private, a failure which he was not backward in ascribing to her indisposition to see him, he had made up his mind to risk everything, even her displeasure; and by making an appeal to her uncle, end the suspense under which he was laboring, definitely and at once. "I want you, Amy," he wrote, "dowered or dowerless, it makes little difference to me. If you will not come of yourself, then I must follow the example of the brave knights, my ancestors; storm the castle that holds you, and carry you off by force of arms."

Neither can I say that I was much surprised, knowing Mary as I did, when in a few days from this she forwarded to me, for copying, this reply: "If Mr. Robbins ever expects to be happy with Amy Belden, let him reconsider the determination of which he speaks. Not only would he by such an action succeed in destroying the happiness of her he professes to love, but run the greater risk of effectually annulling the affection which makes the tie between them endurable."

To this there was neither date nor signature. It was the cry of warning which a spirited, self-contained creature gives when brought to bay. It made even me recoil, though I had known from the first that her pretty willfulness was but the tossing foam floating above the soundless depths of cold resolve and most deliberate purpose.

What its real effect was upon him and her fate I can only conjecture. All I know is that in two weeks thereafter Mr. Leavenworth was found murdered in his room, and Hannah Chester, coming direct to my door from the scene of violence, begged me to take her in and secrete her from public inquiry, as I loved and desired to serve Mary Leavenworth.

CHAPTER 7

Unexpected Testimony

Pol. What do you read, my lord?
Ham. Words, words, words.
—HAMLET.

Mrs. Belden paused, lost in the somber shadow which these words were calculated to evoke, and a short silence fell upon the room. It was broken by my asking for some account of the occurrence she had just mentioned, it being considered a mystery how Hannah could have found entrance into her house without the knowledge of the neighbors.

"Well," said she, "it was a chilly night and I had gone to bed early—I was sleeping then in the room off this—when, at about a quarter to one—the last train goes through R—— at 12.50—there came a low knock on the window-pane at the head of my bed. Thinking that some of the neighbors were sick, I hurriedly rose on my elbow and asked who was there. The answer come in low, muffled tones: 'Hannah, Miss Leavenworth's girl! Please let me in at the kitchen door.' Startled at hearing the well-known voice, and fearing I knew not what, I caught up a lamp and hurried round to the door. 'Is anyone with you?' I asked. 'No,' she replied. 'Then come in.' But no sooner had she done so than all my strength failed me and I had to sit down, for I saw she looked very pale and strange, was without baggage and altogether had the appearance of some wandering spirit. 'Hannah!' I gasped, 'what is it? what has happened? what brings you here in this condition and at this time of night?' 'Miss Leavenworth has sent me,' replied she in the low monotonous tone of one repeating a lesson by rote. 'She told me to come here; said you would keep me. I am not to go out of the house and no one is to know I am here.' 'But why?' I asked, trembling with a thousand undefined fears, 'what has occurred?' 'I dare not say,' she whispered, 'I am forbidden; I am just to stay here and keep quiet.' 'But——' I began, helping her take off her shawl, the dingy blanket advertised for in the papers—'You must tell me. She surely did not forbid you to tell *me*?' 'Yes, she did, everyone,' the girl replied, growing white in her persistence, 'and I never break my word, fire couldn't draw it out of me.' She looked so determined, so utterly unlike herself as I remembered her in the meek, unobtrusive days of our old acquaintance, that I could do nothing but stare at her. 'You will keep me,' she said, 'you will not turn me away?' 'No,' I said, 'I will not turn you away.' 'And tell no one?' she went on. 'And tell no one,' I repeated.

"This seemed to relieve her. Thanking me, she quietly followed me upstairs. I put her into the room in which you found her, because it was the most secret one in the house, and there

she has remained ever since, satisfied and contented as far as I could see till this very same horrible day."

"And is that all?" I asked. "Did you have no explanation with her afterward? Did she never give you any information in regard to the transaction which led to her flight?"

"No, sir. She kept a most persistent silence. Neither then nor when, upon the next day, I confronted her with the papers in my hand and the awful question upon my lips as to whether her flight had been occasioned by the murder which had taken place in Mr. Leavenworth's household, did she do more than acknowledge she had run away on its account. Someone or something had sealed her lips, and as she said, 'Fire and torture should never make her speak.'"

Another short pause followed this, then with my mind still hovering about the one point of intensest interest to me, I said:

"This story, then, this account which you have just given me of Mary Leavenworth's secret marriage and the great strait it put her into—a strait from which nothing but her uncle's death could seem to relieve her—together with this acknowledgment of Hannah's that she had left home and taken refuge here on the insistence of Mary Leavenworth, is the groundwork you have for the suspicions you have mentioned?"

"Yes, sir, that and the proof of her interest in the matter which is given by the letter I received from her yesterday, and which you say you have now in your possession."

Oh, that letter!

"I know," Mrs. Belden went on in a broken voice, "that it is wrong in a serious case like this to draw hasty conclusions: but oh, sir, how can I help it, knowing what I do?"

I did not answer, I was revolving in my mind the old question: was it possible, in face of all these later developments, still to believe Mary Leavenworth's own hand guiltless of her uncle's blood?

"It is dreadful to come to such conclusions," proceeded Mrs. Belden, "and nothing but her own words written in her own hand would ever have driven me to them, but——"

"Mrs. Belden," I interrupted, "pardon me, but you said in the beginning of this interview that you did not believe Mary herself had any direct hand in her uncle's murder. Are you ready to repeat that assertion?"

"Yes, yes, indeed. Whatever I may think of her influence in inducing it, I never could imagine her having anything to do with its actual performance. Oh no, oh no, whatever was done on that dreadful night, Mary Leavenworth never put hand to pistol or ball, or even stood by while they were used, that you may be sure of. Only the man who loved her, longed for her, and felt the impossibility of obtaining her by any other means, could have found nerve for an act so horrible."

"Then you think——"

"Mr. Clavering is the man? I do, and oh, sir, when you consider that he is her husband, is it not dreadful enough?"

"It is indeed," said I, rising to conceal how much I was affected by this conclusion of hers.

Something in my tone or appearance seemed to startle her. "I hope and trust I have not been indiscreet," she cried, eyeing me with something like an incipient distrust. "With this dead girl lying in my house, I ought to be very careful, I know, but——"

"You have said nothing," I cried, edging toward the door in my anxiety to escape if but for a moment from an atmosphere that was stifling me. "No one can blame you for anything you have either said or done today. But"—and here I paused and walked hurriedly back—"I wish to ask one thing more. Have you any reason beyond that of natural repugnance to believing a young and beautiful woman guilty of a great crime for saying what you have of Henry Clavering, a gentleman who has hitherto been mentioned by you with respect?"

"No," she whispered, with a touch of her old agitation, "none but that."

I felt the reason insufficient, and turned away with something of the same sense of suffocation with which I heard that the key sought for had been found in Eleanore Leavenworth's possession. "You must excuse me," I said; "I want to be a moment by myself in order to ponder over the facts which I have just heard; I will soon return"; and without further ceremony, hurried from the room.

By some indefinable impulse I went immediately upstairs, and took my stand at the western window of the large room directly over Mrs. Belden. The blinds were closed; the room was shrouded in funereal gloom, but its somberness and horror were for the moment unfelt: I was engaged in a fearful debate with myself. Was Mary Leavenworth the principal or merely the accessory in this crime? Did the determined prejudice of Mr. Gryce, the convictions of Eleanore, the circumstantial evidence even of such facts as had come to our knowledge, preclude the possibility that Mrs. Belden's conclusions were correct? That all the detectives interested in the affair would regard the question as settled I did not doubt, but need it be? Was it utterly impossible to find evidence yet that Henry Clavering was, after all, the assassin of Mr. Leavenworth?

Filled with the thought, I looked across the room to the closet where lay the body of the girl who, according to all probability, had known the truth of this matter, and a great longing seized me. Oh, why could not the dead be made to speak? Why should she lie there so silent, so pulseless, so inert, when a word from her was enough to decide the awful question? Was there no power to compel those pallid lips to move?

Carried away by the fervor of the moment, I made my way to her side. Ah, God, how still! With what a mockery the closed lips and lids confronted my demanding gaze! A stone could not have been more unresponsive.

With a feeling that was almost like anger I stood there, when—oh, what was it I saw protruding from beneath her shoulders where they crushed against the bed? an envelope, a letter? Yes.

Dizzy with the sudden surprise, overcome with the wild hopes this discovery awakened, I stooped in great agitation and drew the letter out. It was sealed but not directed. Breaking it hastily open, I took a glance at its contents. Good Heavens! It was the work of the girl herself!—its very appearance was enough to make that evident! Feeling as if a miracle had happened, I hastened with it into the other room and set myself to decipher the awkward scrawl.

This is what I saw rudely printed in lead pencil on the inside of a sheet of common writing-paper:

I am a wicked girl. I have known things all the time which I had ought to have told but I didn't dare to he said he would kill me if I did I mene the tall splendud looking gentulman with the black mustash who I met coming out of Mister Leavenworth's room with a key in his hand the night Mr. Leavenworth was murdered. He was so scared he gave me money and made me go away and come here and keep everything secret but I can't do so no longer. I seem to see Miss Elenor all the time crying and asking me if I want her sent to prisun. God knows I'd rathur die. And this is the truth and my last words and I pray everybody's forgiveness and hope nobody will blame me and that they won't bother Miss Elenor any more but go and look after the handsome gentulman with the black mustash.

BOOK IV

THE PROBLEM SOLVED

CHAPTER I

Mr. Gryce Resumes Control

It out-herods Herod.
—HAMLET.

A thing devised by the enemy.
—RICH. III.

A half-hour had passed. The train upon which I had every reason to expect Mr. Gryce had arrived, and I stood in the doorway awaiting with indescribable agitation the slow and labored approach of the motley group of men and women which I had observed leave the station at the departure of the cars. Would he be among them? Was the telegram of a nature peremptory enough to make his presence here, sick as he was, an absolute certainty? The written confession of Hannah throbbing against my heart, a heart all elation now, as but a short half-hour before it had been all doubt and struggle, seemed to rustle distrust, and the prospect of a long afternoon spent in impatience was rising before me, when a portion of the advancing crowd turned off into a side-street, and I saw the form of Mr. Gryce hobbling not on two sticks, but very painfully on one, coming slowly down the street.

His face, as he approached, was a study.

"Well, well, well," exclaimed he, as we met at the gate; "this is a pretty how-d'ye-do, I must say. Hannah dead, eh? and everything turned topsy-turvy! Humph, and what do you think of Mary Leavenworth now?"

It would therefore seem natural, in the conversation which followed his introduction into the house and installation in Mrs. Belden's parlor, I should begin my narration by showing him Hannah's confession; but it was not so. Whether it was I felt anxious to have him go through the same alternations of hope and fear it had been my lot to experience since I came to R——; or, whether in the depravity of human nature there lingered within me sufficient resentment for the persistent disregard he had always paid to my suspicions of Henry Clavering, to make it a matter of moment to me, to spring this knowledge upon him just at the instant his own convictions seemed to have reached the point of absolute certainty, I cannot say. Enough that it was not till I had given him a full account of every other matter connected with my stay in this house; not till I saw his eye beaming and his lip quivering with the excitement incident upon the perusal of the letter from Mary, found in Mrs. Belden's pocket; not, indeed, until I became assured from such expressions as "Tremendous! The deepest game of the season! Nothing like it since the Lafarge affair!" that in another moment he would be uttering some theory or belief that, once heard, would forever stand like a barrier between us, did I allow myself to hand him the letter I had taken from under the dead body of Hannah.

I shall never forget his expression, as he received it. "Good Heavens!" cried he, "what's this?"

"A dying confession," replied I, "of the girl Hannah. I found it lying in her bed, when I went up a half-hour ago to take a second look at her."

Opening it, he glanced over it with an incredulous air, that speedily, however, turned to one of the utmost astonishment, as he hastily read it, and then stood turning it over and over in his hand, examining it.

"A remarkable piece of evidence," exclaimed I, not without a certain feeling of triumph; "quite changes the aspect of affairs!"

"Think so?" answered he sharply; then whilst I stood staring at him in amazement, his manner was so different from what I expected, he looked up and said: "You tell me that you found this in her bed. Whereabouts in her bed?"

"Under the body of the girl herself," returned I. "I saw one corner of it protruding from beneath her shoulders, and drew it out."

He came and stood before me. "Was it folded or open when you first looked at it?"

"Folded; fastened up in this envelope," showing it to him.

He took it, looked at it for a moment, and went on with his questions.

"This envelope has a very crumpled appearance, as well as the letter itself. Were they so when you found them?"

"Yes, not only so, but doubled up as you see."

"Doubled up? You are sure of that? Folded, sealed and then doubled up as if her body had rolled across it while alive?"

"Yes."

"No trickery about it? No look as if the thing had been insinuated there since her death?"

"Not at all; I should rather say that to every appearance she held it in her hand when she lay down, but turning over, dropped it and had lain upon it."

Mr. Gryce's eyes, which had been very bright, ominously clouded; evidently he had been disappointed in my answers. Laying the letter down, he stood musing, but suddenly lifted it again, scrutinized the edges of the paper on which it was written, and, darting me a quick look, vanished with it into the shade of the window-curtain. His manner was so peculiar, I involuntarily rose to follow, but he waved me back, saying: "Amuse yourself with that box on the table, which you had such an ado over; see if everything is there according to Mrs. Belden's telling; I want to be by myself for a moment."

Subduing my astonishment, I proceeded to comply with his request, but scarcely had I lifted the lid of the box before me, when he came hurrying back, flung the letter down on the table with an air of the greatest excitement, and cried:

"Did I say there had never been anything like it since the Lafarge affair? I tell you there has never been anything like it in any affair. It is the rummest case on record! Mr. Raymond"— and his eyes, in his excitement, actually met mine for the first time in my experience of him; "prepare yourself for a disappointment. This pretended confession of Hannah's is a fraud!"

"A fraud?"

"Yes; fraud, forgery, what you will; the girl never wrote it."

Amazed, outraged almost, I bounded from my chair. "How do you know that?" cried I.

Bending forward, he put the letter into my hand. "Look at it," said he, "examine it closely. Now tell me what is the first thing you notice in regard to it."

"Why, the first thing that strikes me is that the words are printed, instead of written, something which might be expected from this girl, according to all accounts."

"Well?"

"That they are printed on the inside of a sheet of ordinary paper——"

"Ordinary paper?"

"Yes."

"That is, a sheet of commercial note of the ordinary quality."

"Of course."

"But is it?"

"Why yes, I should say so."

"Look at the lines."

"What of them? Oh, I see, they run up close to the top of the page; evidently the scissors have been used here."

"In short, it is a large sheet, trimmed down to the size of commercial note?"

"Yes."

"And is that all you see?"

"All but the words."

"Don't you perceive what has been lost by means of this trimming down?"

"No, unless you mean the manufacturer's stamp in the corner." Mr. Gryce's glance took meaning. "But I don't see why the loss of that should be deemed a matter of any importance."

"Don't you? not when you consider that by it we seem to be deprived of all opportunity of tracing this sheet back to the quire of paper from which it was taken?"

"No."

"Humph! then you are more of an amateur than I thought you. Don't you see that as Hannah could have had no motive in concealing where the paper came from on which she wrote her dying words, this sheet must have been prepared by someone else?"

"No," said I, "I cannot say I see all that."

"Can't! Well, then, answer me this. Why should Hannah, a girl about to commit suicide, care whether any clue was furnished in her confession, to the actual desk, drawer, or quire of paper from which the sheet was taken on which she wrote it?"

"She wouldn't."

"Yet especial pains have been taken to destroy that clue.

"But——"

"Then there is another thing. Read the confession itself, Mr. Raymond, and tell me what you gather from it."

"Why," said I, after complying, "that the girl, worn out with constant apprehension, has made up her mind to do away with herself, and that Henry Clavering——"

"Henry Clavering?"

The interrogation was put with so much meaning, I looked up. "Yes," said I.

"Ah, I didn't know that Mr. Clavering's name was mentioned there; excuse me."

"His name is not mentioned, but a description is given so strikingly in accordance——"

Here Mr. Gryce interrupted me. "Does it not seem to you a little surprising that a girl like Hannah should have stopped to describe a man she knew by name?"

I started; it was unnatural surely.

"You believe Mrs. Belden's story, don't you?"

"Yes."

"Consider her accurate in her relation of what took place there a year ago?"

"I do."

"Must believe, then, that Hannah, the go-between, was acquainted with Mr. Clavering, and with his name?"

"Undoubtedly."

"Then why didn't she use it? If her intention was as she here professes, to save Eleanore Leavenworth from the false imputation which had fallen upon her, she would naturally take the most direct method of doing it. This description of a man, whose identity she could have at once put beyond a doubt by the mention of his name, is the work, not of a poor ignorant girl, but of some person who, in attempting to play the role of one, has signally failed. But that is not all. Mrs. Belden, according to you, maintains that Hannah told her upon entering the house that Mary Leavenworth sent her here. But in this document, she declares it to have been the work of Black Moustache."

"I know, but could they not have both been parties to the transaction?"

"Yes," said he, "yet it is always a suspicious circumstance, when there is any discrepancy between the written and spoken declaration of a person. But why do we stand here fooling when a few words from this Mrs. Belden you talk so much about will probably settle the whole matter!"

"A few words from Mrs. Belden," I repeated. "I have had thousands from her today, and find the matter no nearer settled than in the beginning."

"*You* have had," said he, "but not I. Fetch her in, Mr. Raymond."

I rose. "One thing," said I, "before I go. What if Hannah had found the sheet of paper, trimmed just as it is, and used it without any thought of the suspicions it would occasion!"

"Ah!" said he, "that is just what we are going to find out."

Mrs. Belden was in a flutter of impatience when I entered the sitting room. When did I think the coroner would come? and what did I imagine this detective would do for us? It was dreadful waiting there alone for something, she knew not what.

I calmed her as well as I could, telling her the detective had not yet informed me what he could do, having some questions to ask her first. Would she come in and see him? She rose with alacrity. Anything was better than suspense.

Mr. Gryce, who in the short interim of my absence had altered his mood from the severe to the beneficent, received Mrs. Belden with just that show of respectful courtesy likely to impress a woman as dependent as she upon the good opinion of others.

"Ah! and this is the lady in whose house this very disagreeable event has occurred," exclaimed he, partly rising in his enthusiasm to greet her. "May I request you to sit," he asked, "if a stranger may be allowed to take the liberty of inviting a lady to sit in her own house?"

"It does not seem like my own house any longer," said she, but in a sad rather than an aggressive tone, so much had his genial way imposed upon her. "Little better than a prisoner here, I go and come, keep silence or speak, just as I am bidden, and all because an unhappy creature, whom I took in for the most unselfish of motives, has chanced to die in my house!"

"Just so!" exclaimed Mr. Gryce, "it is very unjust. But perhaps we can right matters. I have every reason to believe we can. This sudden death ought to be easily explainable. You say you had no poison in the house?"

"No, sir."

"And that the girl never went out?"

"Never, sir"

"And that no one has ever been here to see her?"

"No one, sir."

"So that she could not have procured any such thing if she had wished?"

"No, sir."

"Unless," he added suavely, "she had it with her when she came here?"

"That couldn't have been, sir. She brought no baggage, and as for her pocket I know everything there was in it, for I looked."

"And what did you find there?"

"Some money in bills, more than you would have expected such a girl to have, some loose pennies, and a common handkerchief."

"Well, then, it is proved the girl didn't die of poison, there being none in the house."

He said this in so convinced a tone, she was deceived. "That is just what I have been telling Mr. Raymond," giving me a triumphant look.

"Must have been heart disease," he went on. "You say she was well yesterday?"

"Yes, sir, or seemed so."

"Though not cheerful?"

"I did not say that; she was, sir, very."

"What, ma'am, this girl?" giving me a look. "I don't understand that. I should think her anxiety about those she had left behind her in the city would have been enough to keep her from being very cheerful."

"So you would," returned Mrs. Belden, "but it wasn't so. On the contrary, she never seemed to worry about them at all."

"What!" cried he, "not about Miss Eleanore, who, according to the papers, stands in so cruel a position before the world? But perhaps she didn't know anything about that—Miss Leavenworth's position, I mean?"

"Yes, she did, for I told her. I was so astonished I could not keep it to myself. You see, I had always considered Eleanore as one above reproach, and it shocked me so to see her name mentioned in the newspaper in such a connection, that I went to Hannah and read the article aloud and watched her face to see how she took it."

"And how did she?"

"I can't say. She looked as if she didn't understand; asked me why I read such things to her, and told me she didn't want to hear any more; that I had promised not to trouble her about this murder, and that if I continued to do so she wouldn't listen."

"Humph! and what else?"

"Nothing else. She put her hands over her ears and frowned in such a sullen way I left the room."

"That was when?"

"About three weeks ago."

"She has, however, mentioned the subject since?"

"No, sir, not once."

"What! not asked what they were going to do with her mistress?"

"No, sir."

"She has shown, however, that something was preying on her mind—fear, remorse, or anxiety?"

"No, sir, on the contrary, she has oftener appeared like one secretly elated."

"But," exclaimed Mr. Gryce with another sidelong look at me, "that was very strange and unnatural; I cannot account for it."

"Nor I, sir. I used to try to explain it by thinking her sensibilities had been blunted, or that she was too ignorant to comprehend the seriousness of what had happened, but as I learned to know her better, I gradually changed my mind. There was too much method in her gaiety for that. I could not help seeing she had some future before her for which she was preparing herself. As, for instance, she asked me one day if I thought she could learn to play on the piano. And I finally came to the conclusion she had been promised money if she kept the secret entrusted to her, and was so pleased with the prospect that she forgot the dreadful past and all connected with it. At all events that was the only explanation I could find for her general industry and desire to improve herself, or for the complacent smiles I detected now and then stealing over her face when she didn't know I was looking."

Not such a smile as crept over the countenance of Mr. Gryce at that moment, I warrant.

"It was all this," continued Mrs. Belden, "which made her death such a shock to me. I couldn't believe that so cheerful and healthy a creature could die like that, all in one night without anybody knowing about it. But——"

"Wait one moment," Mr. Gryce here broke in. "You speak of her endeavors to improve herself. What do you mean by that?"

"Her desire to learn things she didn't know, as for instance to write and read writing. She could only clumsily print when she came here."

I thought Mr. Gryce would take out a piece of my arm, he gripped it so.

"When she came here! Do you mean to say that since she has been with you she has learned to write?"

"Yes, sir. I used to set her copies and——"

"Where are these copies?" broke in Mr. Gryce, subduing his voice to its most professional tone. "And where are her attempts at writing? I'd like to see some of them. Can't you get them for us?"

"I don't know, sir. I always made it a point to destroy them as soon as they had answered their purpose. I didn't like to have such things about. But I will go and see."

"Do," said he, "I will go with you. I want to take a look at things upstairs, anyway." And heedless of his rheumatic feet, he rose and prepared to accompany her.

"This is getting very intense," I whispered as he passed.

The smile he gave me in reply would have made the fortune of a Thespian Mephistopheles.

Of the ten minutes of suspense which I endured in their absence, I say nothing. At the end of that time they returned with their hands full of paper boxes, which they flung down on the table.

"The writing-paper of the household," observed Mr. Gryce; "every scrap and half-sheet which could be found. But before you examine it, look at this." And he held out a sheet of bluish foolscap on which were written some dozen imitations of that time-worn copy: "BE GOOD AND YOU WILL BE HAPPY"; with an occasional *"Beauty soon fades,"* and *"Evil communications corrupt good manners."* "What do you think of that?"

"Very neat and very legible."

"That is Hannah's latest. The only specimens of her writing to be found. Not much like some scrawls we have seen, eh?"

"No."

"Mrs. Belden says this girl has known how to write as good as this for more than a week. Took great pride in it, and was continually talking about how smart she was." Leaning over he whispered in my ear: "This thing you have in your hand must have been scrawled some time ago, if she did it." Then aloud: "But let us look at the paper she used to write on."

Dashing open the covers of the boxes on the table, he took out the loose sheets lying inside, and scattered them out before me. One glance showed they were all of an utterly different quality from that used in the confession. "This is all the paper in the house," said he.

"Are you sure of that?" I asked, looking at Mrs. Belden, who stood in a sort of maze before us. "Wasn't there one stray sheet lying around somewhere, foolscap or something like that, which she might have got hold of and used without your knowing it?"

"No, sir, I don't think so. I had only these kinds; besides, Hannah had a whole pile of paper like this in her room, and wouldn't have been apt to go hunting round after any stray sheets."

"But you don't know what a girl like that might do. Look at

this one," said I, showing her the blank side of the confession. "Couldn't a sheet like this have come from somewhere about the house? Examine it well, the matter is important."

"I have," replied she, "and I say no, I never had a sheet of paper like that in my house."

Mr. Gryce advanced and took the confession from my hand. As he did so, he whispered: "What do you think now? Many chances that Hannah got up this precious document?"

I shook my head, convinced at last, but in another moment turned to him and whispered back: "But if Hannah didn't write it, who did? And how came it to be found where it was?"

"That," said he, "is just what is left for us to learn." And beginning again, he put question after question concerning the girl's life in the house, receiving answers which only tended to show that she could not have brought the confession with her, much less received it from a secret messenger. Unless we doubted Mrs. Belden's word, the mystery seemed impenetrable, and I was beginning to despair of success, when Mr. Gryce, with an askance look at me, leaned toward Mrs. Belden and said:

"You received a letter from Miss Mary Leavenworth yesterday, I hear."

"Yes, sir."

"*This* letter?" continued he, showing it to her.

"Yes, sir."

"Now I want to ask you a question. Was the letter, as you see it, the only contents of the envelope in which it came? Wasn't there one for Hannah enclosed with it?"

"No, sir," replied she, but with strange eagerness. "There was nothing in my letter for her, but she had a letter herself yesterday. It came in the same mail with mine."

"Hannah had a letter!" exclaimed we both, "and in the mail?"

"Yes, but it was not directed to her. It was"—casting me a look full of despair, "directed to me. It was only by a certain mark on the corner of the envelope that I knew——"

"Good Heavens!" interrupted I, "where is this letter? Why didn't you speak of it before? What do you mean by allowing us to flounder about here in the dark, when a glimpse of this letter might have set us right at once?"

"I didn't think anything about it till this minute. I didn't know it was of importance. I——"

But I couldn't restrain myself. "Mrs. Belden," cried I, "where is this letter? Have you got it?"

"No," said she, "I gave it to the girl yesterday, I haven't seen it since."

"It must be upstairs, then. Let us take another look," and I hastened toward the door.

"You won't find it," said Mr. Gryce at my elbow. "*I* have looked. There is nothing but a pile of burned paper in the corner. By the way, what could that have been?" asked he of Mrs. Belden.

"I don't know, sir. She hadn't anything to burn unless it was the letter."

"We will see about that," murmured I, hurrying upstairs and bringing down the washbowl with its contents. "If the letter was the one I saw in your hand at the post office it was in a yellow envelope."

"Yes, sir."

"Yellow envelopes burn differently from white paper. I ought to be able to tell the tinder made by a yellow envelope when I see it. Ah, the letter has been destroyed, here is a piece of the envelope," and I drew out of the heap of charred scraps a small bit less burnt than the rest and held it up.

"Then there is no use looking here for what the letter contained," said Mr. Gryce, putting the washbowl aside. "We will have to ask you, Mrs. Belden."

"But I don't know. It was directed to me to be sure, but Hannah told me when she first requested me to teach her how to write, that she expected such a letter, so I didn't open it when it came, but gave it to her just as it was."

"You, however, stayed by to see her read it?"

"No, sir, I was in too much of a flurry. Mr. Raymond had just come and I had no time to think of her. My own letter, too, was troubling me."

"But you surely asked her some questions about it before the day was out?"

"Yes, sir, when I went up with her tea-things, but she had

nothing to say. Hannah could be as reticent as anyone I ever knew, when she pleased. She didn't even admit it was from her mistress."

"Ah, then you thought it was from Miss Leavenworth?"

"Why, yes, sir, what else was I to think, seeing that mark in the corner? Though to be sure it might have been put there by Mr. Clavering," she added thoughtfully.

"You say she was cheerful yesterday; was she so after receiving this letter?"

"Yes, sir, as far as I could see. I wasn't with her long; the necessity I felt of doing something with the box in my charge— but perhaps Mr. Raymond has told you?"

Mr. Gryce nodded.

"It was an exhaustive evening and quite put Hannah out of my head, but——"

"Wait!" cried Mr. Gryce, and beckoning me into a corner, he whispered: "Now comes in that experience of Q's. While you are gone from the house and before Mrs. Belden sees Hannah again, he has a glimpse of the girl bending over something in the corner of her room which may very fairly be the washbowl we found there. After which, he sees her swallow, in the most lively way, a dose of something from a bit of paper. Was there anything more?"

"No," said I.

"Very well then," cried he, going back to Mrs. Belden. "But——"

"But when I went upstairs to bed, I thought of the girl, and going to her door, opened it. The light was extinguished and she seemed asleep, so I closed it again and came out."

"Without speaking?"

"Yes, sir."

"Did you notice how she was lying?"

"Not particularly. I think on her back."

"In something of the same position in which she was found this morning?"

"Yes, sir."

"And that is all you can tell us either of her letter or her mysterious death?"

"All, sir."

Mr. Gryce straightened himself up.

"Mrs. Belden," said he, "you know Mr. Clavering's hand-writing when you see it?"

"I do."

"And Miss Leavenworth's?"

"Yes, sir."

"Now which of the two was upon the envelope of the letter you gave Hannah?"

"I couldn't say. It was a disguised handwriting and might have been that of either, but I think——"

"Well?"

"That it was more like hers than his, though it wasn't like hers either."

With a smile Mr. Gryce enclosed the confession in his hand in the envelope in which it had been found. "You remember how large the letter was which you gave her?"

"Oh, it was large, very large, one of the largest sort."

"And thick?"

"Oh, yes, thick enough for two letters."

"Large enough and thick enough to contain this?" laying the confession folded and enveloped as it was before her.

"Yes, sir," giving it a look of startled amazement, "large enough and thick enough to contain that."

Mr. Gryce's eyes, bright as diamonds, flashed round the room and finally settled upon a fly traversing my coat-sleeve.

"Do you need to ask now," whispered he in a low voice, "where and from whom this so-called confession comes?"

Mr. Gryce allowed himself one moment of silent triumph, then rising, began folding the papers on the table and putting them in his pocket.

"What are you going to do?" I asked, hurriedly approaching.

He took me by the arm and led me across the hall into the sitting room. "I am going back to New York. I am going to pursue this matter. I am going to find out from whom came the poison that killed this girl, and by whose hand this vile forgery of a confession was written."

"But," said I, rather thrown off my balance by all this, "Q

and the coroner will be here presently; won't you wait to see them?"

"No," said he, "clues such as are given here must be followed while the trail is hot. I can't afford to wait."

"If I am not mistaken they have already come," said I, as a tramping of feet without announced that someone stood at the door.

"That is so," cried he, hastening to let them in.

Judging from common experience, we had every reason to fear that an immediate stop would be put to all proceedings on our part, as soon as the coroner was introduced upon the scene. But happily for us and the interest at stake, Dr. Fink, of R——, proved to be a very sensible man. He had only to hear a true story of the affair, to recognize at once its importance and the necessity of the most cautious action in the matter. Further, by a sort of sympathy with Mr. Gryce, all the more remarkable that he had never seen him before, he expressed himself as willing to enter into our plans, offering not only to allow us the temporary use of such papers as we desired, but even undertaking to conduct the necessary formalities of calling a jury and instituting an inquest, in such a way as to give us time for the investigations we purposed to make.

The delay was therefore short. Mr. Gryce was enabled to take the 6:30 train for New York, and I to follow on the 10 P.M.— the calling of a jury, ordering of an autopsy, and final adjournment of the inquiry till the following Tuesday having all taken place in the interim.

CHAPTER 2

Fine Work

No hinge nor loop
To hang a doubt on!
But yet the pity of it, Iago! O Iago, the pity of it, Iago!
—OTHELLO.

Mr. Gryce had told me enough of his plans before leaving R——for me to understand that the clue he intended to follow was that given by the paper on which the confession was written. "Find in whose possession is the package of paper from which this sheet was taken, and you find the double murderer," he had said.

I was therefore not surprised when upon visiting his house early the next morning, I beheld him seated before a table on which lay a lady's writing-desk and a pile of paper, till he told me the desk was Eleanore's. "What," said I, "are you not yet satisfied of her innocence?"

"Oh, yes, but one must be thorough. No conclusion would be worth anything if the investigation made was not full and complete. Why," he cried, casting his eyes complacently toward the fire-tongs, "I have even been rummaging through Mr. Clavering's effects, unknown to him of course, as though the confession bears the proof upon its face that it could not have been written by him. It is not enough to look for evidence where you expect to find it, you must sometimes search for it where you don't. Now," said he, drawing the desk before him, "I don't anticipate finding anything here that I want, but it is among the possibilities I may, and that is enough for a detective."

"Did you see Miss Leavenworth this morning?" I asked, as he proceeded to fulfill his intention by emptying the contents of the desk upon the table.

"Yes, I was unable to procure what I desired without it. And she behaved very handsome, gave me the desk with her own hands and never raised an objection. To be sure she thought I wished it for the purpose of satisfying myself that she did not keep concealed in it the paper about which so much has been said. But it would have made but little difference if she had known the truth! There's nothing here she need dread having seen."

"Was Miss Leavenworth well?" I inquired, unable to control my anxiety. "And had she heard of Hannah's sudden death?"

"Yes, and was in great agitation concerning it. I should say that her convictions in reference to her cousin were strengthened by it. But let us see what we have here," pursued he, drawing the package of paper toward him with a look of great expectation. "I found this pile just as it is, in the drawer of the library table in Miss Leavenworth's house in Fifth Avenue. If I am not mistaken, it is the thing we want."

"But——"

"But this paper is square, while that of the confession is of the size and shape of commercial note? I know, but you remember the sheet used in the confession was trimmed down. Let us compare the quality."

Taking the confession from his pocket and a sheet from the pile before him, he looked at them closely, then held them out for my inspection. A glance showed they were of the same color.

"Hold them up to the light," said he.

I did so; the appearance presented by both was precisely alike.

"Now let us compare the ruling." And laying them both down on the table, he placed the edges of the two sheets together. The lines on the one accommodated themselves to those on the other, and that question was decided.

His triumph was assured. "I was convinced of it," said he. "From the moment I pulled open that drawer and saw this mass of paper lying within, I knew the end was come."

"But," cried I, in my old spirit of combativeness, "isn't there any room for doubt? This paper is of the commonest kind. Every family on the block might easily have specimens of it in their library."

"That isn't so," he said, "it is letter size, which has gone out.

Mr. Leavenworth used it for his manuscript or I doubt if it would have been found in his library. But if you are still incredulous, let us see what can be done," and jumping up, he carried the confession to the window, looked at it this way and that, and finally discovering what he wanted, came back and, laying it before me, pointed out one of the lines of ruling that was markedly heavier than the rest, and another which was so faint as to be almost indistinguishable. "Defects like these often run through a number of consecutive sheets," said he. "If we could find the identical half-quire from which this was taken, I might show you proof that would dispel every doubt," and taking up the one that lay on top, he rapidly counted the sheets. There were but eight. "It might have been taken from this one," said he, but upon looking closely at the ruling he found that it was uniformly distinct. "Humph! that won't do!" came from his lips.

The remainder of the paper, some dozen or so half-quires, looked undisturbed. Mr. Gryce tapped his fingers on the table and a frown crossed his face. "Such a pretty thing!" exclaimed he, "if it could only have been done!" Suddenly he took up the next half-quire. "Count the sheets," said he, thrusting it toward me, and himself lifting another.

I did as I was bid. "Twelve."

He counted his and laid them down. "Go on with the rest," cried he.

I counted the sheets in the next; twelve. He counted those in the one following and paused. "Eleven!"

He counted again and quietly put them aside. "I made a mistake," observed he.

But he was not to be discouraged. Taking another half-quire he went through with the same operation—in vain. With a sigh of impatience he flung it down on the table and looked up. "Halloo!" cried he, "what is the matter?"

"There are but eleven sheets in this package," I said, placing it in his hand.

The excitement he immediately evinced was contagious. Oppressed as I was I could not resist his eagerness. "Oh, beautiful!" he exclaimed. "Oh, beautiful! see! the light line on the inside, the heavy one on the outside and both in positions precisely corresponding to those on this sheet of Hannah's. What do you think now? Do you wish for any further proof?"

"The veriest doubter could ask for no more," returned I.

With something like a considerate regard for my emotion, he turned away. "I am obliged to congratulate myself," said he, "notwithstanding the gravity of the discovery that has been made. It is so neat, so very neat, and so conclusive. I declare I am astonished, myself, at the perfection of the thing. But what a woman that is!" cried he suddenly, in a tone of the greatest admiration, "what an intellect she has! what shrewdness! what skill! I declare it is almost a pity to entrap a woman who has done as well as this—taken a sheet from the very bottom of the pile, trimmed it into another shape, and then remembering the girl couldn't write, put what she had to say into coarse awkward printing, Hannah-like. *Splendid!* or would have been if any other man than myself had had this thing in charge." And all animated and glowing with his enthusiasm he eyed the chandelier above him as if it were the embodiment of his own sagacity.

Sunk in despair, I let him go on.

"Could she have done any better?" he now asked. "Watched, circumscribed as she was, could she have done any better? I hardly think so. The fact of Hannah's having learned to write after she left here was fatal. No, she could not have provided against that contingency."

"Mr. Gryce," I here interposed, unable to endure this any longer, "did you have an interview with Miss Mary Leavenworth this morning?"

"No," said he, "it was not my purpose to do so. I doubt, indeed, if she knew I was in her house. A servant maid who has a grievance is a very valuable assistance to a detective. With Molly at my side I didn't need to pay my respects to the mistress."

"Mr. Gryce," I said again after another moment of silent self-congratulation on his part and of desperate self-control on mine, "what do you propose to do now? You have followed your clue to the end and are satisfied. Such knowledge as this is the precursor of action."

"Humph! well, we will see," he returned, going to his private desk and bringing out the box of papers which we had no opportunity of looking at while at R——. "First let us examine these documents and see if they do not contain some hint which may be of service to us." And taking out the dozen or so loose sheets which had been torn from Eleanore's diary, he began turning them over.

While he was doing this, I took occasion to examine the other contents of the box. I found them to be just what Mrs. Belden had described them. A certificate of marriage between Mary and Mr. Clavering, and a half-dozen or more letters. While glancing over the former, a short exclamation from Mr. Gryce startled me into looking up.

"What is it?" cried I.

He thrust into my hand the leaves of Eleanore's diary. "Read," said he. "Most of it is a repetition of what you have already heard from Mrs. Belden, though given from a different standpoint, but there is one passage in it which, if I am not mistaken, opens up the way to an explanation of his murder, such as we have not had yet. Begin at the beginning, you won't find it dull."

Dull! Eleanore's feelings and thoughts during that anxious time, dull!

Mustering up my self-possession I spread out the leaves in their order and commenced.

"R——, July 6——"

"Two days after they got there, you perceive," Mr. Gryce explained.

"—A gentleman was introduced to us today upon the piazza whom I cannot forbear mentioning, first, because he is the most perfect specimen of manly beauty I ever beheld, and, secondly, because Mary, who is usually so voluble when gentlemen are concerned, had nothing to say when in the privacy of our own apartment I questioned her as to the effect his appearance and conversation had made upon her. The fact that he is an Englishman may have something to do with this; uncle's antipathy to everyone of that nation being as well known to her as to me. But somehow I cannot feel satisfied of this. That experience of hers with Charlie Somerville has made me suspicious, I fear. What if the story of last summer were to be repeated here with an Englishman for the hero! But I will not allow myself to contemplate such a possibility. Uncle will return in a few days and then all communication with one who, however elegant and prepossessing, is of a family and race with whom it is impossible for us to ally ourselves must of necessity cease. I should not have thought twice of all this if Mr. Clavering had not betrayed upon his introduction to Mary such intense and unrestrained admiration.

"July 8. The old story is to be repeated. Mary not only submits to the attentions of Mr. Clavering, but encourages them. Today she sat two hours at the piano singing over to him her favorite songs and tonight—— But I will not put down every trivial circumstance that comes under my observation; it is unworthy of me. And yet how can I afford to blind my eyes when the happiness of so many I love is at stake!

"July 11. If Mr. Clavering is not absolutely in love with Mary he is on the verge of it. He is now hardly ever absent from her side, making no disguise of his sentiments. He is a very noble-looking man, too much so to be trifled with in this reckless fashion.

"July 13. Mary's beauty blossoms like the rose. She was absolutely wonderful tonight in scarlet and silver. I think she is the sweetest-looking mortal I ever beheld, and in this I am sure Mr. Clavering passionately agrees with me: he never looked away from her tonight. But it is one thing for a woman like Mary to be loved, and another thing for her to return the passion lavished upon her. And yet from certain right true womanly signs, I begin to think that if Mr. Clavering were only an American, Mary would not be indifferent to his fine appearance, strong sense, and devoted affection. But did she not deceive us into believing she loved Charlie Somerville? In her case, blush and smile go for little, I fear. Would it not be wiser under the circumstances to say, I hope?

"July 17. Oh, my heart! Mary came into my room this evening and absolutely startled me by falling at my side and burying her face in my lap. 'Oh, Eleanore, Eleanore!' she murmured, quivering with what seemed to me very happy sobs. But when I strove to lift her head to my breast, she slid from my arms and drawing herself up into her old attitude of reserved pride, raised her hand as if to impose silence, and haughtily left the room.

There is but one interpretation to put upon this. Mr. Clavering has expressed his sentiments, and she is filled with that reckless delight which in its first flush makes one insensible to the existence of barriers which have hitherto been deemed impassable. When will uncle come?

"July 18. Little did I think when I wrote the above that uncle was already in the house. He arrived unexpectedly on the last train and came into my room just as I was putting away my diary. Looking a little careworn, he took me in his arms and then asked for Mary. I dropped my head and could not help stammering as I replied that she was in her own room. Instantly his love took alarm, and leaving me, he hastened to her apartment where I afterward learned he found her sitting abstractedly before her dressing-table with Mr. Clavering's family ring on her finger. I do not know what followed. An unhappy scene I fear, for Mary is ill this morning and uncle exceedingly melancholy and stern.

"Afternoon. We are an unhappy family. Uncle not only refuses to consider for a moment the question of Mary's alliance with Mr. Clavering, but even goes so far as to demand from her his instant and unconditional dismissal on pain of his severest displeasure. The knowledge of this very painful determination of his came to me in the most distressing way. Recognizing the state of affairs but secretly rebelling against the power of a prejudice that could allow itself to separate two persons otherwise fitted for each other, I sought uncle's presence this morning after breakfast, and attempted to plead their cause. But he almost instantly stopped me with the remark: 'You are the last one, Eleanore, that should seek to promote this marriage.' Trembling with apprehension, I asked him why. 'For the reason that by so doing you work entirely for your own interest.' More and more troubled I begged him to explain himself. 'I mean,' said he, 'that if Mary disobeys me by marrying this Englishman, I shall disinherit her and substitute your name in the place of hers in my will as well as in my affection.' For a moment the world swam before my eyes. 'You will never make me so wretched,' exclaimed I. 'I will make you my heiress, if Mary persists in her present determination,' and without further word he sternly left the room. What could I do but fall on my knees and pray. Of all in this miserable house, I am the most wretched. To supplant her! But I shall not be called upon to do it, Mary will give up Mr. Clavering."

"There!" exclaimed Mr. Gryce. "What do you think of that? Isn't it becoming plain enough what was Mary's motive for this murder? But go on, let us hear what followed."

With sinking heart, I continued. "The next entry is dated July 19, and runs thus:

"I was right. After a long struggle with uncle's invincible will, Mary has consented to dismiss Mr. Clavering. I was in the room when she made known her decision, and I shall never forget our uncle's look of gratified pride as he clasped her in his arms and called her his own True Heart. He has evidently been very much exercised over this matter, and I cannot but feel greatly relieved that affairs have terminated so satisfactorily. But Mary? What is there in her manner that vaguely disappoints me? What is there in her action that seems to draw a determining line between us? I cannot say. I only know that I felt a powerful shrinking overwhelm me when she turned her face to me and asked if I were satisfied now. But I conquered my feeling and held out my hand. She did not take it.

"July 26. How long the days are! The shadow of our late trial is upon me yet, I cannot shake it off. I seem to see Mr. Clavering's despairing face wherever I go. How is it that Mary preserves her cheerfulness? If she does not love him I should think the respect which she must feel for his disappointment would keep her from levity at least.

"Uncle has gone away again. Nothing I could say sufficed to keep him.

"July 28. It has all come out. Mary has only nominally separated from Mr. Clavering, she still cherishes the idea of one day allying herself to him in marriage. The fact was revealed to me in a strange way not necessary to mention here; and has since been confirmed by Mary herself. 'I admire the man,' she declared, 'and have no intention of giving him up.' 'Then why not tell uncle so?' I asked. Her only answer was a bitter smile and a short—'I leave that for you to do.'

"July 30. Midnight. Worn completely out, but before my blood cools let me write. Mary Leavenworth is a wedded wife.

I have just returned from seeing her give her hand to Henry Clavering. Strange that I can write it without quivering when my whole soul is one flush of indignation and revolt. But let me state the facts. Having left my room for a few minutes this morning, I returned to find on my dressing-table a note from Mary in which she informed me that she was going to take Mrs. Belden for a drive and would not be back for some hours. Convinced, as I had every reason to be, that she was on her way to meet Mr. Clavering, I only stopped to put on my hat——"

There the diary ceased.

"She was probably interrupted by Mary at that point," exclaimed Mr. Gryce. "But we have heard all we want to know. Mr. Leavenworth threatened to supplant Mary with Eleanore if she persisted in marrying contrary to his wishes, and what other conclusion can we come to than that he, upon hearing some four or five weeks since this marriage had been entered into by her, repeated his threats and so drew down his fate upon him?"

"None," I returned, convinced at last. "It is only too clear."

Mr. Gryce rose.

"But the writer of these words is saved," I went on, trying to grasp the one comfort left me. "No one who reads this diary will ever dare to insinuate she is capable of committing a crime."

"No," said he, "the diary settles that matter effectually."

I tried to be man enough to think of that and nothing else. To rejoice in her deliverance and let every other consideration go, but in this I did not succeed. "But Mary, her cousin, almost her sister, is lost," I muttered.

Mr. Gryce thrust his hands into his pockets and for the first time showed some evidence of secret disturbance. "Yes," he murmured, "I am afraid she is, I really am afraid she is." Then after a pause, during which I felt a certain thrill of vague hope—"Such an entrancing creature, too! it is a pity, it positively is a pity! I declare now the thing is worked up, I begin to feel almost sorry we have succeeded so well. Strange but true. If there was the least loophole out of it," he murmured. "But there isn't. The thing is clear as A, B, C." Suddenly he rose and began pacing the floor very thoughtfully, casting his glances here, there, and everywhere, except at me, though I believe now, as then, I was all he saw.

"Would it be a very great grief to you, Mr. Raymond, if Miss Mary Leavenworth should be arrested on this charge of murder?" he asked, pausing before a sort of tank in which two or three disconsolate-looking fishes were slowly swimming about.

"Yes," said I, "it would, a very great grief."

"Yet it has got to be done," said he, though with a strange lack of his usual decision. "As an honest official trusted to bring the murderer of Mr. Leavenworth to the notice of the proper authorities, I have got to do it."

Again that strange thrill of hope at my heart induced by his peculiar manner.

"Then my reputation as a detective. I ought surely to consider that. I am not so rich or so famous that I can afford to forget all that a success like this may bring me. No, lovely as she is, I have got to push it through." But even as he said this, he became still more thoughtful, gazing down into the murky depths of the wretched tank before him with such an intentness I half-expected the fascinated fishes to rise from the water and return his gaze. What was it? What was in his mind?

After a little while he turned, his indecision utterly gone. "Mr. Raymond," said he, "come here again at three. I shall then have my report ready for the Superintendent. I should like to show it to you first, so don't fail me."

There was something so repressed in his expression, I could not prevent myself from venturing one question. "Is your mind made up?" I asked.

"Yes," returned he, but in a peculiar tone and with a peculiar gesture.

"And you are going to make the arrest you speak of?"

"Come at three!"

CHAPTER 3

Gathered Threads

This is the short and the long of it.
—MERRY WIVES OF WINDSOR.

Promptly at the hour named, I made my appearance at Mr. Gryce's door. I found him awaiting me on the threshold.

"I have met you," said he gravely, "for the purpose of requesting you not to speak during the coming interview under any circumstances whatever. I am to do the talking, you the listening. Neither are you to be surprised at anything I may do or say. I am in a facetious mood"—he did not look so—"and may take it into my head to address you by another name than your own. If I do, don't mind it. Above all, don't talk." And without waiting to meet my look of doubtful astonishment, he led me softly upstairs.

The room in which I had been accustomed to meet him was at the top of the first flight, but he took me past that into what appeared to be the garret story, where after many cautionary signs he ushered me into a room so strange and weird in its appearance, that it produced something of the same effect upon me that a prison cell would have done. In the first place, it was darkly gloomy, being lighted simply by a very dim and dirty skylight. Next, it was hideously empty; a pine table and two hard-backed chairs set face to face at each end of it being the only articles in the room. Lastly it was surrounded by several closed doors with blurred and ghostly ventilators over their tops, which being round, looked like the blank eyes of a row of staring mummies. Altogether it was a lugubrious spot, and in the present state of my mind made me feel as if something unearthly and threatening lay crouched in the very atmosphere. Nor sitting there cold and desolate could I imagine that the sunshine glowed without, or that life, beauty, and pleasure paraded the streets below.

Mr. Gryce's expression as he took a seat and beckoned me to

do the same may have had something to do with this strange sensation, it was so mysteriously and somberly expectant.

"You'll not mind the room," said he in a tone so low and muffled I could scarcely hear him. "It's an awful lonesome spot, I know, but folks with such matters as these to deal with mustn't be too particular as to the places in which they hold their consultations, if they don't want all the world to know as much as they do. Smith?" and he gave me an admonitory shake of his finger while his voice took a more distinct tone, "I have done the business, the reward is mine, the assassin of Mr. Leavenworth is found and in two hours will be in custody. Do you want to know who it is?" leaning forward with every appearance of eagerness in tone and expression.

I stared at him in great amazement. Had anything new come to light? any great change taken place in his conclusions? All this preparation could not be for the purpose of acquainting me with what I already knew, yet——

He cut short my conjectures with a low expressive chuckle. "It was a long chase, I tell you," raising his voice still more, "a tight go; a woman in the business too, but all the women in the world can't pull the wool over the eyes of Ebenezer Gryce when he is on the trail, and the assassin of Mr. Leavenworth and"— here his voice became actually shrill in his excitement—"and of Hannah Chester is found.

"Hush!" he went on, though I had neither spoken nor made any move, "you didn't know Hannah Chester was murdered. Well, she wasn't in one sense of the word, but in another she was, and by the same hand that killed the old gentleman. How do I know this? Look here! This scrap of paper was found on the floor of her room, it had a few particles of a white powder sticking to it, those particles were tested last night and found to be poison. But you say the girl took it herself, that she was a suicide. You are right, she did take it herself and it was a suicide, but who terrified her into committing it? Why, the one who had the most reason to fear her testimony, of course. But the proof? you say. Well, sir, this girl left a confession behind her, throwing the onus of the whole crime on a certain party believed to be innocent. This confession was a forged one, known from three facts, first: that the paper upon which it was written was unobtainable by the girl in the place where she then was; second, that the words used therein were printed in coarse awkward characters, whereas Hannah, thanks to the teaching of the woman under whose care she was, could write very well; third, that the story told in the confession was not that related by the girl herself. Now the fact of a forged confession throwing the guilt upon an innocent party having been found in the keeping of this ignorant girl, killed by a dose of poison, taken with the fact there stated, that on the morning of the day on which she killed herself the girl received, from someone manifestly acquainted with the customs of the Leavenworth family, a letter large enough and thick enough to contain the confession folded as it was when found, makes it almost certain to my mind that the murderer of Mr. Leavenworth sent this powder and this so-called confession to the girl, meaning her to use them precisely as she did, for the purpose of throwing off suspicion from the right track and of destroying herself at the same time; for as you know, dead men tell no tales."

He paused and looked at the dingy skylight above us. Why did the air seem to grow heavier and heavier? Why did I shudder in vague apprehension? I knew all this before; why did it strike me, then, as something new?

"But who was this? you ask. Ah, that is the secret; that is the bit of knowledge which is to bring me fame and fortune. But secret or not, I don't mind telling you," lowering his voice and rapidly raising it again. "The fact is, I can't keep it to myself, it burns like a new dollar in my pocket. Smith, my boy, the murderer of Mr. Leavenworth—but stay, who does the world say it is? Whom do the papers point at and shake their heads over? A woman, a young, beautiful, bewitching woman! Ha, ha, ha! The papers are right, it is a woman, young, beautiful, and bewitching too. But what one? Ah, that's the question. There is more than one woman mixed up with this affair; which, then, of them all is it? Since Hannah's death I have heard it openly advanced that she was the guilty party in the crime; bah! Others cry it is the niece that was so unequally dealt with by her uncle in his will; bah! again. But folks are not without some justification for this latter assertion. Eleanore Leavenworth did know more of this matter than appeared. Worse than that, Eleanore Leavenworth stands in a position of positive peril today. If you don't think so, let me show you what the detectives have against her.

"Firstly: there is the fact that a handkerchief with her name on it was found stained with pistol-grease upon the scene of murder; a place where she explicitly denied having been for twenty-four hours previous to the discovery of the dead body.

"Secondly: the fact that she not only evinced terror when confronted with this bit of circumstantial evidence, but manifested a decided disposition both at this time and others to mislead inquiry, shirking a direct answer to some questions and refusing all answer to others.

"Thirdly: that an attempt was made by her to destroy a certain letter evidently relating to this crime.

"Fourthly: that the key to the library door was seen in her possession.

"All this, taken with the fact that the fragments of the letter which this same lady attempted to destroy within an hour after the inquest were afterward put together and were found to contain a bitter denunciation of one of Mr. Leavenworth's nieces, by a gentleman we will call x—in other words an unknown quantity—makes out a dark case against her, especially as after investigations revealed the fact that a secret underlay the history of the Leavenworth family. That, unknown to the world at large, and Mr. Leavenworth in particular, a marriage ceremony had been performed a year before in a little town called F—— between a Miss Leavenworth and this same x. That, in other words, the unknown gentleman who, in the letter partly destroyed by Miss Eleanore Leavenworth, complained to Mr. Leavenworth of the treatment received by him from one of his nieces was in fact the secret husband of that niece. And that, moreover, this same gentleman, under an assumed name, called on the night of the murder at the house of Mr. Leavenworth and asked for Miss Eleanore.

"Now you see with all this against her, Eleanore Leavenworth is lost if it cannot be proved, firstly that the articles testifying against her, viz.: the handkerchief, letter, and key, passed after the murder through other hands, before reaching hers; and secondly, that someone else had even a stronger reason than she for desiring Mr. Leavenworth's death at this time.

"Smith, my boy, both of these hypotheses have been established by me. By dint of moleing into odd secrets and following up of nice clues, I have finally come to the conclusion that not Eleanore Leavenworth, dark as are the appearances against her, but another woman, beautiful as she and fully as interesting, is the true criminal. In short, that her cousin, the exquisite Mary, is the murderer of Mr. Leavenworth, and by inference of Hannah Chester also."

He brought this out with such force and with such a look of triumph and appearance of having led up to it, that I was for the moment dumbfounded, and started as if I had not known what he was going to say. The stir I made seemed to awake an echo. Something like a suppressed cry was in the air about me. All the room appeared to breathe horror and dismay. Yet when in the excitation of this fancy, I half-turned round to look, I found nothing but the blank eyes of those dull ventilators staring upon me.

"You are taken aback!" Mr. Gryce went on. "I don't wonder. Everyone else is engaged in watching the movements of Eleanore Leavenworth, I only know where to put my hand upon the real culprit. You shake your head?" (Another fiction.) "You don't believe me! Think I am deceived. Ha, ha! Ebenezer Gryce deceived after a month of hard work! You are as bad as Miss Leavenworth herself, who has so little faith in my sagacity that she offered me, of all men, an enormous reward if I would find her out the assassin of her uncle! But that is neither here nor there, you have your doubts and you are waiting for me to solve them. Well, nothing is easier; know first that on the morning of the inquest I made one or two discoveries not to be found in the records, viz.: that the handkerchief picked up as I have said in Mr. Leavenworth's library had, notwithstanding its stains of pistol-grease, a decided perfume lingering about it. Going to the dressing-table of the two ladies, I sought for that perfume and found it in Mary's room, not Eleanore's. This led me to examine the pockets of the dresses respectively worn by them the evening before. In that of Eleanore I found a handkerchief, presumably the one she had carried at that time. But in Mary's there was none, nor did I see any lying about her room as if tossed down on her retiring. The conclusion I drew from this was, that she and not Eleanore had carried the handkerchief into her uncle's room, a conclusion emphasized by the fact privately communicated to me by one of the servants, that Mary was in Eleanore's room when the basket of clean clothes was brought up with this handkerchief lying on top.

"But knowing the liability we are under to mistake in such matters as these I made another search in the library and came across a very curious thing. Lying on the table was a penknife, and scattered on the floor beneath in close proximity to the chair were two or three minute portions of wood freshly chipped off from the leg of the table, all of which looked as if someone of a nervous disposition had been sitting there, whose hand in a moment of self-forgetfulness had caught up the knife and unconsciously whittled the table. A little thing, you say, but when the question is, which of two ladies, one of a calm and self-possessed nature, the other restless in her ways and excitable in her disposition, was in a certain spot at a certain time, it is these little things that become almost deadly in their significance. No one who has been with these two women an hour can hesitate as to whose delicate hand made that cut in Mr. Leavenworth's library table.

"But we are not done. I distinctly overheard Eleanore accuse her cousin of this deed. Now such a woman as Eleanore Leavenworth has proved herself to be never would accuse a relative of crime, without the strongest and most substantial reasons. Firstly, she must have been sure her cousin stood in a position of such emergency, that nothing but the death of her uncle could release her from it; secondly, that her cousin's character was of such a nature she would not hesitate to relieve herself from such an emergency by the most desperate of means; and, lastly, been in possession of some circumstantial evidence against her cousin, seriously corroborative of her suspicions. Smith, all this was true of Eleanore Leavenworth. As to the character of her cousin, she has had ample proof of her ambition, love of money, caprice and deceit, it having been Mary Leavenworth, and not Eleanore as was first supposed, who

had contracted the secret marriage already spoken of. Of the
critical position in which she stood, let the threat once made by
Mr. Leavenworth to substitute her cousin's name for hers in his
will in case she had married this x answer to all who knew the
tenacity with which Mary clung to her hopes of future fortune;
while for the corroborative testimony of her guilt which Eleanore is supposed to have had, remember that previous to the
key having been found in Eleanore's possession, she had spent
some time in her cousin's room, and that it was at Mary's fire-
place the half-burned fragments of that letter were found—and
you have the outline of a report that in an hour's time from this
will lead to the arrest of Mary Leavenworth as the assassin of
her uncle and benefactor."

A silence ensued which, like the darkness of Egypt, could be
felt, then a great and terrible cry rang through the room, and a
man's form, rushing from I knew not where, shot by me and
fell at Mr. Gryce's feet shrieking out:

"It is a lie! a lie! Mary Leavenworth is innocent as a babe
unborn. I am the murderer of Mr. Leavenworth, I! I! I!"

It was Trueman Harwell.

CHAPTER 4

Culmination

Saint seducing gold.
—ROMEO AND JULIET.

When our actions do not,
Our fears do make us traitors.
—MACBETH.

I never saw such a look of mortal triumph on the face of a man
as that which crossed the countenance of the detective.

"Well," said he, "this is unexpected but not wholly unwelcome. I am truly glad to learn Miss Leavenworth is innocent,

but I must hear some few more particulars before I shall be satisfied. Get up, Mr. Harwell, and explain yourself. If you are the murderer of Mr. Leavenworth, how comes it that things look so black against everybody but yourself?"

But in the hot, feverish eyes that sought him from the writhing form at his feet, there was mad anxiety and pain, but little explanation. Seeing him making unavailing efforts to speak, I drew near.

"Lean on me," said I, lifting him to his feet.

His face, relieved forever from its mask of repression, turned toward me with a look of a despairing spirit. "Save!" gasped he. "Save her—Mary—they are sending a report—stop it!"

"Yes," broke in another voice. "If there is a man here who believes in God and prizes woman's honor, let him stop the issue of that report." And Henry Clavering, dignified as ever, but in a state of extreme agitation, stepped into our midst through an open door at our right.

But at the sight of his face, the man in our arms quivered, shrieked, and gave one bound that would have overturned Mr. Clavering, herculean of frame as he was, had not Mr. Gryce interposed.

"Wait!" cried he, and holding back the secretary with one hand—where was his rheumatism now?—he put the other in his pocket and drew thence a document which he held up before Mr. Clavering. "It has not gone yet," said he, "be easy. And you," he went on, turning toward Trueman Harwell, "be quiet or——"

His sentence was cut short by the man springing from his grasp. "Let me go," shrieked he. "Let me have my revenge on him who in face of all I have done for Mary Leavenworth dares to call her his wife! Let me——" But at this point he paused; his frame, which had been one tremble, stiffening into stone, and his clutching hands outstretched for his rival's throat falling heavily back. "Hark!" said he, glaring over Mr. Clavering's shoulder! "it is she! I hear her! I feel her! she is on the stairs: she is at the door! she——" a low shuddering sigh of longing and despair finished the sentence: the door opened, and Mary Leavenworth stood before us.

It was a moment to make young hairs turn gray. To see her

face, so pale, so haggard, so wild in its fixed terror, turned toward Henry Clavering to the utter ignoring of the real actor in this most horrible scene! Trueman Harwell could not stand it.

"Ah, ah!" cried he, "look at her! cold, cold; not one glance for me though I have just drawn the halter from her neck and fastened it about my own!" And breaking from the clasp of the man who in his jealous rage would now have withheld him, he fell on his knees before Mary, clutching her dress with frenzied hands. "You shall look at me," he cried, "you shall listen to me, I will not lose body and soul for nothing. Mary, they said you were in peril; I could not endure that thought, so I uttered the truth—yes, though I knew what the consequence would be—and all I want now is for you to say you believe me when I declare that I only meant to secure to you the fortune you so much desired; that I never dreamed it would come to this, that it was because I loved you and hoped to win your love in return that I——"

But she did not seem to see him, did not seem to hear him. Her eyes were fixed upon Henry Clavering with an awful inquiry in their depths, and none but he could move her.

"You do not hear me!" shrieked the poor wretch. "Ice that you are, you would not turn your head if I should call to you from the depths of hell!"

But even that cry fell unheeded. Pushing her hands down upon his shoulders as though she would sweep some impediment from her path, she endeavored to advance. "Why is that man here?" cried she, indicating her husband with one quivering hand. "What has he done that he should be brought here to confront me at this awful time?"

"I told her to come here to meet her uncle's murderer," whispered Mr. Gryce into my ear.

But before I could reply to her, before Mr. Clavering himself could murmur a word, the guilty wretch before her had started to his feet.

"Don't you know?" cried he. "Then I will tell you. It is because these gentlemen, chivalrous and honorable as they consider themselves, think that you, the beauty and the Sybarite, committed with your own white hand the deed of blood which has brought you freedom and fortune. Yes, yes, this man"—

turning and pointing at me—"friend as he has made himself out to be kindly and honorable as you have doubtless believed him, but who in every look he has bestowed upon you, every word he has uttered in your hearing during all these four horrible weeks, has been weaving a cord for your neck—thinks you the assassin of your uncle, as does, perhaps, this other who calls you wife, unknowing that a man stood at your side, ready to sweep half the world from your path if that same white hand rose in bidding. That I——"

"You?" Ah! now she could see him, now she could hear him!

"Yes," clutching her robe again as she hastily recoiled, "didn't you know it? When in that dreadful hour of your rejection by your uncle, you cried aloud for someone to help you, didn't you know——"

"Don't!" she shrieked, bursting from him with a look of unspeakable horror. "Don't say that! Oh," she gasped, "is the mad cry of a stricken woman for aid and sympathy the call for a murderer?" And turning like a doe struck to the heart by the deadly arrow, she moaned: "Who that ever looks at me now will forget that a man—such a man! a man so low I have ever disdained to let my shadow fall beside his, lest we should seem to walk on a level—thought, dared to think, that because I was in mortal perplexity I would accept the murder of my best friend as a relief from it!" Her horror was unbounded. "Oh, what a chastisement for folly!" she murmured. "What a punishment for the love of money which has always been my curse!"

Henry Clavering could no longer restrain himself. Leaping to her side, he bent above her. "Was it nothing but folly, Mary? Are you guiltless of any deeper wrong? Is there no link of complicity between you two? Have you nothing on your soul but an inordinate desire to preserve your place in your uncle's will, even at the risk of breaking my heart and wronging your noble cousin? Are you innocent in this matter? Tell me!" Laying his hand on her head he pressed it slowly back and gazed into her eyes, then without a word took her to his breast and looked calmly around him.

"She is!" said he.

It was the uplifting of a stifling pall. No one in the room, un-

less it was the wretched criminal shivering before us, but felt a
sudden influx of hope. Even Mary's own countenance caught a
glow. "Oh," she whispered, withdrawing from his arms the
better to look into his face, "and is this the man I have trifled
with, injured, and tortured till the very name of Mary Leavenworth might well make him shudder! Is this he whom I married in a fit of caprice only to forsake and deny? Henry, do
you declare me innocent in face of all you have seen and heard,
in face of that moaning, chattering wretch before us and my
own quaking flesh and manifest terror; with the remembrance
on your heart and in your mind of the letter I wrote you the
morning after the murder, in which I prayed you to keep away
from me as I was in such deadly danger that the least hint given
to the world that I had a secret to conceal would destroy me?
Do you, can you, will you, declare me innocent before God
and the world?"

"I do," said he.

A light such as had never visited her face before passed
slowly over it. "Then God forgive me the wrong I have done
this noble heart, for I can never forgive myself! Wait!" said she
as he opened his lips. "Before I accept any further tokens of
your generous confidence, let me show you what I am. You
shall know the worst of the woman you have taken to your
heart. Mr. Raymond——" And she turned toward me for the
first time. "In those days when with such an earnest desire for
my welfare (as I believe, notwithstanding this man's insinuations), you sought to induce me to speak out and tell all I knew
concerning this dreadful deed, I did not do it because of one
thing: I was afraid. I knew the case looked dark against me,
Eleanore had told me so. Eleanore herself—and it was the
keenest pang I had to endure—believed me guilty. She had her
reasons. She knew first, from the directed envelope she had
found lying underneath my uncle's dead body on the library
table, that he had been engaged at the moment of death in
summoning his lawyer to make that change in his will which
would transfer my claims to her; secondly that I had been down
to his room the night before, though I denied it, for she had
heard my door open and my dress rustle as I passed out. But
that was not all: the key that everyone felt to be a positive

proof of guilt wherever found had been picked up by her from the floor of my room, the letter written by Mr. Clavering to my uncle was found in my fire; and the handkerchief which she had seen me take from the basket of clean clothes was produced at the inquest stained with pistol-grease. I could not account for these things. A web seemed tangled about my feet. I could not stir without encountering some new toil. I knew I was innocent, but if I failed to satisfy of it one who loved me, how could I hope to convince the general public if once called upon to do so? Worse still, if pure-faced Eleanore, with every apparent motive for desiring long life to our uncle, was held in such suspicion because of a few circumstantial evidences against her, what would I not have to fear if the truth concerning these things was told! The tone and manner of the juryman at the inquest that asked who would be most benefited by my uncle's will showed but too plainly. When, therefore, Eleanore, true to her heart's generous instincts, closed her lips and refused to speak when speech would have been my ruin, I let her do it, justifying myself with the thought that she had deemed me capable of crime and so must bear the consequences. Nor when I saw how dreadful these were likely to prove, did I relent. Fear of the ignominy, suspense, and danger that would follow confession sealed my lips. Only once did I hesitate. That was when in the last conversation we had, I saw that, notwithstanding appearances, you believed in Eleanore's innocence, and the thought crossed me you might be induced to believe in mine, if I threw myself upon your mercy. But just then Mr. Clavering came, and as in a flash I seemed to realize what my future life would be, stained by suspicion, and instead of yielding to my impulse, went so far in the other direction as to threaten Mr. Clavering with a denial of our marriage if he approached me again till all danger was over.

"Yes, he will tell you that was my welcome to him when with heart and brain racked by long suspense, he came to my door for one word of assurance that the peril I was in was not of my own making. That was the greeting I gave him after a year of silence, every moment of which was torture to him. But he forgives me; I see it in his eyes, I hear it in his accents; and you—Oh, if in the long years to come you can forget what I have made Eleanore suffer by my selfish fears; if, the shadow of her wrong before you, you can by the grace of some sweet hope think a little less hardly of me, do. I am afraid I shall never be worthy of it, but yet if you can, do. As for this man— torture could not be worse to me than this standing with him in the same room—let him come forward and declare if I by look or word have given him reason to believe I understood his passion, much less returned it."

"Why ask!" gasped he. "Don't you see it was your indifference that drove me mad? To stand before you, to agonize after you, to follow you with my thoughts in every move you made, to know my soul was welded to yours with bands of steel no fire could melt, no force destroy, no strain dissever; to sleep under the same roof, sit at the same table, and yet meet not so much as one look to show me you understood! It was that which made my life a hell. I was determined you should understand. If I had to leap into a pit of flame, you should know what I was, and what my passion for you was. And you do. You comprehend it all now. Shrink as you will from my presence, cower as you may to the weak man you call husband, you can never forget the love of Trueman Harwell; never forget that love, love, love, burning love for your beauty, was the force which led me down into your uncle's room that night and lent me will to pull the trigger which poured all the wealth you hold this day into your lap. Yes," he went on, towering in his preternatural despair till even the noble form of Henry Clavering looked dwarfed beside him, "every dollar that chinks from your purse shall talk of me. Every gew-gaw which flashes on that haughty head, too haughty to bend to me, shall shriek my name into your ears. Fashion, pomp, luxury—you will have them all; but till gold loses its glitter, satin its gloss, and ease its attraction, you will never forget the hand that gave them to you!"

With a look whose evil triumph I cannot describe, he put his hand into the arm of the waiting detective, and in another moment would have been led from the room; when Mary, crushing down the swell of emotion that was seething in her breast, lifted her head and said:

"No, Trueman Harwell, I cannot give you even that thought

for your comfort. Wealth that is laden with such a burden were torture. I cannot accept the torture, so must release the wealth, even if it were mine to dispose of, which it is not. From this day Mary Clavering owns nothing but that which comes to her from the husband she has so long and so basely wronged." And raising her hands to her ears, she tore out the diamonds which hung there, and flung them at the feet of the unfortunate man.

It was the final wrench of the rack. With a yell such as I never thought to listen to from the lips of a man, he flung up his arms, while all the lurid light of madness glared on his face. "And I have given my soul to hell for a shadow!" moaned he. "For a shadow!"

"Well, that is the best day's work I ever did! Your congratulations, Mr. Raymond, upon the success of the most daring game ever played in a detective's office."

I looked at the triumphant countenance of Mr. Gryce in amazement. "What do you mean?" I cried; "did you plan all this?"

"Did I plan it?" he repeated. "Could I stand here, seeing how things have turned out, if I had not? Mr. Raymond, let us be comfortable. You are a gentleman, but we can well shake hands over this. I have never known such a satisfactory conclusion to a bad piece of business in all my professional career."

We did shake hands long and fervently, and then I asked him to explain himself.

"Well," said he; "there has always been one thing that plagued me even in the very moment of my strongest suspicion against this woman, and that was the pistol-cleaning business. I could not reconcile it with what I knew of woman-kind. I could not make it seem the act of a woman. Did you ever know a woman who cleaned a pistol or who ever knew the object or use of doing so? No. They can fire them and do; but after firing them they do not clean them. Now it is a principle which every detective recognizes the truth of, that if of a hundred leading circumstances connected with a crime, ninety-nine of these are acts pointing to the suspected party with unerring certainty but the hundredth equally important act is one which that person could not have performed, the whole fabric of suspicion is destroyed. Recognizing this principle, then, as I have said, I hesitated when it came to the point of arrest. The chain was complete, the links were fastened, but one link was of a different size and material from the rest and in this argued a break in the chain. I resolved to give her a final chance. Summoning Mr. Clavering and Mr. Harwell, two persons whom I had no reason to suspect, but who were the only individuals besides herself who could have committed this crime, being the only persons of intellect who were in the house, or believed to be, at the time of the murder, I notified them separately that the assassin of Mr. Leavenworth was not only found but was about to be arrested in my house, and that if they wished to hear the confession which would be sure to follow, they might have the opportunity of doing so by coming here at such an hour. They were both too much interested, though for very different reasons, to refuse; and I succeeded in inducing them to conceal themselves in the two rooms from which you saw them issue, knowing that if either of them had committed this deed, he had done it for the love of Mary Leavenworth, and consequently could not hear her charged with crime and threatened with arrest, without betraying himself. I did not hope much from the experiment; least of all did I anticipate that Mr. Harwell would prove to be the guilty man—but live and learn, Mr. Raymond, live and learn."

CHAPTER 5

A Full Confession

Between the acting of a dreadful thing,
And the first motion, all the interim is
Like a phantasma or a hideous dream;
The genius and the mortal instruments,
Are then in council; and the state of a man
Like to a little Kingdom, suffers then
The nature of an insurrection.

—JULIUS CÆSAR.

I am not a bad man; I am only an intense one. Ambition, love, jealousy, hatred, revenge—transitory emotions with some, are terrific passions with me. To be sure they are quiet and concealed ones, coiled serpents that make no stir till aroused, but then deadly in their spring and relentless in their action. Those who have known me best, have not known this. My own mother was ignorant of it. Often and often have I heard her say: "If Trueman only had more sensibility! If Trueman were not so indifferent to everything! In short, if Trueman had more power in him!"

It was the same at school. No one understood me. They thought me meek; called me Dough-face. For three years they called me this, then I turned upon them. Choosing out their ringleader, I felled him to the ground, laid him on his back and stamped upon him. He was handsome before my foot came down; afterward—well, it is enough he never called me Dough-face again. In the store I entered soon after, I met with even less appreciation. Regular at my work and exact in my performance of it, they thought me a good machine and nothing more. What heart, soul, and feeling could a man have who never sported, never smoked, and never laughed? I could reckon up figures correctly, but one scarcely needed heart or soul for that. I could even write day by day and month by month without showing a flaw in my copy, but that only argued I was no more than they intimated, a regular automaton. I let them think so, with the certainty before me that they would one day change their minds as others had done. The fact was, I loved nobody well enough, not even myself, to care for any man's opinion. Life was well-nigh a blank for me; a dead level plain that had to be traversed whether I would or not. And such it might have continued to this day if I had never met Mary Leavenworth. But when, some nine months since, I left my desk in the counting-house for a seat in Mr. Leavenworth's library, a blazing torch fell into my soul whose flame has never gone out and never will till the doom before me is accomplished.

She was so beautiful! When on that first evening I followed my new employer into the parlor, and saw this woman standing up before me in her half-alluring, half-appalling charm, I knew as by a lightning flash what my future would be if I remained in that house. She was in one of her haughty moods and bestowed upon me little more than a passing glance. But her indifference made slight impression upon me then. It was enough that I was allowed to stand in her presence and look unrebuked upon her loveliness. To be sure it was like gazing into the flower-wreathed crater of an awakening volcano. Fear and fascination were in each moment I lingered there; but fear and fascination made the moment what it was, and I could not have withdrawn if I would.

And so it was always. Unspeakable pain as well as pleasure was in the emotion with which I regarded her. Yet for all that I did not cease to study her hour by hour and day by day; her smiles, her movement, her way of turning her head or lifting her eyelids. I had a purpose in this; I wished to knit her beauty so firmly into the warp and woof of my being that nothing should ever serve to tear it away. For I saw then as plainly as now, that coquette though she was, she would never stoop to me. No; I might lie down at her feet and let her trample over me, she would not even turn to see what it was she had stepped upon. I might spend days, months, years, learning the alphabet of her wishes, she would not thank me for my pains or even raise the lashes from her cheek to look at me as I passed. I was nothing to her, could not be anything unless—and this thought came slowly—I could in some way become her master.

Meantime I wrote at Mr. Leavenworth's dictation and pleased him. My methodical ways were just to his taste. As for the other member of the family, Miss Eleanore Leavenworth—she treated me just as one of her proud but sympathetic nature might be expected to do. Not familiarly, but kindly; not as a friend, but as a member of the household whom she met every day at table, and who, as she or anyone else could see, was none too happy or hopeful.

Six months went by; I had learned two things; firstly, that Mary Leavenworth loved her position as prospective heiress to a large fortune above every other earthly consideration; and, secondly, that she was in the possession of a secret which endangered that position. What this was, I had for some time no means of knowing. But when later I became convinced it was one of love, I grew hopeful, strange as it may seem. For by this time I had learned Mr. Leavenworth's disposition almost as perfectly as that of his niece, and knew that in a matter of this kind he would be uncompromising; and that in the clashing of these two wills something might occur which would give me a hold upon her. The only thing that troubled me was the fact that I did not know the name of the man in whom she was interested. But chance soon favored me here. One day—a month ago now, I sat down to open Mr. Leavenworth's mail as usual. One letter—shall I ever forget it?—ran thus:

HOFFMAN HOUSE,
March 1st, 1876.

MR. HORATIO LEAVENWORTH:
Dear Sir,

You have a niece whom you love and trust, one too who seems worthy of all the love and trust that you or any other man can give her; so beautiful, so charming, so tender is she in face, form, manner, and conversation. But, dear sir, every rose has its thorn and your rose is no exception to this rule. Lovely as she is, charming as she is, tender as she is, she is not only capable of trampling on the rights of one who trusted her, but of bruising the heart and breaking the spirit of him to whom she owes all duty, honor, and observance.

If you don't believe this, ask her to her cruel, bewitching face,
who and what is her humble servant and yours,

HENRY RITCHIE CLAVERING.

If a bombshell had exploded at my feet, or the evil one himself appeared at my call, I should not have been more astounded.
Not only was the name signed to these remarkable words unknown to me, but the epistle itself was that of one who felt
himself to be her master, a position which, as you know, I was
myself aspiring to occupy. For a few minutes, then, I stood a
prey to feelings of the bitterest wrath and despair; then I grew
calm, realizing that with this letter in my possession, I was vir-
tually the arbitrator of her destiny. Some men would have
sought her there and then, and by threatening to place it in her
uncle's hand, won from her a look of entreaty if no more; but
I—well, my plans went deeper than that. I knew that she must
be in extremity before I could hope to win her. She must feel
herself slipping over the edge of the precipice, before she would
clutch at the first thing offering succour. I decided to allow the
letter to pass into my employer's hands. But it had been opened!
How could I manage to give it to him in this condition without
exciting his suspicion? I knew of but one way; to let him see me
open it for what he would consider the first time. So waiting
till he came into the room, I approached him with the letter,
tearing off the end of the envelope as I came. Opening it, I gave
a cursory glance at its contents and tossed it down on the table
before him.

"That appears to be of a private character," said I, "though
there is no sign to that effect on the envelope."

He took it up while I stood there. At the first word he started,
looked at me, seemed satisfied from my expression that I had
not read far enough to realize its nature, and whirling slowly
around in his chair, devoured the remainder in silence. I waited a
moment, then withdrew to my own desk. One minute, two minutes passed in silence; he was evidently re-reading the letter, then
he hurriedly rose and left the room. As he passed me I caught a
glimpse of his face in the mirror. The expression I saw there did
not tend to lessen the hope that was rising in my breast.

By following him almost immediately upstairs I ascertained

that he went direct to Mary's room, and when in a few hours later the family collected around the dinner table, I perceived, almost without looking up, that a great and insurmountable barrier had been raised between him and his favorite niece.

Two days passed; days that were for me one long and unrelieved suspense. Had Mr. Leavenworth answered that letter? Would it all end as it had begun without the appearance of the mysterious Clavering on the scene? I could not tell.

Meanwhile my monotonous work went on, grinding my heart beneath its relentless wheel. I wrote and wrote and wrote till it seemed as if my life-blood went from me with every drop of ink I used. Always alert and listening, I dared not lift my head or turn my eyes at any unusual sound lest I should seem to be watching. The third night I had a dream; I have already told Mr. Raymond what it was and hence will not repeat it here. One correction, however, I wish to make in regard to it. In my statement to him I declared that the face of the man whom I saw lift his hand against my employer was that of Mr. Clavering. I lied when I said this. The face seen by me in my dream was my own. It was that fact which made it so horrible to me. In the crouching figure stealing warily downstairs, I saw as in a glass the vision of my own form. Otherwise my account of the matter was true.

This vision had a tremendous effect upon me. Was it a premonition—a forewarning of the way in which I was to win this coveted creature for my own? Was the death of her uncle the bridge that was to span the impassable gulf between us? I began to think it might be; to consider the possibilities which could make this the only path to my elysium; even went so far as to picture her lovely face bending gratefully toward me through the glare of a sudden release from some emergency in which she stood. One thing was sure; If that was the way I must go, I had at least been taught how to tread it; and all through the dizzy, blurred day that followed, I saw as I sat at my work, repeated visions of that stealthy, purposeful figure stealing down the stairs and entering with uplifted pistol into the unconscious presence of my employer. I even found myself a dozen times that day turning my eyes upon the door through which it was to come, wondering how long it would be before my actual form would pause there. That the moment was at hand I did not imagine. Even when I left him that night after drinking with him the glass of sherry mentioned at the inquest, I had no idea the hour of action was so near. But when, not three minutes after going upstairs, I caught the sound of a lady's dress rustling through the hall and, listening, heard Mary Leavenworth pass my door on her way to the library, I realized that the fatal hour was come; that something was going to be said or done in that room which would make this deed necessary. What? I determined to ascertain. Casting about in my mind for the means of doing so, I remembered that the ventilator running up through the house opened first into the passage-way connecting Mr. Leavenworth's bedroom and library, and, secondly, into the closet of the large spare room adjoining mine. Hastily unlocking the door of communication between the rooms, I took my position in the closet. Instantly the sound of voices reached my ears; all was open below and, standing there, I was as much an auditor of what went on between Mary and her uncle as if I were in the library itself. And what did I hear? Enough to assure me my suspicions were correct; that it was a moment of vital interest to her; that Mr. Leavenworth, in pursuance of a threat evidently made some time since, was in the act of taking steps to change his will, and that she had come to make an appeal to be forgiven her fault and restored to his favor. What that fault was, I did not learn. No mention was made of Mr. Clavering as her husband. I only heard her declare that her action had been the result of impulse rather than love, that she regretted it and desired nothing more than to be free from all obligations to one she would fain forget, and be again to her uncle what she was before she ever saw this man. I thought, fool that I was, it was a mere engagement she was alluding to, and took the insanest hope from these words, and when in a moment later I heard her uncle reply in his sternest tone, that she had irreparably forfeited her claims to his regard and favor, I did not need her short and bitter cry of shame and disappointment, or that low moan for someone to help her, to sound his death-knell in my heart. Creeping back to my own room, I waited till I heard her re-ascend, then I stole forth. Calm as I had ever been in my life, I went down the stairs just as I had seen myself do in my dream, and knocking lightly at the library door, went in. Mr. Leavenworth was sitting in his usual place writing.

"Excuse me," said I, as he looked up, "I have lost my memorandum book and think it possible I may have dropped it in the passage-way when I went for the wine." He bowed and I hurried past him into the closet. Once there, I proceeded rapidly into the room beyond, procured the pistol, returned, and almost before I realized what I was doing, had taken up my position behind him, aimed and fired. The result was what you know. Without a groan his head fell forward on his hands, and Mary Leavenworth was the virtual possessor of the thousands she coveted.

My first thought was to procure the letter he was writing. Approaching the table, I tore it out from under his hands, looked at it, saw that it was, as I expected, a summons to his lawyer, and thrust it into my pocket together with the letter from Mr. Clavering which I perceived lying spattered with blood on the table before me. Not till this was done did I think of myself or remember the echo which that low, sharp report must have made in the house. Dropping the pistol at the side of the murdered man, I stood ready to shriek to anyone who entered, that Mr. Leavenworth had killed himself. But I was saved from committing such a folly. The report had not been heard, or if so, had evidently failed to create an alarm. No one came, and I was left to contemplate my work undisturbed, and decide upon the best course to be taken to avoid detection. A moment's study of the wound made in his head by the bullet convinced me of the impossibility of passing the affair off as a suicide, or even the work of a burglar. To anyone versed in such matters it was manifestly a murder, and a most deliberate one. My one hope, then, lay in making it as mysterious as it was deliberate, by destroying all clue to the motive and manner of the deed. Picking up the pistol, I carried it into the other room with the intention of cleaning it, but finding nothing there to do it with came back for the handkerchief which I remembered having seen lying on the floor at Mr. Leavenworth's feet. It was Miss Eleanore's; but I did not know it till I had used it to clean the barrel; then the sight of her initials in one corner so shocked me I forgot to clean the cylinder, and only thought of how I could do away with this evidence of her handkerchief having been employed for a purpose so suspicious. Not daring to carry it from the room, I sought for means to destroy it, but finding none, compromised the matter by thrusting it deep down behind the cushion of one of the chairs in the hope of being able to recover it some time next day, when an opportunity would be given to burn it. This done, I reloaded the pistol, locked it up and prepared to leave the room. But here the horror which usually follows such deeds struck me like a thunderbolt, and made me for the first time uncertain in my action. I locked the door on going out, something I should never have done if I had been in the full possession of my faculties. Not till I reached the top of the stairs did I realize what I had done, and then it was too late, for there before me, candle in hand, and surprise written on every feature of her face, stood Hannah, one of the servants, looking at me.

"Lor, sir," she cried, but strange to say, in a low tone, "where have you been? You look as if you had seen a ghost." And her eyes turned suspiciously to the key which I held in my hand.

I felt as if someone had clutched me round the throat. Thrusting the key into my pocket, I took a step toward her. "I will tell you what I have seen if you will come downstairs," I whispered; "the ladies will be disturbed if we talk here." And smoothing my brow as best I could, I put out my hand and drew her toward me. What my motive was I hardly knew; the action was probably instinctive, but when I saw the look which came into her face as I touched her, and the alacrity with which she prepared to follow me, I took courage, remembering the one or two previous tokens I had had of this girl's unreasonable susceptibility to my influence; a susceptibility which I now felt could be utilized and made to serve my purpose.

Taking her down to the parlor floor, I drew her into the depths of the great drawing room and there told her in the least alarming way possible what had happened to Mr. Leavenworth. She was, of course, intensely agitated, but she did not scream—the novelty of her position evidently awing her as much as it bewildered—and greatly relieved I went on to say that I did not know who committed the deed but that folks would declare it was I if they knew I had been seen by her on the stairs with the library key in my hand. "But I won't tell," she whispered, trembling violently in her fright and eagerness. "I will keep it to myself. I will say I didn't see anybody." But I soon convinced her that she could never keep her secret if the police once began to question her, and following up my argument with a little cajolery, succeeded after a long while in winning her consent to leave the house till the storm should be blown over. But that given, it was some little time before I could make her comprehend that she must depart at once and without going back after her things. Not till I brightened up her wits by a promise to marry her some day, if she only obeyed me now, did she begin to look the thing in the face and show any evidence of the real mother-wit she evidently possessed. "Mrs. Belden would take me in," said she, "if I could only get to R——. She takes everybody in who asks her; and she would keep me, too, if I told her Miss Mary sent me. But I can't get there tonight."

I immediately set to work to convince her that she could. The midnight train did not leave the city for a half-hour yet, and the distance to the station could be easily walked by her in fifteen minutes. But she had no money: I easily supplied that. And she was afraid she couldn't find her way: I entered into minutest directions. She still hesitated, but at length consented to go, and with some further understanding of the method I was to employ in communicating with her, we went downstairs. There was found a hat and shawl of the cook's which I put on her and in another moment we were in the carriage-yard. "Remember, you are to say nothing of what has occurred, no matter what happens," I whispered in parting injunction as she turned to leave me. "Remember you are to come and marry me some day," she murmured in reply, throwing her arms about my neck. The movement was sudden, and it was probably at this time she dropped the candle she had held unconsciously clenched in her hand till now. I promised her and she glided out of the gate.

Of the dreadful agitation that followed the disappearance of this girl, I can give no better idea than by saying I not only committed the additional error of locking up the house on my

re-entrance, but omitted to dispose of the key then in my
pocket, by flinging it into the street or dropping it in the hall as
I went up. The fact is, I was so absorbed by the thought of the
danger I stood in from this girl, I forgot everything else. Hannah's pale face, Hannah's look of terror as she turned from my
side and flitted down the street, were continually before me. I
could not escape them; the form of the dead man lying below
was less vivid. It was as though I were tied in fancy to this
woman of the white face fluttering down the midnight streets.
That she would fail in something—come back or be brought
back—that I should find her standing white and horror-stricken
on the front steps when I went down in the morning, was like a
nightmare to me. I began to think it must be so, that she never
would or could win her way unchallenged to that little cottage
in a distant village; that I had but sent a trailing flag of danger
out into the world with this wretched girl—danger that would
come back to me with the first burst of morning light!

But even these thoughts faded after a while before the realization of the peril I was in as long as the key and papers remained in my possession. How to get rid of them! I dared not
leave my room again, or open my window. Someone might see
me and remember it. Indeed I was afraid to move about in my
room. Mr. Leavenworth might hear me. Yes, my morbid terror
had reached that point—I was fearful of one whose ears I myself had forever closed: imagined him in his bed beneath, and
wakeful to the least sound.

But the necessity of doing something with these evidences of
guilt finally overcame this morbid anxiety, and drawing the
two letters from my pocket—I had not yet undressed—I chose
out the most dangerous of the two, that written by Mr. Leavenworth himself, and chewing it till it was mere pulp, threw it
into a corner; but the other had blood on it, and nothing, not
even the hope of safety, could induce me to put it to my lips. I
was forced to lie with it clenched in my hand, and the flitting
image of Hannah before my eyes till the slow morning broke. I
have heard it said that a year in heaven seems like a day; I can
easily believe it; I know that an hour in hell seems an eternity!

But with daylight came hope. Whether it was the sunshine
glancing on the wall made me think of Mary and all I was

ready to do for her sake, or whether it was the mere return of my natural stoicism in the presence of actual necessity, I cannot say. I only know that I arose calm and master of myself. The problem of the letter and key had solved itself also. Hide them! I would try not to! Instead of that I would put them in plain sight, trusting to that very fact for their being overlooked. Making the letter up into lighters I carried them into the spare room and placed them in a vase. Then, taking the key in my hand, went downstairs, intending to insert it in the lock of the library door as I went by. But Miss Eleanore descending almost immediately behind me, made this impossible. I succeeded, however, in thrusting it, without her knowledge, among the filigree work of the gas fixture in the second hall, and thus relieved, went down into the breakfast-room as self-possessed a man as ever crossed its threshold. Mary was there, looking exceedingly pale and disheartened, and as I met her eye, which for a wonder turned upon me as I entered, I could almost have laughed, thinking of the deliverance that had come to her, and of the time when I should proclaim myself to be the man who had accomplished it.

Of the alarm that speedily followed, and my action at that time and afterward, I need not speak in detail. I behaved just as I would have done if I had had no hand in the murder. Indeed, I tried to forget I had I even forbore to touch the key or go to the spare room or make any movement which I was not willing all the world should see. For as things stood, there was not a shadow of evidence against me in the house, neither was I, a hard-working, uncomplaining secretary, whose passion for one of his employer's nieces was not even mistrusted by the lady herself, a person to be suspected of the crime which threw him out of a fair situation. So I performed all the duties of my position, summoning the police, and going for Mr. Veeley, just as I would have done if those hours between my leaving Mr. Leavenworth for the first time and going down to breakfast in the morning had been blotted from my consciousness.

And this was the principle upon which I based my action at the inquest. Leaving that half-hour and its occurrences out of the question, I resolved to answer all queries put me as truthfully as I could; the great fault with men, situated as I was, usually being that they lied too much, committing themselves on unessential matters. But, alas, in thus planning for my own safety, I forgot one thing, and that was the dangerous position in which I should thus place Mary Leavenworth as the one benefited by the crime! Not till the inference was drawn by a juror, from the amount of wine found in Mr. Leavenworth's glass in the morning, that he had come to his death shortly after my leaving him, did I realize what an opening I had made for suspicion in her direction by admitting that I had heard a rustle on the stair a few minutes after going up. That all present believed it to have been made by Eleanore, did not re-assure me. She was so completely disconnected with the crime I could not imagine suspicion holding to her for an instant. But Mary—if a curtain had been let down before me, pictured with the future as it has since developed, I could not have seen more plainly what her position would be, if attention were once directed toward her. So in the vain endeavor to cover up my blunder, I began to lie. Forced to admit that a shadow of disagreement had been latterly visible between Mr. Leavenworth and one of his nieces, I threw the burden of it upon Eleanore, as the one best able to bear it, adding to this denial of the fact that any letter had been received by Mr. Leavenworth which could in any way tend to explain the crime. The consequences were more serious than I anticipated. Direction had been given to suspicion which every additional evidence that now came up seemed by some strange fatality to strengthen. Not only was it proved that Mr. Leavenworth's own pistol had been used in the assassination, and that, too, by a person then in the house, but I myself was brought to acknowledge that Eleanore had learned from me only a little while before how to load, aim, and fire this very pistol—a coincidence mischievous enough to have been of the devil's own making.

Seeing all this, my fear of what the ladies would admit when questioned became very great. Let them in their innocence acknowledge that upon my ascent, Mary had gone to her uncle's room for the purpose of persuading him not to carry into effect the action he contemplated, and what consequences might not ensue! I was in a torment of apprehension. But events of which

I had at that time no knowledge, had occurred to influence them. Eleanore, with some show of reason, as it seems, not only suspected her cousin of the crime, but had informed her of the fact, and Mary, overcome with terror at finding there was more or less circumstantial evidence supporting the suspicion, decided to deny whatever told against herself, trusting to Eleanore's generosity not to be contradicted. Nor was her confidence misplaced. Though, by the course she thus took, Eleanore was forced to deepen the prejudice already rife against herself, she not only forbore to contradict her cousin, but when a true answer would have injured her, actually refused to return any, a lie being something she could not utter, even to save one especially endeared to her.

This conduct of hers had one effect upon me. It aroused my admiration and made me feel that here was a woman worth helping if assistance could be given without danger to myself. Yet I doubt if much would have come of my sympathy, if I had not perceived by the stress laid upon certain well-known matters, that actual danger hovered about us all, while the letter and key remained in the house. Even before the handkerchief was produced, I had made up my mind to attempt their destruction, but when that was brought out and shown, I became so alarmed I immediately rose and, making my way under some pretense or other to the floors above, snatched the key from the gas fixture, the lighters from the vase, and hastening with them down the hall to Mary Leavenworth's room, went in under the expectation of there finding a fire in which to destroy them. But to my heavy disappointment there were only a few smoldering ashes in the grate, and, thwarted in my design, I stood hesitating what to do, when I heard someone coming upstairs. Alive to the consequences of being found in that room at that time, I cast the lighters into the grate and started for the door. But in the quick move I made, the key flew from my hand and slid under a chair. Aghast at the mischance, I paused, but the sound of approaching steps increasing, I lost all control over myself and fled from the room. And indeed I had no time to lose; I had barely reached my own door when Eleanore Leavenworth, followed by two servants, appeared at the top of the staircase and proceeded toward the room I had just left. The sight reassured me; she would see the key and take some means of disposing of it; and indeed I always supposed that she did, for no further word of key or letter ever came to my ears.

This may explain why the questionable position in which Eleanore soon found herself awakened in me no greater anxiety. I thought the suspicions of the police rested upon nothing more tangible than the peculiarity of her manner at the inquest, and the discovery of her handkerchief on the scene of the tragedy. I did not know they possessed what they might call absolute proof of her connection with the crime. But if I had, I doubt if I should have pursued a much different course. Mary's peril was the one thing capable of turning me, and she did not appear to be in peril. On the contrary, everyone by common consent seemed to ignore all appearance of guilt on her part. If Mr. Gryce, whom I soon learned to fear, had given one sign of suspicion, or Mr. Raymond, whom I speedily recognized as my most persistent though unconscious foe, had betrayed the least distrust of her, I should have taken warning. But they did not, and lulled into a false security by their manner, I let the days go by without suffering any fears on her account. But not without many anxieties for myself. Hannah's existence precluded all sense of personal security. Knowing the determination of the police to find her, I trod the verge of an awful suspense continually.

Meantime the wretched certainty was forcing itself upon me that I had lost, instead of gained, a hold on Mary Leavenworth. Not only did she evince the utmost horror of the deed which had made her the mistress of her uncle's wealth, but, owing as I believed to the influence of Mr. Raymond, soon gave evidence that she was losing to a certain extent the characteristics of mind and heart which had made me hopeful of winning her regard by my action. This revelation drove me almost insane. Under the terrible restraint forced upon me, I walked my weary round in a state of mind bordering on frenzy. Many and many a time have I stopped in my work, wiped my pen and laid it down with the idea that I could not repress myself another moment, but I have always taken it up again and gone on with my task. Mr. Raymond has sometimes shown his wonder at my sitting in my dead employer's chair. Great Heaven! it was my only safeguard. By keeping the murder constantly before my mind, I was enabled to restrain my disappointment at its failure to bring me the reward I anticipated.

At last there came a time when my agony could be no longer suppressed. Going down the stairs one evening with Mr. Raymond, I saw a strange gentleman standing in the reception-room, looking at Mary Leavenworth in a way that would have made my blood boil, even if I had not heard him whisper these words: "But you are my wife and know it, whatever you may say or do!"

It was the lightning-stroke of my life. After what I had done to make her mine, to hear another claim her as already his own was stunning, maddening. It forced a demonstration from me. I had either to yell in my fury or deal the man beneath some tremendous blow in my hatred. I did not dare to shriek, so I struck the blow. Demanding his name from Mr. Raymond, and hearing that it was, as I expected, Clavering, I flung caution, reason, common sense, all to the winds, and in a moment of fury denounced him as the murderer of Mr. Leavenworth.

The next instant I would have given worlds to recall my words. What had I done but drawn attention to myself in thus accusing a man against whom nothing could of course be proved! But recall now was impossible. So after a night of thought I did the next best thing, gave a superstitious reason for my action, and so restored myself to my former position without eradicating from the mind of Mr. Raymond that vague doubt of the man which my own safety demanded. But I had no intention of going any further, nor should I have done so if I had not observed that for some reason Mr. Raymond was willing to suspect Mr. Clavering. But that once seen, revenge took possession of me, and I asked myself if the burden of this crime could be thrown on this man. Still I do not believe that any results would have followed if I had not overheard a whispered conversation between two of the servants, in which I learned that Mr. Clavering had been seen to enter the house on the night of the murder, but was not seen to leave it. That determined me. With a fact like that for a starting-point, what might I not hope to accomplish? Hannah alone stood in my way. While she remained alive I saw nothing but ruin before me. I made up my mind to destroy her and satisfy my hatred of Mr. Clavering at one blow. But how? By what means could I reach her without deserting my post, or make away with her without exciting fresh suspicion? The problem seemed insoluble; but Trueman Harwell had not played the part of a machine so long without result. Before I had studied the question a day light broke upon it, and I saw that the only way to accomplish my plans was to inveigle her into destroying herself.

No sooner had the thought matured than I hastened to act upon it. Knowing the tremendous risk I ran, I took every precaution. Locking myself up in my room, I wrote her a letter in printed characters—she having distinctly told me she could not read writing—in which I played upon her ignorance, foolish fondness, and Irish superstition, by telling her I dreamed of her every night and wondered if she did of me, was afraid she didn't, so enclosed her a little charm which if she would use according to directions (which were that she should first destroy my letter by burning it, next take in her hand the packet I was careful to enclose, swallow the powder accompanying it, and go to bed) would give her the most beautiful visions—the powder was a deadly dose of poison and the packet was as you know a forged confession falsely criminating Henry Clavering. Enclosing all these in an envelope in the corner of which I had marked a cross, I directed it according to agreement to Mrs. Belden, and sent it.

Then followed the greatest period of suspense I had yet endured. Though I had purposely refrained from putting my name to the letter, I felt that the chances of detection were very great. The least departure from the course I had marked out for her would prove fatal. If she opened the enclosed packet, or mistrusted the powder, took Mrs. Belden into her confidence, or even failed to burn my letter, all would be lost. I could not be sure of her or know the result of my scheme except through the newspapers. Do you think I kept watch of the countenances about me? devoured the telegraphic news, or started when the bell rang? And when a few days since I read that short paragraph in the paper which assured me that my efforts had at least produced the death of the woman I feared, do you think I experienced any sense of relief?

But of that why speak? In six hours had come the summons from Mr. Gryce, and—let these prison walls, this confession itself, tell the rest. I am no longer capable of speech or action.

CHAPTER 6

The Outcome of A Great Crime

> Leave her to Heaven
> And to those thorns that in her bosom lodge
> To prick and sting her.
>
> —HAMLET.

> For she is wise, if I can judge of her;
> And fair she is, if that mine eyes be true,
> And true she is, as she has proved herself;
> And therefore like herself, wise, fair, and true,
> Shall she be placed in my constant soul.
>
> —MERCHANT OF VENICE.

"Oh, Eleanore!" cried I, making my way into her presence with but little ceremony, I fear, "are you prepared for very good news? News that will brighten these pale cheeks and give the light back to these eyes, and make life hopeful and sweet to you once more? Tell me!" said I, stooping over her where she sat, for she looked ready to faint.

"I don't know," murmured she, "I fear that what you will consider good news will not seem so to me. No news can be good but——"

"What?" asked I, taking her hands in mine with a smile that ought to have reassured her—it was one of such profound happiness. "Tell me; do not be afraid."

But she was. Her dreadful burden had lain upon her so long it had become a part of her being. How could she realize it was founded on a mistake, that she had no cause to fear the past, present, or future!

But when the truth was made known to her, when with all the fervor and gentle tact of which I was capable I showed her that her suspicions had been groundless, and that Trueman Harwell and not Mary had been the perpetrator of this deed, her first words were a prayer to be taken to Mary—"Take me to her! Oh, take me to her! I cannot breathe or think till I have begged pardon of her on my knees. Oh, my unjust accusation! My unjust accusation!"

Seeing the state she was in, I deemed it the wisest thing I could do. So procuring a carriage, I drove with her to her cousin's home.

"Mary will spurn me; she will not even look at me, and she will be right," cried she as we rolled away up the avenue. "An outrage like this can never be forgiven. But God knows I thought myself justified in my suspicions! If you knew——"

"I do know," I interposed. "Mary acknowledges that the circumstantial evidence against her was so overwhelming, she was almost staggered herself, asking if she could be guiltless with such proofs against her. But——"

"Wait! Oh, wait—did Mary say that?"

"Yes."

"Today?"

"Yes."

"Mary must be changed."

I did not answer, I wanted her to see for herself to how great an extent! But when in a few minutes later the carriage stopped, and I hurried with her into the house which had been the scene of so much misery, I was hardly prepared for the difference in her own countenance which the hall-light revealed. Her eyes were bright, her cheeks were brilliant, her brow lifted and free from shadow, so quickly does the ice of despair melt in the sunshine of hope.

Thomas, who had opened the door, was somberly glad to see his mistress again. "Miss Leavenworth is in the drawing room," said he.

I nodded, then seeing that Eleanore could scarcely move for agitation, asked her whether she would go in at once or wait till she was more composed.

"I will go at once, I cannot wait." And slipping from my grasp she crossed the hall and laid her hand upon the drawing room curtain, when it was suddenly lifted from within and Mary stepped out.

"Mary!"

"Eleanore!"

The ring of those voices told everything. I did not need to glance that way to know that Eleanore had fallen at her cousin's feet, and that her cousin had affrightedly lifted her. I did not need to hear—"My sin against you is too great; you cannot forgive me!" followed by the low—"My shame is great enough to lead me to forgive anything!" to know that the life-long shadow between these two had dissolved like a cloud, and that for the future, bright days of mutual confidence and sympathy were in store.

Yet when a half-hour or so later I heard the door of the reception-room into which I had retired softly open, and looking up saw Mary standing on the threshold with the light of true humility on her face, I own that I was surprised at the extent of the softening which had taken place in her haughty beauty. "Blessed is the shame that purifies," I murmured, and advancing, held out my hand with a respect and sympathy I never thought to feel for her again.

The action seemed to touch her. Blushing deeply, she came and stood by my side. "I thank you," said she. "I have much to be grateful for, how much I never realized till tonight, but I cannot speak of it now. What I wish is for you to come in and help me persuade Eleanore to accept this fortune from my hands. It is hers, you know, was willed to her, or would have been if——"

"Wait," said I in the wild trepidation which this appeal to me on such a subject somehow awakened. "Have you weighed this matter well? Is it your determined purpose to transfer your fortune into your cousin's hands?"

Her look was enough without the low: "Ah, how can you ask me?" that followed it.

Mr. Clavering was sitting by the side of Eleanore when we entered the drawing room. He immediately rose.

"Mr. Raymond," said he, drawing me to one side, "before the courtesies of the hour pass between us, allow me to tender you my apology. You have in your possession a document which ought never to have been forced upon you. Founded upon a mistake, the act was an insult which I bitterly regret. If in consideration of my mental misery at that time you can pardon it, I shall feel forever indebted to you: if not——"

"Mr. Clavering," I interrupted, "say no more. The occurrences of that day belong to a past which I, for one, have made up my mind to forget as soon as possible. The future promises too richly for us to dwell on bygone miseries."

And with a look of mutual understanding and friendship we hastened to rejoin the ladies.

Of the conversation that followed, it is only necessary to state the result. Eleanore remaining firm in her refusal to accept property so stained by guilt, it was finally agreed upon that it should be devoted to the erection and sustainment of some charitable institution, of magnitude sufficient to be a recognized benefit to the city and its unfortunate poor. This settled, our thoughts returned to our friends, especially to Mr. Veeley.

"He ought to know," said Mary. "He has grieved like a father over us." And in her spirit of penitence, she would have undertaken the unhappy task of telling him the truth.

But Eleanore, with her accustomed generosity, would not hear of this. "No, Mary," said she, "you have suffered enough. Mr. Raymond and I will go."

And leaving them there, with the light of growing hope and confidence on their faces, we went out again into the night, and so into a dream from which I have never waked, though the shine of her dear eyes has been now the lode-star of my life for many happy, happy months.